SHE WAS [...] OF THE TONG'S BRUTALITY—
OF A MAN'S UNSCRUPULOUS GREED—
AND NOW THEY HAD TAKEN HER BABY . . .

Lem Choy sullenly pulled the blue blanket over the baby's lifeless form. Clutching the basket to himself, he boarded the ferry and returned to San Francisco. Soon he was standing in Bartlett Alley before Ming Lee's crib.

He breathed a heavy sigh and entered the crib. He ignored the half-naked women who were beckoning to him with lewd proposals.

"Where's Ming Lee?" he asked.

Polly pouted and answered, "In the back."

Lem Choy entered the tiny back bedroom. Ming Lee was resting on a flimsy straw mat that lay stretched along a splintered wooden floor. She was awake, just lying there, staring at the cobwebs on the ceiling. Lem Choy stood silently above her, holding the straw basket.

Ming Lee broke the silence. "What is it, Lem Choy? Is he dead, Lem Choy?"

Lem Choy nodded. "I will return all the opium that I accepted as payment. I will pay for what I already smoked."

"Why don't you leave, Lem Choy? Just leave." Ming Lee's gaze remained fixed on the ceiling.

"Yes," Lem Choy responded. "Yes . . . but I want you to know, I'm shipping the body back home for a decent funeral. I'll pay for everything." He paused. "Good-bye, Ming Lee."

"Good-bye." Ming Lee closed her eyes and Lem Choy started out the door. . . .

JOHN ROBINSON

the CHINESE

A Dell/Banbury Book

Published by
Banbury Books, Inc.
37 West Avenue
Wayne, Pennsylvania 19087

Dell ® TM 681510, Dell Publishing Co., Inc.

ISBN: 0-440-01279-1

Printed in the United States of America

First printing—September 1983

For Pamela and Kelsey.

PART I
INITIATION

"From the rooster's head, from the rooster's head, see how fresh blood flows. If loyal and brave my course shall be, my heirs immortal renown shall see. But when base traitor and coward turn I, slain on the road my body shall lie."

—from the Oath of the Chi Sing Tong

Chapter 1

For the first time in weeks, Man Sum could see land. The gently rolling hills, purple through the haze, seemed to be slowly undulating like a dragon restlessly awakening from its sleep. The sight sent Man Sum's blood pulsing.

He shook his head and blinked his eyes. The hills, of course, were not really moving. It was just the steamship rocking with the waves.

"Man Sum, you daydream too much. I wanted you to be a scholar, not a daydreamer. *Ney faat mut yeh mong*? What are you dreaming about?" he remembered his mother saying.

His mother had died a year ago, in March, 1910 . . . of what? He was not sure. Of exhaustion or of a broken heart.

Now there was no time for daydreams. He must concentrate. His clarity of mind in the next few hours would be all-important. If he passed the test, his entrance into the country of gold would be assured. He must again go over all the information he had memorized; he could not afford to overlook even one detail. To forget anything about the life of the man he would claim as his father would mean deportation.

Only the direct offspring of merchants were permitted to immigrate. But since the earthquake of 1906 in San Francisco, all records were destroyed. Thus, merchants could claim to have sons or daughters they really did not have, and then sell the slots. Man Sum's real father, Sing Choy Wu, had bought such a slot. It was given to Sing Man Sum. So Man Sum became a "paper son." His name on that paper was Kwong Bing Win.

He was warned that the authorities would continually ask him his name in order to see if he was lying, but he must also be on guard against his own countrymen. There could be spies among them, so he must always identify himself as Kwong Bing Win to them as well.

The thought of withholding his real name from everyone made Man Sum feel very anxious and disoriented. I am really the son of Sing Choy Wu, he thought, but I must forget that. Concentrate. *Concentrate!* They will try to trip me up!

Remember the coaching papers, word for word:

"The merchant's name is Kwong Pak Yuen. In America, he is a seller of herbs, an apothecary. His store is on Stockton Street, near Washington Street. He has owned this herb store for ten years. Before that, he had been a laundryman. He came to the United States in 1867 and worked for Crocker, building the Western side of the great railroad. He had been one of Crocker's pets, as Chinese railroad builders were called. He is missing the index finger from his left hand as the result of an accident involving a dynamite charge he had set in the side of a cliff in the High Sierras. But he had been lucky. More than ten thousand Chinese had died building the great railroad through the granite-filled High Sierras in the dead of several winters. Remember these facts, Man Sum. You will be held responsible for them."

Strange, Man Sum thought to himself. I know more about this man who is not my father than I do about my real father.

The young man knew very little about Sing Choy Wu, who had visited the village only on two occasions, when Man Sum was too young to remember him clearly. One thing was certain: his father was not a merchant and therefore could not bring his own son over legally, hence, this "paper son" scheme. His father had sent him a large packet of information on the life of this merchant, Kwong Pak Yuen. Man Sum had to read it, memorize it, and be able to put on a perfect act in order to fool the immigration authorities.

He started to review the coaching papers again. He began with the merchant's village, Shang Lok. That part was easy. He had visited the village. It was not unlike his own, Wing Tan Ho.

His mind wandered to his own village. He thought of the dust over everything. The gates, the images of the gods, the large clay pots, straw baskets, bedding, everything. Dust that was impossible not to breathe. There had been a drought. People didn't have enough to eat. Only those who received money from relatives abroad had survived.

He thought of his own mother. Life had treated her hard. She was at the beck and call of her mother-in-law, his father's mother. In the face of his grandmother's condescending remarks, his mother had somehow managed to remain stoic.

Grandmother, crippled with arthritis, could do nothing but sit on the stool in the kitchen all day waiting for Mother to return from the fields.

"The only important thing you ever did was to bear a son," the old woman would say with hostile disdain.

"I'm a little tired," his mother would answer. "We

will talk later.'' A little tired. One day she lay down to rest after his grandmother had made some remark about ''lazy servant girls.'' His mother never got up from her rest. A little tired.

He was letting his mind wander. He must get back to the coaching papers. He formed a picture in his mind of the house where the merchant had lived before emigrating to America. To the left of the merchant's house lived Louie Fook Ping. His wife was Louie An Wei. She had bound feet. Across the street from them was Lau Shuk Kwan. His wife didn't have bound feet. It was of course very important to know which wives had bound feet and which didn't. And it was absolutely necessary to know where the village's shrines, wells, and fields were located.

So much to know. How could he begin to retain it all? He had to keep repeating it, going over it again and again. Had he left anything out? He was sure he had. Each time he ran through it in his mind, he reasoned, he must have left out some details. He wished he had the coaching papers in front of him now, but he had thrown them overboard back at the Hawaiian Islands. If any of the crew or any spies among his countrymen discovered those papers, Man Sum would certainly be pointed out to the authorities. Then he would be singled out immediately for deportation, and he would be returned to China by the next ship out of Gum San, Gold Hill, San Francisco. He couldn't imagine a more terrible fate. Nothing could be worse than the failure to complete his plan. *Nothing.* It would be as if his whole life had been a waste. He would lose face, all respect. He would return to his village, and his kinsmen would see written on his face the characters for failure, *Sut* and *Baai*.

It would be better to commit suicide, to throw himself overboard. That would save what dignity was left to him.

Yes, that's what he must do if the immigration authorities decide against him. That was settled, then. A decision against him would mean suicide; it would be the same as a death sentence.

He was startled out of his thoughts y the ship sounding its deep whistles. It was signaling its approach to the land, and he could hear another whistle far away answering in response. The land mass began to split apart like the dragon opening its mouth sideways. The split widened as the ship moved nearer. He could now see into the bay of San Francisco. The calm waters were dotted by mounds of green islands just now catching the first rays of sunlight breaking the morning gloom.

As the ship slid into the bay, his countrymen began to talk excitedly and gather their belongings.

"We'll be in Gum San soon," one of them said.

"Yes, Gold Hill. But is there any gold left in those hills?" another asked.

"Maybe no gold, but you can make a lot of money. My three uncles are rich. They own a restaurant in Chinatown," still another said.

"And you don't have to be landed gentry to make money, or a bandit. You can do it yourself. Use your hands. Use your mind. Get lucky," another said.

Spirits among the passengers were high. It had been a grueling voyage, and they were thankful to have finally reached San Francisco Bay.

But one of them struck a more pessimistic note. He was a short, wiry man. His eyes were bloodshot, watery. "Don't be so sure you will ever see the land. Your papers better be in order. The immigration authorities will know. They will know if you are lying about your identity!"

His warning caused a leaden silence among the sojourners.

"Mm haih ahhh!" said the one who believed in good luck. "We're going to get lucky! This is our lucky day. The white foreigners will just wave us through their checkpoint, and we will soon be walking down the famous streets of Chinatown, truly free men on the path toward the fortune which awaits the diligent, the strong and the intelligent."

All around were murmurs of agreement.

"There are so many of us, how can they possibly stop to conduct lengthy interrogations with each one?" he asked.

Then, Man Sum thought to himself, all that work memorizing coaching papers until the skull burst with too much information will have been wasted. He would have done better to make plans, to think about his future.

"No, they couldn't possibly interrogate all of us. It would be torture for them. It would take them months, years. No official I ever heard about is willing to work that hard."

The ship's engines went silent suddenly. The crew members lowered the anchor, and the ship stood still in the middle of the bay with the land tantalizingly close. There was an ominous calm.

Anxious buzzing voices asked the same questions:

"*Jo mat yeh*? What is going on?"

"Why are we stopping?"

"What are we waiting for?"

"Is there something wrong with the ship?"

"Somebody ask the white foreigner. Can anybody speak their language?"

But no one could elicit an explanation from the white foreigners, not even the one or two Chinese who could falteringly speak the coarse, barbarian tongue.

The crewmen stood patiently about the ship. The countrymen, mostly men, very few women, sat sullenly on their hastily wrapped possessions. All anyone could do was wait and see what would happen.

The afternoon agonizingly wore on into evening, and the frustrated passengers were told to descend again to their crowded, filthy quarters, which they had hoped never to see again.

The spaces were so narrow that one could not lie flat without touching another's body. One had to lie on one's side. And the tier above was so close that one couldn't sit up. On the nights of the voyage, Man Sum could hear so many sounds of coughing, snoring, weeping and vomiting that he could not sleep. And on this night especially, the confusion and anxiety of everyone on board seemed to thicken the air and deepen the darkness and the oppressiveness of the hold.

He woke to the gruff sound of the foreigner's voice. What was he saying now? Everyone looked toward one of the "interpreters."

"*Lau seang, la*! He's telling us to go up to the top."

Obediently, the passengers piled out of their bunks and made their way to the surface. It was early morning. Again, the travelers arranged themselves on the deck hugging their belongings. Other ships passed them. White men from these ships were yelling something, shaking their fists at them. What was it they were saying? Why did they seem so angry? Why shake an angry fist at us? Man Sum wondered. It probably would be better to avoid these angry, ghostlike people altogether.

His father had written stories about stone-throwing hoodlums encircling Chinatown, and any Chinese who wandered beyond the boundaries of the ghetto became fair game. Those countrymen who returned were covered by bruises or cuts that took months to heal. Chinatown was bounded by Stockton and Kearny Streets, west and east;

Broadway and California, north and south, a total of about ten square blocks. Owing to the malevolent vigilance of these stone-throwing hoodlums, Chinatown had virtually become a prison.

A twin of the steamship Man Sum was on drew alongside. Two very fat men, bulging out of their green uniforms, crossed a plank and came aboard. They carried large, polished sticks attached to their wrists with leather straps. They were white men, but close up they looked red-faced. There were little broken purple veins in their cheeks. They had bulbous, fixed jaws.

These men commanded the recent arrivals through gesture and loud voices to stand in a single line and bring with them their possessions.

Then a third official entered the ship. He looked as tall as a god. His uniform was the same as the others, but medals hung from one breast. Large tufts of red sideburn bracketed his ivory face. Two wooden-looking assistants carried a table on which a pair of rubber stamps and an ink pad were placed.

The tall man began to process the immigrants. Each one was required to show his papers. If the officer stamped the documents, the red-faced men would point with their sticks toward the plank going to the other steamer, and the newcomer would be hurried on board. If he was a little slow, the larger of the two fat men would prod him with his stick just as if the poor fellow were an ox. Those whose papers didn't get stamped were forced again down into the noisome room below the deck.

It was better not to protest, because if you offered resistance, the fat officer was not at all shy about slapping you around with his stick.

It became clear that the other boat was going to shore with its cargo of approved entrants. Stamped papers meant immediate acceptance of the applicant. The unstamped had to mean some problem or other was holding up approval.

This ship must not be going to San Francisco, but someplace else. Perhaps it was going back to China. A number of countrymen tried to push their way past the table, the stamp, the shiny stick. They were struck, kicked, their papers wrenched from them. And they were forcibly ushered back into the bunk room.

Please don't let them send me back to the hold, Man Sum thought. The stench of vomit from the seasickness suffered by many of the passengers still clung to the floorboards. If you didn't get sick from the rocking motions of the ship in rough seas, the smell of the vomit did it to you. All the crew did was to sweep the floor and sprinkle sawdust on it. When the vomit combined with the sickly sweet scent of pine sap, the stench was much worse.

How long would he have to wait if he were sent back? Another day? Another week? Another month? Now his turn came. He summoned all the confidence he could and handed his papers over to the inspector. The inspector looked at the document for an anguishingly long moment, pursing his lips. Man Sum stiffened. His heart was pounding. The inspector looked at him for a moment, then grunted and shrugged.

He pointed with his chin toward the hole below decks. This gesture was immediately followed by the fat immigration officer's shove. It came unexpectedly. Man Sum wasn't ready for it. His head jerked back, causing a sharp pain in his neck. He lost his balance and his knees sank to the deck surface.

"Get up!" the immigration officer growled.

Someone translated. "*Jau la, jau la, giu ney jua la.* Go, go, he's telling you to go."

Man Sum got up and moved toward the metal ladder

that descended to the pit. He struggled to his old bunk, rubbing the pain in his neck. But he had to get up again to retrieve his baggage, which had been thrown down after him. He brought his baggage into his bunk and tried to rest.

Many were rejected after him. There were loud curses as many descended that ladder to join him in the darkness. He realized what the journey back to China would mean. Failure. The scorn of others. No. He would save his face by throwing his life into the ocean.

Somewhere in the middle of his reflections on death, he had fallen into a deep, dreamless sleep. When he awoke, there were officers yelling something in the barbarian tongue. Everyone looked at Chan Lim Yuk because he understood more of the language than anybody, though half the time he was guessing.

"The officer *faan gwai*, foreign ghost, is telling us to get moving again," he said.

Maybe they have had a change of heart and are letting them go ashore, Man Sum thought to himself.

They trudged up the ladder and formed another long line. Once out of the hold, they saw that they had arrived at an island. It was one of the islands in the large bay. Man Sum remembered having seen it when the ship first turned inland. Leading from the pier was a long wooden walkway rising slightly to meet a two-story wooden building. This building was nestled in the hillside, and it was framed by very pretty pine trees.

More men in green uniforms were waiting for the immigrants to disembark. Some held long-handled sticks. Others held clipboards. Two others held rifles in front of them with both hands, ready, it seemed, to use them at any moment. Crew members were already busily cleaning up even before the passengers left the boat.

Then, at last, the plank was let down and the guests set foot for the first time on the firmness of the strange new land. Again, the passengers had more questions than answers.

"What is the meaning of the wooden building?" one asked.

"Are they going to hold interrogations there?" asked another.

But the pessimist said, "This is where we wait for another boat to take us back to China."

"He's right," another agreed gloomily. "We have been crossed off the list of applicants. Those fellows are getting ready to assign us bunks on the next steamship bound for home."

"I won't stand for it! Nobody's putting me on a boat back to China! I'm heading for San Francisco, and nobody's going to stop me," said one youth, shaking with indignation.

A more philosophically inclined older man answered, "That green uniform means power. Do what power dictates, or feel the pain of that stick. Follow orders, obey. That's the best way. No resistance. No complaints. That's the only way. The future will bring improvement in the state of things. Wealth is possible. Yes. Wealth. But, it is a long way off. Wealth worth all of our suffering will be great wealth indeed. One has only to wait and be patient."

"You sound like a Taoist," said the youthful rebel. "I don't believe in Taoist philosophy. I'm a believer in Sun Yat-sen's philosophy. The three principles: nationalism, people's democracy, people's livelihood. And none of that can be accomplished without action."

The old philosopher shook his head. "Non-action, according to Lao Tze's philosophy, is the way. He who pursues the Tao will decrease every day in influence. He will arrive at non-action, and through non-action, everything can be accomplished. Sun Yat-sen doesn't know this, and that's why his revolution will surely fail.''

"And you," the rebel said, "you would let the peasants die of starvation while the wealthy laugh at the food they throw away, just like always."

"One must expect nothing from one's environment," the older man said calmly. "In spite of bad circumstances, non-action must be the rule. The consequences of non-action must be good fortune. That is the law of heaven, the only law that rules all people."

The youth threw up his hands in disgust.

The philosopher continued, "These barbaric people are also dependent on heaven's immutable laws even though they might not know it. They may have power temporarily, but surely their coercive behavior toward others will lead them to destruction. As the sage has said, 'A violent wind cannot last a whole morning; pelting rain cannot last a whole day. But the Tao pervades everywhere and never becomes exhausted.' "

The young rebel looked at the philosopher uncomprehendingly, but Man Sum understood the older man perfectly.

I would be a scholar, Man Sum thought, if I had followed the path my mother set out for me. All those years studying the five classics were wasted as far as she was concerned. I felt that my future was not in scholarship. I felt my true path led to Gold Hill, the way of my father, because that was the way of the world. It was only through this way that success could be attained. The only survivors in China were these relatives of Gold Hill men. But the classics have taught me how to live in the world. And I shall pay close attention to the voices of the sages throughout all the adversity which shall befall me.

Such were Man Sum's thoughts as he walked in short, rapid steps, single file with the others along the wooden walkway toward the white wooden building on the island. A metal fence ran from the shore up to the hill, along the hill and down the other side so that the entire cove was closed off. Man Sum was suddenly struck by a very disturbing thought. This is a prison we are going to. Yes, we're going to prison.

There was a Chinese man at the pier. He was dressed as a Westerner, and he talked through a megaphone. He told the passengers to leave their luggage there, on the pier, and then proceed toward the house. Man Sum hated to leave his belongings in the hands of these foreigners. Possibly, they would pick through the contents of everybody's luggage and take everything of value. Man Sum had jade jewelry his mother had given him, and he didn't want to part with it.

There were about a hundred who disembarked with Sing Man Sum. The men were separated from the women and were immediately led to a hospital room to be examined. The doctors made them give urine and feces samples which, he found out later, were examined for the presence of diseases such as hookworm. Any diseases found in the specimens were grounds for deportation. Man Sum worried over this. Though I have the coaching papers perfectly copied in my mind, he thought, my body's imperfections might yet betray me.

After the physical, the men were led to their separate dormitory rooms by a white guard and an interpreter. Each of the men was assigned a bed not much larger than the berths in the ship. The men, crowded into the dormitory, did nothing. Some lay on their bunks and stared at the ceiling. Others read well-worn Chinese books, books they had read over and over. Still others stared out the window at the chain-link fence, and through the fence at the island sloping toward the bay. The men stared and their faces were full of frustration.

Days passed in monotonous succession. Getting up, washing one's face, eating three dreary meals, lolling about the dormitory, sleeping. Someone was always counting heads. You were only a head to them, nothing more. Your only value was your contribution to the sum of heads the uniform wrote in a column of his clipboard list. He tallied the number of people by bouncing his pencil's eraser end for each head counted. In itself, it was an innocuous ritual, but repeated again and again, it became mean, dispiriting.

Time was broken only by the sound of the bell that called them to meals. Then they rushed down the wide stairs, pushing and shoving. There was always the fear of not getting enough to eat, so they jammed against the doors of the dining hall, each one trying to be first in line. Man Sum held his ears against the shouting.

"*Hoi mun, hoi mun*. Open up!"

Each morning it was the same. Men squeezed together at the foot of the stairs. The body stench was almost unbearable. Nobody had wanted to bathe in the filthy shower room, which was always overcrowded and provided soap that smelled worse than a man's own odor. Moreover, the soap was an abrasive powder that irritated skin already raw from scratching sores caused by soiled bedding and bedbug bites.

Once, Man Sum tried waiting in the dormitory until the dining room doors were opened. That way he avoided the crowds. But when he got down to the dining hall, the food was already passed out and there were no more seatings allowed. So he had to bear the insult of the crowd pressing against him or face starvation. He learned to fight like the others to be closest to the beginning of the line. He felt his spirit begin to coarsen.

The food was all steamed. He could see the vapor billowing out of the kitchen each time the door swung open. Inside, the cooks were all wet from the steam which beaded on their faces. Food prepared in this manner became like mush. The cabbage looked wilted, like old rags. The rice was matted and mashed so the grains ran together into a sticky substance resembling white glue. Everything was overcooked. The inmates ate without appetite.

The bell rang and everyone left the dining hall sullenly, terribly unsatisfied. They all trudged back to the dormitory. There, the guards stood ready to lock the doors after everyone had returned. There was nothing for them to do but read the Chinese newspapers.

The newspaper told of gang warfare in Chinatown, killings in dark alleys. Rival gangs called "Tongs" were constantly picking each other's members off. Professional killers, the "highbinders," also called Tongs for short, were hired by the Tong organizations. They were soldiers, trained to kill quickly, efficiently.

On this particular day, police found yet another body riddled with bullets. It was the body of a laundryman, who apparently was not a rival Tong, but simply a merchant who had refused to pay protection money.

So this was the Chinatown in the America that Man Sum had wanted to enter. How was one to keep from getting caught in the line of fire when Chinatown was so small, when often the dark alleyways were the only paths to the market or to one's home? And then, he thought, if I was lucky enough to get set up in business there, what would be the point if all my profits went to paying off those gangsters?

It was no different from the village back in China. There we always lived in fear of bandits stealing the little food we were able to grow or the little money we were able to save. The constant threat of the bandits had meant total lack of security for Man Sum's family. The drought, too. The weak government in China had utterly failed to control the anarchy into which the country was sinking. Only the families that received money from relatives in America would survive. For the rest, the future was uncertain.

The news of these Tong battles made Man Sum's stomach turn. He must not stay in Chinatown, but go elsewhere. Perhaps, he'd go to the mountain where gold was to be found in chunks as large as one's fist. Staying in Chinatown would be no different than remaining in China.

The others tried to put their minds from it all. They found solace in various forms of escape. Some engaged in storytelling, old fairy tales, stories of heroes from China's history. Others tried to lose themselves in gambling: dominoes, cards, or checkers. Still others idled away the time in political arguments.

Man Sum longed for solitude. He wanted to be alone so he could contemplate his future and devise different strategies for meeting the situations he imagined would confront him. He wanted to begin to learn some words of the white barbarian's language so he would be able to get what he needed from them.

He already sensed what many of the immigrants failed to see: that these white, violent men who imprisoned them on the island were human beings. They weren't simply what the label *faan gwai* implied, namely, foreign devil. *Gwai* meant something like ghost or demon, a dead person without progeny, without anyone to pay him reverence, to light incense sticks for him, to give him food offerings on festival days, to ask for his help in times of need. So a *gwai* had no identity, no name, no "face" in the land of the living. That meant the *gwai* was forced to walk the earth in shadowy form, forever denied entrance to the spirit realm. And so, logically, everything unfamiliar and unknown, everything without a face or a name, became *gwai*. One could have no relationship whatsoever with a faceless being. That's why the term *faan gwai* assigned to the Westerner meant one could have no dealings with him. To Man Sum, this seemed unwise.

But between him and the foreigner there seemed to be an insurmountable gap, which he didn't yet know how to bridge, for it was the *faan gwai* who had assigned him to this place, this prison, this lonely island, where birds sang funeral dirges. The landscape, which once seemed pretty, now sickened the heart. There was the monotonous sound of the surf breaking against the rocks, the sound of the wind rattling the windows. These sounds deadened the mind. Thoughts became idle, listless. Was this calculated? Yes. The waiting, he thought, would make the mind useless so that in the interrogation he would forget. His mind would slip. He would be unable to answer the simplest questions.

He wouldn't be able to refer to the coaching papers. They were torn and buried under miles of ocean. He could feel his own thoughts sinking like those shreds of information he threw overboard back in Hawaii. The scenery outside the dormitory room added to the sorrowful feelings. The landscape was broken up by the chain-link fence. Trees and stones were constantly enshrouded by fog. Clouds massed around the mountain top, choking it. There was the ominous sound of the clicking of horses' hooves, the horses of the American army stationed on the island. The soldiers were prepared to shoot anyone who dared to attempt escape.

The monotony of the long wait in the dormitory was punctured only by meals and by the repeated humiliations at the hands of the doctors. Man Sum had to report to the infirmary on a weekly basis to go through a battery of tests. The first thing they made him do was strip down. Then he had to wait with several others, all naked. All were ashamed of being naked in front of one another and in front of the white doctors and nursing staff.

The waiting room was inadequately heated, so there was always a chill. Those who were healthy had to wait in the same room as those who were sick, so one was always in danger of catching the other's ailment.

On this particular afternoon, the waiting room was especially crowded. He had to sit on the icy linoleum floor because the few chairs were already taken.

Finally, after about two hours, his name was called. The doctor was rude. He ordered Man Sum to turn this way and that. He probed his genitals with a metal stick and made him pass feces in a white bowl, so he could be tested for hookworm. He had heard of cases where an applicant had no hookworm in the first examination. But then several larvae would show up in the feces several weeks later. He suspected that the hookworm was passed from one to another in that place, the wooden building, because the conditions were so unsanitary.

Possibly, the prejudiced among the white people were pleased by the spread of hookworm. Most Americans didn't really want Chinese people in their country, he decided.

Man Sum was dismissed by the doctor and returned to the dormitory to await the results of the exam.

If he had hookworm, he wouldn't be informed or

treated for the illness. What would happen to him had
happened to many others.

He would be wakened in the middle of the night by
several uniformed officials. They would escort him to the
building close to the docks, greyish in color. That was the
building where everyone's baggage was kept. There, he
would be given his baggage and told to wait. Without
ceremony, he and the other deportees would be herded
aboard the steamship of the Pacific Mail and Steamship
Company. It would be bound for China with its cargo of
sadness. Several would never reach China. They would
commit suicide aboard the vessel, as Man Sum himself
planned to do.

But the khaki-clad barbarians never came for him.
Luckily, they had not found any traces of hookworm.

"Watch out for the guards," inmates who had been
there longer warned the recent arrivals.

Stories went around about one of the guards especially,
a real Angel Island hazard named Murphy.

Murphy was Irish. He was about fifty. It was rumored
that he'd spent a good part of his youth as a member of a
hoodlum gang that haunted the docks. The hoodlums,
mostly Irish Catholic, delighted in throwing rocks at the
Chinese as they landed. These hoodlums were the un-
employed. They claimed that because the Chinese were
willing to work for next to nothing, it was impossible for
an honest white man to get a job.

Murphy prided himself on his military bearing and on
his appearance. His uniform was always carefully pressed,
his shoes shined, and his beard combed neatly. He was
known to enjoy trumping up some charge against one of
the detainees and then meting out justice on his own.

The Irish officer always stood at the top of the stairs,

using his long club to herd the bulk, hurry the stragglers and slow down the greedy. It you passed close enough, you would smell liquor on the Irishman's breath. Occasionally, Man Sum would feel Murphy's club in his ribs. Murphy was sometimes given to poking and prodding them, like a child toying with helpless insects.

Mo Fay, as he was known to Man Sum's countrymen, stood one day at his accustomed station when the bell brought the group out to the landing faster than usual. It was Thanksgiving, a holiday of the *faan gwai*, and a little more meat was promised. Man Sum was slight of build. The food they served did little to make up for three months of continual boredom and anxiety. The nourishment did nothing to help him withstand cold nights sleeping under a single blanket. So he looked forward to more substantial fare.

Man Sum gave in to the shoving crowd and let himself be pushed. It was easier than trying to thread his own route at his own pace, and it conserved energy. Energy was always in short supply. The flow of bodies would eventually lead him down the long stairway and into the dining hall. He hoped he'd get there before all the nourishment disappeared down the throats of the starving men. But instead of continuing with the crowd, he was edged by it to the wall, bounced against this wall like a tied up boat that strikes the dock with each wave.

Before he could work his way back into the line, an elbow knocked him backward and square onto the highly polished shoes of Mo Fay.

The Irishman was infuriated. He grabbed Man Sum and threw him so he stumbled back in the other direction, away from the stairs and the crowd.

"Look at these shoes, coolie. Yes. That's right. Open

your slits. Open 'em. Let a little light in. Look what you did.''

Man Sum stared mutely at the man. He knew only that the Irishman was angry over the shoes.

"You don't understand, do you? Yeah, you don't even know what you did. Well, I'll teach you.''

Mo Fay took hold of Man Sum's left ear and hoisted him toward a door at the end of the hall. There were different boxes piled up. It was a storeroom. Mo Fay pushed the Chinese in the room, then came in himself and shut the door behind him. There was a moment of complete darkness before the red-faced giant clicked on a dim, dust-covered bulb.

The white man took time to study this specimen of the race he had despised for twenty years, the race that was responsible for his own poverty, his failures, the drying up of the gold in the hills, and the depression of the eighties and nineties. He considered it his duty to rid the country of the vermin. He wanted to put the fear of God into them so they'd beg for a ticket back the other way, back where they belonged.

He laid his boot across the Oriental's cloth prison shoe and stepped down with all his weight. Man Sum screamed with pain and threw himself backward, grabbing his foot. It throbbed with excruciating pain.

Oh, no! He didn't like that. Evil ghost will die for this, he thought. He and all the bad ghosts like him will die! Man Sum's angry thoughts silently raced behind burning eyes. He thought, I will kill him with my own hands. I will find him, no matter where he is. I will find him and I will kill him. I must be patient. I must bear this suffering in the present. But it will only be for the present. He will pay, eventually. He will pay for my suffering with his life.

"Watch your step next time," Murphy muttered.

Man Sum sat still, glowering at his captor, not moving a muscle.

"Go on, get out of here," Murphy said, opening the door.

"*Jo mut yeh, ney da ngaw ah*? Why did you step on me?" Man Sum barked back at Mo Fay in Chinese.

Murphy ignored what he couldn't understand. "What're you doing in here anyway? Smoking the old opium? Trying to make an opium den out of government property, are you? Go on. Go on down there and lick what's left of your rice bowl."

Others might have kowtowed to this authority, but Man Sum's heart would not bend under this intimidation. It was never in his character to go on his knees. This Mo Fay, this cruel foreign ghost would not receive the gesture of respect which was due only to those who earned it: elders, ancestors, teachers, priests. They were worthy of his respect, but not this white officer. Man Sum stood straight and walked out without a word.

Man Sum limped into the dormitory room. The man in the upper bunk saw him hobbling.

"What happened?" the man asked.

"Mo Fay," Man Sum said. "He stepped on my foot, purposely."

"That white snake!" the man growled. "Listen, I am Tom Lum Po. I want to meet a man who stands up to the *faan gwai*." And Lum Po put out his hand.

Man Sum shook Lum Po's hand. "It is good to shake the hand of a brother and a countryman," Man Sum said.

"Perhaps, one day, we shall fight side by side against this injustice," Lum Po said.

"Yes, I hope we shall," Man Sum said. He had a feeling that this was the beginning of a strong friendship.

Chapter 2

It was three weeks before the foot healed enough so that he could walk without limping, but the pain in his foot was never so great as the pain of humiliation he felt of not being able to exact revenge. He would plot. He would find a way. They would all pay with their lives for this torment visited on him and his countrymen. He would destroy their wicked island. Here, the trees weren't trees, the grass was not grass. Nature herself had abandoned this place a long time ago. Here, all was desolation and coercion.

Awake at night, lost in his bitter thoughts, his mind drifted back to his village. He thought of the familiar people, the paths to the fields he had traversed countless times. Oh, to return! If he could only return to his homeland. It was better to suffer the rigor of the farmer's life, the back bent over a plow for ten to twelve hours. There, together with his countrymen, he could work to make China great again.

Then, once China was the most powerful nation on earth, he would return to Gold Hill, he and his countrymen. They would destroy the wooden building forever, drown the island in the Ocean of Peace, drop large boulders on the island. It would sink all the way down to Yen Lo's world of the demons under the earth. It would never surface again. And that would be the last place a middle kingdom man would ever have to spend wasted, empty time in.

Man Sum had made only one friend since coming to Angel Island. That was Tom Lum Po. For some reason, Man Sum felt instinctively that he could trust this individual, and although Lum Po was not inclined to scholarship, he was very intelligent. He had directness and humor in his eyes. He liked to laugh from deep in the belly like a happy Buddha. When he was angry about something, his voice grew sharp and he shook his fist in quick gestures. Lum Po was muscular. His arms had lifted rice baskets and pulled plows. He was affectionate, too. He would often take Man Sum's arm or slap Man Sum on the shoulder in the spirit of friendship.

Therefore, Lum Po was someone Man Sum didn't fear. He trusted this robustly spirited man. In fact, Lum Po was the one person in the prison with whom he shared his true identity.

"I am not Kwong Bing Win. I am Sing Man Sum. I am, as you would put it, a paper son."

"I will tell no one," Lum Po replied earnestly. "You can have confidence in me."

Man Sum nodded. "I know."

"I am in a different situation than you, Man Sum," Lum Po said. "My father is Tom Lum Ah. He is a bona fide merchant. The papers I received were perfectly legitimate. Yet, for some reason I don't understand, I have been denied entrance. And I cannot figure out why my father has not found me, has not made contact with me."

"I also wonder about my father," Sing Man Sum

said. "He is Sing Choy Wu. He is in San Francisco. I wonder about him. I wonder if and when I shall see him."

"Several times, I have tried to convince the authorities they should try to reach my father, but my requests have been ignored," Lum Po said.

"If China were a powerful country," Man Sum said, "this incarceration would not be happening to us."

"If we can somehow get out of this prison," Lum Po said, "we can make a lot of money here, then go back to China. Help to finance a real revolution."

"Yes, we'll make China great. Then this kind of thing will never happen to our countrymen again," Man Sum agreed.

Man Sum's dream of power did not fade as time wore on. Six months after his arrival on the island, he was talking to his friend Tom Lum Po at the breakfast table.

"When we get out of here, we must remain together, Lum Po," Man Sum said. "We will go to the gold fields together."

"I think we will give each other luck," Lum Po said with a smile.

Then Man Sum was suddenly aware that something peculiar was going on. He felt eyes looking in his direction. There was someone at the kitchen doorway staring at him, a kitchen helper, who was making two signals very fast. Man Sum thought he caught the meaning of the two signals. One was a gesture to the lips which indicated silence, secrecy. The other gesture pointed to the rice bowl in front of Man Sum. With his chopstick, he probed to the bottom of the bowl. Instead of reaching the bottom, the chopstick touched something that felt clearly like a piece of paper.

The expression on Man Sum's face made Lum Po burst out laughing. "It's really tasteless, isn't it?"

"Yes, it is," he answered. "Really tasteless. *Dung mat sik mat.* Animal food."

He was telling the truth. The rice was terrible as always. But he forced himself to eat it so he could find the message at the bottom of his breakfast. Finally, he reached it and read.

It was from the Chi Sing Tong. It said that there was a large stake in getting Man Sum out. It didn't say why. It said there were friends among the kitchen staff, and it warned him to use extreme caution when reading the notes. Do not remove them from the rice bowl. It said that in order to communicate to the Tong, Man Sum should fold his note as small as he could and put it under his tongue. Then, while bringing the bowl level with his mouth, let the note fall into the bowl, all the while continuing to use his chopsticks in the normal manner.

When Man Sun finished reading these instructions, he looked up. One of the kitchen staff promptly came over to Man Sum's table and began clearing the bowls. Man Sum's bowl was now part of a stack of bowls which the helper took back to the kitchen. Man Sum had never lifted the secret note out of the bowl.

"How many times did your father visit your village?" the interrogator asked.

"There were only five visits," Lum Po answered through an interpreter.

"According to the records I have, there were only three visits," the interrogator said.

Lum Po thought definitely it had been five. But one of the visits took place when he was only two years old. Could it be that he mistook another relative for his father?

Lum Po had not thought about it much. He assumed he would be allowed to enter San Francisco immediately. Tom Lum Ah was his true father, Lum Po was the true son. He had not prepared for an examination. He had no reason to expect anyone would doubt his word.

"And where was the kitchen table in your house?" the interrogator asked.

Lum Po asked the interpreter to repeat the question. Yes, the interrogator had asked about the kitchen table. It seemed to Lum Po to be an extremely peculiar question.

The kitchen in his house in Chung San village had been moved around many times because his mother kept on changing her mind, rearranging the kitchen to make things more convenient. What she really needed was a larger kitchen. But that was out of the question. The money Lum Ah sent from America was enough for them to live on day by day, but that was all.

"Well, the kitchen table was moved around a lot," Lum Po tried to explain. "It was in different places at different times."

"That answer isn't good enough," the interrogator said. "Come up with a better one."

"I don't have a better one. It was sometimes in one place and sometimes in another," Lum Po said, frowning.

"Hurry up and decide. Where was it? Against the wall or in the middle of the kitchen? If it was against the wall, what wall? The wall facing the street or the wall facing the yard? Or did you have a yard? I forgot. Come now, surely you who have lived there all your life must remember where your own kitchen table was placed."

"Sometimes—" Lum Po started.

"And don't give me 'sometimes.' I don't want to hear 'sometimes.' Our typist cannot type 'sometimes.' We are dealing with facts here, not fantasy, not conjecture, not your imagination. Translate, please.''

The interpreter leaned toward Lum Po and translated. ''Tell officer where kitchen table was. Don't lie. Only tell truth.''

''The typist is waiting. Hurry up. Hurry up. I have several interviews to do today. I can't waste time. Your sort of people, you always put on that stone-faced expression when you can't answer. Now, if these facts are not at your fingertips, then God help you. Because it simply means you're not who you say you are. Translate.

''*Fai di la. Fai di daap la.* Quickly, quickly, answer.''

''Well, my father would say the wall facing the side yard, by the window. That's where it was his last visit home, I think.''

''He says the wall facing the side yard, by the window.''

The interrogator stopped and waited for the typist to enter the last answer. Then he pulled the sheet out of her typewriter. He joined that sheet with the other sheet, stapled all the papers together, then brought another set of records out of the drawer. This latter set of records was the interrogation of the father, given some years earlier. After comparing the two interviews at length, the interrogator looked at the young man. Fear flitted across Lum Po's face in short twitches. The officer seemed to enjoy watching this.

''Well,'' he said at last, ''there appear to be a number of discrepancies. For one thing, your description of your house, the house you lived in all your life, does not match your father's. But there are other problems as well.'' He nodded to the translator.

The translation ran, ''*Ney gong dai wa.* You don't tell the truth. You're not really the man's son.''

"But I *am*. I *am* his son," Lum Po replied.

The interrogator rose and began pacing and gesticulating with his forefinger. "Your father says, according to this interview, he only visited China three times. Your story makes it five times. You appear to be just guessing at all these answers."

"I am not guessing," Lum Po said hotly.

"They are questions your coaching papers fail to answer."

"What coaching papers? I don't have any coaching papers!"

"I'm very sorry, young man. I hate to have to deny you permission to immigrate. There are laws in the state that must be upheld. Can you imagine what would happen if we allowed all of the Chinese to immigrate who wanted to?"

"I'm a legitimate applicant!"

"The whites in the state would become a minority and California would belong to the Oriental. Now, we can't have that, can we?"

"I am the son, the only son, of the merchant, Tom Lum Ah!"

"And I have a job to do. I'm the one whose responsibility it is to keep his finger in the dike. I'm the one who holds back the flood."

"Why me? Why are you picking on me? There are many paper sons here, and I am not one of them."

"Oh?" The interrogator wheeled around and stopped. "You know about paper sons? You know, in fact, some people who are paper sons."

"I know who is not a paper son, and I tell you, I am not one," Lum Po said emphatically.

"Yes, well, your status may, ahem, be changed . . . to a more favorable one if you were able to supply us with names of those you know to be paper sons," the interrogator said, leaning toward the applicant.

Lum Po was silent.

After a few moments, he said. "That's impossible."

"I see," the interrogator said, and he resumed his pacing.

"I would never do that to my friends," Lum Po said. "Betray my friends, never. I am not that kind of man."

"I have nothing against you as an individual, I'm sure you're a fine young man and you'd make an outstanding contribution to this country. But you see, there are many of you. Too many. And therefore, we have to be selective and careful. You all want to claim you're the sons of merchants. Well, if each merchant had as many sons as they claim, they wouldn't have had any time to develop their businesses, now would they?" He laughed at his joke.

"But I am really my father's son! I am Tom Lum Ah's son. Why don't you contact him? Bring him here. He will tell you."

The immigration officer said nothing. He just stared at Lum Po.

Then, after a pause, he said, "In lieu of perjury proceedings, the order of this board shall be that Tom Lum Po shall be deported. Make arrangements for the deportation of the applicant."

After this judgment was communicated to him, Lum Po stood up, clenching his fists. "It's unfair! You are the unfair ones! I am Lum Ah's legitimate son! His third son! I am his heir! We are tied by blood! I am tied by blood to my family, to my ancestral clan! My clan goes back ten generations, past the Ming to the Han dynasty! My clan is over two thousand years old! It is you who have no lineage, not I! It is you who are the illegitimate ones, the impostors, not I!''

He said all this in a high-pitched scream. The startled interrogator quickly called two guards over. Each took an arm, and they led Tom Lum Po into a small, windowless room with a concrete floor and bare, cement walls. There, they pummeled him until he lost consciousness.

He awakened in his bunk. He was a mass of bruises. His deportation was supposed to take place the following week.

Later that week, Man Sum was awakened by a strange noise in the bunk above him. He got out of his bed and discovered Lum Po with a braided, torn sheet around his neck, and his legs bent and tied. He was just tying the other end of this makeshift rope to the metal bar at the foot of his bunk.

Man Sum quickly jumped to the top tier, ripped away the braided sheet and undid the wrappings around the knees. Lum Po, instead of struggling, put his head in his hands and stifled his sobs. No one awoke.

Man Sum spoke to him with affection. ''Fellow countryman, don't take away this gift of life. You would take all our hopes with you. When a man takes his own life, the peace that he gains he buys with the lifeblood of his brothers. We all have little enough to spare.''

''Brother,'' Lum Po replied. ''Let me go. Let me go. I beg you. I have a wife in the village, a son, mother, uncles. They invested in me. They sold some of their lands and possessions to buy my passage. They gambled heavily in hopes that I would succeed and bring them good fortune. They light incense sticks and make food offerings daily to the god of travelers to insure my safe passage.''

"Yes, brother, what you say about yourself is true for most of our countrymen," Man Sum said.

"I would be going back having failed. I would be subjected to disappointed faces and heads shaking. I would be forced to sit idle and watch wife, mother, son, uncles, suffer hunger and humiliation because I, their best hope in all the world, have utterly let them down."

"You did *not* let them down," Man Sum said vehemently. "You were thrown into circumstances you could not foresee or control!"

"I did not know I would be sent to the Island of Ghosts."

"Of course you did not know."

"I wrote to them letters which were falsehoods, telling them I landed safely. I said I was being treated as a guest, welcome in the beautiful country. I told them I was finding many opportunities to earn money, so many opportunities, I couldn't decide among them. How could I possibly describe to them the reality of the island? I lied to my kinsmen."

"You lied to your kinsmen," Man Sum added, "in order to save them the grief they would certainly feel if they knew the truth of your situation."

"I cannot bear it. I will not return on the deportation ship. What happened was my fault entirely and no one else's. I wasn't at all prepared for the examination. Not at all. I should have been prepared."

"How could you possibly know they would give you this kind of tricky examination?"

"I should have been ready with the answers. I have lost face entirely. There is no face left. I am already like one who is dead."

"Lum Po," Man Sum said reassuringly, "try to realize that this island is only an obstruction lasting for a short time. You have friends here. I am your friend. One must join forces with friends of like mind. This requires the will to persevere."

"Persevere? What are you talking about? They're going to send me back to China, brother!" Lum Po said despondently.

"Unswerving inner purpose will bring good fortune in the end. Just when it appears that all is black, all is lost, is when one must practice perseverance most."

"Look," Lum Po said angrily. "I don't know what you're talking about, but it doesn't have anything to do with me. Why don't you just go back to bed?"

"Suicide does seem like the most rational course of action in a time when the goal looks impossible to realize, but it is just at that moment one must cling to the goal."

"There is no point to clinging to goals that are impossible to realize, brother," Lum Po said. "I have heard enough of this Taoist philosophy! I don't believe in not-doing. I am going to do something about my fate. It is in *my* control, not heaven's. Now, please leave me to do what I must do!"

"There is a better way."

"Not the way of Taoism!"

"There is a better *action*," Man Sum whispered with great seriousness.

"Yes, kill all the demons."

"No."

"What must I do? There is nowhere to hide on the island. They will come for me tomorrow. They will take me to the shed where the belongings are kept. From there I will be led across the wooden walkway to the waiting ship. That ship will be like my coffin, the emblem of my lost life. I talked to Woo Sing. I told him what I meant to do. I paid him in jade pieces to write a note to my family

explaining that I was killed while in the mountains explor-
ing for gold.''

"Tomorrow, you will take your jade pieces back
from Woo Sing," Man Sum said.

"But I gave him money to bribe the ship captain to
bring my body back to my village. I would be given an
honorable burial there. It is all arranged and decided, Man
Sum.''

"It is the wrong decision. It is against the law of
heaven," Man Sum said.

"The law of heaven is broken in the land of the
barbarians. Please do not stand in the path of a man's
pursuit of the one honorable goal he has left.''

"Often," Man Sum spoke slowly, "it seems as though
everything is conspiring against you. You see yourself
hindered in your progress at every turn. You are insulted,
dishonored. But despite the overwhelming opposition, the
matter will end well. Believe me, even though this island has
given us a bad start, it will still be possible for us to make
a new beginning.''

Lum Po answered, "How? How? I have failed the
examination, don't you understand? That is the end of it.
My true father is a merchant, there across the fog-laden
sea. But they only compare papers. They don't contact my
father to make verification. I say, 'Call father. Bring him
here. He will address me as his respected son.' But they
refuse. They choose to disbelieve. They want to extermi-
nate me. They think I am some form of pestilence that
must be done away with. My presence only awakens
disgust in their expressions.''

"The answer to your question of how you will reach
Gold Hill is not immediately clear," Man Sum answered.
"Be patient and persevere while the storm is in progress.
If it is possible to become invisible on a ship, as some of

our countrymen have done in the past, then it is not impossible to attain invisibility in the wooden building.''

"Become invisible? You mean hide somewhere in this building?''

"In the kitchen.''

Lum Po looked astonished. "But to what purpose? To what end? They have decreed I should be deported. You would lock me in a smaller, tighter prison than this one. How will your plan bring me closer to my goal?''

"There are friends among the kitchen help,'' Man Sum responded. "I discovered this truth last week. I found this note in a bowl of red rice at breakfast last Thursday morning.''

Lum Po read the note. It said, "The society of victorious union salutes you. Your success is interesting to us. Kitchen helpers bring coaching information from our Tong to the island. Your father is a brother. Communicate with the helpers carefully as the authorities are always watching.''

Man Sum said, "I looked at the door of the kitchen and saw one of the helpers looking at me. I knew he was the source of the note and I would have to address any letters to him. So you see, Lum Po, you must be made invisible in order to escape deportation. And the helpers, our brothers and friends and the society for victorious union, will serve us. All is not lost. We are not alone.''

"Really?''

"Yes. You see, had I been deported, I vowed the same vow as the one you almost carried out. I too said I would commit suicide rather than lose face in my village of Wing Tan Ho. We are, Lum Po, both men of strong will. If we are joined together, obstacles will be easier to overcome.''

"But how do we defeat the *faan gwai*?''

"The enemy cannot look in two directions at once.

He is blind in the back of his head. He must guard in one direction while in the opposite, work is being undertaken in the shadows to undermine him.''

The following morning at breakfast, Man Sum, seated next to Lum Po, began to drum his metal plate on the table. He was soon joined in chorus by ninety-eight inmates in the dining hall. A frightened guard left the room to call in reinforcements. It appeared to him that this would soon become a full-scale food riot, and it must be quelled.

Lum Po quickly ducked into the kitchen. Man Sum just as quickly stopped the demonstration.

The hallway was peaceful once again, as if no disturbance had happened. The prisoners ate their food contentedly.

Several guards were heard running in the hallway. When they arrived, they quickly swung the double doors open, and they raised their billy clubs, anticipating a terrible confrontation. Instead they were greeted by smiles and bows. One man held up his empty bowl and gestured, by rubbing his stomach, that he was truly satisfied with his meal. Mystified and grumbling, the guards returned to their stations. The meal ended without further incident.

The men in khaki came that bleak morning to bring Lum Po to the first station of his long journey home, but they were disappointed to find no sign of him.

Murphy was among them. ''Where is he? Where is Tom Lum Po?'' Frantically he shook several men in their bunks.

''All right!'' he shouted after one of the men turned on the lights. ''Everyone out! Everybody out of your bunks!''

The men obeyed.

"Who has been answering for Lum Po during the head counts? Who has been responding when his name was called?" Murphy asked, stomping his feet.

No one answered.

"Stone faces. Do you have rocks in your mouths, too?"

The alarm rang and the search was on. The kitchen was highly suspect as usual, but the guards turned it upside down with no result. A certain trap door below a bin full of potatoes was not discovered. There, Lum Po languished, sustained only by the belief and hope that friends were behind him, although he had no idea who they were. The man he had called the philosopher had genuinely inspired him to exercise the will to survive, despite insurmountable obstacles.

The enclosure had a vent through which he could see the outside filtered through strands of overgrown grass.

The search for Lum Po lasted half the day. It was finally called off, but at supper the director of Angel Island Immigration Center delivered a lecture on immigration law, calling attention in particular to the seriousness of the crime of aiding and concealing illegal immigrants.

He paused for the translation. He watched the faces of the inmates for any reactions that might seem to contradict him. But the faces betrayed no emotion whatsoever. He went on.

"The conspiracy to conceal a rejected applicant reflects poorly on all the applicants. Such behavior will adversely affect the results of each of the pending investigations. The Immigration Service is set up to facilitate quick and efficient processing of the immigrant. The service doesn't want delays any more than the detainees. We are, after all, here to serve the newcomer. Don't you ever forget it.''

The director paused as his message was rendered understandable in the tongue of his charges. He paused again after the translation to gauge the effect his words had on the inmates. Then he proceeded to drive his point home.

''I want here and now a full disclosure of the whereabouts of Tom Lum Po. I am sure that a few of you here know perfectly well where, how, and by whom he is hidden. If I am not satisfied in the next few moments, I will be forced to take measures which will, unfortunately, add to the inconvenience you're already suffering.''

He waited. There was no evidence that his words had any effect whatsoever. He stalked out hastily, and with a set, determined face. He left his staff to outline the ''measures'' he had alluded to in his speech: shutting down for an indefinite period of time the stand which had supplied, at a nominal cost, cigarettes, coffee, tea and sundries. Also, Chinese newspapers and other reading materials supplied for detainees would be curtailed. Lights out would be called a half-hour earlier than usual. Stricter limits would be placed on games such as cards, dominoes, and mahjong. Rules forbidding gambling at the center would be more strictly enforced.

These measures were successful in further demoralizing the men in the dormitory, but they didn't succeed in eliciting the whereabouts of Lum Po. The measures stayed in effect long after the search for Lum Po was called off. They became part of the daily hardship. After a while, nobody bothered to regret the lost privileges.

Mo Fay clapped Man Sum's right shoulder. The shoulder was swung around. Instead of being allowed to join the line-up for the evening meal, Man Sum was forced in the direction of the dimly lit storeroom. Mo Fay propelled him there with a shove that almost sent Man Sum sprawling on the hard, wooden hallway floor. In the storeroom, three other immigration officers were waiting for him. Man Sum recognized one of them. He was the proctor at the meal where Man Sum had started the food riot.

"Is this the one?" Mo Fay asked.

"Yes, that's him," the proctor replied.

There was no translator around. Man Sum heard only angry, snarling words. He guessed at their meaning.

"This is the troublemaker," Mo Fay said. "He's got the other Chink hidden somewhere." Then Mo Fay turned to Man Sum.

"Where are you hiding him? Won't you tell us? Where are you hiding the man?" Mo Fay illustrated his meaning by cupping his hands and then opening them to reveal one finger extended. He wriggled the finger that was supposed to represent Lum Po.

"Perhaps he doesn't know," the proctor said.

Mo Fay said, "Come now, you're the plate banger. You bangee platee, no likee breakfast. Guardee leave dining hall, you hidee him Chinese paper son!" Mo Fay spewed mockingly.

Man Sum stared back condescendingly at the enraged Irishman.

"No justice around here, none," Mo Fay roared. "They sneak 'em in any way they can. You know, they're all relatives of each other. For ten deported, they sneak in fifty. They got connections with their relatives in Chinatown, all of 'em."

"It's the Tongs. The highbinders," the proctor said.

"They grease a few palms of greedy politicians.

They've got lawyers working for them. They pay good bucks to corrupt some of the best law firms in the city."

"Or the Immigration Service," the proctor put in.

"Last week a guy with the service was caught with his hand in the file cabinet, getting ready to doctor up a few papers. I tell you, it is a conspiracy. And somebody's got to do something about it!" Murphy yelled.

"What did you bring him in here for?" One of the guards asked Mo Fay.

Mo Fay said, "Well, I thought maybe, just maybe, we could squeeze something out of him, scare him a little."

"Well you succeeded in scaring him all right. Just look at him, will you? I'll tell you, that's one heathen who's thinking he's going to die on the spot."

"Yeah, but that won't pull anything out of him," Mo Fay spat. "These coolies will go through the fires of hell and still come out of it with their jaws clamped shut. Nothing shakes up the cold stone-faced Chinaman."

The guard said, "Well, we've seen enough of him. We know who he is. We'll remember him when his interrogation comes up. Then we'll deal with him. Meanwhile, keep your eyes on him. Likely he's got contacts on the outside. See that he isn't slipped any notes or tries to slip any himself."

They dismissed Man Sum. And when he had turned his back to them, he couldn't help but let a smile cross his face.

Disposing of garbage on Angel Island was a problem. The food was virtually unpalatable, and this meant that much went uneaten. The detainees ate only enough of the gruel to keep them alive.

Once every two weeks, Hal Blakely of the new Sunset Scavenger Company pulled his garbage scow up to the wooden planks that constituted the pier. Just beyond the pier was the walkway leading to the entrance of the detention center. This time the kitchen help had an unusually large amount of leavings, mostly potatoes. The Chinese had found the fare particularly repugnant.

When the kitchen help met Blakely on the pier, they were smiling.

Blakely said, "Hello, you heathens. What d'ya got there? Looks like half the Chinese continent. Little landfill, huh?"

Jack Pong, the head of the kitchen help, said, "You take everything, okay?"

"Yeah, I'll get it. Hey, I'll take this stuff and use it to fill out San Francisco. This'll make up for what she lost in the quake."

"Okay, Hal. You take everything. You dump where?"

"I'll probably dump it couple of miles out to sea, that's what I usually do. Why?"

Jack Pong moved close to Hal Blakely and said, "Hal, you got a passenger. You take good care. You let passenger off Chinatown, okay?"

"Oh, no, not again!" Hal shook his head. "You fellows know I can't be doing favors like this for you anymore. I told you last time, I can't take any more chances. My job is on the line!"

"No chances," Jack Pong whispered. "He hidden very good in potatoes. Nobody see him. You go close to Chinatown on way out to sea. Very good. Passenger slip away, you no see him. He swims good. He knows what to do. You make whistle two times. Nobody suspect you."

He looked fearfully up toward the entrance of the center. A guard was gazing suspiciously toward the kitchen help who were having such an animated discussion with Hal.

Hal relented. "Okay, get the stuff on board, and hurry. I don't know why I take chances for you guys."

They said amongst themselves, "*Koy ho yan. Jun hai ho yan.* He is a good man, a really good man."

As the scow pulled away from the pier, the smiling Chinese men waved to the chubby garbage man reassuringly.

"Bye-bye, Hal. You don't worry, okay? No problem!"

Well into the bay, Hal killed the engine. He turned to a large drum, which Jack Pong had pointed out. He opened the can. It was filled with large, full brown paper bags, but tucked neatly beside the top bag was a jar with the Del Monte tomato sauce label.

Hal fished a wet twenty-dollar bill out of the jar and shook the bill in the breeze.

He walked over to the potatoes, saying, "Okay. You can come out." There was no sound. "Hey, it's okay, you're safe. I'm a friend."

Looking closely at the pile of potatoes, Hal could see where a breathing tube made of cardboard extended. He pulled the potatoes aside and the frightened form of Lum Po was revealed cowering against the garbage surrounding him. Hal attempted to calm the newcomer, then realized the communication gap might be bridged another way.

He put his hand on an imaginary string and jerked it down twice. "Beep, beep, okay?"

He then smiled at Lum Po and repeated the procedure. Lum Po, about to enter the domain of the barbarians in search of fortune, very tentatively smiled back at the sweaty, genial ship's captain.

Chapter 3

Kwan Ming Lee came from an extremely poor family in Nan Hai. In spite of her poverty, she was rather well educated. Her father was a teacher in the village school. He never passed the rigorous exams that would have given him status as a scholar.

Her family was overjoyed when Yuk Wing Ling, a *Gum San Haak*, a guest of Gold Hill, had chosen her to be his bride. On the day declared to be auspicious by the soothsayer, Yuk Wing Ling showered his bride-to-be with gifts. They were Western things: a parasol, a hat, a pearl necklace. More traditional gifts followed. Four red boxes, two containing cakes, one of pork and one of wine, and a gold lacquer box containing the bridegroom's family name character and a marriage contract. This box also held a gift of "big money," in this case, two hundred dollars. Ming Lee's father was the only one permitted to open this box.

Ming Lee, in her turn, gave Wing Ling two large steamed rice cakes with four characters on them, two roots of lotus, and material for a pair of pants which she would be expected to cut and make up under the critical eye of her mother-in-law. She also had to make and embroider shoes for her bridegroom's female relatives to prove her skill at needlework.

Ten days before the date fixed for the wedding, the formal betrothal took place. The bridegroom sent presents of gold accompanied by pork, chickens and wine. The "dragon and phoenix" cakes symbolizing a happy married life were part of the ceremonial process. Red cards embossed with gold characters were sent around to friends and relatives.

On the day before the wedding, the bride's furniture was taken from the home of her parents to her new home, that of the groom's family. In the absence of her husband, she would have to submit to her mother-in-law's authority.

She was placed, then, in ceremonial seclusion, presided over by unmarried girlfriends chosen as bridesmaids. This was a time of weeping over her parting from her family. During her seclusion, she was provided with light literature in the form of a confidential book to prepare her for her married responsibilities.

On the morning of the day of her wedding, she took a ceremonial bath with some pummeloe leaves added. Then she sat in a tray used for drying the family rice while her hair was dressed in the married woman's style.

Before leaving her home for good, she performed ceremonial prostrations to the ancestral tablets and to her parents, thanking them for their care of her all her life. The bridesmaids gave her "lucky money" as pocket money, and she left her parents forever.

The bridegroom's cart was waiting for her. But before he could take her away, he had to pay ransom to the bridesmaids. They demanded a hundred dollars. He countered with fifty, for it was the custom to bargain for the bride. Finally, a deal was struck for the sum of sixty-five dollars, and he was allowed to cart her away.

On the third day after the ceremony, she returned to pay a visit to her own family. She dressed in the red skirt indicating her new status and a black jacket decked with jewelry: rings, bracelets, and gold lockets. Before leaving her husband's house, she bowed before her new family's ancestral tablets. On her arrival at her new home, Yuk Wing Ling tapped her on the head with his fan, then raised her veil with it. Firecrackers signaled the departure from her old home and arrival at that of her new family.

Two weeks later, Yuk Wing Ling returned to the mysterious country across the sea. He bade her a warm good-bye and promised to send for her soon. He said all he had to do was make some arrangements. He did not go into detail. After these arrangements were made, he would send her the necessary papers and passage money.

Her mother-in-law filled her schedule with chores. She was given the bulk of the laundry work, the cooking, and the care and feeding of the poultry and pigs. Evenings, after solid work for fourteen hours and a sore back, she collapsed into a deep sleep.

Her menstrual cramps and bleeding had stopped now for two and a half months. The clan entered into its solemn prayers, supplications for a baby son, in the temple of the gods, or joss house.

Yuk Wing Ling's kinsmen lit joss sticks, which were incense sticks. These were placed in incense holders before the representations of deities and ancestors. The prayers were repeated morning and night.

But at the beginning of the third month of her pregnancy, Ming Lee had begun to find drops of blood on her bedding.

A few days later, at three in the morning, she awoke in great pain. After excruciating agony, the bloodied fetus that had been wrenching her body finally let go. It sat there, her failure, featureless in a clay pot of water. Her mother-in-law beat her about the shoulders and legs during the following day and on successive days, calling her a useless servant girl.

She longed for the letter and passage money redeeming her from this onerous existence with the parents of her husband. When the hoped-for letter arrived six months later, she collapsed in a fit of weeping. Her body shook with the release of its long-suffering tension.

She landed at Angel Island on January 4, 1912. She had expected that her husband would be there to meet her. She had looked forward to his escorting her in a motorcar to their palatial home on some hill or other, surrounded by beautiful trees, brooks and temples. She would not have to lift a finger. He would honor her like a lady. There would be servants. She would dress daily as at her wedding, in golden finery. They would attend the theater together and all sorts of other social events. She would be admired for her beauty, her breeding, and most of all, freed from burdensome chores, she would be able to bear her husband a son. She would give honor to him, and reflect honor back on herself.

But her husband wasn't there to welcome her that day. No one welcomed her. She was assigned a dingy room and a cot. She had to share the room with twenty others. All of their faces echoed her own disappointment and frustration. The initial distress on her face deepened into a mask that blended puzzlement with despair. Where was her husband?

A month passed. At her interrogation, the immigration officer kindly informed her that her papers were totally useless. They had no record in the Labor Department that her husband had ever existed. There was no such person as far as they were concerned.

Would she have to go back to her in-laws then? Would she have to spend the rest of her life in the demeaning service of this ghost's family?

They must have some record of him. They must!

Awaiting her deportation, she awoke nightly from dreams of the grinning face of her mother-in-law, beckoning to her with a bent, arthritic hand. In the background, a river of unwashed laundry, bowls and pigs stretched back toward infinity. They were dreams that would not let her sleep.

The women ate their meals before the men, and as they filed out of the dining hall, they would pass by the men filing in. The men often said things, to the younger women especially. They called them "little chickens." They said things like, "Let's find a quiet place to talk together, just you and me," and "I want to see you."

Ming Lee always shrugged off these comments and kept her eyes downcast, hoping the men would leave her alone after a while if she continued to show no interest, no response. But it was always the same thing, every day.

A couple of times, her avoidance of the situation gave rise to the remark, "Hey, why so gloomy? Look at us, smile! You've got a pretty face, why waste it on the floor?" And they would all laugh together. On occasion, she tried looking back at them with the coldest stare she could conjure, but this only made them laugh more.

Once, however, she caught the eye of someone who seemed much different from the others. He wasn't laughing. His look was friendly, sympathetic, not at all threatening. When their eyes met, the laughter and the remarks receded and became mere background noise. He said his name very softly, but in spite of the din, she understood him.

"I am Kwong Bing Win."

Thereafter, every time the women's line passed the men's, Ming Lee's eyes were downcast except for the look she exchanged with Man Sum. Of course, she knew him only by his "paper name," Kwong Bing Win.

Every morning, her eyes would search out his. And, usually, she would find him, though there were some days when the lines passed each other and the contact was missed. You couldn't stop because the line was always shoving you forward. You couldn't leave the line because a guard was standing by who made sure you didn't.

Man Sum always walked on the far right side of his line. Ming Lee walked on the far left side of hers. They contrived to touch each other's shoulders briefly across the rope. They kept their hands down and out of sight, and sometimes the new friends were able to slip notes to each other.

Passing these notes was easier than finding the privacy to read them. They would have to wait until they returned to their dormitory rooms. Then they slipped their notes behind a newspaper or between the pages of a book.

Kwan Ming Lee thought that this contact with the young man was motivated on his part by genuine friendship. What she did not know was that the Tong had expressly commanded Man Sum to seek her out and aid her escape. He was told in these notes that he would be receiving detailed instructions and information regarding Kwan Ming Lee. In the meantime, he should continue to remain in friendly contact with her.

She wrote him, "The moon has waned three times since I first entered the wooden building. My husband did not greet me after the difficult journey. I sought in vain the succor of his hand. He has disappeared. The *faan gwai* do not know his whereabouts. Or they cruelly torture me by keeping us apart. In the depth of my despair, I raise my eyes to meet your friendly face. I see in you one who, like me, is sad to be in the prison of the wooden building, but who also has the hope of a man whose heart is open to the wisdom of heaven. And in your notes I read words which like your face fill me with pleasant thoughts that keep me among the living. Otherwise I should have very soon entered the kingdom of the dead by my own hand. Our friendship is my only sustenance these long days.''

And he wrote to her, ''I wait endlessly for the *faan gwai* to begin the interrogations. They force me to sit still in the cold of the wind, which little by little eats into my brain. I wonder why, sometimes, hope still pushes me forward. My hope, though, is not without some basis in fact. The gods have granted me a contact to the outside. Though this contact is faceless, I know it to be called the hall of victorious union, the Chi Sing Tong. Already, I have called upon the phantom helper. Tom Lum Po was rescued from certain deportation. He's in Chinatown now, safe among these friends. I have made conveyance of your misfortune to the messengers, and you may put your heart at ease.''

How Ming Lee wished, reading this, that she could talk to Kwong Bing Win face to face.

''The day is approaching when we will be able to talk directly instead of through bamboo slips,'' the note went on. ''When we meet to shake hands and talk freely, we will be landed in the place of our future happiness. Try not to dwell too much on this present suffering, my friend. Your husband will be found. The newsbringers will let us hear of him, and the *faan gwai* must bring him to the island for a reunion with his wife. That is their law. Have no fear. You will be happy."

Man Sum was careful in his note to say that it was *he* who first contacted the Tong. The Chi Sings didn't want her to know that they were aware of her situation and were interested in helping her on their own. What was the Tong's true interest in her? Man Sum wondered.

A communiqué materialized in which the Tong gave him information and instructions, which, he was told, he must pass on to the young woman. He was supposed to tell her that her husband died in an accident. He was also to tell her that the Chi Sing Tong was an organization of Chinese "missionaries" who were taking over her case. She was to go to the interrogations and pretend that her husband was still living. This was only a formality agreed upon by the "missionaries" and the interrogation team. Technically, she was not to be admitted to the country since her husband had died, but these "missionaries" had made arrangements with the Labor Department to allow her to immigrate.

Both men and women volunteers were requested to help Jack Pong, who was head of the kitchen staff, with a huge shipload of abalone. The fishery at Richmond had made its delivery to the city, but only managed to sell half its catch. The boat passed by Angel Island, and the crew members offered Jack the abalone.

The catch was huge and it took three helpers, three shovels and four laundry baskets to haul the catch up to the yard by the kitchen. The unloading took all afternoon. It would have taken the three of them another week to shell, wash and slice the mollusks had they not been given permission to recruit help from among the interned.

The ten temporary additions to the kitchen staff included Man Sum and his friend, Kwan Ming Lee. A guard was dispatched to the work site to guarantee the work proceeded in a systematic and orderly fashion.

Ming Lee repeatedly searched for an answering glance from Man Sum. At one point, she actually contrived to work side by side with him. He was deftly splitting a shell with a large butcher knife. She placed herself next to him so she could take the meat from him and wash it free of blood and gristle, but he didn't return her glance or try to talk to her. He seemed strangely remote. It struck her that something was preoccupying him, some sadness, perhaps. She would very much like to have comforted him, since he had been so kind to her.

"Kwong Bing Win?" she whispered, but still he didn't answer her. She thought she probably had not whispered his name loud enough.

However, Man Sum had heard her whisper his paper son name. Soon, I will tell her my real name, he thought to himself. Something had happened in his emotions in relation to her, a strong feeling which he had never experienced before. He first had that feeling toward her when he found out that her husband was dead. He found himself hoping that as a result, she would be free for someone else. Perhaps him. This realization was accompanied by a mysterious and deep feeling. He knew what that feeling must be. It must be love.

Love was something he had read about in the classics, but it was no longer Chinese custom, this romantic kind of love. Marriages were, for the most part, arranged. The *moy yen,* or matchmaker, was responsible for bringing together suitable partners, and suitability was determined by finances and horoscopes, not affection. Affection came later, after marriage.

Was it because he was such a dreamer that he was having these feelings? He didn't know quite what to do with them. He was embarrassed. Ashamed. So he said nothing.

She thought to herself, He has had the interrogation. He has received the order for deportation. She held up a lump of mollusk flesh and let the water run over it.

"Give it to me, will you?" she heard an impatient voice beside her say. She passed the fish to her left absently. Then she turned to face Man Sum to her right.

She asked him pointblank, "What's wrong?"

"Nothing," he answered after a pause.

"Yes, there is. There is something wrong, Bing Win. I can tell by the lines in your face, there is something wrong. Have you been interrogated? Are they going to deport you?"

"Your husband's dead, Ming Lee. An accident."

"What king of accident?"

"I don't know."

When she heard this news, she felt no emotion whatsoever. She felt no real love for Yuk Wing Ling. Since the day her parents had sold her to him, he had never treated her with affection.

On the other hand, she had deep feelings for the man who gave her the news of her husband's death. That man was Kwong Bing Win. Then let them be deported together, on the same ship. They would reach China together. He wouldn't let her be taken to the home of her mother-in-law. Together, they would manage. They would find work in Hong Kong. They would marry. Yes, let them be deported together.

He turned toward her and whispered, "You will be called in the next few days to a new interrogation. At that time, your papers will be approved and that same day you will be permitted to land. But it will not be, you will not be entirely free, at least not for the present. You will be indebted to certain "missionaries" who have undertaken to sponsor you."

"Missionaries? What do you mean?"

"The Chi Sing Tong. Chinese missionaries."

"Oh."

"You are to behave in the interrogation as if your husband were still living. They have to say in your file that your husband is still alive."

"Why?"

"I don't know why, Ming Lee. If I did, I would tell you."

"So now I am indebted to this missionary organization? But what do they want me for? Some kind of work?"

Man Sum answered her question with silence. He already wanted to tell her that he loved her, but he did not know how. He knew only that there was nothing he could do for her now. He must abandon her to whatever fate the Chi Sing Tong had in store for her.

The friendliness in his face remained, but the hope had gone out of his eyes. His words and his coldness mirrored her own deepest fears.

For the next few days, Man Sum passed Ming Lee in the dining hall, but there were no exchanges of either notes or smiles. Ming Lee's eyes remained riveted to the floor.

The interrogating officer looked over Ming Lee's papers.

"Yes, your husband is Yuk Wing Ling. What kind of business is he in these days, Miss Lee?"

"He has a gift shop on Grant Avenue."

"How's business?"

"Oh, I hear from him that it's quite prosperous."

"A fortunate man, is he, your husband?"

"Very fortunate," she answered courteously.

"He's what you would call a crafty businessman, then, wouldn't you say so, Miss Lee?"

The interpreter had trouble translating "crafty" into Cantonese. He settled for *ho gey soot*, "skillful."

"Well," said the interrogator. "Well, I suppose you have to be, if you're a Celestial. There are a lot of you. You have a way of coming from nowhere. But most of you seem to manage. It helps, of course, to have acquaintances with influence. Aren't I right, Miss Lee? Does it not help to have friends among the Celestials already well established in their seven heavens?"

"Do you have friends helping you?" the interpreter asked.

She denied this vehemently. "No, no."

Her interrogator smiled pleasantly at her and then, still grinning, picked up the stamp, rocked it on the stamp pad and proceeded to mark the official seal on each of her papers. "Approved, May 13, 1912."

He perfunctorily handed the documents to a clerk, who typed something on a small blue card. The clerk took the documents and placed them in a drawer, then took the blue card out of the typewriter and handed it to the interrogator. The interrogator, still grinning, handed the card to Ming Lee.

"This is your Alien Registration Card, Miss Lee. You must keep it on your person at all times and show it to an officer of the Labor Department where and whenever he should ask you to produce it."

"*Mm goy,* thank you," she said, bowing, and receiving the card with both hands.

He then leaned forward, took her hands in both of his, winked at her with inappropriate familiarity, and said, "Welcome to the United States of America."

* * *

Her departure from the island would occur any day now.

I must tell her my real name and I must tell her of my love, thought Sing Man Sum. "When we see one another again, that's how you will address me," he wrote to her. "I have tender regard for the sweet grass wherever you go. With thoughts of you my mind is obsessed. In my dreams I see the light of your face. Now you are started on your long journey. Each day will take you farther from me. Oh, that I had bird's wings, and flying high, could follow you."

Reading these words of love filled Ming Lee with happiness. When they saw each other in the line again, they beamed with joy. She passed him a poem of her own. As their hands touched, she felt her body tremble with passionate longing for Sing Man Sum.

She passed him a short verse from the poet Chien T'ang, of the Ch'ing Dynasty: "Look, love of mine, fading light still issues from the waning moon. Listen. That lovely bird is singing for the dawning light. It is so sad, that bird, forlorn. It misses its nest. It longs for its mate. You are not mine, yet, my dearest, my own, you beam in my heart like the faded moon. And, when the dawn comes, you will be with me. We will be as one."

He wrote to her, "Tears cannot be shed for secret departures. Secret lovers cannot speak openly. Other than our two hearts, no one must know. The solitary bird sleeps restlessly in its locked cage. Spring brings the workers to the fields, pruning the overgrown branches. Rivers clouded with silt may run again like crystal waters. The head of the black crow may grow white feathers. Secret, parted lovers we, we must sustain our fervent hope, that time will bring us back together at last."

*   *   *

A handful of newly approved sojourners waited at the pier for the ferry. Their belongings were neatly packed. A teen-age boy was there with an elderly woman who was very protective of him. She looked at Ming Lee as if to say, "Keep your hands off my boy."

Ming Lee thought about the women's fear and about the immigration officer's lewd glance. They believe I am a woman without morals. They don't realize how I intend to work. If the missionaries have found a job for me, then I will do that job to the best of my ability. I will prove I have ability. I will show them that I am worthy to be a citizen of this country.

She watched the white building recede into the distance and thought of Man Sum. Would she ever see him again? She looked at the pine trees growing on the side of Angel Island Hill, flanking the wooden building, and one of the odes of T'sin came to her.

> My lover grew like the pine tree
> And his bearing was like a lord's.
> Oh, I am sad. I will never see him again.
> My lover stood like a pine tree
> And bent toward my lowered eyes.
> Oh, I am sad. I will never see him again.
> My lover sighed like a pine tree.
> Every breeze brought me words of his love.
> Oh, I am sad. I will never see him again.

Yet, how she hoped. She prayed to Kuan Yin, the goddess of mercy. She prayed she would see her Man Sum again. And it would not turn out like a poem of lost love.

Chapter 4

Man Sum's interrogation day had finally arrived. He was led to the small interrogation room in the basement of the wooden building. However, he was not greeted by an immigration officer. Instead, a well-dressed gentleman with a neat beard greeted him. This man politely stood up when Man Sum entered the room, and shook Man Sum's hand, then graciously offered him a seat. This man spoke softly and more courteously than the other staff members.

"I am J.B. Densmore. I am undertaking an investigation of graft among officials of the immigration service. It has been alleged that some of these officials have been conspiring with certain Chinese organizations to doctor, falsify, and in some cases, to steal, documents that are material evidence in immigration cases."

"I wish you success in your investigation," Man Sum said through the interpreter.

"I am here to see that all of us abide by the rules and to make sure these interrogations run smoothly and thoroughly. And most of all, I am here to see that they are conducted impartially, so that each case may be determined in a fair and just manner."

"Yes, fairness and justice are very important," Man Sum said.

"Now, Man Sum, we might as well tell you from the outset that suspicion has fallen on you."

"Suspicion has fallen on me?" Man Sum said indignantly. "Why me?"

"You have been watched over the last few months, watched carefully, and your behavior has been suspect. Our informants have seen you passing and receiving notes of great length, and destroying secret documents."

"I have never received notes, read notes, or destroyed documents," Man Sum said calmly and forcefully.

"It has been alleged, by our informants, that you have been in secret communication with the Chi Sing Tong, a Chinatown benevolent society. You have given that organization the names of those who might be willing to receive graft payments in exchange for favors to applicants. You have told the Chi Sings the names of those who have access to the files. And you, together with your cohorts, have attempted to induce our clerks to meddle with those files."

"I deny all the charges you have made against me," Man Sum said softly.

"Is it not true," the investigator continued, "that you arranged to have one Tom Lum Po hidden in this detention center?"

"Not true."

"Then you illegally arranged for him to be shipped to Chinatown. Didn't he illegally enter United States territory wtih no status whatsoever? You certainly were a key figure, weren't you? A key figure in the arrangements."

"That is false," Man Sum replied.

"Well, Jack Pong, the kitchen worker involved in these capers, and the others who were involved, have all been replaced. The skipper of the Sunset Scavenger garbage scow *Columbia*, Hal Blakely, has been indicted for violation of immigration law. A search is still going on for Tom Lum Po. But I'm sure we'll find him. And then of course, you know Kwan Ming Lee.''

"No. I don't know her.''

"Are you quite certain?''

"Yes, I am completely certain.''

"Didn't you make yourself available to the Tong society to help them realize their objective of placing Kwan Ming Lee, a young woman approximately eighteen years of age, into service as a 'singsong girl,' a slave-girl prostitute?''

Inwardly Man Sum flinched at this statement. A prostitute? Was that what the Chi Sings wanted her for? If it was true, the situation was much worse than he thought.

"I deny it.''

"What do you mean, you deny it?''

"I have had no dealings with the individual you mention.''

"I am sorry, but you were overheard to explain to her that she had been sold by her husband to the Chi Sing Tong. You told her that she was going to enter the United States with the status of a slave.''

"That is a complete lie! I said no such thing to her!''

"Aha,'' Densmore said, a self-satisfied grin crossing his face, "then you *do* know Kwan Ming Lee.''

"All right, I know her,'' Man Sum admitted.

"And you were instrumental in having her sold into slavery.''

"No! That's a lie!'' Man Sum said.

"This, of course, is most illegal. We have outlawed slavery in this country. We fought a very bloody war over that very issue. And all good Christians must condemn this despicable Chinatown prostitution trade. What explanation do you have to offer, Mr. Kwong?''

"None."

"None?"

"I am in no way involved."

"Well, we have witnesses to the contrary."

"They are not telling the truth," Man Sum said with simple conviction.

J.B. Densmore threw up his hands and let them fall with a loud thud on the desk. A silence followed, after which he leaned toward Man Sum and said, "You are a paper son."

The applicant said, "I am the legitimate son of Kwong Pak Yuen, who immigrated here in 1875 and who is an apothecary on Stockton Street between Jackson and Washington Streets."

At this point, Densmore gave up his seat, and a new immigration officer, whom Man Sum had never seen before, continued the questioning. Densmore withdrew to a chair next to the wall and lit a pipe.

The new interrogator asked, "What is the name of the village where you were born and raised?"

"Shang Lok," Man Sum answered.

"And Shang Lok village has how many inhabitants?"

"Two hundred fifty-six."

"How many rows of houses?"

"Eight."

"Your house, which row?"

"Second."

"The rows run north to south or east to west?"

"North to south."

"The central shrine of the gods is in which direction from the village?"

"To the east."

"Your house was how many from the corner?"

"Third."

"Who lives across the street from you?"

"Lau Shuk Kwan."

"Married?"

"Yes."

"Wife's name?"

"Lau Mui Toy."

"Bound or unbound feet?"

"Unbound."

"Next door to the Laus?"

"Left or right side?" Man Sum asked.

"Left," the interrogator barked

"Lim Sung Wong."

"The well was located?"

"I believe south of the village "

"Southwest?"

"Yes, southwest."

"Which is it, south or southwest?"

"Southwest."

"You said south."

"I meant southwest."

"But you said, *south*."

"South is southwest."

"Listen to me. You lived there all your life, right? You would know if the well was to the south or southwest. If you walked directly south, you wouldn't find the well. You'd get no water."

"I meant southwest."

"You're quite sure you did?"

"Yes."

"Well, you're wrong. It was south."

"That's what I said the first time."

"You changed you mind. You changed to southwest.

If you had been so certain, you wouldn't have changed your mind.''

"I was always certain it was south."

"You changed your testimony."

"You're trying to confuse me. I always knew it to be south."

"Your chicken loft had how many partitions?"

"Eight."

"Your father testified seven."

"Yes, there were seven stalls for the seven chickens, but eight partitions."

"There we have yet another discrepancy." The officer noted it.

"Now, look. Draw eight lines on a piece of paper and count the spaces between the lines. Eight partitions divide the loft into seven stalls for the hens. We had seven laying hens. Seven hens laid eggs."

"Which one laid the most eggs?"

"The second one from the left."

"Not the third one from the right?"

"No!"

"Not the third one from the right." The officer made another note. "Did your mother have any unusual markings?"

"Yes, she had a mole on her left cheek."

"Her mole was approximately how large?"

"About like that." Man Sum held his fingers parted a sixteenth of an inch.

"That all?"

"That is all. That is the extent of the size of her mole."

"Very good. Very good answers."

For a moment the investigator seemed genuinely impressed. Then he took all of the documents before him, tore them up and put them in the wastebasket. He looked toward Man Sum and smiled.

"What are you doing?" Man Sum asked. "Those are my papers."

"But the well was directly south of the village of Shang Lok, not southwest."

The interrogator then took out of the drawer of the desk another form. He stamped something on it.

"The order of this hearing is that you shall be deported within the week." He handed the forms to the secretary. "We do not admit criminals into the United States or its territories."

It was the middle of the night. The moon was hidden. The room was pitch black. The waves of the sea washed blackness over his spirit. And the gods? The gods of fortune were far away. The cold, whistling winds spiraled about the wooden building deafeningly. The walls and floors creaked somberly All was hopeless.

Man Sum forced himself to stay awake. He didn't want to be surprised in his sleep by the foreign devil.

The waves of the sea. There was nothing sweet or soothing in the sound of the waves to assuage his melancholy He had taken pity on others, had he not? Hadn't he done everything in his power to help others make their landings? But now there was no one to either help or pity him. The waves of the sea and the wind in the walls scorned him.

His eyes scanned the inert forms of his countrymen sleeping soundly on their narrow bunks At least one of them had been a spy, had betrayed him Someone did it to get a better deal for himself It was not worthwhile to harbor resentment What was done was done He might even forgive them. After all, they were as desperate as he to enter Gold Hill.

Man Sum buried his face in the pillow to muffle the sound of his voice. "Now, I invite death," he said. "I do not fear it. I will not hang myself by makeshift ropes as Lum Po tried to do. In the company of other condemned souls, I will use the sea in my journey to the kingdom of the dead."

Through eyes now grown accustomed to the darkness, he dreamily skimmed the lines of poetry his countrymen had penned or carved into the walls of the dormitory, and in some cases, into the floors.

"Sitting here uselessly, delayed for months and years, I am like a pigeon in a cage."

"It is very sad for the innocent to be imprisoned in the wooden building."

"We are as one, fellow sufferers with mutual sympathy."

"My only hope is that my compatriots will avenge this grievance."

"How was I to know the Western barbarians had lost their ears and reason?"

"A thousand sorrows and a hatred ten thousandfold burns between my brows."

Man Sum had no writing implement other than a knife he had taken from the dining hall and sharpened for use as a defensive weapon. Now he began to carve into the wall next to his bunk. The wood was soft and the characters emerged under the careful and determined strokes of the blade.

This was the poem he wrote: "I have failed the interrogation. The devils now will throw me to the land of the hungry ghosts. I will be carried there like a leaf blown aimlessly. My life-long ambition has been swallowed up by the monster enemy, the purple dragon, dimly visible through mists. The nightingale is quietly weeping now. The only sound is her tears. The only character left to write in this poem is sorrow.''

As he finished carving, the room began to grow slightly luminescent. Though it was still dark, the sky signaled the morning's approach from the east. He heard faraway footfalls coming in his direction. He knew they were coming for him now. His life was over, the life of this world. What kind of life would the next world bring? That was a mystery.

No! He refused to yield passively to such a fate! Suddenly his desire for life had grown stronger than his desire for death.

The windows on the outside of the building were barred. He couldn't escape that way. He ran out into the hallway. The men in the khaki were not yet visible. He crouched in a corner of the hallway adjacent to the stairs so that he was not in their line of vision when they attained the landing. Then, as they entered the dorm, he silently made his way down the stairs and out of the building. He quickly scaled the fence to his left and soon was running through the woods. The wooded forest floor, tangled with underbrush and sharp twigs, bit his feet. Behind him he heard the sound of the alarm. His escape had been discovered.

He had on a prison shirt and pants, making him easily identifiable as an escapee from the detention center. He had one chance in a thousand now. But since he had considered himself already a dead man, he decided that he had nothing to lose, and only one deep regret. He had to leave his belongings back there. His mother's jade. The precious jade, given to him in love. He hated to part with it. Leaving it behind meant leaving all that was left of her.

How sad that had made him feel But still he must try to escape. He must try

He thrust aside thickets of brush and branches to reach the crest of the hill just as the sun reached partway past the horizon.

The characters of "I" and "Ming came to his mind from the *Book of Changes* "The darkening of the light." His situation was that of "the darkening of the light." The greatest of adversities was now upon him The *Book of Changes* said that in such circumstances, it furthered one to be persevering. One must not permit one's steadfastness to be shaken. Perseverance must dwell in inmost consciousness. In a time of darkness it was essential to be cautious and reserved. When flight becomes necessary, one must "lower one's wings." Without rest, he must hurry along. There is no permanent abiding place. Never mind. One must just fix one's attention on one's goal.

Man Sum looked across the bay to the nearest land. It wasn't San Francisco, but land in the opposite direction. He could see a few houses and a road. If only he could reach it. He would have to swim, and to reach the water, he'd have to sneak past the army compound located on the northeast side of the island "With great resolve, a man endeavors to soar above all obstacles, but thus encounters a hostile fate "

On the fifth floor in a large red-brick building located on the Clay Street hill between Powell and Stockton Streets, San Francisco Chinatown, there stretched a large, long room with high ceilings It was the Hall of the Victorious Union, the Chi Sing Tong The word *chi* meant "combine" or "together " The *sing* ideogram stood for "successful" or "victorious "

A huge hand-carved ebony table, with the emblem of

the warrior god Kwan Kung at each of the legs, stood in the center of the room. The top of this table was marble, inlaid with mother-of-pearl, bordered by the same pitch black ebony that composed the legs. Straight-backed chairs surrounded it. They were also placed around the room, against the wall.

In front of the chairs around the wall there were small tables made of the same wood and marble as the larger table. A chair with a higher back than the others, reserved for the exalted master of the secret society, stood at the head of the table. All the chairs had matching red cushions at the back and the seat.

On the fourth wall, there was an immense shrine, an altar to the Tong's several gods, on which sat a lotus-shaped bowl. It contained peanut oil and a small, burning wick. Eight pewter hand-wrought incense containers sat on the altar. These were covered with quotes from Confucian and Taoist scriptures. From the high ceiling dangled ornate chandeliers.

The walls were covered with photographs of the brotherhood, paintings of scenes from Chinese mountains, and many scrolls in which, with the finest and most pains-taking calligraphy, passages from the five classics were rendered.

The incense sticks were lit so that what would be said at this meeting would gain the favor of the gods. But the smell of tobacco competed with the incense, and the to-bacco fumes soon displaced the incense fragrance.

The officers and members of the Tong, called by the exalted master to an emergency session, took chairs accord-ing to their several ranks. The exalted master sat at the head of the table, the secretary to his right and the treasurer to his left. The six honorable elders occupied the other seats. In the chairs around the room, other members of less exalted status sat. All were served tea by young men in neatly pressed white jackets.

At the far end of the room sat a number of men dressed in black. They looked cool and tough. They were the "highbinders" or the professional soldiers hired by the Tong to deal with the enemy forthrightly and with immediacy. The highbinders functioned both as bodyguards and assassins.

A nod of the head from the exalted master was a signal to two of the highbinders, who promptly rose, exited and closed the door behind them. They stood outside the room, at the head of stairs that descended to the street. Their hands rested calmly on their revolvers, which were tucked neatly in their belts.

On the table before the exalted master stood an incense bowl, and next to it was a pile of incense sticks—or "joss" sticks, as they were called. Incense bearers, men wearing red sashes, waited at either side of the exalted master's chair for a sign from him. When the sign was given, the incense bearers solemnly issued three of the joss sticks to each member. When everyone received his sticks, the exalted master lifted one of his own and in a droning voice said, "Let the first oath be recited."

Each man lifted one of his joss sticks and, led by the secretary, repeated together the first of the three oaths of the Tong.

"By this incense stick, we swear to avenge any wrong committed against any brother of this Tong."

Lighting his incense stick and placing it in the incense jar before him, the exalted master intoned, "He who violates this oath, let the dragon of misfortune annihilate him."

"Let the second oath be recited," the exalted master droned again.

Following the lead of the secretary, each man lifted a second joss stick and intoned, "By this incense stick, we swear to fight resolutely and fearlessly the battles of this Tong."

Again the voice of the exalted master rang solemnly as he lit a second joss stick and placed it in a jar before him. "He who violates this oath, let him suffer a horrible death by ten thousand swords.

"Let the third oath be recited."

They all lit their third joss stick and with somber voices repeated, "By this incense stick, we swear to kill without mercy all who lift their hands against any member of this Tong."

"He who fails to keep this oath," droned the exalted master, placing the third lighted joss stick in the jar, "shall without fail die at the hands of the salaried assassin."

Then the exalted master gave the incense bowl with the three smoldering incense sticks to one of the incense bearers, who placed it upon the altar. After that, the exalted master again droned, "Some who take oaths are true, but others are false. True brethren are alike the world over. Those who are true are honored. Those who are false die the death."

The ceremonial part of the meeting being over, the exalted master bade all in the room be seated. He pursed his lips slightly and began speaking in an unhurried and formal way, as if he were speaking to a crowd of thousands. He paused frequently, allowing his words to sink into his listeners' minds and hearts.

"We are assembled here today at this emergency session of our great society to consider a matter of grave importance to us all. This matter concerns my son, Sing Man Sum. As you know, the foreign devil pays your exalted master no honor, bestows on him no favor, gives him no respect. And so, your exalted master, in order to bring his only son here to this land of wealth, has had to purchase papers from the merchant Kwong Pak Yuen at great cost. And I have had to endure the humiliation of saying that I have no son!''

His body shook with anger and he brought his fist down on the table. He paused to regain his composure.

"This was a great effrontery to the gods of heaven and to the spirits of my ancestors. May the great pestilences strike dead the foreign devils who have forced this action on me, who have imposed the law of 1882, the Exclusion Law, which has been created to all but eliminate the Chinese people from the American continent.

"We who are proud of our race and who refuse to go down on our knees before this pale man who lets women rule him, we have come to honor our Tong all the more. Our Tong has grown stronger because we who belong to the Tong fear not the fight to the death. We do not bend the knee to foreign rule or feel we must obey laws created by barbarian devils to subject us. We do not require the consent of the foreigners to do what we know is right. Do I speak your hearts, brothers?''

"All power to our Tong!'' the brethren said, raising their voices enthusiastically in chorus.

Sing Choy Wu continued, "Let the Chinese merchant companies continue to make bargains with the foreign snakes. The merchant companies frame contracts whereby laborers are hired by the devil's factories and the devil's farms. But our livelihood is independent of the barbarians. We survive without their help. We stand on our own. Daily our coffers grow with the proceeds from the sale of opium, our gambling interests and our singsong girls. We are men doing men's business. We are not washerwomen; we are not cooks; we are not maids! What are we, brothers?''

"We are men! We are men!"

Sing Choy Wu smiled at his ability to stir the emotions of his membership. They were hanging on his every word.

"And since *faan gwai* only lets the Chinese do women's work in his land, we who insist on doing men's business remain outside *faan gwai's* law. We are proud of our people. Our gods, our ancestral spirits, our five classics and all of our twenty-four rules of filial piety, the cornerstone of civilization. *Faan gwai* would seek to destroy all that. We shall not let them. Through various means at our disposal, we have managed to stay one step beyond the barbarian. It has not been very difficult! *Faan gwai* are a sleepy people, ignorant, prone to fits of womanish silliness, and easily tempted by coins."

He did a little pantomime of a *faan gwai* holding out his hand for a bribe that brought down the house.

"Do but touch his palm with the currency of the land, and he'll look the other way when the message is lifted from the rice bowl."

The laughter reached a crescendo. Sing Choy Wu gestured for silence.

"And so, we have been completely successful in our infiltration of the hated and inhuman prison at Angel Island where my son has been interned these many months and where he has been subjected to the greatest loneliness and suffering imaginable. May the wrath of the insane monkey descend to stamp his foot down and crush the island of the black angel!"

"Down with Angel Island!" the membership intoned.

"My son has received messages, and through the aid of our agents, he has succeeded in helping two of the inmates reach the warming bosom of our fellowship. Yes, my son has proven himself to be a true and loyal Tong even before he has become a member. Lum Po was the first. His is currently being trained by our highbinders in the arts of war. And he is learning quickly and proving to be an asset to our organization.''

Now Sing Choy Wu paused, and as he spoke quietly, his eyes seemed far away.

''The finest prize of all, the one who is dearest to my heart, my own little nightingale is Kwan Ming Lee. She is the greatest gift a son has ever bestowed upon his father. Kwan Ming Lee, until the careful and considerate and loving instruction of her exalted master, was a stranger to the lute. She is now learning to accompany her beautiful singing voice with that musical instrument and others to which I have introduced her. I have placed her also under the tutelage of Chu Mae Pong, lady of the finest culture. Madame Chu can tame even the foreign devil with one look of eyes that glow like fine white jade wrought in heaven's palaces. And the younger lady is like raw jade, freshly cut out of the mountain side, that awaits the skilled application of the jade worker's art. It is to Man Sum we owe this great and heavenly gift.''

Then he paused and looked each brother in the eyes.

''Now we must go to his aid, for he is in the deepest trouble.''

The exalted master paused and nodded to the highbinders standing at the far side of the large hall. They obediently opened the door and ushered in a short, portly man. This man entered the room stumbling. His attempts at controlling his nervousness were evident and unsuccessful. His eyes darted in all directions as if expecting ghosts to jump out at him from the furniture. One could hardly blame him for being frightened. Here among those assembled were some of the most renowned hired assassins in Chinatown. The silent atmosphere of the dark chamber, the wisps of incense smoke winding their way to the dimmed chandeliers, all created in him a sense of gloomy foreboding.

He was Kwong Long Kwok, the new head cook who had replaced Jack Pong after the arrests on Angel Island.

The exalted master now performed the chicken-killing ceremony. This was the tradition prior to hearing important testimony.

Sing Choy Wu said, "Let the chicken be brought in."

The secretary moved off to the left, disappearing into the shadows, then returned with the chicken, which was happily picking at grains of rice in its cage. The treasurer placed a bowl on the table and a knife on the moist towel. At a nod from the exalted master, the secretary opened the door of the cage. Then Sing Choy Wu reached in quickly and brought the startled bird's neck in line with the edge of the bowl. With his other hand, he raised the knife, stretching his arm out and upward.

The secretary addressed Long Kwok, speaking with ritualistic inflection. "Do you swear to this Tong that what you have in your heart will match without flaw the utterance of your mouth? Do you swear upon the full expectation that if you are discovered lying to this organization, your fate will be the same as that of this fowl? Swear it."

"I swear it, I swear it," Long Kwok said.

"Upon the bones and the ashes of your esteemed great-grandfather?"

"Yes, yes."

Satisfied that the oath of truthfulness had been made correctly, the exalted master brought the blade down on the chicken, stifling its squawks. A full two minutes passed as the company impassively watched the dead bird flutter frantically in its attempts to escape the blow that had already taken its life. Chicken blood covered the exalted master's arms to the elbows, and the bowl was half filled with it. The secretary and the treasurer aided the exalted master with cleaning his hands. The dead bird was laid on a large sheet of red paper, the head a few inches from its body. The bowl was removed.

An odd, uncharacteristic smile crossed the exalted master's face as he very quietly and naturally said, "Let the testimony be heard."

He sat down. The cook was left standing, his widened eyes staring without focusing at the space of red paper between the chicken's body and its head.

The secretary began the cross-examination. "Your name?"

"Kwong Long Kwok."

"Your duties on Angel Island?"

"I am a cook."

"Did you, in accordance with the instructions given to you by this society, find out the fate of Sing Man Sum?"

"I did."

"Will you now tell this entire organization what news you have of our brother? What is his present situation?"

"The order of the interrogation committee was that Man Sum must be immediately deported."

A gasp filled the chamber from all sides. The members began to talk to each other excitedly.

"Silence." The exalted master's face reddened, and his voice shook. "Deported?" He growled. "But did you not present the envelope with the gift of money to the authorities? They have always accepted payment. Why have they made an exception in the case of my son?"

In a quavering voice, the new cook replied, "All of

the investigators who had accepted gifts of money have been expelled from the service and replaced. I offered the payments to the new investigators. I left the usual notes under the blotters of their desks. I was careful to conceal my own identity. But they did not make the correct signals. They did not convey their acceptance as I instructed in my notes to them.''

The exalted master reflected a moment, then said, ''Evidently, they are still being watched by the higher authorities, the officials dispatched by the central government in Washington. When is my son due to be deported, then?''

''As soon as he is caught,'' the cook answered.

''Caught?''

''He has escaped from the confinement of the wooden building.''

''When did this happen?''

''This morning, early.''

''Why did you not tell us sooner?'' the exalted master growled.

'' I . . . I was scared. You frightened me. You made me think that if I told you bad news you would hurt me. You brought me here by force. I had no time to talk. You wouldn't let me talk. Everyone was looking at me as if they wanted to kill me. Please don't kill me. I have a family and two sons. Two sons! I was afraid. I don't know what I was afraid of. I . . .''

''Silence,'' the exalted master rang out. ''Escaped? Where?''

''He's somewhere in the woods on the island. They were searching for him when I left. They had no sign of him. He's somewhere in the woods. There's a search party with dogs. As of the hour my shift was up, they still had not located him.''

The exalted master addressed the entire room. "Is it possible to rescue him? I open this meeting to general discussion among the membership. My son must be aided in his escape from the island of the immortal ghost. We cannot waste time. We are an army. This is a soldier brotherhood. We must fight."

The general membership was now excited by Choy Wu's fighting words. Only the highbinders sat silently.

"We are ready to fight."

"We will rescue him. Rescue him for the Tong!"

"Go to Angel Island. Yes. Free all incarcerated immigrants."

"Yes. Fight the foreign devil himself if necessary!" Sing Choy Wu continued, topping the voices of the members. "We must go to the island. Light incense sticks to make sacrifices to the warrior god. We shall do battle." Both the exalted master's fists drummed down hard on the black wood, and the chicken carcass jumped.

The silence that followed was broken by the sliding of a chair in the rear of the hall. A large man rose. He had eyes that seemed not to blink, and his cheeks looked as though he were holding them sucked in. He was tall, thin. His long arms hung fully extended downward to his thighs. He gestured only with his left hand, and as he made his points, his arms remained inert. He was Duk Fong, Chinatown's most feared and elusive hired assassin. His movements were almost feline, and his voice was very gentle, almost kind.

"I beg the exalted master's permission to speak," he said humbly.

The exalted master nodded.

Duk Fong spoke in a dry, factual manner. "It is possible to make an escape from the island, but extremely difficult. One of our paper sons had attempted such a swim. His corpse was found washed up on the beach near the army garrison the following day. But the swim *is* possible.''

"Are there not sharks?" Choy Wu asked sharply.

"There are sharks, but with good fortune and frequent supplications and sacrifices to the sea gods, the predatory shark may be kept away. The nearest land on which a swimmer might hope to find refuge would be the small peninsula called Tiberon.''

"Tiberon? Tiberon is a wilderness, is it not?" Choy Wu declared hotly.

"Tiberon is not reachable except by the ferry that goes as far as Sausalito. Then a narrow, badly maintained road leads as far as the point. From the road to the beach opposite Angel Island stretches a length of several hundred yards. Under cover of darkness, we might reach an advantageous spot there and hide among the rocks. In the event he tries the bay, we would be able to supply the needed support from Tiberon Point onward.''

"Hmm." Choy Wu folded his hands meditatively. "The plan is not ideal, but lacking a better one, it is acceptable.''

A vote was taken that unanimously approved Duk Fong's plan. Volunteers from among the membership and the soldiers were selected for the venture. Oaths, binding the membership to secrecy, the violation of which meant certain death, were droned in chorus responsively, after the exalted master.

The meeting was ritually ended by the extinguishing of the joss sticks in the cool sand of the large pewter vase before the altar of the gods, and the Tong dispersed into the fog that clouded Clay Street

*   *   *

Murphy stood in the forest at sunset. He was not used to walking around in wooded areas, but he was strong and stubborn and would not give up the chase. The dogs were searching through another part of the woods, but Murphy could have sworn he'd seen something move in this direction. If he was right, if the fleeting form was Man Sum, he, Murphy, was sure he could chase the heathen down. The sun was gone now and overhead, the twisting branches stood out sharply against the pale grey sky.

Murphy clicked on his flashlight. There was enough darkness now that he could see the beam's point of light dance among bushes, trees and rocks. A pair of dark eyes, set wide apart, caught the beacon for a split second. Then the eyes were gone in a quick rustle of tan oak leaves.

Murphy ran, his massive legs pumping and his angular chin knifing its way through the forest. He dodged, and stiff-armed the brush aside. Man Sum was struggling to keep a distance between them, but he was staggering from exhaustion. He was ahead of the Irishman only by a few feet.

The brush was thick and thorns cut at both the hunter and his prey. Murphy was closing the gap between himself and the Chinese. There was only a single row of vegetation now separating them. Murphy yanked this last barrier aside and hurled himself with one motion into a small clearing. The fugitive wasn't there. He was nowhere to be found. It was somewhat darker now. A squirrel screamed and skittered up a nearby pine.

Murphy suddenly felt something sting the skin between his shoulder blades to the right of his spinal column. The sting widened and broadened. Murphy tripped as the sting of his back yawned. The pit grew so large that all around Murphy was pain and blood. He fell into it screaming.

A sharp knife stuck in Murphy's unmoving back. It

was the knife Man Sum had used to carve poetry on the wooden walls of the barracks.

Man Sum was shocked to see what he had done. He quickly pulled the knife out of Murphy's back. Then he tore off his shirt, ripped it into strips, and made a wad of cloth, with which he stanched the wound. Then he tied pieces of the shirt together to form a very crude bandage. He would have tried to do more, but just then he heard dogs and men coming closer He would have to get away quickly

Chapter 5

Now, Man Sum thought, they would do more than deport him. A Chinese murdering a white would certainly be a crime punishable by death. He had not wanted to kill the Irishman. It was the only time he had ever harmed another human being. The thought kept repeating in his mind. *You killed a man, you killed a man.* How do you live when you are cursed with the reality, the fact that you have taken the life of another human being? he wondered. Murder was against the law in every civilization.

Man Sum was exhausted. He could hardly move. Something pressed him, however, to keep up the flight, even though he had hardly any strength left at all. It didn't matter that he had no strength. The will to survive pressed him onward.

Flashlights shone through the branches and the darkness, casting twisted, grotesque shadows. The shadows seemed to howl. It was the dogs. They were coming this way, the guards. How many of them were there? They had heard Murphy's shout and it would be only moments before they would discover the dead Irishman. Man Sum would have to make a move quickly or be caught. But he didn't have the strength to rise up. All he could do was crawl. He slowly put his hands in front of him and brought his knees forward. Every move brought him pain But he kept going. He lost track of time. It was dark Flashlight beams. He didn't know what direction they were coming from. The dogs were barking. The men's heavy boots cracked twigs, kicked aside the thick underbrush. He heard these noises, but couldn't tell how far off they were.

The cloth on his pants above the knees had worn through. His skin was exposed to the sharp teeth of rocks and brush. They ripped through his pants and dug into his flesh. His knees and shins were skinned raw, and dirt filled the scratches. He was growing more and more dizzy from exhaustion. The ground beneath him teetered and spun. He got sick to his stomach, as if he were seasick. He grasped the ground in front of him to pull himself forward, but his arms shook uncontrollably. He had no power to pull his body forward. He could no longer crawl.

Now he was certain to die. He could no longer move. The dogs, guards and guns were closing in. They would have shackles to bind him, and they would drag him off to their prison. He would die there He would not have the blessing of a funeral in his village No one would be there to extol his virtues There would be no ceremony to implore the bad spirits to show leniency in their punishments. No *Feng Seui*, or diviner, to determine from the horoscope the most favorable site for the burial. No paper offerings burned to placate demons. No coffin. No chanting of the offices of the dead by priests. No weeping relatives. Just the wandering spirits, here in the forest in the demon stranger's land. Hungry bad spirits like birds of prey, plucking up what little goodness his soul had gathered in this short life.

Worst of all, he would die without offspring He

would be doomed to wander the earth, forever searching for a home where he could rest his weary spirit.

He, Sing Man Sum, would be a "hungry ghost."

Then a face floated toward him. It came from the dark, a shadowy suggestion of branches and leaves. It was the face of Kwan Ming Lee. Now, at the point of death, it was clear to him how much he loved her. He had seen very little of her, but that didn't matter. She had expressed to him more tender feelings than he had read about in all the love poetry of the classics. Her lettering had had the grace and charm of a sparrow's footprints. And his brush and ink had poured forth feelings he never thought he had. His calligraphy had never looked so perfect.

How he longed to touch her hand once more and feel her soothing stroke on his pain-racked body. If only his shoulder could brush hers once more before he set his feet upon the pathway to the land of the dead.

He wondered of her fate. Would she be taken and used by the Tongs for profit? Would she be reduced to the status of a common whore? That's what the interrogation officer had said. If he had gone to Gold Hill and found gold, he would have been able to save her from that life. But that dream would never be realized. There would be no Man Sum to buy her from the Tong. She would sink deeper and deeper into the prostitution trade. She'd become more and more degraded as time went by. That lovely, innocent face would be powdered and painted until nothing was left of it but a bitter mask. Her beauty would be drowned in the sordid memories of bodily abuse.

That thought stuck in his mind. It would not leave his mind in spite of his efforts to cast it out. He was responsible for her fate, he thought. He and no one else. It was he who delivered her into the hands of the Tong. On the other hand, she had no hopes either way. Without the

Tong, she would have been deported, and had she returned to China, there would have been nothing for her but life as a slave to her in-laws. They were probably participants in the slave-girl trade. What would prevent them from selling her again? Perhaps to another broker? The thought made him sick. Either alternative—staying here or going back to China—was unthinkable.

And here, dying on this forest floor, there was nothing he could do for her. This would be the true failure of his life In this failure, he would die and lose face for all eternity. He could not die in such a fashion. He could not. He could not! He could die only if his life had meant something To die incomplete, to die having lived only half a life, without a mate, without wealth, without offspring or a name, was unthinkable. He must escape this island of the angel of death. No strength left, yet he must find the strength. No chance to surmount the obstacle, yet he must discover the way.

His physical powers had totally lapsed, but he poured his will into one last break for freedom.

Ahead of him, a few feet away, there was an edge of a bluff. He couldn't tell what was beyond it or how steep it was. He would just have to take a chance. He lunged toward the rise and rolled over the edge. His body spun until a bush stopped it. Then he adjusted the angle of his body and rolled again. This happened several times until he had rolled all the way to the foot of the hill. Now he could hear the lapping of the water of the bay upon the shore, and the sound of birds in the forest. Bats screeched overhead, and little invisible animals scurried around him. Gradually, these sounds faded from his senses, and sleep overtook him.

* * *

"They found Murphy. The Chink knifed him. Murphy's still alive. He's being shipped to Frisco General Hospital."

The immigration officer, Peter Brannan, was on the phone to his immediate supervisor, Bill Saxon. Both men were new to their jobs.

Brannan continued, "Yeah, well, he's still out there, the Chink. But we'll get him before long. We've notified the military stationed at Fort McDowell. They're going to comb the island first thing in the morning."

"You can't get those boys on the hunt faster?" Saxon replied in an irritated tone.

"Well, you can hardly ask them to lose sleep over a Chink, sir. It's not exactly their jurisdiction. I mean, their job is to defend the port of San Francisco."

"Sure, sure," Saxon said. "Now, what happened to the fence? How did that fellow get out?"

"Went right over the top of the barbed wire. The entire complex here is enclosed by fencing. The kid scaled it, that's all," Brannan said nervously.

"What's to prevent somebody else from doing the same thing?" Saxon barked.

"What? Yes, well, the fencing's not strong or extensive enough to keep them in. We need wire netting with barbs on it, going all the way up to the top of the building. That row of barbed wire on top of the chain link just isn't enough."

"You're giving me a new idea? That recommendation was approved a year ago. What happened to it?" Saxon asked.

"My predecessor had the wire netting on order for over six months. When he first put in for it, they said it'd only be a couple of weeks. I've got his memo right here to that effect.'' Brannan was growing progressively more tense.

''Great,'' Saxon grumbled.

''Now, it doesn't surprise me someone escaped. It was bound to happen. I'm amazed it didn't happen sooner. The service can't stand this kind of publicity, much less the Department of Labor.''

''Looks real bad,'' Saxon said numbly. He was getting tired of this conversation.

''I know it looks bad, real bad.''

''Anybody besides Murphy wounded out there?'' Saxon asked.

''No. Wasn't Murphy enough? He almost got himself killed.''

''Anybody on the outside get wind of this?''

''I'm afraid so.''

''Who?''

''The papers. We tried to keep it quiet, keep it in the family, so to speak, but you know how that goes. So now we've got to call in the military, and that will create an even bigger stir. The papers are going to get hold of this thing . . .''

''And make us look like a bunch of idiots,'' Saxon added.

''Well, we don't have much choice in the matter, I'm afraid. The Chinaman has flown the coop.''

It was still dark when Man Sum awoke. He found pine and fir needles stuck to his pants and embedded in his shoes. The gulls were circling overhead. It seemed to him that they were getting ready to pick the flesh off his corpse. Thorny bushes impeded his progress through the forest, but the blackberries growing on them provided needed nourishment and refreshed him.

While it was dark, he felt he still had a chance to swim off the island. In the morning, the guards and dogs would be back. They had failed to catch up to him the previous day. Today they probably would send two or three times as many men and many more dogs. After all, he thought, he had already killed one man.

The shrubbery here grew so thick that it was impossible to walk through it without a huge knife, but the vegetation gave way somewhat in a small brook that worked meanderingly toward the seashore. He used the brook as his path. His bare feet were already scarred with thorn stabs. Now, sharp rocks cut into him as he slid off the slippery stones in the stream bed. He groped along until the welcoming sound of the surf grew louder.

After a time that seemed to go on forever, he reached the shore. He didn't lose so much as a moment before he disrobed. A dark land mass, half a mile away, was dimly visible through the early morning light. He lumbered into the surf and flopped his slim, muscular body into the water.

Immediately, his strong, wiry arms went to work in a battle with the waves that were fighting to return him to the shore and death. But with persistence he won over the tide and kept his arms steadily arching toward his goal.

Thoughts of Kwan Ming Lee succeeded one another. They lent some measure of calm and comfort to a body racked with muscular exhaustion and cold. She was the true driving force behind his aching arm muscles. Her face created in him the overwhelming desire to once more behold her beauty. But all his strength was gone.

As the dawn broke fully over the bay, the light faded from his senses. His arms ceased rhythmically cupping the water. His inert form drifted at the whim of the sea. His senses rapidly drifted away from consciousness.

In his dreams he saw the island rising from the waves. On the beach there was a fire. Three deities stood around the fire, warming themselves.

He heard a voice say, "This fire is for you. There are warm clothes here. There is warm tea and rice."

Then all three stretched their hands toward him. "You are safe now. You are with us. Come closer. Come closer. There is nothing to fear. We are your kinsmen."

He tried to swim to the shore, but with each stroke, the undertow pulled him back out to sea. "We are sending help," the deities said. "Help is coming."

Man Sum answered, "But my mouth is full of salt water, and the salt is stinging my wounds. I will dissolve when I wash up on shore. I will be nothing more than a wisp of sea foam, and then I will be carried away by the wind."

One of the deities began to walk toward him. He was large. In his left hand he carried something that looked like a net. His body moved from side to side as he attempted to push his way out to sea. More and more of his body became submerged so that finally there was only his head left. The head of the deity was now inches away from Man Sum's.

He studied the deity's face. The face was calm, angelic, kindly.

"I am your kinsman," the voice that came from the face said. "I am your brother. We are of the same family."

Man Sum replied, "But I don't know you."

"You will, soon enough," the face in the waves said. "I am taking you to the exalted master. He's your father, your true father."

"I have been studying the coaching papers so long, I had forgotten that I had a real father."

"Come with us now," the voice in the sea commanded. "*Mm ho pa, mm ho pa*, don't be afraid."

Man Sum felt the net enclose him. He tried to break free. He struck the net with both fists, but the more he struck it, the tighter it seemed to bind him. These deities, he thought, are not heaven-sent. They have been dispatched from below the earth. They have come to deliver me to a place reserved for me in the underworld, presided over by the ghostly Yen Lo. If they were taking me to the golden palaces of heaven, I would go willingly. But since it is to the nefarious regions I will be going, they must of course drag me there against my will, using force, and using this net.

Suddenly the sound of the waves was no longer apparent. Moreover, Man Sum was dry. He was naked, but warm and dry. He was contained in cloth, in a cloth bag. He could see nothing. Beneath him, he felt vibrations and heard the sound of a motor. He was in a car. But where were they taking him? He heard their voices. They weren't deities, but men. He wasn't dreaming. This was all very real. These men were speaking his dialect. They were not only his countrymen, they were also from one of the three districts that constituted the Sam Yup, or Cantonese speaking area.

One of them said, "When we get to Sausalito, we'll call the exalted master, tell him we have been successful in our rescue mission."

Man Sum heard himself say, "Who are you? Why am I being kept in this bag? Why am I being held naked and trapped? Why may I not see your faces?"

The voices next to him responded, "Have patience, young comrade and kinsman. You will be released soon enough. We are taking you to the Hall of Victorious Union, the Chi Sing Tong. You must be shielded from the light of day until the rite of initiation has begun. When you pass the initiation and become officially a member of our Tong, you will see your true father face to face, he who has worked and prayed these long months to release you from the *faan gwai*.''

The car stopped. He heard the door open and one of his rescuers got out. Less than a minute later, the car door closed and the car started again. ''Now, kinsman, we are going to enter a ferryboat that will take us to San Francisco. Don't move. The *sai yan*, Western people, must not think this sack contains a living man. To them, it must appear to be just a sack of fish, for we ourselves are masquerading as fishermen. This precaution is for your protection. Your description and the fact that you escaped from Angel Island have probably reached the police. Now, silence, brother, until we are well past this checkpoint.''

In a few minutes, the car stopped. Words he didn't understand were exchanged between one of his kinsmen and a voice outside the car window. The car started again, and he heard it move over what sounded like loose planks. Then the car's engine was turned off, and he heard another engine start up. Also, he heard the sound of lapping water. A few minutes later, the engine sound ceased, and the car motor started up again. Man Sum and his captors were now in the city of San Francisco. He heard cars around him, and horses' hooves.

After a short while, his ears told him that he was in a different part of the city. The sounds from the street were no longer in the foreign tongue, but in his own Cantonese. Also, he heard people speaking Sey Yup, a more guttural and slurred dialect.

The car swerved and pulled to a standstill. The doors were opened and hands reached in the car to take hold of Man Sum. He felt himself being lifted and carried. Suddenly the noise of the street ebbed. There were steps of a stairway, smells of incense, a long ascent, doors opening and closing. He must now be in a large room, for he heard the murmuring of many excited voices, followed by the sound of someone hushing them, "*Mm ho gong.*" He felt himself carried by many hands now. Another door closed. Then he was put down.

For a long time he lay in the sack in the darkness on the floor. This must be the place of the Chi Sing Tong. He was afraid. He knew nothing of these people, only that the men who called themselves his kinsmen had said that his father, his own father, was the exalted master, or the head of this Chi Sing Tong.

The sides of the bag began to move. He looked up. Light, and freedom. But no sooner was he let out of the bag than blindfolds were placed on him. Still blind, he thought. He smelled food. A plate of rice, vegetables and meat was set before him. Though he could not see it, it tasted wonderful. As he ate, hands were dressing his wounds, and he was being clothed. Finally he was placed on a soft bed, and there he went to sleep almost immediately. When he awoke, he felt himself being led to another room. Doors opened and closed again.

All at once, his blindfold was removed. He was standing in a small room. There was a statue of Kwan Kung, the god of war, on a small altar, brandishing a sword. The hilt was decorated with characters that signified "death to the enemy." At the feet of Kwan Kung were small skulls of men and animals. The room was lit with candles and lanterns inscribed with the Tong's insignia.

There was a man dressed as a vermilion phoenix standing by the door and gazing at Man Sum with great seriousness, but also swaying a little, side to side. On the walls were ancient swords and plaques inscribed with the words, "Death to the invader Manchu, restore the Mings."

The Manchus had deposed the Ming Dynasty two hundred fifty years ago, but the Chinese, particularly the Chinese of the south, had always seen the Manchu as an invader. Almost from the outset, the tribes of southern China had revolted against these interlopers.

The vermilion-phoenix doorkeeper stared at the lone initiation candidate and spoke solemnly. "You will be admitted to membership in our Tong only after a difficult examination. Only those whose hearts are fearless in the face of death can pass, but first you must learn the story of the beginning of our Tong. Be assured that if ever you divulge to an outsider any of the information I am about to impart to you, your betrayal will cost you not only your life, but also the memory of your name among the living."

This last threat was stated by the vermilion phoenix as though he were performing a tragic role in a stage play. His voice rasped loud and deep inside his throat. He stood on tiptoe and appeared to be leaning at about a forty-five-degree angle with the floor. He leaned toward Man Sum. His facial muscles quivered dramatically while his eyes bulged.

Thus, he continued, "In the days when the Manchus first took power, fearless warriors from the south challenged their rule.

"The government troops were unable to conquer these great warriors. But dwelling in the monastery of Shui Lum in the mountains of Fookien Province was a company of warrior Buddhist priests. Impressed by the miraculous strength of these priests, the emperor commissioned them to help him quell the rebels in the south.

"The monks fought with such skill and intrepidity that the rebels were seized with panic and fled. Not one of the one hundred twenty-eight priests lost his life. They were honored by the emperor himself in the ornate and sumptuous palace at Peking. But having renounced the world with its pleasures, riches and honors, and having taken the vow of poverty, the priests refused the emperor's gifts. They would not partake of the elaborate feast set out before them, except to sample the excellent imperial wine. This behavior of the priests annoyed the emperor greatly.

"Moreover, the military was jealous of the Buddhists' prowess in the arena of war. And So Chan Man Yew, the emperor's minister, under some pretext or other, had the priests secretly accused of high treason.

" 'These priests are invincible, are they not?' " Chan Man Yew said to the emperor. 'What is to hinder them carrying out some seditious plot to seize the government and overthrow the state?'

"And so the emperor sent his minister to the monastery at Shui Lum with a case of the imperial wine laced with deadly poison. The priests were surprised to receive a gift of wine, but when the jars were opened, a huge black cloud rose out, filling the room with a noxious odor.

"The monks queried, 'Why does the wine have such a terrible odor? Bring forth our founder's sword and let the wine be tested.'

"The test revealed the true nature of the substance in the jars. The abbot, infuriated, demanded to know why the emperor was treating his loyal subjects this way. While he spoke, an explosion shook the monastery. Of those who escaped the blast, most were cut down by waiting soldiers. Only eighteen escaped, fleeing to the desert. Most of those died of exposure, cutting the number of survivors to five These five became begging wanderers.

"One day, the wanderers came upon a stone tripod on which was engraved the words, '*Fan tsing, fuk Ming* '

These words called them to work for the downfall of the Manchus and the restoration of the Ming Dynasty, which the Tartars had deposed. These persecuted priests became the first elders of our Victorious Union, our Chi Sing Tong.''

When the vermilion phoenix finished his story, he paused to weigh the effect of his words on the candidate. Man Sum was nonplused. He had read the story before, it was no secret to him. But he tried his best to look impressed for the benefit of these kinsmen of his father.

He said, ''I think it's—''

''Don't answer until I give you the sign. After I give you the sign, you may repeat what I tell you. You may not repeat the password until I, the doorkeeper of the first portal, the Eastern Gate, tell you the password. It is''—he paused to walk over to Man Sum, then whispered in his ear—''*Fan Tsing, Fuk Ming.*'' Then he walked back to his station with a ponderous, ritualized gait. He ended up by the door, and there, puffing himself up like a vermilion phoenix ruffling its feathers, he said, ''Now, what is the password?''

''*Fan tsing, fuk Ming,*'' Man Sum answered simply.

''Perfectly stated. You may pass this portal. Remember, the secrets of this chamber may not pass your lips, not in this life or in the life to come.'' The vermilion phoenix creaked open the door and admitted the weary immigrant to his next series of tests.

The portal of the Eastern Gate was opened. There, he found himself in the hall of fidelity and loyalty. A statue of the god of wealth, Ch'ao Kung Ming, standing on the altar to the left, was depicted astride his black tiger. In one hand, he held pearls, which in his life he had used as missiles, hurling them at his enemies with devastating success. In the other, he wielded a steel whip.

He was accompanied by two small boys with fierce expressions on their faces. Each held high a miniature sword, as if attacking an invisible enemy.

Man Sum was approached by a man in a white silk robe. The robe was tied with a bright red silken sash. The characters for loyalty and fidelity decorated both the robe and the sash.

"I am the *Heng Do*, the guide of the Eastern Gate," the man said. "Behold the two sons of Ch'ao Kung Ming. You see how they fight on their father's behalf, even at their tender age? What virtue do they express, Man Sum?"

"The virtues of filial piety and loyalty," Man Sum said.

The *Heng Do* smiled. "That is correct." He paused. "Now, I will show you the tools of our Tong. You will have to learn the tools and their uses. You must not forget! For when you reach the last portal, you will have to tell all that you have learned in your journey through the previous portals."

The *Heng Do* showed him a mirror five feet high and five feet wide.

"This mirror is made of brass, and it has the virtue of immediately healing anyone who loses his reason at the sight of a ghost."

"Yes, I understand," Man Sum said obediently.

Next, the *Heng Do* pointed to an ornate red and purple vase. It stood next to the altar. It was about four feet high from base to rim. "This vase contains the elixir of life." The *Heng Do* reached into the vase and pulled out a much smaller vase, similarly decorated. He held this up for Man Sum's inspection.

This elixir was distilled from the venom of five poisonous animals: the viper, the scorpion, the centipede, the toad and the spider. Chang Ten Shih, the master of heaven, riding on a tiger, conquered all the poisonous animals. Each one gave up its essence, making the true dragon-tiger elixir. The Tong soldiers drink this elixir before going into battle. It gives them invincibility on the battlefield. You will drink?''

The *Heng Do* held the bottle to Man Sum's lips. The young man drank. Never in his life had he tasted anything as foul.

The *Heng Do* then produced a tiger's claw from behind the statue of the master of heaven. ''This instrument,'' he said, ''is called the *Hu Chao*. It wards off sudden fits of fright such as one experiences in the moment before battle. Wearing the tiger's claw, the warrior merges with the animal's spirit and achieves the requisite state of 'no thought' in which his energy becomes pure, bright, and perfectly balanced.''

The *Heng Do* solemnly placed the tiger's claw around the neck of the initiate, then he led Man Sum to the left side of the room. There, the *Heng Do* opened the large chest inscribed with the characters, ''Tool box, Chi Sing Tong.'' From it, he hoisted a large iron lock.

''This is the hundred-family lock,'' he said. ''The hundred-family lock clasps the child in filial obedience to the parents for life. It withstands the hundred negative influences which threaten to rupture the child's bond with the parents. The hundred-family lock in the Chi Sing's tool chest is the symbol of the highbinder's never-flagging fidelity to this Tong.''

The candidate was then introduced to several spells, some written on triangular red paper. The triangle, serving as the symbol of the Triad Society, represented the cosmic trinity: man, heaven, earth. Other spells, designed to ward off evil influences, both visible and invisible, were stitched into expensive-looking silk banners.

The *Heng Do* said, "It is time, having learned the talismans and their significance, to enter the Northern Gate, realm of the tortoise and the black-faced warrior. But first, you must dress in sack cloth and ashes in mourning for the defeated and departed Mings."

At his guide's order, Man Sum stripped down, and the *Heng Do* examined carefully the candidate's naked body.

"I am looking for birthmarks. When I find them, I write them down."

"May I respectfully ask why?"

"It is a way to identify a corpse. Sometimes the only way," the *Heng Do* said, smiling. He didn't elaborate.

Man Sum dressed himself according to the *Heng Do's* instructions. Then he passed through the Northern Gate, alone.

A coffin, in which an effigy of the Ming emperor was placed, lay in the center of the room. The body of the emperor was dressed as a Buddhist priest. There were five vessels on an altar at the head of the body. In the vases were blue and white paper flowers and two illuminated candles. They were reinforced with a pagoda-shaped lamp stand containing a bowl of sesame oil in which floated a wick of twisted cotton. A spirit tablet inscribed with the name "Ming" was in the center of the side of the altar next to the coffin.

A husky man, short of stature, entered the room from behind a thick black curtain. He was dressed in black from head to foot. Bright steel armor covered his garments. The armor protected his entire body. He wore a helmet that left a slit for the eyes and a small hole for the mouth.

"I am the black warrior," said a voice muffled by the helmet. "You will kneel at the left shoulder of the corpse. It is the position of the eldest son."

Man Sum didn't hesitate to do as he was instructed

At the head of the coffin, there was an altar heavy with the usual odor of incense from a score of lit punk sticks. The Ming emperor was replicated on this altar, riding on the back of the tortoise.

"The tortoiseshell is the symbol of the universe," the black warrior said. "The tortoise's dome-shaped back represents the vault of heaven while its flat belly is the earth floating on the waters. Lotus flowers surround the tortoise. Their leaves and roots signify progeny and steadfastness in the family When you join our Tong, our Tong becomes your family, replaces your original family."

Man Sum was told by the warrior to kneel four times before the coffin of the Ming emperor. Then the black warrior himself knelt at the head of the coffin, and an attendant served him a brass wine cup on a tray. The warrior, in turn, poured the wine into a bowl set on the floor for the purposes of the libation Man Sum followed him in making three prostrations

The ritual prostrations having been completed, the candidate was dressed in the clothing of the Ming Dynasty in five colors: blue, green, yellow, with a white girdle and a red turban.

Beyond the third portal, Man Sum was immediately confronted with an arch of drawn swords. He quickly ducked down as five swordsmen began a dance in the small room. They waved their swords and purposely moved very close to the candidate so that he had to use all the defensive skills his agile body knew to avoid being wounded At one point, he was cornered. All the swords were flailing at once, and he realized they were going to cut him.

One of the men brought his sword down across Man Sum's body, but at the last second turned the blade so that the flat side of the sword struck the candidate It hit Man

Sum with such force that if it had been the blade's edge, it would have cut him in half. Then suddenly they stopped.

An older man dressed in feminine garments stood in the center of the room. Since the ascension of the Manchus, all Chinese had cut off their queues, but this man had an old-style queue, and it was unplaited. Perhaps it was a wig, Man Sum thought.

This man looked the prospective member over very carefully. To his left was another elderly man dressed in a dark grey long Chinese robe unrelieved by any ornament. This was the secretary of the organization, Man Sum was to find out later. For a man, his hands were exceedingly small and beautifully formed. But they were strong and capable, as the firmness of his grip testified. His clean-shaven, kindly face had all the marks of centuries of good breeding, and his charm of manner put Man Sum at ease for the moment.

The secretary spoke. "You are going to be examined, candidate, by the *Ah Mah*, the mother. You will die and be reborn through him. But first you must be put through the examination."

This *Ah Mah* then began an endless series of questions, which ranged over Man Sum's life, his parents, his memories of his father, his reasons for coming to the United States. Also, he was asked questions based on the events of the last hour or so, since the initial proceedings began.

Then the swordplay began again. As before, Man Sum had to use all his agility to dodge the blades. At one point, he was cornered, and one of the swordsmen began thrusting. He felt a sharp pain in his ribs. One of the swords had penetrated the Ming robe and broken through to his skin. The swordsman, however, checked the thrust and withdrew.

Man Sum wondered if this slight bloodletting was part of the ceremony.

"Have you carefully considered the step you are about to take?" the secretary then asked.

"I have," Man Sum answered.

"Are you ready to storm the Great Wall?"

"Quite ready," the candidate said.

"Have you been prepared with weapons?"

"Not as yet."

"How can a child be born without a mother?"

"She is seated upon my left," Man Sum said, designating the *Ah Mah*

"Are you ready to become a blood brother?"

"All ready," Man Sum said.

"Then let thy mother proceed to shed the blood of maternity," the secretary said.

The examination was finally concluded and the *Ah Mah's* face took on a kindlier disposition.

The secretary announced, "The candidate has successfully answered the three hundred thirty-three questions required by the Chi Sing Tong initiation requirements."

The swordsmen sheathed their weapons in ornate brass scabbards and these were placed on hooks on the wall. Man Sum was allowed to rest He thought to himself, If I had known it would be this difficult to immigrate to the United States, I probably would have reconsidered.

The *Ah Mah* seated himself on a throne situated at a doorway.

The secretary gently clasped Man Sum's hand and bade him crawl beneath the throne. The swordsmen, meanwhile, had withdrawn their swords again from their scabbards, and were placing them low to the ground so that Man Sum had to crawl on his belly in order to keep himself from touching and being scratched by the down-turned blades. Straining to keep himself as flush as possible with the floor, the candidate bellied his way to the small space made by the *Ah Mah's* robes.

"This ritual," the secretary said softly, "signifies your renunciation of all previous allegiances: father, mother, kin, clan, and emperor. *Ah Mah* represents the mother who will give you birth as a new being, newly born child of the Tong. Your reappearance on the other side of the throne coincides with your entrance into the Tong's sacred chamber, your rebirth as a Tong member."

When Man Sum emerged, he found himself in a large council chamber furnished with a teakwood table in the center and teakwood chairs along the sides. Eighty or so men stood in a circle. He was made to join the circle also. A three-legged brass caldron was carried from man to man in the circle.

The secretary said, "This *ting* symbolizes the vessel containing that which provides men with nourishment."

Each member of the Tong was given a needle with which he pricked his own finger, then let a couple of drops of blood fall into the *ting*. The same act was repeated by everyone as the caldron was ritually handed around the circle. Lastly, the vessel came around to Man Sum. Before mingling his blood with the others, Man Sum was made to repeat after the exalted master on the opposite end of the circle the following verse: "By this red drop of blood on fingertip, I, Sing Man Sum, swear the secrets of this Tong I never will declare. Seven gaping wounds shall drain my life away should I dare to alien ears my sacred trust betray."

A little wine was added to the blood. Man Sum was made to take a drink of it. Each member around the sacred circle drank from the same cup until all had been served. The exalted master led all present in the rites of worship.

Incense sticks were lit, libations poured, and dishes of food were offered to heaven, earth, the spirits of the slaughtered priests, and the ancient kings. Further secrets were revealed, and more oaths of allegiance were solemnly repeated.

A rooster was sacrificed upon the high altar to bind the new member to his sacred trust, never to betray his Tong. He repeated after the grand master, ''From the rooster's head, from the rooster's head, see how fresh blood flows. If loyal and brave my course shall be, my heirs immortal renown shall see. But when base traitor and coward turn I, slain on the road my body shall lie.''

Chapter 6

A special banquet room at Shanghai Low, at the corner of Grant and Clay Streets, was reserved for the brotherhood. Round tables, each seating ten people, were set up in the back room of the restaurant's second floor. Man Sum was escorted to the seat of honor, next to the exalted master. The leader introduced the new member to the others at the table.

"These are several of our good *boo how doy*."

"*Boo how doy*?" Man Sum didn't understand.

"Yes, *boo how doy* means hatchet sons. These are the highbinders."

"Yes," one of the highbinders said. "The *sai yan*, Western people, call us 'highbinders' because we wear our belts high up."

The exalted master continued, "They are called hatchet men because hatchets and knives were used in the Tong wars of the '60s, '70s and '80s. Now the highbinders mostly use the Colt .45 revolver. The term *boo how doy* is used anyway, even though the style of combat and type of weapon changed since the earthquake of '06."

The *boo how doy* at Man Sum's table included the three men who rescued him. He recognized their voices.

Now they introduced themselves to him. They were the shallow-cheeked Duk Fong, the short, muscular Ah Foon, who squinted constantly, and the wiry Lok Wing. The exalted master had not yet introduced himself.

All stood around and drank a toast of rice wine out of the tiny porcelain cups.

"To our Tong, the great Chi Sing Tong!" the exalted master said.

"To our Tong," the members repeated.

These cups, once drunk, were promptly filled again by pretty young maidens dressed in black velvet with headpieces full of bangles and brooches. They wore heavy rings on their earlobes that dangled almost to their shoulders. Jade bracelets decorated their wrists.

The highbinder on Man Sum's right, Ah Foon, smiled at seeing the new member's interest in these young women.

"They are our singsong girls," Ah Foon explained. "Prostitutes purchased for high prices. On the occasions of special banquets, they wait on us, pouring wine and tea, making pleasant conversation, and singing melodies from the home country."

Man Sum wondered if Ming Lee was among them. He searched for her, but she was nowhere to be seen. Was she now, at this very moment, selling her body? He quickly tried to repress this thought.

Now they were being served melon soup made from chicken stock with lotus seed, mushrooms and bamboo shoots. The soup was served in the melon itself, the rind acting as a lid to hold the flavor in. All ate in silence.

Other festive dishes were brought on: grilled Peking duck served in plum sauce, walnut chicken, roast pigeon, barbecued pork with hearts of cabbage. Talk was strictly confined to the merits of the meal or the beauty and graciousness of the singsong girls, much more beautiful, it was pointed out, than the girls of the other Tong.

One of them sat on Ah Foon's lap and licentiously put her tongue in his ear. Man Sum blushed, but the other highbinders seemed not to notice the girl's bawdy behavior.

The meal was concluded. The guests were wiping their faces and fingers with steaming towels, and the exalted master turned toward Man Sum and asked simply, "Don't you recognize me, Man Sum? I am your father. I am Sing Choy Wu."

"My father?" He looked at this elderly gentleman in disbelief. It had been many years since he had seen his father, but the man he saw before him did not at all resemble the photographs that had always hung over the stove in the house.

"Yes, Man Sum, it is I who am responsible for obtaining your coaching papers. And it is I who, through contacts at Angel Island, have been attempting to aid you. It has been a very difficult task, breaking the steel cord that binds the sufferers of our race."

Man Sum said enthusiastically, "What a relief it is for me to have found you at last, Father!"

"Oh, Man Sum," Choy Wu said, embracing his son. "How I have supplicated the gods for this bright day!"

"It is hard to believe it is really you."

Choy Wu brushed away a tear.

"Your mother!"

"Yes."

"How her death saddened me! I wept for a week. I went nowhere. How I loved her! Curse the barbarian country that would not permit us to be united. I missed her. I missed her so much when I first left China. I carried her picture next to my heart. You, you must have been quite grieved at her death, son, yes?"

"Oh, yes, Father, yes. We were so very close."

"You must have been. You must have been. Ah, but that's all done now. All over."

"I am glad, at least, I have found my father."

"I caution you, however, to never tell anyone outside this brotherhood that I am your real father," Sing Choy Wu said in low tones.

"But, why?" Man Sum asked. "Must I continue this paper son charade?"

"For a while, yes. This is not our land, my son. This is a land ruled by barbarians who govern by laws they write themselves, then claim the laws give them no choice in matters. It is as if their laws were framed in heaven and not by their own hands. That is what this immigration law is. It does not allow true sons to openly acknowledge their true fathers."

"But do all their laws restrict our people?" Man Sum asked. Is there any law that protects us?"

"At one time, there was. Up to about twenty years ago. At that time, the only place a Chinese person could turn for justice was the Chinese merchant companies. Each company represented one of the districts in Gwong Jau from which most of the immigrants came. These Chinese merchant companies ruled Chinatown. They had all the power because they had the most influence with the *faan gwai*."

"Why don't the Chinese merchant companies help the Chinese now?" Man Sum asked.

"They were ruled by the large families: the Wongs, the Lees, the Chins, and the Woos. The claims of the smaller family groups were almost always passed over. Or, where there was a dispute between a small family and a large one, the larger, established family always won out because they had the most pull."

"You mean, just because your name was Sing, the Chinese merchant companies treated you differently?" Man Sum asked.

"I had a cigar store and a small factory here in Chinatown on Jackson Street between Stockton and Dupont. When I visited China, I entrusted my store to those whom I thought were my friends. I went back to China and visited you and your mother. When I came back here, I discovered that my so-called friends had completely taken over my business and had my name struck from the deed. In other words, they had stolen it."

"I never knew anything like that happened to you, Father."

"I never told your mother. I didn't want her or you to worry about me."

"I see," Man Sum nodded. "But how could these bandits take your business away from you?"

"They had other papers drawn up that claimed they were the sole legitimate owners. Because one of them belonged to the Wong family, their claim was upheld by the Chinese merchant companies and then rubber-stamped by the *faan gwai* court."

"What did you do about it?"

"I took my complaint to the Chinese merchant companies. I appealed to their sense of justice. I told them how much that business meant to me. You see, I found much gold in the Sierras, but the tax collectors stole everything I found. Then I came to Chinatown and became a vegetable peddler. I made only ten cents a day, but I saved and hoarded. Gradually, from nothing, I built up that business."

"Was there nothing you could do to get your business back?"

"I was out of luck, that's all, just plain out of luck.

That's what I was told. One thing I did know, though: I was in the right and they were in the wrong. I also knew then and there that all justice for Chinese was dead in Chinatown. I never again returned to the merchant companies. There was no justice for Sings. Sings were a small family.''

"And then you joined the Chi Sing Tong?"

"Yes. I met some men who were in the Triad Society, soldiers from the T'ai Ping rebellion who had had similar experiences with justice here. We decided to form a society where we could protect each other, help each other.''

"Then that's how the Tongs really came into existence?''

"That's right, we were the first Tong, modeled after the secret societies in China that go back two thousand years. The Tong was a benevolent society to begin with. You see, just about all the immigrants were bachelors. They had to leave their families behind. The Tong became like a family for them.''

"And now the Chi Sing Tong is very strong?" Man Sum asked.

Choy Wu nodded. "We got enough money together and set up a gambling house on Ross Alley, started a very profitable fan-tan game. Everybody came to our gambling house. We expanded. When we made enough money, we were able to get some opium trade and even buy some girls.''

"But all those activities must be in violation of the laws of this country.''

"The gambling, opium and the girls were ways to build up capital fast and make more investments, and eventually buy property. Not too far in the future, we'll own enough, get enough ahead to buy the *faan gwai* court system and get some justice for Chinese people.''

"But do you think you will ever be able to buy the court system of this large country?"

"Yes, we will. Then this barbarian law will not be able to hurt us any longer We'd get the 1882 exclusion law repealed. Then we can bring our families here to the United States and live prosperously together with our families again."

Sing Choy Wu was speaking loudly and all were listening and nodding. He took out another cigarette. A singsong girl promptly lit it

"I wanted you, my son, here by my side, to help me wage the battles that will be coming. If we win these struggles against our rival Tongs and the big families, we will become the strongest and most wealthy organization in Chinatown."

The highbinders nodded and grunted with approval.

"You will carry forth this Tong after I am dead. In you I am investing the future of this Tong and in no one else."

This statement shocked Sing Choy Wu's son. "Me? You mean you want me to be . . . ?"

"Yes, but before you can become leader, you must first learn the *boo how doy* If you don't have a reputation as a tough highbinder the salaried soldiers will never respect you. That's why I'm putting you into training with Duk Fong, our number-one fighter."

Man Sum looked across the table at Duk Fong. The highbinder seemed to be sizing him up, doubtfully.

Sing Choy Wu continued, "We won't be able to win the revolution in this *faan gwai* land in my lifetime. It will take time, maybe many lifetimes before a place will be carved out here for our clan and kinsmen. But you will see, our glorious Tong will win. The merchant companies and large families and even the *faan gwai* will know defeat at our hands. Then they will respect us. Then there will be justice for our people.''

Man Sum said, ''But I . . . I don't know if I can ever learn to fight with a gun. It is not in my nature, it is not . . .''

''You, Man Sum, have proven your strength and bravery in your escape from the hated Island of the Angel of Death. Maybe you are the only one who has ever gotten away from that place. I am not worried about your ability to become a *boo how doy*!''

''Father, I am not as sure of myself as I would like to be. Try to understand how long it has been since I knew my position in the world. For months I had been drumming into my mind that I was the son of another father. I was very confused all that time. I was lost because I was living a lie and even I had trouble distinguishing the true from the false. In order to tell lies to the Immigration Service, I also had to tell lies to myself.''

''You'll never be misled by falseness again. You never have to be untruthful again except of course with your enemies and the foreign ghosts. There is no blame in that. You must keep the truth from them. They would do everything in their power to use the truth against you.''

There was a pause. The highbinders were all looking at him now, as if expecting him to say something.

Finally, Ah Foon prompted him, ''Well, Man Sum, what do you have to say to all this?''

Duk Fong said, ''Are you with us or not? We must know your decision.''

Man Sum knew that there was only one decision open to him.

''I pledge myself in filial piety to you, my true father. You will always know the truth of what I think and what I do And I will become a *boo how doy*, if that is your wish."

"That is good, my son I knew I saw in you a lad I could count on."

"And we'll make a good fighter out of you, boy," Duk Fong added, picking his teeth.

"Yes, soon you will be able to fight side by side with them. They are your new family, Man Sum, your kinsmen to whom you now owe absolute obedience Just as you owe it to me, your father and your exalted master "

"But Father, something yet troubles me My entire background has been study, scholarship, the classics Not warfare," Man Sum said.

"I don't ask you to forget your classic training. It is good that your mother attempted to make a scholar out of you. I am pleased to have a son so knowledgeable, a son who can compose a poem, make intelligent references to the great thinkers of our history But more important for the present crisis is to learn to fight. There are enemies everywhere, and if you don't know how to fight, this town will crumble you like a moth "

"Father, there is something else on my mind It has been worrying me greatly The subject of my concern is Kwan Ming Lee. She is the woman I, through the secret contacts in the Tong, was able to help to free What has become of her? Is she all right?"

Sing Choy Wu started to say something but was interrupted by his son

"Because, Father, I love her. I don't want her to be a prostitute, Father. I love her and want to marry her "

The expression on Choy Wu's face darkened "She is . . she is all right, yes," he said with hesitation

"I never want Ming Lee to be one of those singsong girls I plan to be successful, and make some money I want Ming Lee to be my bride. I don't want other men touching her, degrading her. She's so pure, so beautiful. I know that you wouldn't think of putting her out for hire now that I have told you this, but I just wanted to be sure she was all right.''

"She's all right. Nothing's going to happen to her. We will never ask her to do anything she would not do willingly."

"But what about our investment in her?" Ah Foon asked. He was half drunk. "She's got to pay us back, with interest. Now, how she gets it is unimportant, but it's quite a debt. We helped her husband bring her over here. It was all quite expensive, not the passage only, but the bribe money too. Well, he died, you see? So he won't ever be able to pay us the money we're owed.''

"I'll pay her debt for her," Man Sum said.

"How's that?" Choy Wu said in surprise.

"I said, I'll find a way to raise enough money to pay you back everything she owes you."

The *boo how doy* allowed slightly mocking smiles to cross their faces as they took sips of their after-dinner tea.

"That's very noble of you, son," Choy Wu said, smiling. "I respect you. You've got passion and ambition. These qualities are essential in a good Tong man. You're going to do very well for us. And as I said, one day, you will become an exalted master like me. Yes, I see you love the woman very much, but you will meet many beautiful women in Chinatown. Not a few of them will turn your young head, much more than this large-footed Ming Lee."

"It is she and she alone whom I want to marry, Father. Please, tell me where she is so that I might see her and talk to her face to face. We could never talk freely at Angel Island. The men were separated from the women.

All contact was prohibited. But now, surely, we will be able to see each other, touch each other!''

Duk Fong couldn't resist making a joke at the immigrant's expense. "You might have to stand in line," he said pointedly.

Man Sum didn't appreciate his humor. "No, no, she must never become a common whore. Never. I will see her die first, and then I will die."

Man Sum, realizing that he was losing his composure, tried to calm himself. "I will find a way to pay you back, make good your losses."

His father, after looking at the *boo how doy* and then back at Man Sum, gently put his hand on his son's arm and said, "Remember, your first duty is to your Tong. Your Tong comes first, before all other relationships, including your parents! The girl is not a priority. Please, try to remember that. You have to think of yourself. She is in good hands. We are taking good care of her. You needn't worry."

"Where is she? May I see her?"

"No, you may not. Not at this time. You must be patient. You will have the opportunity to see her soon enough. She is a little sick now."

"Sick?"

"It's nothing serious. Don't concern yourself too much. She just needs to rest for the time being. After a while, you'll be able to see her. And when you see her, you might find that you'll have a change of heart."

"What do you mean, Father?"

"You see, at the island, you spoke to each other through notes only. There is much to be learned from a woman. But when you find out what you want to know, you may realize you were wrong about her. She may turn out to be someone very different than you thought."

"No," Man Sum protested. "I believe I know her very well. It feels like I have known her all my life." Man Sum's emotions started to get the better of him, and he began to weep. It made him feel very ashamed to weep in front of those men.

His father was sympathetic. "You are young, Man Sum I am old. I have had much experience with women in my time. There is much I can teach you. And here in Chinatown there are plenty of places to learn what you need to learn. Wipe away those tears, boy. You're going to have a good time here, you know. Okay? Now we'll break up for the evening, and you will be shown your quarters."

As they were leaving the restaurant, Duk Fong said, "You will see Lum Po."

"Lum Po? Here?" Man Sum said in a surprised tone.

Duk Fong answered, "He was initiated into the Chi Sing Tong when he arrived in Chinatown. Like you, he swam to freedom. But his swim was shorter than yours. He only had to make the distance between an anchored garbage skiff and the shore. We fished him out, brought him here, saw that he was a strong fellow, and so we gave him a chance, tested his strength, endurance, intelligence He did very well indeed."

"Since you're my son, membership was automatic with you," Choy Wu added. "The same was not true for him. He wasn't anyone's relative in the Tong, so we had to test his powers. If we'd rejected him, he'd be in a bad way The authorities would pick him up. He'd have no protection, no way to get past the 'green uniform.'"

Duk Fong interrupted, "We tested Lum Po and didn't test you That means you have to work harder You have good basic strength, a hard and well-developed body, but your mind is still too full of the cobwebs of classic training

And we don't as yet have any idea what kind of fighting spirit you have. We know Lum Po that way a little better than we know you. We'll have to start putting you through some tests. Then we'll get some idea.''

"Yes, it's time the paper son became a hatchet son,'' Ah Foon added.

"You know what we are?'' Lum Po said. "We are soldiers. We may not want to be soldiers, but that is what has become of us. We have no choice. The only alternative to our present condition is abandonment to the American court justice system. You know where we would go then. Prison.''

Lum Po and Man Sum occupied a tiny room together in the Tong building's fourth floor. The room overlooked Clay Street hill. They could see the lights of Powell Street outside their small window. To look out the window of their room, they had to move the shade slightly, but for security purposes, they were not permitted to open the dirty yellow shade. However, they could open the window just a crack to get a little air.

Lum Po said, "I've talked with the *boo how doy* and they gave me their contract to read. You and I are going to have to sign this thing. It's like this: You act only when orders are given. Without orders, you don't act. You try to be the best highbinder, and if you're only second best, you have good reason to fear for your life.''

"I'd say then we have good reason to fear for our lives!'' Man Sum said, somewhat sarcastically.

"You must never back away from the field of battle. Never turn back when you're told to make a kill.''

"What do you do when you're not killing people?'' Man Sum asked.

"Spend days on the pier receiving prostitutes and

escorting them to their work places," Lum Po said. Smirking, he added, "I don't mind that part of it."

"I could take it or leave it," Man Sum said, thinking of Ming Lee.

"Listen to this: 'If, in the discharge of your duties you are slain, the Tong undertakes to pay five hundred dollars' sympathy money to your family. If you're wounded, the Tong will hire a surgeon to take care of your wounds. If you're sick and have to be laid up for any length of time, you get ten dollars a month.' "

"In case your face is so disfigured that they can't identify you, they know where your birthmarks are," Man Sum said.

Man Sum leaned his head back on the grimy wall. His mattress was thin and his only covering was a worn brown blanket. The new soldiers' only source of light was a piece of tallow in a jar in which a string had been dunked.

Man Sum said, "Maybe it was better back on Angel Island. At least there, they didn't require you to get yourself involved in situations where you might get yourself killed."

Lum Po continued reading the contract. "Well, if you're maimed for life and incapacitated for service, you shall receive the additional sum of two hundred fifty dollars. A subscription shall be opened to defray the expense of your passage back to China. But it is further stipulated that you, in common with your comrades, shall exert yourself to kill or wound anyone at the direction of this Tong. And if in so doing, you are arrested and have to endure the miseries of imprisonment . . ."

"As if I haven't already had enough of that!" Man Sum snarled.

"This society undertakes to send the sum of one

hundred dollars every year to your family during the term of your incarceration.''

"If I'm sent to prison, I'll have the money sent to Kwan Ming Lee! It'll help defray her indebtedness to the Tong.''

"Listen, Man Sum, what do you think of this Tong business? I didn't expect to become a Chi Sing Tong when I emigrated. My father, I know, is somewhere here in America, perhaps Chinatown. But I have not been able to find him. Moreover, the Tong has made me one of its members. That means I forswear all other relationships. I have made a vow to the Chi Sing Tong to renounce my real father. I felt that I had to do so or they would turn me over to the authorities.''

"That's right. We pretty much have to do as the Tong directs. We don't have any other alternatives.''

"But having renounced my father, I still can't stop thinking about him, wondering where he is. He must not even know I am here. What is the point of all this? If I can't rejoin my father, what can I do?''

"What can either of us do?''

"Perhaps it would have been better if you had let me carry my suicide plan to completion back on the island.''

"No.'' Man Sum shook his head.

"Self-inflicted death is the easy way out. We both have too much courage for that way. We will learn the *boo how doy* skills. Yes. That's what we will do, Lum Po!''

Lum Po squinted at Man Sum through the dim candlelight of the tiny room above Clay Street.

Man Sum went on, "Never fear. You are my very good friend. There is power in the fighting skills of the highbinders. And as my father said, the toughest men in Chinatown have been assigned to be our mentors. We will be their good students.''

"Yes, we will learn the *boo how doy* skills. But then?"

"We must not entirely give our hearts over to them. Our hearts belong more truly to others. Mine belongs to my love, Kwan Ming Lee. Yours belongs to your father in filial piety. These powers that the highbinders will instruct us in will eventually result in our freedom. We will even become better fighters than they are. We are younger, and we are stronger."

Lum Po said, "But will we not have to kill others of our own race!"

"I have already killed a man. It is not so hard. He was only a *faan gwai* policeman, but I think it was no different than killing an enemy Tong." Man Sum spoke without conviction. He had not yet really reconciled himself to the blood on his hands.

"But you did not kill him," Lum Po said. "He survived."

Man Sum's heart became light at the words of his friend. The white had not died. He, Man Sum, was not a murderer. But in his relief, another problem arose. If he had not killed before, he never would now. Perhaps he could learn the skills of the *boo how doy*, but he would never use them. Never. "Perhaps time will show us our path," he said to Lum Po. "Perhaps we will never be called upon to kill our brothers."

Duk Fong stood with Lum Po and Man Sum in the second room in the cellar under brother Yat How's fish market. The room looked ordinary enough. Wooden boxes were stacked along the walls. From the ceiling, a lamp dangled by a slightly frayed wire. A green translucent shade covered the rather weak bulb. There was a table beneath the lamp. It had a dusty account book on it, which looked as if nobody had written in it for a while. Under the table, a threadbare antique rug lay on the concrete floor.

Duk Fong pushed the table aside. He reached down and lifted the threadbare rug. There was a keyhole underneath the rug.

Duk Fong addressed two other men. "After we have gone below the earth, you will replace the rug and the table."

Having given the order to the two apprentices, the sallow-cheeked killer put a key in the keyhole and opened a trap door. The opening led to a flight of stairs.

Duk Fong lit the wick of an oil lamp he had been carrying and said to his students, "Follow me."

They started down the stairs, and promptly the door was shut behind them. No sounds from above could be heard. At that point Man Sum realized that the two apprentices left above were putting back the rug and the table.

The stairway ended at a passageway not much higher than an average man's height.

Suddenly a flash and a loud noise issued from Duk Fong's left hand. He pocketed his revolver and led them twenty yards farther, where they found a large dead rat. A bullet had entered its neck.

"That was a poor shot," Duk Fong said. "I was aiming for its left eye." He put away his gun. Then he took out his keys and opened a thick metal door on their right. They passed through the door and found themselves in a large room, about seventy yards long. Small paper targets were tacked to the wall at the end of the room. From a bag he was carrying, Duk Fong's assistant carefully lifted two bull-nosed .45 automatic pistols.

For the next few hours, in that shooting range underground, Man Sum and Lum Po took turns loading the pistol clips for each other and firing hundreds of rounds of cartridges.

"The *boo how doy* is not born with the ability to create a three-bullet pattern six inches in diameter at a range of fifty yards," Duk Fong said. "Tong killings are sometimes midnight jobs. Midnight marksmanship means long weeks of practice boiled down to where accuracy becomes instinct. You are shooting now with your arm extended. Otherwise, you wouldn't be able to come even close to the target. But you're going to learn how to shoot the way I do, with your arm close against your side. That's much more difficult, but if you can't do it with ninety percent accuracy, you're no *boo how doy*, and you're a corpse if you try to be one."

Man Sum and Lum Po spent days and weeks going down to the Chi Sing labyrinth under Yat How's fish market and practicing marksmanship. Before and after, they would occasionally practice on the rats, firing from the hip. But they invariably missed. Neither of them was very successful at the pistol range either.

The regimen of the practice and the inability to learn difficult marksmanship skills were wearing on Man Sum. He found that he had less and less to say to his friend and roommate, Lum Po. Sharing the tiny room was getting on his nerves.

That's why it was a relief when, one Saturday night, the highbinders decided it was time to show the pledges a game of fan-tan at the club on Ross Alley. Man Sum had about five dollars altogether from the meager salary doled out to apprentice hatchet men. Over the entrance to a dingy-looking vestibule on Ross Alley was a sign that read, "*Pay Hoy Yuh Yat*, this place is open both day and night."

They climbed stairs that had thick, dusty vermilion carpets and a single dim bulb at the top. It was strangely quiet as they climbed. When they reached the second floor, they turned to the right, down a narrow hallway, then left. At the end of this corridor, a watchman sat on a stool, smoking a long bamboo pipe. He was half dozing in the dim light, but when he saw Duk Fong, one of Chinatown's most notorious *boo how doy*, he practically jumped three feet in the air. He forced his lips, stiff with fear, to make a thin smile.

"Honored *boo how doy*, we are most honored that you come to the game tonight."

"Quickly, open the door for us!"

"Yes, sir. Yes, esteemed sir."

Then he nodded and bowed obsequiously and opened the steel door.

The sounds of the excited crowd rushed out to dispel the silence of the carpeted corridor. The room was crowded, smoke-filled. A long table was in the center. Two lamps with conical green lamp shades were suspended by rope from the high ceiling. The proprietor sat on a high stool at the head of this table. Duk Fong exchanged quick nods with him. Customers ranged on both sides of the table. They were constantly jockeying for position at the table's edge to get the best view of the play and gain the greatest access to the betting squares. In the center of the table was a mound of Chinese coins, the kind with square holes in the center.

The game of fan-tan consisted of the simple procedure of betting whether the heap of coins in the center of the table contained an odd or an even number of coins. At the edge of the table, each customer playing at the time had two betting squares, one for odd, one for even. He'd place his money in one of the squares.

If he lost, the proprietor would scoop his bet away with a long, ivory-handled rake. If the bettor won, the proprietor would push double the amount of the bet toward the customer.

Suddenly, three players at the center of the table were politely asked to give up their places. They protested, but once they saw they were speaking to highbinders, they quickly acquiesced. Man Sum all at once found himself in betting position. The wicker basket containing the square-holed coins was upturned and the coins cascaded into a pile.

Duk Fong sneered, "A game of pure chance, no skill involved whatsoever. Not much different from the lottery."

Man Sum put his quarter on an even square. The rake clicked the coins off. Two were gone, then four, then six, eight, until Man Sum could count them. Forty-eight. He found that he could count the coins in groups of eight. He had won fifty cents.

"Seung so, seung so, la." Even number.

Forty-eight coins had appeared to him clearly before the other gamblers were certain. Would it be possible to see the number of coins in the entire pile? He quickly dismissed the thought. No. Too many coins. To make real money gambling, he'd have to find the right game, the game where he could eliminate chance by knowing with certainty the outcome before anyone else.

Man Sum continued to play, straining his eyes on the pile of coins, furiously trying to count groups of eight, but it was futile.

Through pure guesswork, he managed to pull ahead ten dollars, but lost another five. Duk Fong had lost six dollars. Altogether, Lum Po managed to come out fifty cents ahead.

Duk Fong said, "Here, nobody wins too much. It's

Chi Sing Tong's gambling place. The bank's winnings go in the Tong's war chest. Money from the war chest pays my salary. It buys your rice, too, and your shooting lessons.'' Smiling at Man Sum, he said, ''You'd better not get too good at this game, or you'll be taking rice out of my bowl.''

''Hai la,'' Ah Foon said. ''You play fan-tan too good, and we'll send you to Gin Kong Tong's place on Commercial Street, let you rob from their war chest.''

Man Sum enjoyed the excitement of the game. He found himself looking very carefully at every move of the proprietor, the gamblers and the coins. He noticed faces. He kept track of consistent winners, those whose winnings steadily increased, and there were some.

There was one very quiet man in particular who never called out numbers, but who managed to win more times than anyone else.

''That's Mow Lem Choy, otherwise known as 'the trick.' He's a Gin Kong man,'' Duk Fong said. ''He's a gambler, just like I'm a warrior. He can pull money out of fan-tan like a fish pulling breath out of water, but he knows he can never win *too* much. Many a great gambler grows a hatchet in his backbone in Sullivan's Alley. I'm keeping my eye on Mow Lem Choy.''

''The only straight snake is a dead snake,'' Ah Foon said.

Lok Wing whispered, ''But at this point there is no reason to go after Mow Lem Choy. He isn't winning enough. He's discreet. His winnings don't tally enough to embarrass the Tong's house bank. Yet he always wins enough to make the game profitable.''

Man Sum wondered what exactly was the gambler's secret.

Man Sum and Lum Po returned to the fan-tan game

several times over the next month. It was their only recreation, and they had to be accompanied by the highbinders whenever they went.

One night, during a very exciting game, a loud, clanging bell rang.

"Raid! It's a raid!" several players shouted simultaneously.

"What's going on?" Man Sum asked Duk Fong.

"Police raid. No time to explain!" Duk Fong said, pushing Man Sum before him.

The table was immediately cleared of all evidence of gaming. The tan markers were quickly burned or flushed down the toilet. Man Sum saw a number of secret trap doors open as if by magic. There were trap doors under the big table, under a small carpet, behind a tapestry. Man Sum was pushed by the highbinders through a door hidden by decorative wallpaper. He found himself on a ladder that led down to a basement area.

"The room is now completely empty," Duk Fong said, catching his breath when they reached the basement. "The policeman will be shown an innocent, nondescript room. He knows perfectly well gambling was going on there, but he took his time coming down the hallway. He gave us the chance to clear it out because we pay him well."

"They always pretend to do their job," Lok Wing added, "but it's all for show."

But this raid was different.

PART II
WAR

"When orders are given, you shall advance valiantly, striving to be first and only fearing to be laggard. Never turn your back upon the battlefield."

—from the Oath of the Chi Sing Tong

Chapter 7

No warning bell was sounded. There was only the sound of axes chopping at the iron and oak doors. The gamblers took the usual escape routes. Trap doors were opened and the evidence was hidden. But this time, the police were waiting for them in the barber shop below the gambling house.

The entire group was taken to the Chinatown Precinct Police Station and locked up. Because there were so many of them, they were let out after a few hours. However, when some of them tried to return to the club, they found it boarded up.

The sign that said, "This place is open all day and all night" was replaced with a piece of paper that read, "*San mun*," closed.

Duk Fong was infuriated. "What is this?" he demanded.

"Looks like this raid was a real one. They shut our place down," Ah Foon replied.

"Hey," Lok Wing called out. He was running toward them, out of breath. "I checked our places in Bartlett Alley and Saint Louis Alley. They've been closed by the police, too."

"Bartlett Alley? Saint Louis Alley? Closed?" Duk Fong said in disbelief. Then a sudden realization dawned on him. "We've been paying off the special police. Something else is going on here. This business smells very suspicious. We had better get a hold of Sing Choy Wu immediately."

A week after the closing of the fan-tan clubs belonging to the Chi Sing Tong, they were reopened under the management of Lam Wong, an influential member of the Wong guild. The Wongs were one of the families which had been ruling the merchant companies. But after the 1882 exclusion law, the Chinese merchant companies began to lose the respect of the people. So Wong joined the Suey Duck Tong.

When he was not able to take over the Suey Duck Tong, as he had wished, he split from the Suey Ducks, taking some of the membership with him. He convinced some and bought others, and formed his own society, the Suey Sing Tong.

He had paid his own protection money to the *faan gwai* police, and it was more than the Chi Sings had been able to pay. The Wong clan was the most powerful family guild. It had a war chest a hundred times greater than that of the Chi Sings and a membership three or four times as large. In the merchant class alone, there were several thousand Wongs in San Francisco and scattered all over California.

After opening the gambling houses again, Lam Wong began publicly to boast that he could do with the Chi Sings as he liked. They were "as eggs in a basket, which I can shake up and smash at will." His followers in the Suey Sings, aping their leader, began to harass Chi Sing men, beating and robbing them whenever they ventured near a gambling house.

The feeling between the Suey Sings and the Chi Sing Tong was gradually turning to blood lust.

Then, one night, came the final straw. A group of young warriors of the Suey Sing Tong were making merry in a house of singsong girls in Sullivan's Alley.

Duk Fong called wiry Lok Wing and short, muscular Ah Foon and big Som Hom, and they all went to the party, looking for a fight.

It was a fashionably decorated parlor. There were fern plants in large Chinese vases. Velvet drapes, deep maroon in color, hung the length of Victorian windows. Cigarette smoke waved about the high ceiling.

Three girls were there, and eight of the young Suey Sing bachelors. One of the girls poured drinks, while a young man standing behind her held her waist and rubbed against her. He was drunk. Two more youths sat on the divan with a second girl. They were competing with each other for her attention and her favors. She tried her best to accommodate both of them. Now she embraced one, then the other.

The other young men just stood around watching. There was clearly a pecking order among the young men. When one went up to a girl, he was pushed away by a tougher man.

The Suey Sings' focus was so much directed toward the women that they didn't notice the Chi Sings entering the house.

For a while, the Chi Sings just joined the other bachelors who were standing around doing nothing.

Then Duk Fong started to insult the Suey Sings. "Beside these rats," he said, "the cats have spent too much time sleeping."

A Suey Sing Tong man replied threateningly, "Words are the color of blood. A whisper can bring on a war!"

And Ah Foon spat, "It furthers one to repel robbers."

"Snakes!" a Suey Sing hurled back, drawing a knife. "Snakes cannot creep when they have no heads."

Wiry Lok Wing in turn drew his knife, saying, "Good medicine is bitter to the taste."

When the singsong girls saw the knives, they ran out into the street and huddled together, terrified.

A scuffle followed. Duk Fong smashed in a young man's nose with his fist after ripping away the knife. Lok Wing sliced another's ear.

No one drew guns during this skirmish. But Duk Fong knew the young Suey Sings would go to their Tong leaders. They would tell what happened. The leaders would send their *boo how doy* to the scene to seek justice. The less powerful were supposed to owe something to the more powerful. The weaker were always in debt. This was the law of Chinatown.

Both the Suey Sings and the Chi Sings called councils. The same decision was reached by both groups independently from each other. War was on, and it must be fought to the finish.

"And so," Sing Choy Wu announced, "the order of the Chi Sing Special Council is as follows: a *Chun Hung* will be posted on the 'dead wall' immediately."

"What is a *Chun Hung*?" Man Sum asked Duk Fong.

"A declaration of war."

Ah Foon added, "The war is to be fought until the Suey Sings give up. Then they must pay for the gambling houses or return them to us. If they return them, they have to reimburse us for our business losses. They can pay in the form of slave girls, or opium, or other property."

"They can also pay with their lives," Duk Fong threw in. "The number of Suey Sing lives acceptable for payment would depend on the status of the countryman. If he is one of the better *boo how doy,* that life is considered more valuable than a laborer's, for example."

The *Chun Hung* was posted at the bulletin board on the "dead wall" corner of Grant Avenue and Clay Street. When the Chi Sings posted their *Chun Hung,* a large crowd gathered. For most of them, the symbols written in black ink on red paper created a great deal of excitement.

A poet, Chin Lim, was adept at reading the texts on the dead wall aloud for the illiterate because he had a fine, melodic voice reminiscent of a priest's. The crowd chanted, "Chin Lim, Chin Lim. Read the *Chun Hung.*"

"Interpret the characters for us!"

He at once obliged them. Standing on the box and raising his hand for silence, he intoned, "The Suey Sing Tong is hereby sincerely and earnestly requested to send out its best fighting men to Waverly Place at midnight tomorrow to meet our *boo how doy.*"

The crowd reacted with a hushed, "Ahhhh."

Chin Lim put up his hand for silence and resumed, "If this challenge is ignored, the Suey Sings must admit defeat and make adequate compensation for the expropriation of the gambling house, legitimate deeded businesses of the Chi Sing Tong. However, we sincerely hope the Suey Sing Tong will accept this challenge and paste alongside this poster its own *Chun Hung.*"

Five hours later, a messenger from the Suey Sing Tong, bearing a red poster with fresh characters on it, could be seen walking down Grant Avenue. Men left their meals and their barber chairs. Merchants closed shop. A procession formed behind the Suey Sing messenger. He reached the dead wall and slapped onto it the red *Chun Hung* of his Tong. The message was terse, but it made its point: "The Suey Sing Tong would be pleased to send its fighting men the following night to the designated place."

Man Sum and Lum Po were consistently hitting the bull's eye on their respective targets.

"Well," Duk Fong concluded, "you can't as yet hit the left eye of a rat at fifty yards in the dark, but your aim is sufficient to kill a man."

Lok Wing was also present that day underneath Yat How's fish store. "Yes," he said, "we need them tonight. They'll make good back-up support. The Suey Sings will outnumber us. Especially if they enlist Wong family members as back-up men."

Duk Fong abruptly terminated target practice for that particular day. "Lum Po and Man Sum, this will be your first Tong battle," he said. "You are ready now to become highbinders. Your aim is fairly accurate. It remains to prepare your spirits."

They went to the joss house. There, Lum Po and Man Sum made offerings to the god of war, Kwan Kung.

A few minutes before midnight, not a soul could be found stirring on Waverly Place. Even Sacramento and Clay were deserted between Stockton and Grant. All businesses were closed and the streets were dark. All the doors on first floors were locked. But people could be seen peering through windows and occasionally stepping out onto the balconies of the second floors. Some who lived on Waverly Place had invited friends and relatives to join them in witnessing the battle which was to take place below.

Ah Foon, Lum Po, Man Sum, Duk Fong and Lok Wing were on their way up Sacramento toward Waverly.

As they walked up Sacramento, Man Sum turned to Lum Po and whispered, "The journey has been short for us. We have not found the famous Gold Hill."

He felt his dreams lay crumpled like so much soggy paper lying in the gutters with the discarded vegetables.

Lum Po was equally frightened. "Look at all the people hiding behind the steel grills of their stores. They're placing bets on who will die."

"Yes," Man Sum said bitterly. "We'll be lying in the street in pools of blood while men smoking cigars collect on their bets. Merchants, already rich, will grow richer from our deaths!"

"How much do you think is riding on it?" Lum Po asked.

"I don't know. Fifty, a hundred, two hundred."

"We're good bets to be the first knocked off," Lum Po said sadly. "We have the least experience."

Man Sum did not even know why he was there. What was the purpose of it all? To die in an alley, a beginner *boo how doy*, for some ridiculous grudge war? He thought of Ming Lee. They all wanted her. They all had money. They could buy her. Once he was dead, who would stop them?

Five Suey Sings were headed down Clay. Meanwhile, a truck was pulling off Grant and onto Clay. The truck was being driven by An Ho, a Suey Sing. It was going very slowly and its lights were turned off. The Suey Sings turned onto Waverly Place. It was midnight. The moon was at its waning quarter and Orion's belt shone clearly. The five Chi Sings entered Waverly Place from the Sacramento side. It was too dark to make out the figures at the far side of the alley. The two groups would have to come much closer.

Nobody dared to make a move. Silence except for shuffling of feet. Then, the insults.

"Chi Sings have no mothers. Chi Sings are motherless."

"The Wongs eat rat dung!"

Another pause. Then a voice was heard above them. An impatient onlooker called, "Let's get on with the battle. Enough of this cackling!"

The Suey Sings ignored the complaint.

"Show your stupid, blunt fish noses, Chi Sings."

Duk Fong fired. The five Chi Sings went for doorways. The truck driven by the Suey Sing entered the alley, its lights blaring.

"Hey, what's the truck doing there? Suey Sings have to hide behind a truck?"

"What's wrong with your war chest, Chi Sings? Can't afford your own truck?"

With the light in Man Sum's eyes, he could not see the shadows of the Suey Sings. Bullets broke shards off the buildings where the Chi Sings were dug in. Ah Foon stepped out of the doorway and fired several times. He caught a Suey Sing in the leg, but at the same time, he was cut down. He lay there in agony, dying. It had all happened much too fast.

The truck pulled out. The Suey Sings jumped on it and were gone. The shouts of victory of the Suey Sing Tong men gave way to the piercing sound of police whistles.

A small squad had been there at the beginning of the fight, but had not dared to charge the combatants. The police gathered up the wounded and took them to hospitals without making a single arrest. Ah Foon died on the way.

*   *   *

A pair of massive lions, carved from Honan marble and adorned with gold leaf, flanked the portal of the Chi Sing temple, which adjoined the meeting house. The exterior was richly decorated with bronze and porcelain. It suggested the lavish ornamentation of the interior. The outer door was a single plate of polished steel whose mirrored surface was covered with engravings. The inner surface of the door was made up of six plates of white jade pierced with filigree. The design was so delicate, one needed a magnifying glass to appreciate it. The floor of the outer hall was a mosaic of amethyst crystals set on purple silk. A light overhead, blazing through the rose quartz prisms, kindled purple flames in the polished ebony walls.

There were three doors. The middle one gave upon the anteroom of the hall of sorrows, where Ah Foon's coffin lay. At the head of the coffin, in a white jade bowl, a dwarf cypress tree had been set. The tree would soothe the soul on its journey through the cold skies after it had abandoned its residence of flesh. A robe of quilted silk lay folded at the coffin's head.

Sing Choy Wu stood at the altar erected against the east wall of the hall of sorrows. He was clad in a flowing gown of blue, brocaded silk on which, in gold thread, the symbol of eternal life had been embroidered. An incense vase of white jade formed the central ornament upon the altar. From it, a fragrant, quivering ribbon spun upward to be lost in the blue haze of aromatic vapor that lay against the turquoise tiles of the ceiling.

The exalted master's voice spoke in a tone of tenderness. "Sweet brother Ah Foon, we have known each other for many years. You have always been one of the most loyal and filial sons. You have always spoken kindly of your exalted master and of your kinsmen. How great has been your respect for the victorious union! Your word has been good, both in small matters and in great. We shall remember you for saving my son, Sing Man Sum, from the shark-infested waters of Angel Island. We shall remember your kindly and valiant deeds throughout the rest of our days and throughout eternity. As a highbinder and a Tong man, you have shown strength, wisdom, and great skill.''

Sing Choy Wu's eyes left the coffin. They now focused on the face of each man in the room in turn.

''Finally, Ah Foon, we of the Chi Sing Tong pledge to continue the war against our enemies the Suey Sings. This heinous crime of theirs, taking your life while you were yet a young man, will be avenged. And we shall not rest until every last Suey Sing has learned the price of what your death must cost them. Justice shall be done, brother. Your spirit may rest in that knowledge. And you may proceed peacefully in that knowledge toward your final resting place. Justice shall be done!''

Chapter 8

Kwan Ming Lee was welcomed at the port of San Francisco by a very sweet woman in her mid-fifties. The woman's kindness of expression and the straightforward simplicity of her dress were very reassuring. It was a relief to be away from the confinement of the island. The only fact Ming Lee regretted was having to leave Sing Man Sum behind. She had fallen deeply in love with him. It seemed to her that she had never been as close to anyone in her life, even though they'd only exchanged notes with each other. These notes were the sweet remembrances she took away from Angel Island, jewels in what was otherwise a sojourn in a hall of sorrow.

Chu Mae Pong recognized Ming Lee and approached her just as she disembarked. With her she brought a gift of flowers for the new immigrant.

"These are a welcoming gift," she said, "from Sing Choy Wu, your new sponsor. I am Chu Mae Pong, Mr. Sing's housekeeper. It is Mr. Sing's wish that you stay as long as you like at the residence of Sing Choy Wu."

Blushing, Ming Lee replied, "That is very kind of Sing Choy Wu, but . . ."

"Employment and opportunities for education will be provided for you."

"I can pay you nothing for any of this," Ming Lee said in an embarrassed tone of voice.

"Never mind. Be assured, every effort will be made to make your stay in Chinatown comfortable," Chu Mae Pong said affectionately.

"I can't thank you enough," Ming Lee replied, bowing.

"You are among your own people now," Mae Pong added. "You needn't fear you will be taken back to Angel Island or anywhere else by the foreign devil. Your new family will protect you from the *faan gwai*."

The more the young woman listened to the older, the more her fears were laid to rest. She had dreaded her arrival at the port of San Francisco. She had imagined filthy hands of crude laborers, Caucasians and Chinese, all competing to grab her body.

But here she was made to feel welcome, and she experienced nothing in the way of a threat. Ming Lee's heart immediately went out to this woman with the friendly countenance. Mrs. Chu took her for a ride in a taxi. The taxi driver was Chinese and seemed to know Mrs. Chu. So it looked to Ming Lee as if everyone knew one another in Chinatown. Everyone was glad to see her. Everyone was friendly.

They pulled up to a brand-new, three-story brick building on Clay Street. The driver helped Ming Lee with her baggage, and soon she was comfortably settled in a room with curtains, a dresser, a chest of drawers, and a spacious bed. The room had a dressing table and a comfortable chair with a footrest, too. And there was a large closet with a sliding door. Though she wanted to open it, she didn't dare.

"This is Mr. Sing's house," the housekeeper said. "As you can see, he is very wealthy and very generous. Yes, you will learn a great deal from Mr. Sing. You listen to what he says and do as he says, then you'll see. The foreign devil will never again harm you. And you too will be wealthy."

"I, wealthy?" Ming Lee looked perplexed. "Oh, I don't think I will ever be wealthy, Mrs. Chu. I'm from a poor family. I'm just a poor country girl."

"This is the land of opportunity," Mrs. Chu said. "You don't need to come from a wealthy family to find wealth here."

"Well," Ming Lee answered, "I was married to a man of wealth, but as you must know, he died while I was in the island prison. That's why I was delayed. There was no one to vouch for me. That is, not until the missionary was able to find your kind master who was willing to act as my sponsor."

"Yes, we are not Christians, but we are religious people and so it is natural for us to work hand in hand with those who believe in God. It was for the purpose of helping one who was in need, such as yourself. Tea?"

"Oh, thank you very much."

Mrs. Chu slowly put out the tea while Ming Lee sat in the parlor admiring the potted palm, the beautifully carved statuette in jade of Kuan Yin, and the pretty silk screen with the design of a mountain stream and the character of longevity. It seemed peaceful there among the tasteful artifacts from her country. But these were objects only the very wealthy owned.

Mrs. Chu served the tea and cake.

Ming Lee asked, "What of your husband, Mrs. Chu?"

"I am, alas, a poor widow like yourself. No. I have never remarried. My husband died while working on the

Trans-Pacific Railroad. He died of wounds from explosives, as did so many of our countrymen who cut tracks across the high mountains in the wintertime.''

"I am very sorry to hear that.''

"I am old enough to realize it's useless to question the will of heaven, my dear. It was very generous of Mr. Sing to take me on as a housekeeper. Otherwise, I would have had no idea where to go. I would not have had any means at all for making a livelihood. Yes, it would have been my end. I thank the goddess of mercy. She has seen fit to allow me modestly to continue my days in the service of youth.''

"Youth?''

"Yes, youth, my dear. You are not the only young person Mr. Sing and I have aided in the hour of need. As long as this evil exclusion law remains in effect, many will continue to be threatened with deportation.''

Ming Lee said, "Well, it's very kind of you. You must have helped many newcomers. I hope I shall have an opportunity to repay you for your kindness.''

The modest Mrs. Chu looked at Ming Lee with a slight frown, took another sip of the jasmine tea and then brightened her face in a generous, wide smile. "Yes, you shall have that opportunity if you wish. But that would be a matter to take up with Mr. Sing. The whole question of repayment would be something to talk to Mr. Sing about.''

Ming Lee said, "Yes, well, I look forward to meeting him. Only, I'm a little afraid.''

"Oh, there's nothing to be afraid of.''

"I feel so out of place here. I'm just a country girl with little cultural refinement. But my father is a school-teacher, and I have a little knowledge of the classics.''

"Well, that's impressive!'' Madame Chu said with enthusiasm.

"I'm afraid Mr. Sing will find me dull, dull and without breeding or charm."

Mrs. Chu said, "Please, dear, don't be afraid of Mr. Sing. He is a charitable man, believe me. He is well acquainted with your situation, your grief. He understands. And don't fret on account of your breeding. It is of less importance here than in your homeland. The rich and poor are equal in America, you know. There are no dividing lines according to class. It is money that counts."

"Money? More important than anything?"

The Chu woman sipped her tea. "Yes, and you have the opportunity to make a lot of money, more than you ever dreamed possible, more even than you imagined your husband had. I have seen new immigrants with no breeding, no background, do very well for themselves. Young people such as yourself, with a pleasant appearance, learn how to be successful."

"Of course, I intend to remarry some day," the young woman said.

"You do?"

"Yes, of course."

"But I never remarried. I never thought it was fitting that I should remarry. Of course, these are modern times. An unmarried woman has such freedom, particularly here, in Chinatown. You can dress in fine clothes, go to plays, music recitals. You don't have to worry about house, chores, children. Yes, I think if I were a young widow, like yourself, I wouldn't at all mind not marrying for a while."

Kwan Ming Lee laughed. Never had she heard such ideas expressed by someone of an older generation. Marriage and family had always been the way she was taught. It never occurred to her that it would be at all different in the United States, though she would be dishonest with herself, she thought, if she didn't acknowledge that these new ideas held some appeal for her. But they seemed fraught with danger.

Ming Lee said, speaking softly, "It is a frightening thought, the idea of being without a husband. There would be no security. If a marriage is arranged in China by one's parents, and the man is wealthy, then the woman knows she will be cared for. Provision will always be made for herself and her children through inheritance. In the event her husband died, his property would go to his sons. Through the sons, the mother would attain status as a mother-in-law, and then an esteemed Ah Mah, earning the respect of her daughter-in-law and her grandchildren. Through her immediate family, she would earn the respect of her clan."

"In the United States," Chu Mae Pong said, "the foreign barbarians have a different custom entirely. They say that it is love between the man and woman which should lead to marriage, not a prearrangement by parents. In China, this love is secondary to one's duty to one's husband and children, but I think if I were younger, I would be curious about the experience, and I might experiment and see if I might find this love on my own, without my parents or anyone else making arrangements."

Ming Lee brought her hands together and looked toward her teacup modestly. "I have found someone I really and truly love. I met him on Angel Island. And if it is the will of heaven, and oh, I do hope it is, I will marry him."

"And what would this man's name be?" Chu Mae Pong asked.

"Sing Man Sum."

Madame Chu was startled by the name and inadvertently knocked over her teacup. "I'm very sorry, how clumsy of me."

She immediately knelt down, picked up the pieces of the teacup and placed them in a napkin. Her movements puzzled the young immigrant. These movements were not a housekeeper's. The manners of Madame Chu were too refined. How could her occupation consist of doing menial household chores? It must be because she had been a new immigrant. Life in the new land was hard. That was what Madame Chu meant by "equality." Those who lived poorly in China may find that their fortunes grow beyond their wildest dreams, while those who were rich and educated such as Madame Chu may find that they must accept positions as menial laborers.

Ming Lee suspected that she would see many more strange things in this country. Now she was outside of the Middle Kingdom where customs and class had been orderly and predictable.

Chu Mae Pong said, "For a minute I had thought you meant someone else. But of course you didn't. You see, I thought you were talking about a relative of Sing Choy Wu—his son, as a matter of fact. But of course you weren't. He doesn't have a son. He never had sons. Getting back to your friend, this Sing Man Sum. He has no relatives here?"

"He has papers," Ming Lee insisted, "proving he is the son of Kwong Pak Yuen, a seller of herbs on Stockton Street, an apothecary from the village of Shang Lok. At first, he told me his name was Kwong Bing Win. I always addressed my notes to Kwong Bing Win. But the day before I departed, he told me his real name. He said he would use his real name again when he reached the shore of Gold Hill. I should never forget that name, he said. He assured me we would unite here, in this city."

"A paper son, then, that's what he is. He is not the son of the apothecary Kwong Pak Yuen."

"No, he is not."

"And so he is trying to enter this country through illegal means, misrepresentation."

"I suppose you're right."

"I know I'm right," replied a smiling Madame Chu. "But there is something you might not know. Recently there has been a crackdown on these paper son schemes at Angel Island. There has been a federal investigation. That means that the emperor of this country has sent his secret spies to Angel Island. They are investigating illegal methods employed by the Chinese, just like your Sing Man Sum."

While listening to the older woman's words, Ming Lee had begun to feel a little lightheaded. She attributed the feeling to her excitement. Yes, she had arrived in the beautiful flowered country at last. She had even seen the flowers! She did not know that her lightheadedness was the result of opium flakes added to her tea. The opium was supposed to make her lightheaded and consequently more vulnerable to suggestion.

Madame Chu had "worked" on a number of women in her ten-year career as matron of the Chi Sing Tong's string of brothels. Each girl had presented her with a different challenge. A thousand years of conditioning had to be severed in the young prostitute's mind.

Most slave girls were not volunteers for the trade. They were brought over to America under false pretenses. Without being aware of it, they were already flesh for hire. It was Madame Chu's task to gain the young women's trust, then, through more and more persuasive means, to transform them. She must turn them from innocent virgins into sultry sex objects. They must become open to the embrace of whoever might knock on their parlor door, of whoever had cash for desired favors.

At first, Madame Chu had to subtly teach her new trainees that marriage was not important. There were better avenues for social expression open to pretty young ladies. Opium in very tiny amounts, barely noticeable, helped. Opium blocked pathways to the seats of fear. Fear was the one emotion that checked the expansive feeling of pleasure in abandoning oneself.

Madame Chu said, "I am afraid your young man, Sing Man Sum, will be deported and you will never see him again."

Ming Lee suddenly burst into tears. "No, no. If I can't see him again, then I would rather be dead."

The older woman gently placed her jade-ringed hand on the younger woman's shoulder. "I am sorry I spoke so plainly. I should have made an effort to state the fact more carefully, so I have been too disrespectful of your feelings in this situation. I am so sorry."

"I love him so," Ming Lee said.

"But you must understand, even though it is hard, that you will never see him again unless you also return to China, and that is impossible. Even in that event, to find Man Sum would be, well, you know the saying. 'To find someone without an address is like looking for a needle at the bottom of the sea.' "

"You are right," Ming Lee sighed. "I will never see him again. What should I do then with my life? My husband is dead, my loved one is as good as dead. I am lost. I am completely lost. What should I do? Please, advise me."

"How beautiful you are," the older woman said suddenly.

"I am beautiful?"

"You are the only person with whom I am now speaking."

"I do not understand." Ming Lee shook her head in disbelief. "How can you say I am beautiful when my feet are as large as a man's?"

"Large feet do not matter in this country. What is important here are the features you possess now: a shapely, full lip, an oval, perfectly formed face, pretty eyes, gleaming, luxuriant hair. You should let me play with your eyes and your hair. I am an expert at adorning a woman. I can bring out qualities of beauty you probably never noticed before."

As Madame Chu spoke, she held a mirror up to Ming Lee's face. The words of the dignified matron seemed to flow out of the mirror. They had a scent like sandalwood incense, yet sweet like mulberry blossoms in early spring. As Mrs. Chu spoke, Ming Lee saw her own face as if for the first time. There was a charm to her features that surprised her. She looked at herself as she imagined a man would see her. She watched her face change. A little flare of confidence crept into her expression, making the rivulets of tears seem incongruous.

As if reading her thoughts, Madame Chu gently and skillfully applied tissue paper to the young woman's skin, wiping the tears away. "Won't you come with me into your room for a moment? I would like to see if this country girl's face could change into a city girl's face."

"Oh, no, never. It will never be anything but a country girl's face, I'm afraid," Ming Lee said shyly.

"I bet it could be much more. It really needs very little. Only a few slight touches. And while I am working away on that sweet face of yours, I would like to switch beverages. I would like a little *sau jau*, rice wine."

"I have never had a drink of rice wine before."

"I think you would enjoy it. When we're done with

our make-up, I have some beautiful dresses for you. I used to wear them, but no longer.''

"I couldn't wear your dresses! I just couldn't!''

"Never mind! They are more suitable for a younger woman, like yourself. So I will give them to you. Tonight you will be dressed in the finest of garments. You will see how your new appearance will impress your benefactor.''

So Ming Lee and Chu Mae Pong sat in Ming Lee's bedroom at the dressing table. A maid, a girl of thirteen or fourteen, known as a *mui jai*, or servant girl, served them rice wine. The two ladies chatted and giggled, and Ming Lee felt as though Madame Chu was one of the nicest people she had ever known.

The wine felt hot in Ming Lee's throat and all the way down. It jolted her on the first sip, but gradually the taste of it grew on her. She felt happier than she had since reading Man Sum's last love poem.

The lines of the poem were vague now. She made an effort to remember it, but could not. That was strange because she thought it had been engraved in her mind. She had read it over so many times to herself.

The changes that came over her appearance under Madame Chu's deft hand made her laugh. She looked silly to herself, like an actress in a play, so she made faces at herself in the glass. Her antics made them both giggle like schoolgirls.

Her face painted, her hair done up in ribbons and bangles, Ming Lee was led to Madame Chu's bedroom. There, she swung open the closet to reveal a collection of some of the loveliest dresses Ming Lee had ever seen.

"Try one, any one,'' Madame Chu offered.

"I'd like this one.'' Ming Lee tentatively reached into the closet and pulled out a green silk robe. It was embroidered with the motif of little vermilion tigers. The embroidery was all done by hand, as was the stitching. Ming Lee hadn't seen anyone but the richest of the rich wear such a fine dress. When bidden to try it on, her mouth dropped open in disbelief.

"Go on, try it," Madame Chu urged. "Oh, Ming Lee, you need not be so careful with it. The silk is very strong. It's not going to tear."

"I have never worn anything this beautiful!"

"Not everything beautiful is delicate. Beautiful jade is strong. Beautiful dresses. Beautiful women."

"Nothing has ever felt so pleasant against my body. This garment seems to caress me every time I take a step!"

"Ha, ha! That's the way you should feel *all* the time, my dear."

Madame Chu had three full-length mirrors set at angles to each other so that the young beauty could view herself from all sides. Ming Lee bathed in the compliments of the matron and primped casually before the mirror. She tilted her head this way and that. She lifted the garment's hem a little to expose the lower leg.

She did not see standing in the doorway a well-built man in his mid-fifties staring at her, captivated. Then Ming Lee chanced to turn so that the stranger was visible out of the corner of her eye. Her first impulse was to run and hide, but for some reason, the fear evaporated immediately. She was dumfounded to find herself turning with utter confidence toward her benefactor and executing a most graceful bow.

"I am Kwan Ming Lee, sir. I am deeply honored to be welcomed as a guest into your most wonderful house." Blood throbbed in her temples as she spoke to the gentleman.

He replied graciously, "*Ho fun ying.* You are most welcome, beautiful woman. Madame Chu, I see, has been showing you around, making you feel at home in my unkempt little shack. That is good.''

Ming Lee looked into Sing Choy Wu's eyes. She experienced a strange shock of recognition. Man Sum! This man was Man Sum. Full jowls, flecks of grey, a light, almost monkeylike expression in the eyes, these were the only traits that separated this man from the man she loved. But no, it must have been the wine. Shadows on Sing Choy Wu's face were playing tricks on her. This could not be Man Sum's father. Madame Chu had said this man had no son. Now Ming Lee could see the gentleman in a better light. He had stepped from the hallway into the room. The shadow that had hidden his face from full view was gone. No, there was not, could not, be a resemblance. Too much rice wine.

They settled around a black wood table. The plate settings were laid out with care. They included the *faai ji*, or chopsticks, as they were known to Westerners, made from ebony. The plates were delicately decorated with filigree patterns.

The *mui jai* brought steamed rice, a succulent vegetable dish of snow peas and broccoli, an ample plate of beef and black mushrooms, a plate of fried prawns, and more rice wine. Never had Ming Lee been served with such effort to please, and never had she tasted such excellently prepared cuisine. Most of the meal was spent eating in silence, but Ming Lee felt Sing Choy Wu's eyes on her. She blushed.

Madame Chu remarked, smiling sweetly, ''You blush when you feel a man's eyes on you? But I am sure you have never looked so beautiful. You probably have never had the sensation of a man looking at you with such obvious pleasure.''

Ming Lee had to admit Madame Chu was right. Her

husband had never really looked at her with desire. To him, she was simply a piece of property. Man Sum, also, had not really responded to her physical beauty. It was their written messages that drew and held them together. But here, it was sensual desire that emanated from the eyes of the older man.

"Have more wine," Madame Chu said. "It's all right. There's no need for nervousness. He is your benefactor. He only wants what is right for you. You have been stranded. You're a widow with no inheritance because you have not had a son. You need not be afraid. It was very kind of him to help you, don't you agree?"

"Yes, I agree."

"He responds naturally, as a man should, to your pleasant appearance. That is no reason for making your cheeks red." She reached over and caressed the girl's cheek. "Now where is that wonderful self-confidence we saw only a moment ago? Where is that bright shining star? Let it twinkle in the high heavens for a while. Youth is short. You will lose your luster soon enough, as I have. Why give it up before you need to? It's the spark of happiness, the spark of joy."

"Would you sing for us, Ming Lee?" Choy Wu asked. "It has been customary for us to request our guests to sing something. Perhaps you have learned some song while in Middle School in China. Madame Chu plays delightfully on the bamboo harp. Perhaps, Mrs. Chu, you would be good enough to accompany Ming Lee."

"I would be glad to, sir."

Shyly at first, but then with growing sureness, a song came to her lips. She did, indeed, have a fine singing voice. The song was one of her favorites. It was a song of the river people. It reminded her of her childhood and the simple pleasures she had experienced in those rare moments when she had been alone and at peace with the river. She sang of the long grass growing along the banks of the estuaries. The water birds. The men and their nets. Fires in the early evening dotting the hillsides. The decorative boats of the festivals sporting straw statuettes and multicolored flags. She sang of the ripples made by the junks passing by. The gay laughter of men and women at their wedding rites. She sang of the nights. The stars of the heavens shedding beneficent beams, casting their reflections on the stream.

She became unaware anyone was listening to her, so caught up was she in the images evoked by her song. They reminded her of home. They comforted her.

The *mui jai*, upon completion of the song, was heard to be softly weeping in the kitchen. The song created a nostalgia for southern China. It brought back the beauty and simplicity of its countryside.

Sing Choy Wu knew, even as she had been singing, that he had to possess her, hold her, keep her only for himself. She would belong to no one else. Not even for a moment. Madame Chu had done her job well. She had decorated this songbird magnificently. She had made the girl feel at home, relaxed. That was good. This was going to be the place she would remain.

Her feet were strong enough to carry her outside. Big feet. Did it matter? Not really. Other than her feet, she was magnificent. She could run with those feet, run away, but her body wasn't strong enough to break through the steel chain of guards posted downstairs.

Yes, only when he was absolutely sure it was safe, and then accompanied by Madame Chu and a *boo how doy*, could she go out, perhaps as far as Grand Avenue, to do some shopping or run an errand. But always accompanied, always under guard. When indoors, strict lock and key would hold her.

He loved her. He wanted her. She was his one and only desire, the blessing of his declining years. She would be his only love, his great love, even after death. She would accompany him to heaven on the back of the dragon. They would share their great love even after death. Was he not the emperor?

There would be a great wedding feast. He was planning it, even now. His son would be there. His son. His filial son would not allow another to come near his father's wife. He could trust his son. The others might become disloyal. The Wongs might name Duk Fong's price, but his own son would never betray him. His son was bound by rules of double obedience. Filial obedience and loyalty to the Tong. The laws of filial piety were written from the beginning of time in heaven's eternal, frozen arch.

Yes, Madame Chu has done her job excellently. Now it was time to dismiss her for the day. He would take over.

Having nodded to Madame Chu, he turned to Ming Lee and said, "Your lovely voice has made us all most happy this evening. Our little supper was but poor payment for such rich entertainment as you have provided."

Ming Lee, bowing profusely, replied, "No, no. You shouldn't say that. You really shouldn't. I have never dined so well in my life. And as for my singing voice, I am afraid it is very poor indeed."

Madame Chu then turned toward the young woman and spoke very slowly and carefully to her. "I am going to leave you now. You have many things to talk over with your benefactor. Listen to what he says. He understands many things. Your benefactor is wise. If you do as he advises, you will achieve your goal. Obey him as you

would your own father. Your best interests are his upper-
most desires.''

With that, the genteel dowager took her leave. She
bowed to her exalted master with her palms and fingers
brought together. It was the worshipful attitude reserved
for dignitaries, gods, and revered ancestors.

Madame Chu had cultivated a great deal of feeling for
Ming Lee even in the short time they had been together.
No other girl for whom she had been responsible had
awakened such sympathetic feelings in her. She knew the
kind of man Sing Choy Wu was. So she had a sense of
foreboding about the fate of the new singsong girl. The
exalted master was showing an unusual amount of interest
in the new prize. She reflected over the years she had been
in the service of the Chi Sings. Whenever Choy Wu had
been attracted to one of the girls, one or another kind of
disaster had always taken place. The girls rarely survived.

She left the red brick building and entered the fog. It
was mixed with the smoke from a hundred chimneys. It
was very thick. The cobblestones on Clay Street were
moist. It seemed as if the stones were bleeding.

Ming Lee was feeling the cumulative effects of her
day. The rice wine, the opium-laced tea and the general
excitement were making her very tired. For a long while,
Sing Choy Wu stared at her without speaking or moving.
She began to doze off.

When she awoke, she was in a different room. It was
a bedroom. The bed was huge with satin pillows and
sheets and a silk bedspread. Potted palms encircled the
room, too. Mirrors were everywhere. Intricately designed
porcelain vases contained sticks of incense. The tips glowed
bright red. The fragrance was that of pine forests after a

rain, steaming under a bright hot sun. She was lying on the bed. He was sitting on its edge.

He was holding a box swathed in windings of yellow silk. He was gazing at her body. She sat up instantly, embarrassed. She drew the cover over her exposed legs. He smiled at her and began to unwind the yellow silk covering. Revealed beneath the silk was a flat box of polished teakwood. He opened this and picked out of it carefully a thin case of bright gold. He lifted the lid of this case. On the lining of yellow velvet, Ming Lee saw a flat ring of clean green jade.

"This ring belonged to a Ming emperor. It was hidden from the Manchus and became the possession of the secret Triad Societies in China. I was a member of the Tong where this ring was entrusted. I rescued it before the temple was sacked by Manchu troops during the T'ai Ping rebellion. It's of priceless value."

"It is so beautiful!" she said admiringly.

"I worked many long, hard years in the gold fields. The tax collectors took everything we mined, and more. They never took this jade, however. They didn't know what it was. Many times, I was tempted to trade this piece to my friend Ok Wah, the jeweler on Grant Avenue. He recognized its value immediately. He would have paid me thousands for it. Yet, rather than give it away at any price, I have chosen to endure poverty and suffering. No, I have had no good reason to let go of this treasure until now. Please, accept this gift as a small token of my love and esteem."

"I cannot! I cannot accept this gift. I am not worthy of it. I am poor."

"I want you to be my wife," he said after a pause. "You will live here with me. All this will be yours, all this wealth. I have wealth that even the *faan gwai* would envy. It has not been easy. I have endured much. It is useless for me to live alone here. This wealth means nothing when one is lonely. I look at this art around me from China and only feel homesickness.''

''Why do you not return to China? There you would be greatly honored. With your wealth, you would be able to buy a palace. You would be able to buy a wife, several wives.''

''No, Ming Lee. I would only sit around and rot. My business interests are all here. I have made this country and Chinatown my home. Now I want you to complete this life for me by accepting my hand in marriage.''

''I am afraid,'' she said, replacing the ring in its yellow container, ''you have had much rice wine and are speaking with the voice of the wine. I would not have you hand your empire over to a poor peasant girl. Tomorrow morning, you would wake up with nothing but regret in your thoughts. And before I could accept such a proposal, I would have to make offerings and say prayers to the supreme powers, for only they are the ultimate guides to right conduct. To set forth without being thus prepared would be disastrous. As I consult with the gods, you should also.''

''I always consult the gods, my dear,'' he said, taking her hand in his.

''You might discover, then, that you really don't want this marriage after all. Making such a weighty decision after hearing a pretty song was unwise. But forgive me. I don't want to displease you, sir, by being the voice of criticism.''

''The rabbit does not comment on the prowess of the tiger.''

"I am a humble guest in your house, that is all. Only please, I beg your forgiveness for my bold talk and offer all due respect for your position and your kindness, dear sir, but I am unable at this time, please forgive me, to accept your proposal of marriage."

Choy Wu answered, "I shall tell you the story of this ring. Both the emperor and his servant deeply loved one of the emperor's wives. She favored the servant, but the servant desired her with a passion that often broke loose from the bounds of the middle way. She feared that he, overstepping his bounds, would soon be found out and killed by the jealous emperor."

"Is this a true story or a fable?"

"Which do you prefer?"

"I prefer true stories."

"This is a true story."

"Thank you. Please, continue."

"Now, the emperor gave her this precious gift so she would know she was his favorite. He needed no other, and anyone else who took an interest in her would pay with his life. So the next time she saw the servant, she told him he would have to leave the palace. His life was in grave danger. Now the servant had no means of livelihood. He had no way to support himself. Released into the world, he would soon die of starvation."

"Like many new immigrants."

"That's right. You're enjoying this story?"

"Yes."

"So she gave him the ring. 'Take this ring to the jeweler in the city,' she told him. 'From the sale of it, you will be able to live.' He accepted her gift of the ring and ran away. But the emperor's soldiers soon caught up with him. To make the story shorter, the favored wife was presented with the ring a second time. When she opened the gold box, she discovered the ring placed on the severed finger of the disobedient servant.''

"That's terrible."

"Yes, it is."

"I hope nothing like that ever happens to me."

"I'm sure it won't. You're much smarter than the emperor's wife."

"I'm not so sure."

"The theme of this story should be clear to a girl of your intelligence. A man of power does not ask for what he wants. He gets what he wants. Only beggars hold out their bowls in hopes of alms. My asking you to marry me is ceremony after the fact. You are my wife already. I own you.''

"You what?" she asked, her mood turning suddenly dark.

"I own you."

"I don't understand."

He opened the box again, took out the ring and placed it on a trembling finger. "You will wear this ring as a symbol of our union. I don't need to make supplication to Kuan Yin to ascertain her will. The will of heaven is already clear enough. It is identified with my own. Fate has delivered you into my hands for a reason. That reason is very clear to me. Shall I tell you what it is? You shall bear my sons.''

"I was sold to you?"

"That is correct."

"But that's impossible. I belong to no one now. I was married and my husband died, and that's the end of my belonging to a man."

The exalted master shrugged. "Your husband purchased you in China for three hundred dollars. He sold you to us for four thousand dollars, we, the Chi Sing Tong. You would have belonged to me whether he had lived or died. All along, his intention was to make a profit by selling you. If that meant you would become a prostitute, that was not his concern. All that mattered to him was collecting his coins. Your husband sold you with the full knowledge that you would become a singsong girl, a daughter of joy. It is very fortunate that he sold you to me, because I have no desire to put you to work in a brothel. I have made deals like that with other women, yes. But when I saw the photograph your husband brought with him, I knew right away fate had other plans for you.'' He spoke more gently now because he saw that Ming Lee was pressing her face against the coverlet and was beginning to sob.

Everyone had betrayed her, she was thinking. Everyone had let her down. Her husband had sold her. Sold her! Man Sum had gotten himself deported. She was utterly alone with this stranger who now owned her. But matters might have been much worse, she reasoned. At least she was the property of only one. She didn't belong to the world of the faceless. How she now hated the memory of this false husband. And her parents? They must have known, too, that this man was a broker of whores. Was he not well known to them? They had only wanted to get rid of her, big-footed peasant girl that she was. They were pleased to obtain such a bargain, weren't they?

"No, I will not marry you, or anyone else!"

"You would rather work in a brothel?"

"I will return to China."

"Are you really sure that's what you want to do?"

She turned away without answering.

"There is plenty of time, fortunately. You can think it over. I have to go on a business trip. You will stay here. You'll be well taken care of. Consider well my offer. Remember, the alternatives aren't too pleasant."

Choy Wu gently escorted her to her bedroom. Then he left her to cry herself to sleep.

For the next three days, she spoke to no one. The *mui jai* cooked her meals, but would not talk to her. Madame Chu didn't return. The guards answered her questions with icy silence. They would not let her leave. Ming Lee sank into a deep depression.

She gritted her teeth at the thought of the fine sentiments expressed in the poems she had exchanged with Man Sum. So much air. So much thick fog. He had gone and gotten himself deported! Who was he, anyway? Another faceless man in the legions of the powerless. Another nobody. It was only the wealthy and powerful who mattered. They were the only ones who could save her from being dragged down in the mire. She didn't want to be rolled around in the mud. She didn't want to be the object of the crass desires of work gangs, bad-smelling men. No, the poets' words could do nothing for her. To listen to them seriously was mere foolishness. She had learned a lesson in the school of reality. She counted herself lucky to find a place where rice would fill her bowl without fail.

Choy Wu returned on the fourth day. He gave her a gift of flowers. They had a delicious meal together. He told her a story. He was very kind to her. Perhaps it would not be so terrible living here after all.

Yet, her heart felt empty.

"Well, Ming Lee," he finally asked, "did you consult the deities?"

"Yes," she heard herself say in a dead, wooden voice. "I will marry you."

"I am happy," the stranger answered. He bent over her face and gently brushed his lips on her cheek. She did not resist. What would be the point? She looked at the beautiful, clear jade that ringed her finger. She thought of Madame Chu's advice.

Am I really beautiful? she wondered.

Her betrothed took her into his bedroom. They lay on the bed together. He undid the top two clasps of her dress. He kissed her neck and bare shoulder. But the kisses from the lips of her benefactor were not those of the poet she had wanted on the island.

Forget him! she told herself. Forget him, he no longer exists!

Kisses played along her arm as she forced her mind to dispel the image Man Sum had grafted on her heart.

Forget him!

"Loosen now the clothing that separates your body from my touch, Ming Lee."

She obeyed, and as she undressed herself, he followed suit. Naked together now, their images reflected in the mirrors, he held her and stroked her back, legs, breasts. She watched him in the mirrors and listened to his heavy breathing. This was the great price one must pay for being a woman alone in a world ruled by men and their money. I must pay the price now, she thought, but one day, I will be rich, and then no one will be able to demand the payment of my body. It will be mine and mine alone.

As his passion for her grew and became more urgent, she suddenly became possessed by a wild rage. She hadn't intended to feel this. She had intended to submit. But how angry she was, angry at all of them. She broke away from

Choy Wu and ran toward the door. Locked. She struck it with both fists until flakes of paint from the molding loosened and fell to the floor. He slowly moved toward her and leaned forward to grasp her. She screamed and hit him in the chest with all her strength. His grasp only tightened. She kicked and screamed more loudly until she was hoarse with anger and fear. He finally released her. She went at his face with her fingernails, but he waved her arms aside.

Then, she bit him on the arm, drawing blood, all the while yelling, "I won't, I won't submit. I would rather die. I would rather die, die, die."

The effort of resistance sapped her strength entirely. She crumbled on the floor, exhausted. Gently, Choy Wu lifted her again onto his bed and tentatively resumed the love play. After a time, she offered no more resistance, and he mounted her. Her thighs opened to receive him, but mechanically. As he was taking his pleasure, she felt nothing but disgust, and then was relieved when sleep overtook her. It was a sleep in which faces of Sing Choy Wu surrounded her, leered at her, pressed their lips on her.

Over the next few days, Madame Chu spent all of her time with Ming Lee, chattering about wedding plans. Ming Lee tried on different wedding gowns. She was not permitted to leave the house except for an occasional trip to Grant Avenue for shopping. When she went out, she was always accompanied by Mrs. Chu and at least one guard. Apart from certain members of the Chi Sings, her presence in the house of Sing Choy Wu was kept a strict secret. Ming Lee felt restless and oppressed.

On her rare trips to the store, she had carefully scrutinized all the male faces she saw. It was a vain effort to search out Man Sum, but her heart cultivated a dim glimmer of hope. He may have passed the immigration check-point after all.

She spent many listless hours at the third floor window, peering down into the street below with the remote chance of discovering him, but she never saw anyone who looked like him.

Chinatown fascinated her. She enjoyed the bazaars north of California Street, the windows heaped with pink and green Canton vases, the teakwood tables inlaid with mother-of-pearl, the processional umbrellas made from old cherry silk studded with sequins, the ebony screens framing porcelain panels bearing pictures of court ladies. There were vermilion chests on whose surfaces scores of fantastic flowers bloomed. Statesmen's robes embroidered in apple green and lined with white fur. Buddha in gold shrines. Milo Fo, the god of wealth, with his large belly. And the goddess of mercy in white porcelain and ivory, chaste and serene. There were, too, trays of red lacquer with inch-thick carvings on them: paintings of mountain peaks, cascades of water running down them.

On the corner of Clay and Grant, she saw in the shallow window the dried food shop delicacies that made her mouth water. Half a score of sun-dried eatables hung in long rows on a wire: duck that had first been salted, then pressed in oil; dried pig livers; pork spare ribs, first barbecued, then dipped in soy sauce. Dried oysters were strung on bamboo sticks.

"Do they look good to you, my dear?" Madame Chu asked her one day. "You shall savor them at your wedding banquet."

"Madame Chu, I am frightened," Ming Lee said. Who else could she confide in?

"I know, my dear, I know you are," the older woman replied sympathetically.

"Tell me about Sing Choy Wu. What kind of man is he? Who is this man who is to be my husband?" Ming Lee asked.

"A wealthy man," Madame Chu said. "Temperamental," she added, looking at Ming Lee as if to warn her.

"Temperamental?"

"Exercise caution, my dear," Mae Pong said. "Do not displease him."

A wave of fear went through Ming Lee. Would she survive?

Chapter 9

Murphy sat in Mooney's Irish Pub with three other police officers: Wilber Price, Jack O'Reilly and Jesse Cook. The surgeons at General Hospital had done a good job on the Irishman. He was in perfect health, as good as new. Murphy had had himself transferred to the Chinatown beat. He was determined to personally take charge of the investigation into the whereabouts of his assailant. The detectives who had been on the case had turned up nothing, but Murphy was convinced he would get results where others had failed. He had a personal stake in the outcome of the case.

"I'm gonna nail that Chinaman if it's the last thing I do," he said.

"He's got it coming to him," added Jesse Cook.

"He practically finished me, didn't he? Didn't he practically finish me?"

"That he did," Jack O'Reilly agreed.

"Well, I didn't have a fighting chance, did I?"

"Not a breath of chance," Price said.

"I wouldn't take that from a white man. I wouldn't let a white man do that to me, you hear?"

"Yes, we hear ya, Murph," Jack and Jesse said together.

"But a Chink. A Chink! I'm gonna track that son of a bitch down," Murphy said, drumming a big hand down on the table.

"How're ya gonna do that, Murph?" Price asked, squinching his eyes doubtfully.

"Hit the beat, what else? Scour the ghetto. I'll put in twelve-hour days," Murphy said. "How about you? Are you with me?"

"We're with you, Murph," Price replied. "All the way."

Before the week was out, the three lawmen had gathered again to plan more sober strategies. Their stakeout of the Chi Sings yielded nothing. A few elderly men entered and exited, but that was about it. Then followed a visit to the famous apothecary on Stockton Street.

"Kwong Pak Yuen?" Murphy called out, knocking on the apothecary's door.

No answer.

"Kwong Pak Yuen!" Murphy knocked louder and yelled.

"What you want?" returned a frightened voice from inside.

"Police. Open up!" Murphy called.

"I no do wrong thing, I no do wrong thing," Pak Yuen said, opening the door.

Murphy, Price and Cook entered hastily, closing the door behind them.

The apothecary was petrified. "What you want? I no do wrong thing. It late. Store close. What you want?"

"Calm down, Mr. Kwong. Calm down. We have a few questions for you, that's all."

"Question? What question? All right. You ask question. I answer question. Then, you go home. Okay?"

"We happen to know," Murphy began, "you sold a paper son slot to somebody. We got a kid at Angel claiming you were his father, but he couldn't answer simple questions in the interrogation."

"*Ngaw mm ming bahk*! I don't understand!"

"Now come on, Mr. Kwong, we know you sold a paper son slot to somebody. Who bought it?"

"I no sell nothing. I don't understand paper son. What you mean? I sell dlug. All I sell, dlug. Okay? You go home now?"

"Mr. Kwong," Murphy said, impatience creeping into his husky voice, "be assured that if you tell us the truth, we won't do anything to you. We won't arrest you. We won't harm you. In fact, we will protect you. Every day, all day if necessary."

"All I sell dlug, no paper. I no do wrong thing!"

"Mr. Kwong! If you don't tell us who you sold the papers to, you're going to get into trouble. Big trouble."

"No. No tlouble."

"Big trouble! Understand that? You tell, no trouble. You no tell, big trouble. Understand me?"

"You're scared, aren't you, Mr. Kwong?" Price put in.

"I scared. I scared," Pak Yuen said, the muscles in his neck trembling.

"Why don't you sit down, Mr. Kwong. Take a seat. That's okay. Take a seat behind your counter, there."

"I scared sit down. I stand. I scared sit down."

"What are you scared of exactly, Mr. Kwong? Tongs? The Chi Sing Tong? Are they the ones got you scared? What about it, Mr. Kwong?"

The apothecary cleared his throat twice. He was

trembling all over. "I no talk policeman. They kill me, I talk."

"Who?"

"They kill me. Kill family. I no talk policeman. I scared. I sell you dlug, okay? I no talk. All my family dead, I talk policeman. *Do mm yiu. Mm dak. Mm dak a la. Ho pay pa sey lawwww*."

"Who would kill you?" Murphy asked. "The Chi Sing Tong?"

"I don't know Tong," Kwong insisted, then shut his mouth like a clam.

"You know, Mr. Kwong," Murphy said, "we are the arm of the law. The law declares that these Tongs are illegal organizations. We intend to rid Chinatown of them, and that would make the lives of merchants like yourself a lot easier, wouldn't it? But we cannot touch these Tongs without your help. We need testimony against them in a court of law."

"I don't know Tong. Chinatown, no more Tong," Kwong said, shaking his head.

This denial infuriated Murphy. He grabbed the terrified apothecary's shirt lapels and pinned him to the counter. "Now look, Chinaman! We know you're paying protection money to the Chi Sing Tong. Otherwise, they'll blow your joint to high heaven. So you're paying out protection, can't make ends meet, right? Sell paper son slot. Make ten thousand dollars. That keeps you going. Maybe you lose lotta money in the lottery or fan-tan. Sell paper son, no more debt! Right? Right? We'll give you police protection around the clock. Won't let the Chi Sings near you!"

"I don't know Tong. No more Tong."

"Ahhhh." Disgusted, Murphy let the apothecary go and stalked out.

Price turned to Kwong and said, "Listen, Kwong.

We're serious. We want to help the merchants in Chinatown. If you change your mind, you know where the precinct office is. Columbus and Broadway, okay?''

With that, Price turned and left. He was joined by Cook.

At two o'clock in the morning, the apothecary rose from his bed and crept past his sleeping wife and three-year-old child. He descended the back stairway of the store into a thick cover of darkness outside. The fog was so dense that he could see only a few feet ahead. He slid across town to the precinct station on Broadway, near Columbus.

He asked for an interpreter. He made his statement. After imparting the information necessary for the recovery of the fugitive, the apothecary returned to his family.

Man Sum and Lum Po had been warned by the spies that the *faan gwai* were on the lookout for them. Agents had even begun to stake out the Tong headquarters on Clay Street. By this time, the young men had become real assets to the Chi Sing army. Their services were needed, so the Tong could not afford to give them up to the authorities. It didn't take much to move the new immigrants. They had few possessions.

They were set up in the basement of Yat How's fish store. That way, if they were discovered, they could go down to the tunnels. Duk Fong gave them a set of keys to the trap door. Yat How himself could be counted on to replace the rug and the table after them.

Unfortunately for the two refugees, the emergency that they had been preparing for was upon them. The apothecary had given the police Yat How's name. The police knew How's store was a front for the highbinders.

The apothecary didn't know exactly what went on in the basement of Yat How's, but he knew illegal immigrants could be found there.

The stakeout of Yat How's began the following day. This time, Murphy would be on the lookout himself. For the purposes of anonymity, the Irishman made up a disguise for himself. He looked passably Oriental when he was finished. He decided to pose as a beggar. That made him look less ferocious. He walked stooped over, wore a tattered coat and sported a felt hat.

He made the mistake of trying out his disguise around Union Square. It was such a successful masquerade that several hoodlums threw shards of brick at him. He cursed at them in fluent English, with an Irish accent no less. That surprised them. They stopped throwing for a moment.

Some strange heathen Chinaman this was, they thought.

"They're getting so clever, they can even imitate Christian talk," one of the hoodlums murmured and then the missile-tossing resumed.

But Murphy used his speedy legs to get himself to safety within the confines of Chinatown.

If it's so safe here, why do they call it the most dangerous ghetto in the world? he asked himself.

Murphy posed as a peddler of limp vegetables instead of a beggar. There was more dignity in that. He set himself up catty-cornered from the fish store. After several hours of waiting, he saw no one he recognized. He decided that the apothecary must have given him a bad lead. Young "Kwong" was nowhere to be found.

The frustrating day was now drawing to a close. Murphy had put so much effort into getting his man that he surprised himself. If he failed, having worked this hard, there was no justice left.

Murphy gave himself a quick rush of courage. He took a big breath and let it out through his teeth. Then he charged the store. Without pausing at the counter, he immediately seized the back room.

Yat How's assistants were there, cleaning and cutting the fish. They instantly recognized the invader as a *faan gwai*.

"Police," Murphy barked as he divested himself of his costume, then yanked out a Colt .45. The workers held their hands up and tried to smile.

"I'm looking for Kwong. Bing Win Kwong. Where is he?"

They looked at him uncomprehendingly.

"You got other rooms in here? You got a basement here?"

No response.

Murphy looked about, and his eyes settled on a pantry door at the far end of the room. That must be it, he thought. He had grown used to spotting innocuous-looking doors like that from his experiences at Angel Island. He charged the door and found the stairway. He practically fell down the steps, he was so eager to consummate his revenge. He reached the basement just as Yat How was straightening the carpet. A table stood there with a ledger book.

Not everything was as it should be. There was something wrong with the appearance of things, something curious.

He waved Yat How away from the table and the carpet, but the Chinese hesitated. That was a dead giveaway. Murphy threateningly pointed the Colt .45 at him, and the fish seller backed off. Murphy made a few swift moves. He sent carpet, book and table flying, uncovering a trap door.

"Keys," he demanded.

But when the Irishman opened the trap door, his prey was nowhere in sight. Instead, there were stairs descending into blackness.

"Reinforcement is necessary," he told himself.

He ran upstairs and called Cook and Price. They were there in minutes. Together, the three men descended the underground stairway.

"I didn't know they really had tunnels down here," Cook said, barely concealing the quaver in his voice.

"Yeah, they're real all right," Price replied.

They reached the underground hallway. There appeared to be no end to the passageway.

Then Murphy's light caught a crack in the wall of the hallway. It intrigued him. Pressing his knife in to try to widen this crack, he was surprised to find a door there. Behind that door, Sing Man Sum was playing dominoes with himself in dim candlelight.

Preparations for Sing Man Sum's trial were elaborate. Jeremy W. Porter, a Caucasian with a lucrative law practice, was chosen to represent the immigrant. The Chi Sing interpreter, Tom Ah Lung, spent long days in consultation with Porter in the lawyer's posh Montgomery Street office. They hit upon a plan.

The trial was held on the fourth floor of the brand-new City Hall on Polk Street. Willard B. Clark declared the Superior Court of the County of San Francisco in session. It took three days to choose a jury.

Finally, on the fourth day, the prosecutor, Matt Davis, got around to his introductory remarks. "The prosecution will show beyond a doubt that the defendant is a liar. The defendant is not who he says he is. He is not the son of the merchant, Kwong Pak Yuen. He is a paper son. In short, he is here illegally. This young man, we will show, is a hired assassin. He was hired by the Chi Sing Tong. Trained in China in the skills of street crime. The paper son scheme was used to import him. He is a dangerous criminal, this nameless Chinese. We will show that he is guilty of attempted murder. And we will seek the strongest penalty available to the law."

Murphy, in attendance at the trial, leaned over to his friend Price and asked, "What the hell is wrong with Matt Davis?"

"What do you mean?" Price whispered.

"I don't know. Something's off. He doesn't have any enthusiasm."

"He's not the one who got knifed. You can't expect everybody to be as hot as you are."

"I still say there's something off in the manner of his speech."

"Don't worry so much, Murph," Price said, frowning.

"He acts like he'd rather be someplace else," Murphy grumbled.

"The defense will show," Porter began, "that what we have here is simply a case of mistaken identity. And when you realize that, ladies and gentlemen, you will wonder why the prosecution has wasted your time. It was impossible for the accused to have perpetrated these terrible crimes. He was nowhere in the vicinity of Angel Island when the Irishman felt the back stab. In fact, the defendant, as you will soon realize, has never been to Angel Island. No. His immigration was perfectly legal. We have the papers to prove it. He lives happily with his father, Kwong Pak Yuen, the apothecary."

Price, Cook and Murphy were stunned by Porter's introductory remarks. The prosecutor acted as though he hadn't heard them.

Murphy slapped his big hand down on the good book. He took the solemn oath against deceit and lumbered to the stand.

The large officer told the story of how the young Chinese mastered him physically.

"He came from nowhere. I tell you, from nowhere. I was following him. I saw him. I saw him ahead of me in the forest, there. I ran after him. He just disappeared, that's all. Then, from nowhere comes this attack. Got me in the back. Didn't have a fair chance for a fair fight."

"And who," Matt Davis asked, "is that man that stabbed you?"

"Well, I don't know. He goes under an assumed name."

"But officer, can you point him out in this courtroom?"

"Yes, I can. He's that man. Over there." Murphy pointed at Sing Man Sum.

"Do you know what his assumed name is, officer?"

"I believe I do," Murphy said. "I believe he goes under the name Kwong Bing Win. That's his paper son name. He's posing as the apothecary's son."

"I have no more questions. Your witness," Matt Davis said, gesturing to the defense attorney.

Next, Jeremy W. Porter cross-examined the witness.

"Now, exactly what time was it, Officer Murphy, when you caught up with the fugitive in the woods at Angel Island?"

"I would put it at about seven-thirty p.m."

"Of course, you realize, do you not, that we are talking about total darkness? Did you *positively* see the defendant's face?"

"Well, no, I didn't see his face, all I saw was the shape of a man. But there was—"

"You only saw a shape, is that what you said?"

"But there was only one Chinaman in the woods. It had to be that Chinaman."

"If you only saw his shape, how did you know he was of Chinese descent?"

"Look, there was only one fugitive in the woods and he was Chinese. Why would anybody attack me in the woods if he wasn't a fugitive? First of all, there was just me and the search party and the dogs. Me and the searchers and the dogs, that's all there was out there. Now, some searcher isn't going to jump on me in the woods. They're my colleagues, so it'd have to be the heathen. And he's the only heathen escaped."

"The positive identification you have just made is based on your experience—"

"Yes, it is."

"With one of Chinese descent who was at the detention center—"

"Yes, that's right."

"Whom you recognize in this courtroom."

"He's right over there."

"And whose name you assume is Kwong Bing Win."

"I don't assume anything. I know who he is."

"But this identification is not based in any way whatsoever on your experience in the woods. In those woods on the island, you were attacked by the shape of a man. His distinguishing features were in no way available to your senses because it was dark."

"Okay, okay, whatever you say. But it sounds real picky to me, what you're saying."

"Try to stick to the facts, Officer Murphy, and keep your opinions to yourself, please," the judge admonished.

"Mr. Murphy, approximately how many males of Chinese descent were you responsible for in the exercise of your duties at Angel Island?" Porter asked.

"About a hundred and fifty, I would say."

"A hundred and fifty at any given time. But didn't the configuration of the hundred and fifty go through almost daily changes? Some were deported, others accepted. And there were always new ones interned. Isn't that right?"

"Yes. The group kept changing."

"There were always new faces. New faces and new names."

"That's right."

"And I believe—correct me if I'm wrong—but I believe you once said to a colleague of yours that the faces of the newcomers 'all ran together like pea soup.' Weren't you heard to be making a remark of that nature?"

"Well, it's true. Especially when you see how they stick together."

"If they are so indistinguishable, the one from the other, what makes this instance an exception? Why is it that, in this instance rather than all the other hundreds of instances, you actually managed to connect a face to a name out of the 'soup,' as you put it?"

Murphy leaned in the direction of Sing Man Sum and squinted at him slightly, then replied, "He stepped on my feet."

Porter echoed incredulously, "He stepped on your feet?"

"Yes, I remember that very well because the little wife had just spent a good part of the previous evening buffing a real nice sheen into my shoes. They were already a year old, those shoes, but she got a real nice shine out of them. That's why I was so annoyed when that Chinaman carelessly walked all over them."

"Which Chinaman?"

"That fellow sitting right there. He's the one started that food riot. One of my friends pointed him out to me. He started throwing food around. Don't try to mix me up. I know who I'm talking about. He's the one."

"You did not actually see him start a food riot, did you?"

"Stop trying to mix me up."

"We're just trying to limit your testimony to the information which is immediately available to your senses, Officer Murphy. I would like the testimony of the witness related to 'food riots' stricken from the record."

"The court reporter is so ordered." The judge nodded to the court reporter.

"What did you do when your shoes were stepped on? Did you immediately ask to see the man's papers? His I.D. card, his number?"

"No, I took him on down the hall and gave him a dressing-down. Told him to keep his feet to himself because that was how Christians behaved. Christians, I said, respect the bodies of each other, the privacy of each other. That was the custom of this country. The Chinese have got to learn that because they're always on top of each other. That's what the cubic air ordinance was about, to protect the Chinaman. I mean, too many of them in a room and nobody can breathe."

"Too many of them in a room, and apparently you, Officer Murphy, cannot tell one from another. No further questions for the time being, Your Honor."

The prosecuting attorney then called various Immigration Service officers. They were at Angel Island at the time Sing Man Sum was there. He was identified by them as the one who started the food riot. They all said he had been suspected of being in contact with Tongs on the mainland.

J.B. Densmore was called to the stand.

"Now, Mr. Densmore, you had contact with the defendant?"

"Yes, I did."

"What was the nature of your contact with him?"

"I interviewed him. Then I heard the interrogator ask him questions. He was unable to answer questions pertaining to the village, Shang Lok. That was Kwong Pak Yuen's village. Since he couldn't answer simple questions, we decided he must be a 'paper son.' We determined that his claims of relationship were worthless. He had been using coaching papers, apparently. He had not learned them well enough, however."

"Your witness."

Jeremy W. Porter didn't attempt to discredit Densmore. His strategy was simply to drive a wedge between face and name. It had worked with Murphy. It was certain to work with Densmore.

"And you are quite certain, Officer Densmore, the man at that table is the same one you interviewed on the second of May?"

"Absolutely, he would have to be the one. He was pointed out to me as a troublemaker. I would have to remember him."

"By troublemaker you mean one of those Chinese who were in touch with Tongs or other organizations on the mainland."

"That's right."

"Now, how many Chinese do you estimate at that time were being helped by Tongs in San Francisco's Chinatown?"

"Well—"

"It is the case, is it not, that there were many? In fact, so many that the island had become famous for its corruption? The immigration officials were all being bribed. Graft was rampant. And so, you were dispatched by the Labor Department to investigate."

"That's true," replied Densmore. "And we went a long way toward cleaning up that mess, you can believe that."

"The gentleman you interviewed was not the only troublemaker. That's the point I'm trying to make. The island was rife with trouble of this sort, am I not correct?"

"Well, it's true. There were more paper sons than you could shake a stick at. And a lot of them slipped through because of bribes. And, I must say, you white lawyers were partly responsible. You were all paid by the Tongs. You helped the immigrants violate the law!"

"The witness will please confine his remarks to the case at hand, thank you very much," the bench admonished blandly.

Murphy turned toward Price and said, "Why the hell aren't they calling Kwong Pak Yuen to the stand? They have the statement he made out at the station. All he has to do is say the guy ain't his son. That'll cinch the case against the Chink."

"Patience, Murph, patience," Price said.

The prosecutor, Matt Davis, yawned. Then he put the apothecary on the stand.

After putting together some of the preliminaries, the prosecutor moved to the question of the identity of the man at the defense attorney's table.

Kwong Pak Yuen spoke through an interpreter. Kwong's neck muscles quivered as he said, "That man is my son, Kwong Dong Lam."

The prosecutor blinked. "Who?"

"My son, Kwong Dong Lam," the apothecary reiterated. "Kwong Bing Win, he was my son, too. They are brothers, twins. They were both born in China, in Shang Lok. Only, Kwong Dong Lam came to the United States with me after my third visit to Shang Lok. No, that man, my son, never went to Angel Island. The other one did, Kwong Bing Win, but he never left. I read he tried to kill an officer. And then tried to swim to shore. But apparently he didn't make it. I have never seen him. My son Kwong Dong Lam has never seen him, either."

The prosecutor simply shrugged and yielded to his colleague.

Murphy stood up in the courtroom and said, "Wait a minute, Matt. The statement. The statement he made out at the station. Aren't you going to refer to the statement?"

"Sit down, Officer Murphy. We'll have order in this courtroom," the judge said.

Murphy, red-faced, continued. "Matt, what are you doing? This witness ain't telling the truth. You know that. That statement. He signed that statement. It's all there."

"Bailiff, will you remove Officer Murphy from this courtroom?" the judge said in an irritated tone.

Murphy sat down and pushed air through his teeth.

"Take it easy, Murphy. It's just a trial," Price whispered, trying to calm his friend down. Murphy just looked at him.

Jeremy W. Porter addressed the jury, holding records with his left hand. "According to these records, the apothecary has four sons. One of them is Kwong Dong Lam. The name is right here, and it states clearly that Kwong Bing Win was born the same day. They are twins. It is a case of mistaken identity."

Much to Murphy's dismay, the prosecutor did not follow up this point.

"That's just another slot," Murphy said in a hoarse whisper. "Kwong didn't sell it yet. The Tongs got to him somehow, got him to change his story."

Jeremy W. Porter then called Chinese witness after Chinese witness to the stand. Each one testified through the court-appointed interpreter that indeed the accused was Kwong Dong Lam. Dong Lam had lived in Chinatown for ten years. He had worked side by side with his father in the family herb business. They had heard the apothecary speak of the twin with fondness. The twin had been on his way from China to Gold Hill, but then he was interned at Angel Island. And then after a rumored escape, he had never been heard from again. With remarkable uniformity and without a hint of doubt, each witness who was called repeated the same story.

It took the jury only five minutes to deliver to the bench a verdict of "not guilty by reason of mistaken identity."

Murphy, Price and Cook retired to Mooney's Irish Pub in North Beach to drown their disappointment.

"Some kind of magic is working for the Tongs," Price said. "Chinese magic."

"Money," Murphy replied glumly.

Cook said, "We've got to rid San Francisco of these Tongs for good."

Price tried to strike a note of encouragement. "You know, I think they're already losing a little power. I mean, the apothecary did go to the station and make a statement."

"We let him down," Murphy said sullenly.

"If the department hadn't been so short-handed, we could have had him covered better."

"The jokers were too busy collecting their graft," Murphy said bitterly.

"Yep," Cook said, "the Chi Sings must have pressured Kwong to fill the extra slot. Must have cost them a bunch."

"Thing that gets me is Matt Davis," Murphy said, taking a slug of ale. "Didn't do much of a job. I think the Tong greased his palm, too."

Chapter 10

Duk Fong said to Sing Man Sum, "You should be a very happy man. You're fortunate to be part of this brotherhood. We don't let our brothers down. You needed us, and we came through for you. So don't look so glum."

Man Sum, surrounded by his fellow highbinders, didn't feel much better than he felt in the county jail. It was difficult for him to make sense out of the experience. He found the whole trial very depressing. So much of it he didn't understand. He had wanted to tell everyone how he had tried to save Murphy's life. Because of the first aid he administered, Murphy was alive today. But he couldn't say anything. That was the frustrating part. He wasn't even allowed to testify. All he could do was sit there.

Man Sum sullenly pushed away the cup of *sau jau* that Duk Fong had offered him. They were celebrating their victory over the *faan gwai* courts. To Man Sum, it wasn't much of a victory. The highbinders were just trying to bolster their spirits. They were trying to forget the Suey Sing defeat. The Suey Sing Tong was tougher than the *faan gwai*.

The highbinders couldn't figure out why their cadet

wasn't having more fun. Then Duk Fong thought of something that would make the young man feel much better.

"Hey, Man Sam, how would you like a girl?" he offered.

"What do you mean, how would I like a girl?"

"I told you when you were satisfactorily trained, you could visit the singsong girls with us."

Man Sum shook his head. "Not tonight."

"When?"

"I don't know. Maybe tomorrow."

He knew he wouldn't really be interested tomorrow either. He didn't want to visit the singsong girls. He was afraid he might find Ming Lee among them.

Sing Choy Wu and Duk Fong were having tea at Tung Fung's on Pacific Avenue. The subject of discussion was Choy Wu's son. The exalted master was concerned.

"I had hoped that Man Sum would be able to enjoy himself more. It increases a highbinder's loyalty to the Tong when he lets himself have a good life."

"He has been despondent since his release from jail," said Duk Fong.

"I know. And I am disappointed in his spirits. I wish my son to have pleasure with the singsong girls."

"Perhaps it is lack of experience in these matters. That could be his problem," Duk Fong said thoughtfully.

"I hold you, Duk Fong, personally responsible. Your job is to introduce Man Sum to the singsong girls and make sure the young man has a good time."

"I shall try to serve you better, exalted master," Duk Fong said.

"Yes, see that you do."

"I will do everything I can."

"I wonder if the problem is not Kwan Ming Lee," Choy Wu said.

"Does he know you intend to marry the young lady?" Duk Fong asked.

"I am concerned about the conversation at Shanghai Low. He said he loved her, then, so I didn't want to tell him my intentions. It was too early. He wasn't ready to hear that news. I told him she was sick and that he couldn't see her."

"I thought that was a wise choice," Duk Fong said.

"He didn't believe me, but I don't want him to dwell on the woman. I intend to marry her! I feel very badly about taking his woman away from him, but it's my last chance for happiness. He will have plenty of other chances. He is young. I am old. Anyway, she will be his stepmother, won't she?

"This sullen behavior of his must be stopped. It does not become a son of mine. It is not a professional frame of mind for a warrior. A soldier must be serious, but not out of sorts. We are technically at war, are we not?"

"Yes, sir," Duk Fong said.

"It is time my son learned the truth about Ming Lee. Under the laws governing filial piety, he must bow to my will cheerfully."

"I am sure he will."

"He must come out of this childish mental state. It could be a longing for what he cannot possess. That's dangerous. I don't like it."

"You must speak to him, sir. You must tell him your mind."

"Yes. I will settle accounts with my son. Then he must understand his duties completely. Then we arrange a wedding feast. Set a date for the ceremony."

"We must have a feast in honor of the couple. A three-day feast."

It was late in the afternoon on a rainy day in February when Duk Fong broke off a *boo how doy* training session and the highbinders left the underground warrior gym and headed down Stockton toward Clay Street. The simple felt fedora hats were all that kept them covered from the rain.

The two guards admitted the Tong men inside. The guests were met by two more guards on the carpeted stairs. They were admitted to the exalted master's private chambers. There, pastries and tea were laid out on the decoratively carved teakwood table. A few jokes and other pleasantries were exchanged. Then Choy Wu leaned forward and cleared his throat, a sign that serious business was at hand.

"I know we have discussed these matters in previous meetings," the exalted master began. "Many suggestions were offered on those occasions. But I am not satisfied with any of the solutions. We must even the score with the Suey Sings. And time is against us. The community is talking. They say the Chi Sings have lost face. The longer we wait, the more face we will lose. We owe it also to our fallen brother, Ah Foon, to take action. We must do so without delay."

Duk Fong rose to the challenge. "Kill Yuk Dai Gong. That's the answer. He's their toughest *boo how doy*. He's at least Ah Foon's equivalent, if not stronger. He may be more my equal than anybody's. Therefore, I should be the one to get him. It should be a surprise. No *Chun Hung*. Just take him."

Lok Wing expressed doubts. "He's too careful. He's never seen. Keeps himself invisible pretty much, unless he's on the attack."

"We will find him," Choy Wu promised. "We'll

assign Duk Fong to deal with killing Yuk Dai Gong. Then we'll even with the Suey Sings on the life for a life question. But there's still the problem of the property. Lam Wong has taken three of our fan-tan clubs with the aid of the *faan gwai* law. I want to make a truce with the Suey Sing Tong. But I can't make any kind of peace when things are so uneven.''

Duk Fong put in, "But Lam Wong, their leader, must feel that he has no defense against the Chi Sings. That is the key.''

"Well, Duk Fong,'' Choy Wu asked, "what is the first step?''

"It is time for the Chi Sing *boo how doy* to withdraw into secret barracks. We come onto the street only to fight a battle, but for no other purpose.''

Sing Choy Wu was very thoughtful for several long moments. Then he said, "Yes, Duk Fong's proposals are the most reasonable so far. His suggestions are clearly thought out. Well presented. Should get the job done. Man Sum, do you agree?''

"Yes, Father, of course,'' Man Sum replied.

"You *have* been listening?''

"Yes, I have been listening.''

"You seem . . . distracted.''

"I was thinking about all that has been said.''

The exalted master turned to the others. "We will hold our formal meeting this coming Thursday night. At that time, let these proposals be brought up to the entire membership. The recommendations of the special war committee. But don't wait for the approval of the general membership. Implement the recommendations now. The approval of the membership is a matter of ceremony.

"Now, let us turn to the next urgent matter on our agenda. That concerns our son, Sing Man Sum.''

As all eyes present turned on him, Man Sum felt extremely uncomfortable. The eyes were registering disapproval. They didn't like the way he had been conducting himself. He saw disapproval in the eyes of his father as well. They were upset with him for not wenching and drinking like the rest.

Choy Wu spoke to his son after a pause. "My good *boo how doy* tell me your spirits have not been very high lately. You seem unhappy."

"True. I have not been feeling very well lately," Man Sum said, his eyes averted.

"What's the trouble? Let's clear the air."

"I don't know," Man Sum said.

"I wonder if you understand just how happy you should be. Your Tong has saved you from an unhappiness worse than death itself. If it weren't for our legal intervention, you would now be languishing in a *faan gwai* prison cell."

"I realize my Tong has saved me, and I am thankful," Man Sum said. But he was unable to strike the gloom from the tone in his voice.

So Choy Wu continued, "They would put you on death row. That is reserved for criminals awaiting the death sentence. It would be a very simple matter to reverse the decision that was made at your trial. The *faan gwai* immigration officer, Mo Fay, will try to get a retrial of your case. He wants revenge very badly. He won't stop until he gets a conviction. We can see to it that he will never succeed. We can always keep Kwong Pak Yuen terrorized."

"It doesn't take much to terrorize Kwong Pak Yuen," Duk Fong added.

"On the other hand, we can always influence Kwong Pak Yuen to tell the truth. Which is that you're not his son at all. We can always pull our support out from under you, my son. How would you like that?''

"No, Father, I would not like that at all," Man Sum said. Irritation was in his voice. He resented being lectured to.

"And believe me, if we did that, you would take a very heavy fall. Your very existence in Gold Hill is dependent on our support, whether you like it or not. Are you aware how much your trial cost us?''

Man Sum said nothing.

"I repeat, are you aware how much your defense cost us?'' Sing Choy Wu barked.

"No, I am not," Man Sum replied, blushing.

"We paid for your defense out of the Chi Sing war chest. We paid over ten thousand dollars to the *faan gwai* lawyer, Jeremy Porter, and paid over six thousand dollars to the prosecutor to bribe him not to press for a conviction.''

"I appreciate what you have done, Father.''

Choy Wu continued, "I hope you appreciate our Tong, but I'm afraid you don't. Lately I am told you have been depressed. I don't like depressed people. That's not the way to succeed in America. I think if my *boo how doy* is depressed, he must not like his Tong. That makes me nervous. It indicates he maybe is thinking about betraying his Tong.''

"I wouldn't think of betraying my Tong, Father!'' Man Sum protested.

"Maybe he wants to join another Tong. He thinks it may make him happier.''

"No.''

"Maybe you're thinking you'd like to join the Suey Sing Tong. A man acts depressed, that's the kind of thought that may be brewing in his brain. We can't afford to be made nervous by your bad moods!''

"I will forsake my bad moods, then," Man Sum said, desperately trying to pacify his father.

"Learn to be cheerful. Make others feel cheerful in your presence. If you don't learn how to love your Tong and its leaders, we'll abandon you to *faan gwai* justice. Then we'll see how you do before the devil's law, without anybody to hold you up. Now, have I made my point?"

"Yes, Father," Man Sum said simply, but inside his guts were churning. He thought to himself, I must control myself, I must concentrate and control my feelings. I must stop daydreaming, I must forget my feelings of revulsion about turning girls into slaves.

"You better say something better than, 'Yes, Father.' "

"Father," Man Sum said, reaching for words, "I don't think violence is a good thing!"

Choy Wu stood up, enraged. "What? You dare to contradict your exalted master? Shame. Shame on you."

"I . . . I will obey you, though. I will do anything you say!"

"Then you will change your philosophy. You are a soldier! You will love war! Go to it gladly! We do not do women's work! We do men's work here!" Choy Wu seated himself and tried to regain his composure.

"I will," Man Sum said. "I will change my philosophy. I will be filial. I will obey."

"I think you want to be a filial son. I think you have just had bad training. Your mother, may the heavens give peace to her soul, was too innocent. No, I don't think you will be a traitor."

Duk Fong frowned. He had his doubts.

Man Sum said, "I will honor my Tong pledge. My life belongs to my brothers."

"That's better. Now. You will smile. You will be happy. And I will tell you some news. It is news of my happiness. I will do this thing properly." He called out, "Ming Lee?" Then, to the others, "You will welcome her with cups raised. Welcome, Kwan Ming Lee, who is to become my wife. The new Sing Tai Tai, Mrs. Sing!"

With his announcement, Kwan Ming Lee entered the room.

Man Sum's heart jumped. His head throbbed. What? Kwan Ming Lee? My father's wife? My future stepmother? No. No! This must be a nightmare. It cannot be. It cannot! The world's falling apart!

She looked more beautiful than Man Sum had remembered her. In fact, she looked more beautiful than any woman he'd ever met. But he immediately sensed that a vast change had come over her. She glanced at him briefly, then quickly looked away. Had she recognized him?

He longed to be alone with her, but he knew that was impossible now. Now he must show no feelings. He must smile. He must be cheerful.

This was not a nightmare. This was reality. Poetry, philosophy, were nothing but air, nothing to hang on to. All was empty. To lose Ming Lee, and lose her to his own father! He felt he was going to die. His legs shook. He dug his fingernails into his palms until they hurt.

He must show filial affection for his father and mother-to-be! He must be happy in their happiness. He could not demonstrate feelings of grief or inner torment. To be anything less than cheerful meant he was a traitor to them. If they cast him aside now, all would be lost. So he smiled.

It was like forcing a steel mask onto his face. Sharp spikes pointed inward, dug into his cheeks. He wanted to cry out in pain from the ache of the smile on his face. It was a new kind of smile that he put on then, a broad, false smile. He had to learn to put it on. If he failed, he could expect the worst.

He forced his mind to obey. His thoughts. He must control his thoughts. It was possible, wasn't it? Control. Taoists could control thoughts. Buddhists could control thoughts. So he must. He must control. Non-action. Not doing. Erase the mind of its crippling illusions.

He told himself, Yes, he was happy for his father. Yes, it was wonderful that he, Man Sum, had had a small part to play in his father's newfound happiness. No, he no longer felt anything for Ming Lee. It was all an illusion anyway, based on love poetry, based also on the circumstances at Angel Island. He must no longer feel anything for Ming Lee. Only for his father. His father and his Tong.

Man Sum raised his cup as high as he could. Be filial. Yes. Filial. His duty. He was a soldier. Yes. He must preserve his father and his father's marriage.

"To the future Sing Tai Tai," Sing Choy Wu intoned.

"To the future Sing Tai Tai," Man Sum repeated, holding his cup toward Ming Lee, smiling.

Don't think. He must tear the image of Ming Lee out of his heart, though his heart would be left bleeding from it. Hopes and dreams belonged to the past. He must be filial. Loyal. True. And above all cheerful. No more sentiment. Sentiment was air. He was a killer. A Tong man.

Chapter 11

The Gin Kong Tong had a reputation for espionage. Little Lem Choy had made that reputation. He was nicknamed "The Trick." He was both the exalted master and the chief highbinder of his Tong. The Gin Kongs only rostered a membership of five. None of these were *boo how doy*. Lem Choy had to let his salaried soldiers go. He lost a lot of money gambling when Lam Wong took over the Chi Sing clubs. The Gin Kong war chest had been depleted.

Duk Fong nodded to Lem Choy across the fan-tan table, a sign he wanted to talk. Lem Choy was losing anyway, so he left the table. Duk Fong followed. They walked to a dark recess of Ross Alley. No light there to speak of. A good place to talk.

Duk Fong said, "We need the whereabouts of Yuk Dai Gong."

"Oh? Why?" Lem Choy asked.

"Business."

"I see. Well it won't be easy. Yuk Dai Gong is known as 'The Invisible One.' "

Duk Fong asked, "How much will it run us?"

"Two thousand dollars."

"All right," Duk Fong agreed.

"Then you won't need a *Chun Hung* to get him out."

Duk Fong didn't see the ironic smile cross Lem Choy's face. "The Trick" knew the Suey Sing was a dead man once the Chi Sings could place him.

Duk Fong said, "If he's gone back to China, the deal's off."

"*Ho la*. Good," Lem Choy said.

No American highbinder war could be carried to China. That was Tong war policy.

To find Yuk Dai Gong, "The Trick" had to infiltrate the Suey Sing war council. That would be impossible. Lem Choy had a reputation as a neutral.

That meant Lem Choy would have to hire a spy, but he could lose no time. Duk Fong was in a hurry. The Chi Sings had been removed to their barracks. Action was imminent. Wait a minute, Lem Choy thought. Lee Hong Fun. Of course. He borrowed money from me to play the lottery. He lost everything. Never paid me back. And he's a Suey Sing man. Not a highbinder. Not on the war council. But he is a very close friend of Lam Wong's! He might know something. He must know about "The Invisible One."

Lem Choy contrived to run into Hong Fun at a small fan-tan game. It was held every Wednesday in the back of Yat Gar's merchandise store on Washington Street.

It won't be easy, Lem Choy thought. He won't be so willing to betray his Tong. He's a Suey Sing, after all. I might have to twist his arm a little.

Lem Choy quietly stood at Hong Fun's shoulder. While the coins were being scooped up, he said, "You know, Hong Fun, New Year's is approaching and it is bad luck not to pay your debts by year's end."

"You know also that it is bad luck to bring up a

man's indebtedness while he is gambling. Can you please wait until I finish this round?'' Hong Fun requested.

"Unfortunately, there are matters in this world that will not wait, Hong Fun. You have a chance to not only clear your debt with me but make a little extra besides. Interested? This offer will last only ten seconds. I will begin counting.''

"How much extra?''

"Only one thousand dollars. I have already counted up to seven.''

"All right, I'm interested.''

"We must talk privately for the protection of all of us.''

"We can talk on the roof that is accessible by fire escape. It is the roof of the building where I reside on Jackson Street. Go down Saint Louis Alley. Two hundred yards. Wait until three hours after midnight. Bring the money with you then, or the agreement is canceled.''

A dark shape scaled a fire escape ladder in pitch blackness. No one saw the shape. It was Lem Choy, "The Trick.'' Hong Fun, the Suey Sing Tong, was waiting for him.

"What is this offer you have to make to me, Lem Choy?''

"It is very simple. I need to know the whereabouts of the famous invisible one. He has only to be visible for a split second. I await with pleasurable anticipation your answer to my question.''

"I want you to know something. I am not the kind of man who thinks every day how he can best betray his Tong. My Tong means more to me than anything in this life, besides my own family in China. I would not ordinarily put a brother's life in jeopardy, but I am no highbinder.''

"That is true," Lem Choy nodded. "And praise heaven for it!"

"I am a gambler who has run into very bad losing times."

"You have my sympathy, my friend," Lem Choy said.

"My Tong still depends on my monthly contributions to the war chest. I can no longer make such contributions without hardship. I have a wife and two children in China. I must think of them. Lately I have been able to send them nothing. Nothing!"

Lem Choy put his hand on Hong Fun's shoulder comfortingly. "Well, now you'll be able to help your family."

Hong Fun nodded. "Now I will be able to send them something. It may be my last gift."

Poor Hong Fun, Lem Choy thought. People like him are too emotional. They are always getting into trouble of one kind or another. Yet, for some strange reason, he had always found such people very helpful when he needed them.

The following day, Duk Fong picked up the pay phone at the corner of Bay and Harrison Streets. He listened silently, intently. He then returned to the barracks. He requested three volunteers to join him. All volunteered, so he chose Som Hom, Som Hom's brother Som Yuen Ling, and Man Sum.

"We will 'let out the horses' this evening," Duk Fong said.

Lok Wing explained the expression to the new cadets. " 'Letting out the horses' means sending highbinders into battle."

"Tonight, we're going to 'eat pie,' " Duk Fong said.

Lok Wing explained, " 'Eat pie' means to make a killing. 'Eat pie' comes from highbinder legend. Some highbinders who ate pie before a battle were successful. Others who didn't eat pie were killed. That's why it's good luck to say, 'Eat pie.' "

"It will be mince pie," Duk Fong said.

"Mince pie," Lok Wing explained, "is the best kind. So to eat mince pie means to kill a hatchet man of high standing."

"We are going to the theater," Duk Fong said.

"That one I don't understand," Lok Wing said. "Going to the theater?"

Duk Fong laughed, "No, that's where we're really going. I just heard from 'The Trick.' He found out that Yuk Dai Gong is an actor."

"An actor?" Lok Wing exclaimed.

"Yuk Dai Gong is not invisible at all, just the opposite. Yuk Dai Gong can be seen every night at the Chinese Theater on Jackson Street. The Silver Phoenix. He's an actor. He's unrecognizable as Yuk Dai Gong the highbinder. His make-up and costume conceal his identity. It seemed that Yuk Dai Gong had been brought over from China to perform a killing for the Suey Sings, but in order to bring Yuk Dai Gong over to the United States, an excuse had to be found to let him in the country. One of the Suey Sings had a contact in the theater. Yuk Dai Gong was hired to fill an important role."

"Very odd. Very, very peculiar," Lok Wing mused.

"No one knew about his acting except his brother Tongs," Duk Fong went on. "No one knew he existed. That's how he earned the name, 'Invisible One.' "

* * *

That evening, the "horses" who were to go into battle performed preparatory rituals. They ate wildcat meat for dinner.

"We eat wildcat, and that way, we take from the wildcat his prowess and strength," Duk Fong said.

"You are privileged to have such a meal," said Lok Wing. "Wildcat meat is rare, therefore expensive."

Man Sum found the meat stringy and impossible to digest. It sat in his stomach like a lead weight.

Then Lok Wing passed to each highbinder a tiger's claw. Each man was to keep the claw on his person while engaged in the battle.

"Now, drink the elixir of the five poisonous animals," Duk Fong said, offering a cup to his "horses." All drank some of the substance. Then they were ready to go.

The play was to begin at eight-thirty. Duk Fong sported a beard and affected a stoop. He didn't want to be recognized in the theater.

The highbinders arrived at the Silver Phoenix right on time. Duk Fong, Man Sum, Som Hom and his little brother all slipped in unnoticed and took seats on the aisles. They sat at a distance from each other. But they were still in visual range of one another.

There was a hush as the house lights went out. In the darkness, the *boo how doy* lifted out their guns. They were concealed in handkerchiefs.

Sing Man Sum's hand was shaking as he held the pistol. What am I doing here? he asked himself. He would have to stand to fire. The entire audience would be witness to his act. To kill an actor, an artist. That was unthinkable! I must not do this thing, Man Sum thought. Yet I must. My pledge of loyalty. If I do not, they'll abandon me to the *faan gwai*! If this were only a dream!

The curtain rose. The character Chung-li stood there, an immense figure of striking appearance. It was Yuk Dai Gong! He held a beaker in his hand. He walked toward a stove.

"When he stops at the stove," Duk Fong had said, "that's when you fire. Not later. Not sooner."

Man Sum's hand shook uncontrollably. He would have to fire that gun. They would be watching to make sure. But how could they watch him? he thought. How could they watch him and still concentrate on hitting Dai Gong? They could count the shots!

The actor reached the stove. He stopped. He was about to put a rice wine beaker on top. Four shots rang out! Man Sum's was not one of them. He had not fired!

The actor was not able to say his first line. The four Chi Sings dropped their weapons and left the theater. They slipped into Stouts Alley, which led them through a circuitous route of interconnecting alleyways to Washington and Kearny Streets. There they separated, each following a different route back to their barracks by the bay.

When Lem Choy saw the Suey Sing highbinders coming after him, he did not try to escape down the dark alley. He knew that if he had tried to do that, he would be a dead man now. The *boo how doy* were trained to see and fire in the dark.

Lem Choy sat trembling in the Suey Sing's war council. "The Trick" was surrounded by five of the salaried soldiers of the Tong. He was seated in the center of a circle. Sitting, facing him, was Lam Wong, the Tong's exalted master, smiling broadly, coldly. Other highbinders in the circle included the three highest ranking Suey Sings besides Yuk Dai Gong.

"Well, Lem Choy," Lam Wong began, "it is getting difficult to tell which Tong you belong to these days. You are the exalted master of the distinguished Gin Kong Tong, I am given to understand. You have no fighters yet on your payroll, but your war chest is gathering the fruit of your prosperous fields."

"The Gin Kong will never be able to compete with the Suey Sing. The Suey Sing will always be greater. The greatest!" Lem Choy said.

"I have no doubts whatsoever. But it appears now that you have abandoned your Tong and joined a more recognized organization. Is it true what I hear? Have you in fact left the fledgling Tong of your own creation for an older, better established order, namely, the Chi Sings? Or was it only a vicious rumor that I heard?"

"It—it is untrue," Lem Choy protested, stammering. "I am a member of no other order than the Gin Kong."

"Then I am terribly mistaken. I was under the impression you obtained for the Chi Sing Tong the secret identity of our invisible one. You used the agency of our unfortunate weakest link, one Lee Hong Fun."

"That is absolutely false," Lem Choy protested.

"That was what he made us understand. We have had a long conversation with Mr. Lee. Now, are we to assume from what you have said that Mr. Lee was not telling us the truth?"

Lem Choy's eyes darted about the room. He fixed for a split second on each of the highbinders' faces. They were all turned in his direction. All were intently concentrating on his words. "No, I do not like to dispute the word of Mr. Lee Hong Fun because I respect him very much. He did approach me and ask me to do a job for him."

"What kind of job?" Lam Wong leaned forward.

"He wanted me to perform a robbery for him. He was going to tell me the whereabouts of a lot of Suey Sing gold he knew about. Then I was supposed to go and rob it. From the stolen money, I would first take out what he owed me. I had loaned him some money he failed to pay back. We would split the remainder of the take down the middle."

"I see," Lam Wong said. "And that is how Hong Fun planned to pay off his debt to you?"

"Hong Fun was in debt, not only to me, but to a lot of other people as well, so he needed a lot of money. That was his problem, and it was a pretty big one. He figured I also could use a lot of money since I was building a Tong of my own. But I, of course, refused to be mixed up in such a thing."

"That's very honest of you, Lem Choy," Lam Wong said.

"Well, then, I heard that he hooked up with the Chi Sings for the sale of secrets. He figured he could get a good five thousand dollars out of the Chi Sings for selling them secrets vital to their war with you Suey Sings. That's what I heard. I don't know if it was true or not."

"Not according to Lee Hong Fun. He says it was you—"

"But I never got involved with the Chi Sings. It was Hong Fun all the time. Hong Fun dealt with them directly. I wasn't ever involved with the Chi Sings. Now, if Hong Fun is trying to tell you that I was, he's only trying to get me in trouble with you good friends. You're all good friends of mine."

Lam Wong could see how Lem Choy earned his reputation as "The Trick." But he covered his true feelings and said, "I am glad, Lem Choy, that you are not an enemy of our Tong as Hong Fun had led us to believe."

"Where is Hong Fun now? Let him come forward and tell this lie in my presence! Then we'll see what the truth is."

"That, unfortunately, is impossible," Lam Wong said, shaking his head. "Lee Hong Fun is no more."

Lem Choy suspected as much, but he was relieved to hear that it was fact. "Oh," he said.

"But now let's get down to the true matter of this war council. How does the sum of five thousand dollars look to you?"

"It looks very good, but it would depend on what sort of work would be attached to the earning of such a sum."

"The work we have cut out for you cannot fail to be of interest. It involves a woman. Like the Christian *faan gwai* missionaries, we Suey Sings are very concerned with the plight of slave girls. One Kwan Ming Lee is being held captive by Sing Choy Wu. He has expressed his intention to marry her. But we all know what kind of marriage that tyrant has in mind. He has married other singsong girls. He has held large feasts such as the one he is planning now. He has made these 'marriages' occasions for lavish celebrations."

"Yes," Lem Choy said. "His marriage feasts are a legend in Chinatown."

"But the marriages are very short! They last one, two years at the most," Lam Wong continued. "His wives disappear. Who knows what happens to them? But they are no longer there, no longer living in Mr. Sing's brick townhouse on Clay Street."

"His wives just disappear? One cannot help suspecting the worst," Lem Choy said, thankful that their attention had shifted away from himself.

"Our interest in his latest find is strictly humanitarian. She is Kwan Ming Lee. This is her photograph."

"Yes, she is quite lovely," Lem Choy said.

"We certainly don't want a perfect treasure like this to disappear from Chinatown. We don't want to be deprived. We would take too much pleasure in looking at her. We shall see that such perfect jade is well taken care of."

"I see what you have in mind," Lem Choy said, leering somewhat. "An excellent idea!"

"She will have her own parlor, tastefully decorated. It will be as nice as the parlors of the railroad barons. It will be modeled after the sumptuous mansions on Nob Hill, up Sacramento Street. Her customers will be none but the best, the wealthiest. They will be hand-picked. She will not starve. But naturally we first must have her."

"I see you must," Lem Choy said.

"You, Lem Choy, have secured a well-earned reputation in Chinatown as a clever fellow, to say the least. So we therefore have determined that we should require your services. Crack the brick building on Clay Street. This ample five thousand dollars will be yours to add to your Gin Kong war chest."

"Of course," "The Trick" answered. "I am sure something can be arranged."

Chapter 12

"The Trick" visited a certain house of prostitution and made some inquiries.

"Yes," one of the girls to whom he spoke began, "Madame Chu is very well liked. She takes a personal interest in all the girls here. She treats us with respect and dignity."

"What is your name," Lem Choy asked her.

"I am Mei Tim Moy. But if you want to talk to someone who knows her better than I, you should speak to Shei Wai Tam. But I'm afraid you will have to pay as much as a customer."

"I am prepared to pay," Lem Choy said.

He was admitted to Shei Wai Tam's parlor. The heavily made-up woman told him she would be glad to answer his questions, if she could.

In the course of Lem Choy's questions, she said, "Madame Chu spends most of her time at the *daaih-ngok*, as it is called, the mansion."

"Has she spoken to you about the new girl?"

"Yes. *Chu Tai Tai ho daam sam,* Madame Chu is very worried about the new girl."

"Is Madame Chu fearful that Ming Lee could be hurt?"

"Yes. The uncontrollable temper of Sing Choy Wu has always been a problem. It accounts for the failure of some of his marriages. He just drives his wives crazy, I guess. And then has to get rid of them. They usually turn up here, or in the 'cribs.' "

"Does he ever kill them?"

"I don't really know about that. You should talk to Madame Chu. She would know. That *would* be terrible, wouldn't it?"

Lem Choy knew that he must himself contact Madame Chu. And he knew precisely what he would communicate to her. He thanked Wai Tam for her information and left the house.

The next time he saw Chu Mae Pong leave the Sing mansion, he followed her. Before she entered a clothing store on Grant, he stopped her.

"Madame Chu," he said, blocking her way, "I am Kwan Ming Lee's cousin. I have heard rumors that she is being mistreated by her fiancé, Sing Choy Wu. I want to help her."

Madame Chu didn't answer. She took one look at Lem Choy, turned the other way and walked on.

Running after her, he kept up a patter like a radio that couldn't be turned off. "You have to believe me. I *am* her cousin. She didn't know that she even had a cousin in America. Would I lie about such a thing? I have heard rumors that she could be killed any minute by this maniacal tyrant. You must be concerned about her welfare also."

"Of course I am concerned about her welfare, sir," Madame Chu said, trying to get away from him.

"Listen, I want to rescue her from that man. I don't

want her around him another minute. It is my duty as her kinsman. I won't stop until I take care of this matter. I don't care what it takes. Will you help me? Will you help our family?''

Madame Chu spoke to him sharply, but in a trembling voice. "It is dangerous to talk that way. Very dangerous! Please, leave me alone."

But Lem Choy wouldn't let up on her.

"We are interested only in saving her life. We wish to do harm to no one else. We only want to get her away from that madman who threatens her at every turn. We have a small family organization here in Chinatown. The Kwan family. It is a benevolent organization. We take care of family members. You know, we find good jobs for our family members.''

All this time, Madame Chu did not look back, but she did speak to him. She said, "I am also very worried about her. But we cannot talk here on the street. There are eyes and ears everywhere that belong to Sing Choy Wu. If he suspected me for one minute of conspiring with another to help her, he'd put a price on my head immediately."

"We must talk," Lem Choy said in an urgent tone.

Madame Chu whispered, "Descend the stairs into the dry goods store I am about to enter. Come after a quarter of an hour and make sure you are not being followed. I will be behind one of the shelves."

Lem Choy did as he was told. When they were behind the shelves together, she said, "I fear very much for the life of Kwan Ming Lee. She greets the prospect of marriage to the old man with despair and grief, although sometimes he is very kind to her. And there are times when they seem happy together. But Sing Choy Wu is a very jealous man."

"Jealous, yes! And he has a violent temper," Lem Choy added.

"He allows himself to feel envious even of the attention given her by another woman. He began to be terrified that she would be stolen. So he would not even allow her to go out."

"Caged like a bird," Lem Choy said.

"She cannot conceal her despair and boredom, but she must behave according to the rules he has set up for his women. If she does not, I am afraid the rumors you have heard are all true. Her life would be in danger."

"We must do something right away. There is no time to lose."

"But the highbinders are always watching," Mae Pong said.

"I know what we must do, please trust me. It is a matter of a life!"

Mae Pong thought for a minute. Finally she said, "All right. But we must be careful. It is so dangerous."

"Don't be afraid," Lem Choy said. "You will meet me at 811 Stockton Street in twenty-five minutes."

Yuk Lum Tom stood in the basement of a small storefront on Stockton Street. It used to be a chair factory.

Against one wall of the basement Lem Choy had set up a table with a mirror. A light had been placed over the mirror, like the make-up room at the Silver Phoenix. At one end of the table, Lem Choy had accumulated a bunch of wigs, various lipsticks, eye liners, false eyebrows and false eyelashes.

Yuk Lum Tom, brother of the slain "Invisible One," had gained the immediate cooperation of the theater. They were asked for the make-up materials. Slender Yuk Lum Tom could be made up to look like Madame Chu. He would resemble her well enough to pass by the often inattentive guards of the brick castle. That was Lem Choy's plan.

Madame Chu sat on one of the chairs and modeled for them. Lem Choy wasn't an experienced make-up artist, but he worked hard that afternoon, rummaging through the wigs, eyelashes and eyebrows, trying to match the exact color and texture of Madame Chu's hair.

Lem Choy was a perfectionist. He tried and failed several times. His make-up job just wouldn't come up to standard. For his part, Yuk Lum Tom was getting exhausted. His face itched and burned from the repeated scrubbings and applications. But he didn't complain. The plot must succeed. He must get revenge for his brother's murder.

It was around three o'clock. Lem Choy had finished yet another make-up job. He looked at Lum Tom, then at Madame Chu, then back at Lum Tom. He said nothing.

"I think I look like her now," Lum Tom said in a hopeful tone.

"Not good enough," Lem Choy said. Lum Tom felt his heart sink. "But," Lem Choy continued, "I think it is the best we can do. We will stop." Then he turned to Madame Chu. "Mae Pong, you will please change into this silk robe. There is a screen over there. When you are dressed in the robe, bring your clothes to Lum Tom. He will change into yours."

"All right," she said. She proceeded to do as she had been asked.

Yuk Lum Tom put on Madame Chu's flower-patterned dress. Tissue paper and cotton cloth were stuffed into the dress. It was secured with pins. The woman's curvature was thereby simulated.

When the whole was completed, Yuk Lum Tom took his revolver out of his coat. He looked for a place in the dress where it could be concealed. He settled on its bodice. He practiced drawing it from its hiding place and aiming. This practice consumed an hour. By this time, Madame Chu had been moved upstairs. She was not permitted to witness the *boo how doy* practicing.

Another hour was taken up practicing the feminine gait of Chu Mae Pong. Her walk was graceful, not self-conscious or accentuated at all. He did well, even though he was not an actor like his brother.

"Yes," Lem Choy said, "it is an irony. To take revenge for the actor's murder, Lum Tom, you must take up your brother's skill."

It was the tenth of February. The quarter was gearing up for its New Year celebrations. The Chinese New Year was held according to the lunar calendar. New Year's Day was celebrated on the first new moon after the sun entered the sign Aquarius. Therefore, New Year's Day was never earlier than January 21 or later than February 19.

Stockpiles of firecrackers were built up by children and adults alike. Stalls were set up along Grant Avenue. Entrepreneurs came from nowhere to satisfy the special needs of New Year celebrants. There was a demand for fragrant, blossoming lilies, sweetmeats, and, of course, firecrackers.

The crowds bargained from one end of Grant to the other. They grabbed up sprigs of cherry blossoms, bags of salted plums, or boxes of candied kumquats. There were other delicacies appropriate to the season as well. There were mounds of litchi nuts, lily seeds and melon seeds. The tables were heaped with tiny dried figs, and pickled almonds the size of plums, as if there were any lack of plums. There were in fact plenty of plums: dried purple plums, candied green plums. Plums were pickled, too, both purple and green, in luscious plum syrup. There were strips of candied winter melon and thin slices of sugared coconut piled in bright white mounds.

And then there were the decorations. Quince blossoms decked the windows and balconies of Waverly Place with red flames. Within their homes, families set up altars with vermilion candles. They cut fantastic butterflies out of silver and gilt paper. The altars were set atop teakwood tables. Pewter incense jars stood on them, as did exquisitely sculpted lions. Platters of mandarin oranges were arranged on these tables. Bouquets of paper flowers of every color and type rose out of soft green or pink vases.

In the bakery shop windows, one saw pastries and cakes flavored with many different kinds of bean pastes. There were coconut cakes, almond cakes, and pastries stuffed with brown sugar.

Toward the late afternoon of the first day of the New Year, the firecrackers began exploding. They rattled and crackled up and down Jackson, Clay, Pacific, Broadway, Stockton. They exploded in gutters, garbage pails. They detonated on balconies, in dim corridors and on rooftops. Firecrackers exploded by the thousands from the headquarters of the Tongs. They resonated from the family associations, merchant companies, and from the stores of the wealthier merchants. Some were only an inch in length. Others were huge, measuring eight to ten inches and strung on fuses thirty feet long. These were let out of third story windows and dangled to the street.

It was early in the evening when the din reached its loudest. Yuk Lum Tom, masquerading as Madame Chu, entered the *daaih-ngok*. There he found Kwan Ming Lee staring out the window. The guards didn't know that the intruder was not who he pretended to be. They were too busy watching and listening to the New Year's festivities.

The disguised Yuk Lum Tom was admitted to the parlor in the Sing residence. Ming Lee was ignoring the New Year's festivities. She was broodingly staring at a piece of pottery. It was a representation of a watchdog. It had an iridescent glaze.

Yuk Lum Tom said, addressing her, "It used to be, an emperor was buried with his watchdogs and his slave girls."

Ming Lee looked up and saw the man dressed as Madame Chu.

"Who are you?" she whispered in fright.

"A friend," he said. "A friend who does not want to see you buried alive with your emperor."

"What must I do to escape such a fate?" Ming Lee asked.

"You must accompany me out that door. Act as if I am indeed the person I am imitating. Act very naturally, and your freedom is assured."

"I am afraid," Ming Lee said. "How can I be assured I will not be walking into a worse destiny? I don't know who you are. Give me some proof my safety will be maintained."

"Don't delay, Ming Lee. I am armed. I am fully ready and able to engage these watchdogs. You could be caught in the middle and killed. I would not like to see that happen."

"What has become of Madame Chu? Have you killed her to obtain her garments?"

"No, Ming Lee. She offered them to us. She aided us in our rescue plan. She is with us. You trust her, don't you?" Yuk Lum Tom's tone was calm but insistent.

"Yes, but how can I know you have not taken these garments by force?"

"You cannot know," the highbinder said. "You must come with me now. You have no choice!"

"I can take my things?"

"You can take nothing," the highbinder said. With that, he gripped her arm strongly. It hurt her. He lifted her to a standing position. "You will come with me."

Ming Lee didn't know what else to do. She obeyed.

As Yuk Lum Tom started to leave the house of the Chi Sing exalted master with Kwan Ming Lee, one of the bodyguards stopped them.

"I am sorry, Madame Chu, but Sing Choy Wu gave strict orders Ming Lee may not leave the building."

There was a pause. The impostor said nothing.

"Did you hear me, Madame Chu?"

Yuk Lum Tom looked over at Ming Lee.

"Oh, I will be safe with Madame Chu," Ming Lee said. "We just want to see some of the firecrackers explode. I have never seen New Year's in Chinatown before. Please, let me go. We'll be right back."

The other bodyguard said, "Let them go. It's okay. I'll go with them."

"All right, but don't let them out of your sight."

So the three of them left the brick building and walked toward Stockton. Nearby, somebody had just lit a string of one hundred firecrackers. As they started exploding, Yuk Lum Tom drew his revolver, swiveled, and shot the bodyguard at close range.

"This damn drunk," he said aloud, shoving the dead man into the nearest doorway. The body tumbled into a heap.

Yuk Lum Tom and Kwan Ming Lee crossed the street at Stockton, then turned left and entered Lam Wong's merchandise store. They had come two blocks from the intersection of Clay and Stockton.

* * *

Duk Fong, experienced in dealing with the violent temper of his exalted master, spoke softly on his end of the phone. "Attack now? I don't think that would be wise. I think the Suey Sings would be prepared for such an attack. They would have the advantage. We would be in their territory with only the arsenal we could bring with us there. If they were cornered, they'd use the girl's life as a shield. We should let out the horses only for getting individuals. That's been my strategy from the beginning."

"I don't want strategy, I want results!" Choy Wu yelled.

"We have had results. We have so far cut down three of their highbinders using this approach."

"I don't want a long, drawn out war," Choy Wu barked. "I want you to take the Suey Sings now. Even if you have to post a *Chun Hung* to get them out of hiding."

"That's how Ah Foon died. If we all go out on the attack, I guarantee there will be more Ah Foons! It will be a waste of men and those good *boo how doy* skills we worked so hard to learn and teach."

"You are my highbinders. You will not be defeated. You will win. Why do you talk about failure? Defeat?"

"The Suey Sings have highbinders, too. Most of them, I am afraid to say, are our equals or better."

Choy Wu wasn't listening. All he could do was feel outrage, anger. He wanted immediate results, and he didn't care how he got them. "The man who kills Chu Mae Pong gets fifteen hundred dollars. She is the traitor. Why did she betray us to the Suey Sings? Why? She came here and they went out together. That was the last time either of them was seen at the mansion."

"She is probably in hiding. The Suey Sings would be hiding Mae Pong and Ming Lee. They may even be hiding them out of the city. They wouldn't be taking any chances,'' Duk Fong said.

Then he had to hold the phone away from his ear again. Choy Wu let fly an earsplitting expletive.

It was important to be able to convince Choy Wu that Duk Fong's method was the best. Duk Fong was concerned with the lives of his men. He knew that a Tong could lose all its power overnight with a bad strategy. He had seen it happen. When a Tong lost its strength, nobody honored his obligations to it. Thus, if it sustained significant military losses, the erosion of its economic base would soon follow.

Fortunately, for the time being, Sing Choy Wu held off giving any rash orders. He allowed Duk Fong to resume command of the soldiers.

"All right," Choy Wu said, "don't order an attack, but I want quick action. I want the recovery of both women. And I want you to find all the Suey Sings you can, discover who is responsible for this, and assassinate them."

Sing Man Sum spent many hours in the Chi Sing's highbinder barracks in deep thought. He had lost all that he had hoped for in this world. He had wanted Kwan Ming Lee above anything, but she was not to be his. Was it heaven's will? Were the gods depriving him of his great desire? It would follow that if he did something to please heaven, he would attain his wish. Heaven would reward his right conduct.

But how was that possible? How could he do right? Here he was, a salaried soldier, a hired killer. As far as any of his fellow Tong men knew, he had already fired one of the shots that brought down the actor, Yuk Dai Gong, though he never fired the gun. A killer he was not, and a killer he would never be. Yet the result was the same as if he *had* fired. Yuk Dai Gong lay dead. The next time around, he might be ordered to act alone. He might have to kill in order not to get killed himself.

Then he would have to fire that gun at another human being. He could refuse to accept the assignment. Yes, that's what he would do. But wouldn't that be considered unfilial? If he disobeyed Duk Fong, that would be the same as defying his father. He would have no choice. He was the son of his father. He must be an obedient son.

It was as Confucius had said, "The first duty of a son is to pay careful attention to every want of his parents. If one is a farmer, then his first duty is to do his utmost to make the lands fertile. The farmer must be frugal in spending money. That is so he can keep his parents in comfort. This is the filial duty of the most common people. And everyone has the same duty imposed on him, from the Emperor down."

He dreaded the next time he would be asked to "eat pie." He would be handed a red envelope and sent on his way to some meeting place. Death would either choose him or the other person, depending on heaven's whim.

Over and over again he pondered Confucius' maxim, "Resist when wrongly commanded."

The great sage told the story of a certain emperor who would have lost his empire through his wickedness, but he had seven good ministers who checked his illegal actions by strong protests. There was a feudal baron who would have lost his feudal estate through wantonness, but he had five good men who kept an eye on him. There was also a statesman who would have brought frightful calamity upon his family, but he had three good servants who strongly advised him against doing wrong.

Confucius had gone on to say, "If a man has a good friend to resist him in doing bad actions, he will have his reputation preserved. So, if a father has a son to resist his wrong commands, he will be saved from committing serious faults.''

But Man Sum had already tried to convince his father that the way of killing was wrong. His father had not listened.

If Man Sum disobeyed, he would not change his father's ways at all. That was clear from the facts. At the same time, if he resisted the Tong, they would abandon him very quickly to the *faan gwai* courts. He would spend the rest of his days in prison for attempted murder. He felt trapped and deeply confused. No matter which way he turned, he was a victim. He felt helpless, like a blade of drooping millet waiting to be harvested.

Duk Fong entered the barracks. His cold exterior revealed nothing. But all the soldiers sensed that something was wrong. It was, however, not the custom to ask questions of Duk Fong. He would speak only when he was ready.

He ate a meal of rice and vegetables in silence. Then after the dishes had been cleared, the head highbinder addressed them all. ''The war has taken an ugly turn,'' he began. ''The duplicitous Suey Sings have not answered our requests for peace. They did not respond to our exalted master's invitation to the feast of truce. Instead, they have acted in such a way that can only cause more battles and more deaths on both sides. Kwan Ming Lee, our exalted master's betrothed, has been kidnapped by the Suey Sings.''

''Kidnapped?'' several of the soldiers said at once. Each one mirrored the other's astonishment.

''How could the Suey Sings be so bold?'' one asked.

''Bold? How did they manage to do it in the first place? The *daaih-ngok* was well guarded, was it not?'' another said.

Man Sum stood and walked over to the dusty window. He looked out. There was a Pacific Mail Steamship moving slowly across the water. Were there immigrants on it? he wondered. Would they, too, endure imprisonment on Angel Island? Then be brought to Gold Hill and find work spilling blood on street corners? Or whoring? He wanted to yell out at the ship, tell it to turn around and go back.

He thought of poor Kwan Ming Lee. She would be passed around like a rice bowl from mouth to mouth, house to house. That's what her life would be like now. She was the property of this enemy Tong. She would be reduced to the status of a common prostitute. And when she was too old to serve in that capacity, she would end up in a "sick house," a room where prostitutes were left to die.

It would be good to be deported. Even sweet. One evening, when all were sleeping, he'd climb onto the deck, leaving the vomit stench of the crowded hold behind. Then he'd reach for the ship's railing. He'd fly over into darkness. The waves would engulf him. He'd be like a shred of paper. It would not take much to part with this fragment of a false life.

Duk Fong shot his voice sharply at Man Sum, like a bullet. "The dreamer again, it appears, is squandering his time and ours. What is it this time, Man Sum? Confucius? Lao Tze? Mencius? Or is it more of Kwan Ming Lee, your unattainable love? Oh, unpitying great heaven, is there no end to disorder? You would do better, Man Sum, to behave humbly, as a filial son. Do not your five classics tell you to do so?"

The others laughed mockingly at him, but their laughter was not especially robust. They weren't taking much pleasure in the joke.

Duk Fong said, "Remember this bit of the classics

next time you decide to waste our time: 'Do not try to cultivate fields too large. The weeds will only grow luxuriantly. Do not think of winning people far away. Your toiling heart will become grieved.' "

The remarks made Man Sum hot with anger, but he repressed it. He supposed, in a way, Duk Fong was right. To forget Ming Lee was best.

At that moment, Som Yuen Ling said, "I don't want to add to the bad news, but I have something to report."

"I should explain," Duk Fong added, "Som Yuen Ling has been assigned to keep track of all Lem Choy's movements. Lem Choy is useful because he's clever, but he's not a brother. He could betray us to the Suey Sings."

Som Yuen Ling nodded. "It appears that is precisely what he did. I saw 'The Trick' enter a boarded up storefront on Stockton Street. A few minutes later, Madame Chu entered by the same door. I didn't see any of the Suey Sings at that time, but I could smell them. I only realize now that Lem Choy must have been behind the kidnapping."

"Yes," Duk Fong said. "Lem Choy and the Suey Sings must have paid Madame Chu plenty to do that job for them."

Duk Fong, enraged, fired a shot into the wall, striking a water main. Water spewed out all over the floor. Luckily, someone had the presence of mind to find the valve and turn off the water.

Duk Fong said, "The betrayal by Lem Choy is a very bad indication of how the war is going. It means we can't use neutral Tong men for the purposes of espionage. The Suey Sings can always outbid us."

"What if Lem Choy has given them the location of our barracks?" Som Hom asked.

"He doesn't know the location. We wouldn't be so

foolish as to give 'The Trick' that kind of knowledge,'' Duk Fong said.

Som Yuen Ling added, "What the Suey Sings wouldn't give for the whole Chi Sing army at one time. What a banquet that would be."

Duk Fong shook his head. "No, we've been careful to keep in contact with Lem Choy only by phone. Therefore, he couldn't know where we are."

"What can we do?" Som Yuen Ling said. "We can't go after the Suey Sings as a group. They would have the advantage. They would pick us off like so many ducks. We'd be in the open. They'd blow our heads off. It'd be easier than lighting firecrackers. We'd be lucky if we got one of them. It would be the end of our Tong!"

Duk Fong paused, then said in a low voice, "If our exalted master insists on that course of action, we must follow it."

"*Gung Hay Fat Choy*," Som Hom said sarcastically.

No one responded to the New Year's greeting.

Man Sum turned to Lum Po and whispered, "You know, in a way, we aren't much different from the sing-song girls. Only they have it better than we do. They can buy their freedom with money. We can only buy ours with our lives."

Lum Po slowly turned his head and faced Man Sum. "What's the matter, Man Sum, don't you want to get your hands wet with Suey Sing blood?"

"I am not very fond of killing," Man Sum said. "And from what I know of you, you aren't, either."

"Then I don't think you know me very well," Lum Po said.

"I know you are a goodhearted man. You like to laugh and you have a good mind. That is why we're friends, I think."

"I am not so sure, Man Sum."

"What do you mean, Lum Po?"

"I have changed. I have changed a great deal in the last few months."

"Well, we both have. It is this confinement in the barracks. It is worse than the wooden building! And it is the war."

"It is not just the war. I didn't tell you this, but my father is dead," Lum Po said, barely containing the emotion in his voice.

"Dead?"

"Yes. Two weeks ago, I went looking for him. I found his store on Stockton Street. But there was another owner. He told me my father had been killed. Tongs did it. My father had refused to pay any more protection money," Lum Po said. Now his voice betrayed rage.

"But what Tong?" Man Sum asked.

"The Suey Sing Tong," Lum Po said. "The Suey Sing Tong killed my father. That is why he never contacted me on the island. But of course the *faan gwai* never told me."

"Lum Po," Man Sum said, putting his hand on Lum Po's arm, "I am sorry this terrible thing has happened to you."

Lum Po just looked at Man Sum's hand. Then he abruptly pulled his arm away. "I will avenge my father's death if it's the last thing I do," he said with conviction.

Lum Po turned away. Man Sum suddenly felt a great distance had come between them. It was like a giant, yawning chasm. He could think of nothing more to say to his friend.

Chapter 13

It was a grey day when they left the barracks by the wharf. It drizzled and they wore black. They could hear the sound of exploding firecrackers in the distance. It already sounded like a war zone.

They approached Jackson and Kearny. The sound of firecrackers was deafening. The sidewalks were already thick with the shattered red, green and yellow paper from hundreds of thousands of exploded, harmless charges. It was as though a giant migration of butterflies had settled there.

They waited to be noticed, just stood there, looking calm and tough and mean. Someone in a barber chair spotted them. "It's the Chi Sing Tong!" he said to the barber excitedly. "It looks like war."

When the man left the shop, the barber quickly locked the door and put up boards.

The six highbinders' fedoras were pulled over their foreheads, masking their eyes in shadow. It was good that their eyes were masked. Otherwise the people of Chinatown would have seen the fear in those eyes.

The firecracker blasts were becoming less frequent. After a few minutes, only an occasional explosion could be heard. Finally, the streets were totally silent. The New Year's festivities had suddenly, dramatically been brought to a halt. Shutters were thrown over windows and heavy steel grills were latched over storefronts. The populace took cover against the bullets they feared would be flying in all directions at once.

Duk Fong, Lum Po, Som Hom, Som Yuen Ling, Man Sum and Lok Wing started up Jackson toward Grant. It was eerie to walk on a deserted Jackson Street during Chinatown's biggest festival week, wading through firecracker paper thick as autumn leaves.

Several loud cracking sounds ripped the street next to them. The six men dug into the walls or the sunken staircases leading to basement shops. It had only been a firecracker. They slowly unglued themselves from the false security of the brick walls and resumed their fatal march on Jackson toward Waverly. They knew that by this time the *Chun Hung* would have reached the headquarters of the Suey Sings and Wong would have let out his horses. They were on their way to the banquet of Chi Sing highbinders now.

"I heard something," Som Hom said.

"Just another *paau-jeung*, firecracker," his brother reassured him.

"No, something up there," Som Hom said, pointing to the roofs over some shops in the next block, on the right side of Jackson, between Grant and Stockton. "Somebody's up there watching us. I heard running feet."

"Keep walking," Duk Fong ordered. Sweat was running down his face, falling onto his black shirt. The sky darkened and a light rain began to fall.

"Up there, something is up there watching us," Som Hom repeated. "We should get onto the roof. They're on the roof of that shoe repair shop."

Duk Fong tried to calm him. "We'll walk on the same side of the street as the roof. They won't be able to see us."

"They're on both sides of the street! I mean, they're on both roof tops. I can see them," Som Hom said.

His brother, Yuen Ling, said, "Come on, Hom. Nobody's up there. You're seeing things. You're looking at your hat. Stop looking up there."

"Keep walking," Duk Fong said.

They kept walking. Now they were in the middle of the block. The drops of rain blended with the sweat on their faces, cooling them off.

Som Hom was becoming increasingly agitated. "We should get up there on those roof tops. We keep walking, they'll just pick us off down here. Why should we keep walking? I know they're up there."

Man Sum had not heard any sounds on the roof tops other than the wind.

Just then, a rock dropped in the center of the street from somewhere. There was a piece of red paper with black ink lettering on it. The paper was secured to the rock with a piece of wire used to bind crates for shipping. Duk Fong picked up the rock. They all huddled in a doorway to read the *Chun Hung* that had been delivered to them from the sky. Som Hom had been correct. They were indeed on the roof.

The enemy's *Chun Hung* listed each of them by name and then concluded by saying, "These are corpses of men."

"We can get up there by using that fire escape," Lum Po said, pointing to a ladder about ten feet off the street. The ladder led to a second store apartment. Then metal stairs went to another landing before a last ladder attained the roof.

"That'd be too risky," Duk Fong decided. "We'll go through these flats." They went up to the landing and Duk Fong knocked on the door. A few moments went by without anyone having answered the knock. Duk Fong was impatient. He blasted the door with three weighty cartridges.

The highbinders entered and went up the stairs. There were about twenty people living in that flat, all men. They huddled, terrified, in the corners of the hallways, in the kitchen and in the bathroom.

"Get a board. We need a board, a plank to cross the roofs. You, there, get a board!" But the man being spoken to was too terrified to do anything. He just sat there, shaking.

Duk Fong charged into another room. There he saw ten people, all grabbing whatever furniture they could to shield themselves from these intruders. Duk Fong roughly swung open doors to shelves and tore the shelves out of the wall.

"Take these," he ordered his apprentices. "This way." Duk Fong beckoned them to the door that led to a stairway going up to a door to the roof.

They all followed Duk Fong up the stairs. The roof was as silent as the street.

"This is a trap. This is a trap. This is a trap," Man Sum heard himself saying over and over. He felt steel fingers grip his arm.

"Quiet," Duk Fong said.

"Nothing's up here. Nothing," Lum Po put in. "We should have stayed on the street. There would be somebody on the street we could deal with. Here, there's nothing."

"He's right!" Som Hom screeched through his throat.

"I'm going down to the street. I'm going down to the street." He went for the door they had just come out of. It had been locked behind them. Som Hom emptied his Colt .45 into the door. It was still stuck. Then another gunshot rang out. Two, then three bullets struck the chimney. The Chi Sings quickly flattened themselves against the roof. Again, silence.

Som Hom crawled over to the other men and peered across the street. "They're out there somewhere, on the other roof top. It must be that one." He pointed across the street.

"There!" Lum Po pointed to two shapes crossing a plank from the next building to the third building over. Duk Fong and Yuen Ling fired, but the Suey Sings ducked mysteriously out of sight before they could get their shots off. They left their plank behind them. Duk Fong's soldiers all felt greatly relieved. At least they had seen the Suey Sing men. It made them feel less like they were battling ghosts.

Hurriedly they threw the planks down between the two buildings, then crossed to the next building. The rain had made the planks wet. They were flimsy, too. Man Sum slipped and almost fell to the street. He lay prostrate on the plank, gripping the edges, and pulled himself forward.

After all were safely landed on the next building, they pulled up the planks behind them. Then they dug for the cover of chimney or vents. Now the Chi Sings were on the offensive. Several minutes passed in which nothing happened. No Suey Sings were seen anywhere.

Voices were heard on the street. People were laughing, resuming the celebration. They thought that the *boo how doy* skirmish was over and that they no longer needed to hide themselves from the flying bullets. People were again lighting firecrackers on the street. Every time they went off, the highbinders would turn in the direction of the sound and look for the evidence of bullets hitting fixtures on the roof.

"Go for the next building over. One at a time." Duk Fong pointed to the plank the Suey Sings had abandoned that went to the next building. Lok Wing was the first to assay the plank.

He was cut to shreds. Bullets came from everywhere. His body fell to the alleyway below after sliding off the wet plank.

Bullets were coming from behind them, too. And now, the Suey Sings came out of their hiding places. They didn't worry about concealing themselves. They had the Chi Sing army pinned down. Planks were yanked away before the Chi Sings knew what had happened.

Duk Fong's voice, under the circumstances, was strangely calm, "We've got to get out of here. Fire escape."

They ran, heads ducked, to the ladder. Bullets whizzed over them. They knew their chances of getting down to the street alive were slim at best.

Duk Fong was hit before reaching the first landing. He was followed by Som Hom and his brother. All lay on the street, dead.

Lum Po had disappeared.

Man Sum, wounded badly in the leg, staggered down Waverly Place. He was stalked by shadows. Every firecracker sounded like a gunshot. He felt each one rip into his body. Duk Fong, Som Hom, Som Yuen Ling, all were dead. The Suey Sings were after *him* now. He could hear their steps running behind him. They knew who he was, *what* he was.

He grabbed a lion head out of the hands of a lion

dancer and began whirling wildly in the street, in spite of his wounded leg. He danced up to a doorway where a merchant was dangling a lettuce leaf by a string. He played the role of the New Year's lion to perfection. He halted, shivering and shimmying with delight. The lion loved lettuce leaves because money was hidden beneath them. A barrage of exploding firecrackers sent out blue smoke clouds to meet his gyrations. Attendants blew the smoke away from his nostrils with their palm-leaf fans. The orchestra, mounted on a truck, played a lion dance tune. It consisted of a cacophony of beating drums and crashing cymbals. The lion's body undulated and plunged, circling around the lettuce leaf with rhythmic anticipation. Then, drawing near to the feast, the insatiable monster leapt upward. He closed his jaws over the lettuce leaf. The string snapped and he moved on to the next doorway. Under the lettuce leaf was a five-dollar bill. This was the merchant's donation to the charity the lion dancers represented, probably the Chinese Hospital.

Once he consumed the lettuce leaves, Man Sum immediately handed the money over to the attendants. He didn't want them to think he had donned the lion's head in order to steal the money.

"I felt like dancing," he told them. "And the other dancer looked like he needed a rest."

"We accept your explanation," a representative said. "You're doing a very good job!"

The ruse worked. Through the lion's mouth, he could see the Suey Sing highbinders looking through the crowd for him, baffled. The lion sniffed the air, proudly shaking his mane and keeping a lookout for those lettuce leaves which were his consuming passion. Man Sum had to keep up the act even though his leg was bothering him more and more and he continued to grow weaker. He felt a wet oozing under the spot where his pants stuck to his leg. He looked down and saw blood dropping from his cuff, merging with the red firecracker paper. Yet he danced on through the late afternoon.

Now it was early evening and Man Sum was still dancing. He had collected more than two hundred dollars for the Chinese Hospital, but his strength was giving out. The fog was rolling in. All around him, the shapes of people started looking more and more vague. The vagueness of their shapes was his last memory before blacking out.

When he awoke, he was in a room in his father's house. His leg had been bandaged. Sing Choy Wu was standing next to his bed, looking down at him.

Sing Choy Wu held some tea out to him and said, "Drink this. You are still very weak. You almost lost your life out there. This tea will help replenish your blood. Don't try to talk. The important thing now is to rest."

"But how did you find me? I thought I was well hidden under the mane of the New Year's lion."

His father answered, "When I learned of the battle's outcome, I found out that you were not one of the victims. Your body was not among the dead. I reasoned that you had probably been wounded, so the Chinese Hospital was the first place I looked. I spoke with the attendants and the orchestra who were with you. They said that you had been quite an excellent lion dancer."

"I'm afraid that I am a better lion dancer than I am a gunman," he said, lowering his eyes.

"Don't think about that now, son. You need to rest," Choy Wu said. "You did the lion dance to escape the

Suey Sings. But in the process, you came very close to losing your life, or at the very least, to losing that strong leg of yours.''

"What of my friend Lum Po? What became of him? I didn't see him fall in battle with the rest of them.''

"Lum Po is in Fresno. He is in hiding because the Suey Sings know who he is and are gunning for him. Duk Fong made a big mistake in contracting for the services of Lem Choy. That deceiver is easily bought. He would betray his own parents. He doesn't know the meaning of duty or loyalty. He is worse than an animal. But enough of him. Yes, Lum Po is in Fresno. We are all going there,'' Choy Wu said.

"We are all going to Fresno? We're leaving San Francisco? But why?'' Man Sum asked.

"Our lives are in great danger now. The Suey Sings have a price on all our heads,'' Choy Wu said, frowning, "The highbinders are gearing up for an attack on my *daaih-ngok*, my mansion, even now. We were waiting for you to grow strong enough, then we were all going to get out of Chinatown.''

"And Kwan Ming Lee? What about her?''

"I thought you would bring up her name. Listen, there is no point worrying yourself now. You are still weak. You need to rest, to get back your strength. We can talk more later if you wish.''

His father was right. He was indeed quite tired. The last part of his father's sentence was lost as Man Sum drifted again into unconsciousness.

When he awoke, he felt a little stronger. The bitter-tasting herbal tea must have had some positive effects. He was alone, but he could hear bustling going on in the other room. They were packing up, getting ready to move. He thought that his father seemed different. He was friendlier, softer. But the lines on his face were deeper. And his countenance betrayed a deep sadness and remorse.

Man Sum spent about a half-hour lying there. He felt useless and bored. He wanted to get up and help his father with the packing. He pulled the covers aside and swung his legs over the side of the bed. Then he stood, favoring his good leg, and hobbled toward the doorway of the bedroom. He looked into the living room and saw his father carefully wrapping a precious porcelain vase in tissue paper. His father looked up and saw him standing there.

"What are you doing?" his father demanded. Then the older man came to the doorway and did an unusual thing. He lifted Man Sum and carried him in his arms gently to bed, then laid him down and drew the covers over him very much like a caring nurse would. Choy Wu stroked the top of Man Sum's head. It was a spontaneous, unguarded moment. Choy Wu quickly withdrew his hand when he started to realize what he was doing.

"Father," Man Sum said, looking up at him. "Perhaps . . ." Man Sum felt himself reaching for words. "Perhaps we could become close friends through all this suffering."

"Yes," Choy Wu said. "Because you're my son, you're my friend. That goes without saying."

"I just wanted to say it, that's all," Man Sum replied.

"And because you are my son and my friend, I want you to get well. Do you understand?" Choy Wu said, holding back his emotion.

"Yes, Father."

Choy Wu had learned through hard experience never to leave himself open. Even when there was obviously no threat around. He always assumed that an attack could come from anywhere, at any time. One could not cease to maintain vigilance. He assumed a stricter tone, saying, "Now, I order you to stay in that bed. You will obey me!"

"All right, Father. I won't move until I'm ready," Man Sum said.

PART III
THE RESCUE

"Do not try to cultivate fields too large. The weeds will only grow luxuriantly. Do not think of winning people far away. Your toiling heart will become grieved."

—Anonymous Chinese Proverb, Ming Dynasty

Chapter 14

After three months, Man Sum's leg had almost completely healed. He enjoyed going with Lum Po up to the nearby Sierra mountains. There they would work out with their revolvers. They would attempt to improve their marksmanship by shooting chipmunks or squirrels.

"I haven't yet been able to hit the left eye at a range of even thirty yards," Man Sam said. "We have a long way to go before our skill will ever match Duk Fong's. But that's probably just as well. I never want to use this gun on another human being as long as I live."

"You'd better keep practicing," Lum Po returned. "We might be required to draw on our *boo how doy* skills sooner than you think."

Man Sum was greatly enjoying the beauty of the mountains and the clear air. He liked hiking over long distances in the forests. It was easy to walk there without a trail, for the trees were far apart and the ground was matted down with pine needles.

Lum Po practiced his *boo how doy* skills more religiously than Man Sum. Often, when Man Sum wanted to walk, Lum Po would continue his target practice. In Lum

Po's mind, he wasn't just hunting deer or raccoons. He was shooting down Suey Sings.

Sing Choy Wu never joined the younger men. He preferred staying in the rented flat in Fresno's Chinatown. He spent long afternoons brooding over the fate of his Tong. Lum Po and he often talked about taking revenge on the Suey Sings. They devised various schemes for getting back his bride-to-be, Kwan Ming Lee.

As his father spoke of his love for this woman, Man Sum felt very uncomfortable. He wanted also to talk to someone of *his* love for her, but he could not. It greatly pained him to think of what Ming Lee must now become. After her experiences in the Suey Sing house of easy virtue with hundreds of men, she would not be the Ming Lee he remembered. Her innocence would be gone. Her mouth would be full of coarseness. Her heart would be full of great bitterness. She would be like a delicate flower crushed by the heel of a heavy boot.

One day in the woods, Lum Po reprimanded his friend for his lack of perseverance in the art of killing. "Your leg is again as strong as it was before you were shot, Man Sum. Your marksmanship, however, has not much improved. You have not been practicing. We are in the middle of a war. Your aim must be better. We must take on the Suey Sings and win."

"What? The two of us?"

"Yes, the two of us. We are the only Chi Sing highbinders left. When we are ordered to kill, we must obey. There is no turning back. And the exalted master, your father, will order us to kill Suey Sings just as soon as he feels we are ready. The Suey Sings may have won the battle of the roof tops, but the war is not over yet."

"But Lum Po, my father will not send two novices

against the strongest Tong in Chinatown. I can't imagine it. It would be suicide. The roof-top battle was enough of a suicide," Man Sum said.

Lum Po, frowning, seemed not to be listening to Man Sum. He nervously dug into the ground with a stick.

"Yes." Now he raised his voice. "He will send us back to San Francisco. And we will give the Suey Sings the justice they deserve. I hope only that he does it soon. I'm getting tired of waiting around in this wilderness for something to happen. I'd go tomorrow. I'm ready to kill them at any time. I would like nothing better than to show them their own blood on the pavement and make them lie in it. How I hate the Suey Sings!"

"Think, Lum Po, think. It would be suicide to go back there with revenge in mind. We wouldn't have a chance against their skill and numbers. My father foolishly threw away our best strength in the New Year's fiasco. The Chi Sings need more men. Perhaps my father is planning to bring soldiers over from China. Only then will the Chi Sings have the strength to get back at the Suey Sings."

"I don't think you want to achieve victory for our Tong at all," Lum Po said angrily. "You just want to stay in these woods and talk to the animals. Tell me, are you a coward?"

Now Man Sum felt angry. "I just don't want to throw my life away in some crazy war."

"Because if you are a coward, I will go to Chinatown by myself!"

"Is it not a crazy war, Lum Po? Is it not madness?" Man Sum demanded, practically pleading with him. "Come now, you must see the madness of it. Don't you? Many lives are lost but nothing is gained."

Lum Po would not be persuaded. "I will let you lose

your face, and I will take on the Suey Sing *boo how doy* strength without you.''

"But Lum Po, why die a meaningless death? They'll scrape up your dried blood with firecracker paper and forget you. Nobody cares after the wagers are paid off!''

"I want to eat a lot of pie. I'm hungry, Man Sum. I want my banquet now. See what a killer I've become?''

With that, Lum Po drew his gun and fired from his hip. He brought down a squirrel climbing a tree some forty-five yards away. Lum Po went and got the squirrel and brought it back. Where it's left eye ought to have been, there was a large hole.

"Now it only remains," Lum Po said, "to do the same thing under the cover of darkness.''

Man Sum was more impressed—and disturbed—by Lum Po's attitude of mind than his marksmanship.

"Lum Po, I hope you have not forgotten the time that I saved you from taking your own life. We are friends. You should not call me a coward.''

Lum Po turned toward him and for the first time Man Sum noticed how grim Lum Po's face had become. "My life means nothing to me if it is not in the service of my Tong.''

They spent the rest of that afternoon in silence. The Tong and its philosophy of violence had driven the two men apart. Yet what was the Tong at this point? It consisted of only three men: his father, Lum Po and himself. The other highbinders had been cut down. The rest had quit rather than remaining in a Tong that had lost so much face. But Lum Po had become a fanatic. He was ready to throw his life away for the remnant of the Chi Sing Tong.

Man Sum had decided that the time had come to really counsel his father. He must stop his father from trying to take revenge on the Suey Sings. It was time to do exactly what Confucius had advised. Now the position of the Chi Sings had become weak. So perhaps his father would pay attention to common sense and right philosophy.

That evening, as was customary, no talk was permitted during the meal. But afterward, Man Sum addressed his father.

"Father," Man Sum began somewhat hesitantly, "Lum Po has been telling me that you want to send the two of us into Suey Sing territory. Yet again, you would have us engage Lam Wong and his stable of professional killers."

"Lum Po and I have discussed the possibility," Choy Wu admitted.

Man Sum responded, "I have always tried to remain a dutiful and obedient son. But I must also speak my mind. It is my duty to counsel you. For it appears to my reason that you are taking the wrong course of action."

Man Sum looked at his father across the table to gauge his reaction. His father simply looked back at him. No emotion whatsoever registered on his face. But he didn't interrupt or object to what Man Sum was saying. Man Sum felt it was all right for him to continue.

"Father, the war must be brought to an end. It is senseless. Even if we did succeed in defeating the Suey Sing strength, they would soon try to take revenge on us, or some other Tong would attempt to undermine our position."

Lum Po looked at Man Sum with hatred. Then he turned to Choy Wu and said, "Sir, with all due respect, I must tell you that your son is a coward."

"Why coward?" Choy Wu asked, startled.

"I spoke to Som Yuen Ling after the assassination of the actor, Yuk Dai Gong. I learned from him that Man Sum did not fire his gun. He did not even lift it with the intention of firing. Perhaps he was more interested in watching the play about dreamers.''

Now it was Man Sum who grew angry. "It is true I didn't fire my gun at that helpless, defenseless actor. I should have spoken up and said how utterly disgusted I felt at that murder. We didn't even give the highbinder a chance to defend himself. Three bullets were more than enough to kill him. There were four shots in any case.''

"Yes, because Som Yuen Ling shot twice. He did it to cover for you. He didn't want you to get into trouble. He should have reported you, though,'' Lum Po said.

"I question the whole reason for killing the actor in the first place,'' Man Sum said.

Lum Po stood up. He was livid. "Your place was not to question, but obey. You were chosen for a job. You were not supposed to think or have opinions. You are a *soldier*!''

Man Sum stood, too, facing Lum Po. "I have never forgiven myself for having participated in that atrocity. No, I want nothing more to do with highbinderism. Do you hear? Nothing!''

"Not so angry, both of you. Sit down. Sit down,'' Choy Wu commanded.

They both sat down.

Choy Wu turned to Man Sum and spoke quietly but firmly to him. "Is it true that you did not shoot to kill when you were ordered to do so by your Tong?''

"It is true, Father,'' Man Sum acknowledged after a pause.

Choy Wu's look turned cold. "It means that you have violated the Tong's trust. You have failed to live up to the oath.''

"I know that, Father. I accept that judgment. I have

no desire to continue in this madness. I want nothing to do with killing. I want only to do what is right."

Again, Choy Wu spoke very quietly. "Do you think you know what is right? Do you imagine you know better than I what the right thing to do is? Do you think that I like violence? I have lived in this country since the last century. I have tried to live by its laws. I have legally removed gold from under the earth, only to have it wrenched out of my hands by whites who claimed to be 'tax collectors.' "

Suddenly Choy Wu rose his voice. His face was trembling with emotion. "I have worked on the railroad, doing the same work as the white, getting a fraction of the pay. When the railroad was completed, our countrymen, who bore the great part of the burden of the construction on the Western side, were not even invited to the opening ceremony. Our work was not even acknowledged."

"Father, I understand all that, but—"

"You don't understand! Yes, I have tried to live a moral life. But I had to survive. One has to live. The barbarian insists you live in a half-alive state. You must fight back. Fight for your right to live a full life. You say you abhor violence. If you are married, would you not defend your home? Your wife? Your child?"

"But the highbinders are the attackers. They hunt people and kill them!" Man Sum countered.

Now Choy Wu stood. He was practically screaming at his son. "We have never initiated violence. We have only responded when attacked, like the head of a family defends his home from the robbers. Now, my son, I have this to say to you." Choy Wu sat back down at the table and pointed a finger directly at Man Sum's face. "Our Tong is still in existence. I am still its exalted master. I am holding you to your highbinder's oath and contract. If I choose to let out the horses, you will go.''

"But Father—'' Man Sum started to protest.

"If I order you to shoot to kill, you will do so. You have disobeyed once. That is a terrible blemish on your record of service. You may not be able to wipe it clean. But if you refuse again, my son, though I am your father and I love you, I will still put a price on your head. And it will be a high enough price. You will not last beyond the sunset of the day I post the red paper!''

Hearing this, Man Sum felt his heart go numb. Not since his period of incarceration on Angel Island had he felt so powerless and empty of hope. He had failed to move his father one inch.

His father stood up from the table and went out the back door. Soon, he re-entered. He was carrying a live rooster. He reached for a bowl and put it on the table. Then he picked up a large kitchen knife.

"It is time we renewed our oath,'' he said.

After both Lum Po and Man Sum repeated the oaths of obedience to the Tong, Sing Choy Wu laid before them their assignment. He even set a time limit for the accomplishment of the task. It was to be completed within the following five weeks.

He said, "I want my bride returned to me here, in Fresno. That's right, my good young men. You will retrieve my lost treasure. She is all that I have, all that I hold dear. I want her. I want her desperately. You will bring her to me.''

He then dismissed his two salaried soldiers. "You need to sleep well. Tomorrow I'm putting you on a train to San Francisco.''

* * *

The Suey Sings were completely contented with their victory over the Chi Sings. Duk Fong, the killer of their beloved Yuk Dai Gong, was dead. "Wickedness has a bad recompense." The rest of the highbinders were dead, too. Or they had fled the quarter holding on to the shirt sleeves of their exalted master.

The Suey Sings were not tempting fortune with their spoils of war. Kwan Ming Lee was carefully watched and accompanied wherever she went. Three highbinders alternated guard duty, and all her customers were carefully screened.

As for Madame Chu, she was freer than Ming Lee. It did not matter to them what happened to her, but she preferred to stay close by. She feared retribution from Sing Choy Wu for having betrayed him. The Suey Sing highbinders were willing to oblige her request for protection. Kwan Ming Lee did not mind having Madame Chu around. It gave her feminine companionship. They shared a room in the Suey Sing Tong headquarters.

The feeling of degradation Ming Lee suffered for her acts of prostitution made her hate her body. As time went on, that hatred turned into indifference. She ignored her body and gave all her attention to her spirit.

Accompanied by the dependable highbinder guard, she went daily to the temple. Usually, she went for two hours in the early morning. She had to return to her parlor before her customers started arriving.

The temple was called the joss house. Joss sticks were lit before the many gods. These large incense sticks emitted every imaginable scent. The smoke of the incense was supposed to bear the words of the prayers up to heaven.

Ming Lee fell on her knees before Kuan Yin, the goddess of mercy. Kuan Yin's name literally meant, "She who hears the cries of the world.'' Her image was enthroned on a lotus. She was represented holding a vase. This symbolized a receptacle for the tears of the worshippers whom her presence consoled.

In life, the goddess had experienced suffering in great abundance. That's why, when she became a goddess, she sympathized so much with the plight of other women.

Today was a special day. It was the nineteenth day of the Second Moon, the birthday of the goddess. Ming Lee brought to the joss house an assortment of food, paper clothing and money. Through her religious devotion, Ming Lee unburdened her heart of all its remorse and shame. Her sacrifices to Kuan Yin insured that the goddess would listen intently and sympathetically.

The highbinder, Huang King Lep, stood at the door as Ming Lee prostrated herself before the goddess.

''Kuan Yin,'' she whispered, her face close to the wooden floor, her body rocking slightly, ''Kuan Yin, I am so deeply ashamed of what I must do with my body. I am carried in the arms of strangers. They bear me in their arms disrespectfully. They throw me on the couch that smells only of their desires. I have no place there. I am nothing to them. Kuan Yin, transport me, carry me away from this place. For only a moment, take away my torment.''

She extended her body fully against the floor, face down, and sobbed for a long time. Her sobs were loud and deep enough to attract Huang King Lep's attention, and he reasoned that something might be seriously wrong with Ming Lee's mind. He decided to report this matter to the exalted master.

Lam Wong would have a remedy for her spiritual distress. Opium.

Chapter 15

Lam Wong contacted Yan Chui Lee, a young prostitute who was about the same age as Kwan Ming Lee. Chui Lee would introduce the new slave girl to the succor which the pipe could provide.

It had been a particularly degrading day. It seemed all the men who visited Kwan Ming Lee derived pleasure from dispensing pain. The highbinder guarding the parlor admitted a young woman. Kwan Ming Lee was very surprised to see a woman instead of the usual customer, but Yan Chui Lee immediately put her at ease. The two women began talking and sharing their experiences.

"I have been at the trade for a long time," Chui Lee said. "Since I was fourteen. When I was twelve, I was sold to a family living in the Tai Ping San district of Hong Kong. There, I performed the duties of *mui jai*."

Ming Lee understood that being a *mui jai* meant being burdened with all the housework, including the cooking and the child care. In the streets of both Hong Kong and San Francisco Chinatown, the *mui jai* could be seen carrying babies and groceries on their backs. The loads they had to carry often weighed as much as they did. By the age of fourteen, the *mui jai* could be sold to the Tongs. A poor family could make a profit that way. Often, however, the *mui jai* was too sick or crippled by the age of fourteen. Then the family would have to find another way to get rid of her.

Chui Lee continued, "I was bought by the Suey Sings in Hong Kong and brought here to work for them."

"You are still quite young, Chui Lee. That couldn't have been very long ago," Ming Lee noted. "How do you feel now about what you do?"

"You can get used to anything," Chui Lee said offhandedly.

"I don't think I will ever get used to it," Ming Lee said.

"It isn't so bad. It can be made bearable by little moments of peace. And peace is easy to find. I just go to the Palace of Heavenly Peace."

"The Palace of Heavenly Peace? What is that?"

"You would like the Palace of Heavenly Peace," Chui Lee told her new friend. "Only women like us go there. Lam Wong is very good about not letting any men in the place. He makes sure we're not bothered when we're smoking."

"Smoking? You mean opium?" Ming Lee asked.

"Of course, opium," Chui Lee said.

Ming Lee looked shocked.

"Don't act so surprised," Chui Lee said. "All the singsong girls take opium."

"I have never smoked it," Ming Lee protested.

"You've probably tasted it. The Tongs slip it to the new girls all the time. You've probably had it with your tea," Chui Lee said.

"Tell me more about this Palace of Heavenly Peace," Ming Lee pressed.

"Well, I will do better than tell you. I will take you there tonight."

Kwan Ming Lee felt skeptical. She had never smoked opium. She imagined opium smokers sitting around half-dead in filthy basements by open sewers infested with rats.

But the room Yan Chui Lee took her to was clean. There were five bunks covered with clean cotton bedspreads, wool blankets and white sheets. Next to each bed was a table that held the opium equipment: the pipe itself, the lamp, the little pillbox, and the various shapes of wires and hooks for holding and manipulating the paste.

"I am afraid," Ming Lee confessed. "I am afraid of what it might do to my health."

"There is no need to be afraid. I heard of a ninety-year-old man who had worked on the railroad. One of my customers told me about him. He had smoked opium every day for seventy years. His mind is still as clear as crystal."

"But I am not an old man. I am a young woman," Ming Lee said. "And so are you."

Chui Lee laughed at her friend's hesitancy. "If you eat well, and you can afford to buy the best quality opium, you will be all right."

"What will it do to my mind?" Ming Lee asked, still frightened.

"As I said, it will give you peace," Chui Lee answered. "And there is an added benefit to opium that makes it very popular among the girls. You should know about that."

"What's that, Chui Lee?"

"If you take opium every so often, you reduce your chances of getting pregnant. You know, if you get pregnant, the Tong doesn't like it much. It means you can't work."

At first Ming Lee had been put off by Chui Lee's frank talk, but now she grew to like her. It was refreshing to have someone to share information and anxieties with. And it was encouraging to meet someone who, though hardened to her profession, was still kind and friendly. In spite of great suffering, Chui Lee had retained her sense of humor, her femininity and her humanity.

As Ming Lee watched Chui Lee's deft hands prepare the pipe for her, she felt baffled. To Ming Lee, the procedure for cooking the gummy paste seemed hopelessly complicated.

Finally, after several long minutes, Chui Lee handed Ming Lee the pipe.

"Breathe the smoke deeply into your lungs, Ming Lee."

She did so, and as she took the smoke in, she felt a wave of relaxation take over her entire body. She felt her veins grow hot, like they were on fire. But at the same time, her extremities were tingling as if she had suddenly dived into a pool of ice water. She could not remember a more pleasant feeling in her body. She felt for the first time that her body truly belonged to her. It was not something that could be bought or sold, bargained for or married off, processed or incarcerated.

"Well, how did you like your first real taste of opium peace, Ming Lee?" Chui Lee asked, when she came to visit a few days later.

"It was all right, but I wouldn't want to do it again," Ming Lee answered.

Chui Lee smiled knowingly at her friend. "We'll see about that."

Ming Lee was definite. "I doubt I will ever come to the Palace of Heavenly Peace again."

However, as the days stretched into weeks, the repetitive wearisomeness of her life continued, and Ming Lee looked forward to her visits to the place. When she went, she always partook of the ivory-tipped pipe. Opium dreams had become the only dreams in her life that held meaning.

Unfortunately, the opium habit in which she was indulging more and more was expensive. The more she took the drug, the more money she spent, diverting it from the purchase of her freedom. It was a conflict that she had trouble resolving. She needed the opium to get through her onerous nightly chore, but the more she spent for opium, the longer her release date was postponed. The only way to resolve the conflict was to increase her income, make more money, lots more. But how? She reflected on this dilemma. Then she had an idea. She thought of the woman who was a dealer of opium at the Palace of Heavenly Peace. Couldn't Ming Lee also become a dealer? Perhaps in addition to the pleasures her body afforded her customers, she could sell them a few pillboxes.

For a month, Lum Po and Man Sum blended into their surroundings on the streets of Chinatown. They discarded their highbinder-style Western sport coats, black shirts, pants and fedoras. They adopted the typical Chinese dress of the time, which included a quilted blue jacket embroidered with circular symbols of longevity. These jackets were good protection from the chilly air. San Francisco summers were characterized by coastal low-lying clouds and dense fog.

They took jobs as kitchen helpers in the newly opened Nam Jung Restaurant on Jackson Street between Stockton and Grant. They lived in a small rented room above the restaurant with the other workers. There were about ten employees living together. They shared a small stove. They also had to share the bathroom at the end of the hall with two other families. They had to work ten hours a day.

They only had Tuesdays off. They adopted this situation to become anonymous, but it was typical of Chinese immigrants of the time: long hours, low pay, crowded living quarters.

When their work schedule permitted, they walked over to Sullivan's Alley. There they tried to find out where the Suey Sings were keeping Kwan Ming Lee. They had as yet seen no sign of her. None of the girls they spoke to knew of her, or if they did, they wouldn't tell these inquisitive strangers. Occasionally Man Sum and Lum Po saw the Suey Sing *boo how doy*. But the Suey Sings did not recognize them.

They had not yet been fortunate enough to find the object of their mission. Two weeks had passed since they started working at Nam Jung. It was Tuesday afternoon. Lum Po was on his way to a fan-tan club on Stout's Alley when he suddenly spotted Ming Lee with another singsong girl. They were walking on Clay toward Kearny. Following close behind was a highbinder bodyguard, the deadly Huang King Lep.

Lum Po pursued them. He held himself at a distance to avoid being noticed. The ladies stopped between Grant and Kearny. Then they descended stairs that led to a basement under a storefront. Lum Po slowly and cautiously walked to a spot opposite the store. The storefront simply had the characters *Tai Ping Gung Si,* Pacific Trading Company. The characters were written on a plaque hung by hooks above the door. There didn't seem to be any business activity there. The windows and doors were covered by wide sheets of gritty, yellowish paper. The door to which the stairs descended was heavy oak.

Lum Po didn't try the door. He waited outside for at least two hours to see if anyone emerged or anyone else entered. Nothing happened. Finally he grew tired of waiting around. There would be other chances. He made a mental note of the location of this mysterious establishment. He noted the time of day he saw the two women and the Suey Sing enter. It was fortunate that there was only one highbinder assigned to accompany the women. He and Man Sum together could wrestle the Suey Sing man to the pavement. They could disarm him if they took him by surprise. And they would have to. All of Chinatown knew of Huang King Lep's marksmanship.

The following day, Lum Po reported what he had seen.

Man Sum was very excited. "This is our chance," he said.

"Yes, it looks that way," Lum Po replied.

"We shouldn't move right away," Man Sum said. "Not until we've watched *Tai Ping Gung Si* very carefully."

"It's only one bodyguard, but he's one of their best. Lam Wong won't take any chances with his best slave girl."

Man Sum swallowed hard. Lum Po noticed this.

Sing Man Sum had been doing a lot of thinking. He wanted to see Ming Lee again. Also, he wanted to get her away from the Suey Sings. That was the most important task. But he didn't want to turn her over to his father.

On the other hand, what was the alternative? He would have to go along with Lum Po's plan. It would be impossible for him alone to rescue Ming Lee from the Suey Sings and hide her.

However, something happened in Ross Alley which gave him an idea. One night after a hard day at the restaurant, he heard screams coming from the end of the alley. There he saw two highbinders forcibly dragging a woman around the corner. A police whistle sounded. Immediately a large Caucasian woman and two policemen were traversing the alley toward the corner around which the girl had been dragged.

Man Sum recognized the large woman. She was Sylvia Damon. She ran the Presbyterian Mission Home for runaway prostitutes. The Tong men all hated her. They called her *daaih sehk*, or "big rock," because she was built like a large rock. She stood some six feet tall, all muscle. By looking at her, one wouldn't think she was built for speed, but she could keep up with any *ging chaat*, policeman.

Often she would be accompanied by at least two policemen on her "raids," staged for the purpose of rescuing slave girls. When the "big rock" started rolling down those hills, it was said, everybody had better get out of the way. Upon Sylvia Damon's knock on any given door, the Tong men would whisk any slave girl present away, using any means of escape available, including windows, trap doors, fire escapes, roof tops, ledges, alleys, streets, and if necessary, underground passageways.

Man Sum ran around the corner to witness the girl calling out to Sylvia Damon. It was as if the large foreign devil were her mother. She called out, "*Ah Mah, Ah Mah*," the name one uses to address one's mother on the most intimate level. The policemen were pulling away the Tong men who were cursing at the top of their lungs.

"She is our property, she is our property. We paid good money for her. She's ours! You can't just steal her like this. You are thieves. Ah yah! *Faan gwai* thieves!"

Simultaneously, the girl was calling out to Sylvia Damon, calling her, "*Ah Mah*," and saying, "Save me, *Ah Mah*, save me!"

Finally, the police succeeded in prying the girl away from the highbinders. She rushed into the arms of "big rock." Sylvia Damon held her tightly, as though the girl were a long-lost daughter. She kissed the girl, saying something in English which Man Sum did not understand. The police worked over the two Tong men with their clubs.

The highbinders were left sprawled on the street, mumbling, "You fools, you idiots, we'll see you in court!"

The policemen had no idea what the heathens were saying to them. The Christian woman and the policemen left the scene in a large black squad car. The happy, rescued slave girl curled up in the loving arms of her protector.

This incident made an impression on Man Sum. After being a witness to it, he made some inquiries among the girls about the mission home. Almost without exception, the girls greeted the name with fear and revulsion. Obviously, the girls had been sufficiently warned off by the Tongs they worked for.

It was a place overrun by devils. They enticed girls into the mission home, pretending to rescue them. But in reality they enjoyed torturing young girls from China. If the girls ever hoped to marry at some point in the future, they had better not end up at Sylvia Damon's palace. There, under her direction, the white devils removed women's genitalia. This was punishment for their having been prostitutes.

Man Sum, however, succeeded in talking to one prostitute who had actually spent some time at the mission home.

"Yes, I was there for about a year," she said.

"Why did you leave?" Man Sum asked.

"I didn't want to leave. The Tong pulled a legal trick. They got me out through a writ of habeas corpus," she said.

"How could they do that legally?"

"They simply charged me with a theft. I was put in jail to await trial, and they posted my bail. The judge forgot about the trial. I was back in the Tong's hands. There was nothing I could do."

"Would you like to go back to the mission home?"

"Oh, yes, if I could, but I am so closely watched over now that I don't have a chance to breathe. I wish I could see *Ah Mah* again. She was so good and kind."

"That's not what the other girls say," Man Sum protested.

"Those stories are Tong lies! The Tongs lose from two to five thousand on the initial investment in the slave girl. Then they lose up to three hundred a month in revenue. So naturally they don't want their girls to end up in the mission home."

"Then the girls are treated well?" Man Sum asked.

"The stories of torture are completely false. We were well fed and clothed. We could develop skills and learn English. Children were treated very well, too. They could learn English and have plenty of space for recreation. Mostly, we learned about Christianity. Everybody who goes to the mission home becomes a Christian," she said.

"Christian? You mean the *faan gwai* religion?" Man Sum frowned. That part of it he didn't like.

"It is the only religion. All other religions are false. Only the Christian faith is true. That's what we were taught at the mission home."

Man Sum had now heard enough to convince him. The mission home was a paradise compared to the bagnio. Kwan Ming Lee would be absolutely safe there. He certainly did not want her to embrace the *faan gwai's* strange religion, but even if she did, her stay there would only be temporary. Afterward he could make her forget the foreign deity. Yes, Man Sum thought, it would be possible to take

Ming Lee to the mission home. He could leave her there for safekeeping. Then he'd try to raise enough money to take her out of Chinatown altogether.

He would not return her to his father.

The only difficulty with his plan was Lum Po. Man Sum needed Lum Po to undertake the initial rescue, but then Man Sum would have to rescue Ming Lee a second time. That meant eluding Lum Po after the successful rescue from the Suey Sings. He only hoped he would not have to harm Lum Po.

A week after Lum Po told Man Sum about the storefront on Clay, the two of them went there after work. They watched for movements in or out. They saw only women go in. Each one had her own key.

Then Man Sum saw Ming Lee.

"It is she," he said. The words came out involuntarily.

"That's right," Lum Po replied, looking at him.

She had been on Man Sum's thoughts for so long. He dared not count the days his mind had been preoccupied with her image.

She came with the other woman Lum Po had mentioned. The highbinder was there, too, like a dog trailing behind them. He looked mean and bored. All three descended the stairs together, but before they entered the place, the highbinder looked back. He saw the two men observing them.

"We've been spotted," Lum Po said. "We can't stay here. He'll call the Tong for reinforcements. He suspects us. Let's get out of here."

Confirming Lum Po's fears, Huang King Lep poked his head out the door and again looked at them. Then he immediately closed the door.

Man Sum said, "If we've been noticed, they'll have

more Suey Sings posted to guard her. We've got to move now while there's an opening.''

"No, no. You must be crazy. How can we move now?''

Man Sum was already making his way toward the short stairway.

"Are you a crazy idiot? What are you doing?''

Lum Po barely kept himself from yelling at Man Sum. But by this time Man Sum was at the door. He tried it. Locked. He smelled opium.

"You fool, Man Sum. What did you expect? You idiot. Have you gone mad? Get away from that door. Now!''

Man Sum pulled out his revolver and was about to fire at the door to destroy the lock, but Lum Po pulled out his own weapon and aimed it at Man Sum.

"Just a minute. Turn around, Man Sum, what do you think you're trying to do, get us both killed? That marksman will be on the other side of the door. You're a dead man if you go in there. Now come away from there. You'll get us both killed.''

Lum Po was right, Man Sum decided. He quickly backtracked to the other side of the street.

The expression on Lum Po's face blended sheer amazement with rage. How could anyone act so stupidly as Man Sum just had?

Lum Po whispered angrily, "We've got to get out of here. You're being impulsive. You're a hopeless novice!''

They climbed to the roof top over their room. They could talk privately there. Even with their jackets on, it was chilly on the roof. A billowy blanket of fog moved slowly on the bay toward them. Foghorns sounded mournfully.

"All right, I admit it," Man Sum said after a pause. "I acted stupidly."

"Why? Why did you do it?" Lum Po implored.

"I don't know," Man Sum answered. "I saw her and I—"

"You what?" Lum Po asked suspiciously. "Do you still have feelings for this woman? Is it some sort of love sickness that's driving you crazy, or what?"

Man Sum had to be careful. He could not be honest with Lum Po. He suddenly straightened and said, "How could I? I know she is to be my father's wife, my future stepmother."

"Don't lie! You are a fool in love with that whore. That's what's turned you into a coward and foolhardy idiot! Now stop being crazy," Lum Po said. "I mean it." He stared at Man Sum with narrowed eyes.

Man Sum looked away.

Lum Po took out his revolver and pointed it directly at Man Sum's heart. There was a pause. In spite of the chill, Man Sum felt himself breaking out in a sweat.

"No more craziness," Lum Po said. "You saw me take the eye out of the squirrel. I can do the same to you. You won't see me coming either. It will be dark. There will be a flash of light and you will be a corpse in the alley. Don't be tempted to play the traitor with me. Do you understand?"

"I understand," Man Sum replied. He was beginning to wish he had let Lum Po finish hanging himself on the island.

Lum Po put away the revolver. He walked to the other side of the roof and looked down on Clay Street. "We might have to stand off a whole Suey Sing army to rescue the girl." He wheeled around, facing Man Sum. "Are you ready for that?"

"Whatever it takes," Man Sum said, "to accomplish the rescue."

Chapter 16

The next day, during their break, they huddled in a corner of the restaurant and Lum Po began drawing a sketch of the storefront on a paper napkin.

"It will be a difficult task," Lum Po said. "We are very far from accomplishing it. Easy for one and all to die in the attempt. Including Kwan Ming Lee."

"This is the best way. Plan it out. Think it out on paper. Now we both have an idea of what the layout looks like," Man Sum said.

"That's why we went there in the first place," Lum Po said, looking at Man Sum. "We didn't go there to make an unplanned attack."

"I know, Lum Po. I made a mistake. It won't happen again," Man Sum said for the hundredth time.

"You said you smelled opium?" Lum Po asked.

"It is an opium place," Man Sum told him. "I'm sure of it."

"Since there are only women, it must be for the singsong girls alone," Lum Pro reasoned.

"That means that Ming Lee is taking the drug," Man Sum said. All the more reason to get her away from the Tongs, he thought to himself. The longer she continues that habit, the more difficult it will be to break it. Also, it would make her weaker and weaker. She must be pulled away from it, and quickly.

Lum Po made a sketch of the *Tai Ping Gung Si* on the paper napkin. He drew in Clay Street, Kearny and Grant. He noted, "The basement appears to have no windows at all. The only entrance is the oak door at the foot of the short stairway."

"But isn't there an entrance to the basement from the inside of the store? That would be another possibility."

"There's probably a stairway on the inside, but most likely it leads to a locked door to the basement," Lum Po answered.

"We must get inside that store. Our entrance from the inside of the store would not be expected. We would have the advantage of surprise," Man Sum contended.

"But there is still the problem of the Suey Sing highbinder, Huang King Lep," Lum Po said, "and maybe others."

"I have an idea," Man Sum said, hitting the table with his palm. "Suppose we posted a *Chun Hung* on the dead wall? We could make an arrangement to meet the Suey Sings at Waverly Place. We'd affix the Chi Sing seal to the document. In that way, we could divert the Suey Sing highbinders to the location of the battle. Except no one would be there to fight them."

"Hmm. That's not a bad strategy, Man Sum," Lum Po said. He seemed genuinely impressed.

"Once they got to Waverly, they'd realize they were tricked. They'd go back to Clay real quick. But meanwhile, we could enter the store. We'd blast our way through the basement door if necessary. Then we would have our prize."

"Sounds like a good enough plan," Lum Po agreed.

"Maybe you're not so dumb after all, Man Sum." His face broke into a smile.

At that moment, it seemed to Man Sum that the old Lum Po was back.

They proceeded to purchase the red paper, the brush and the ink for the *Chun Hung*. Man Sum carefully brushed on the elaborate calligraphy necessary for a convincing challenge.

The Suey Sings lost no time entering their answer. The typical highbinder threats were repeated in their own *Chun Hung*. Curses were drawn in perfect penmanship. Their *Chun Hung* was as artistically rendered as any wedding invitation.

Secretly, Man Sum wrote another letter. He addressed it to "*Ah Mah*, 910 Sacramento." The letter was written in Chinese. Man Sum hoped it would be translated by one of the reformed singsong girls at the mission home.

The letter said, "Please come to 325 Clay Street at ten a.m. on July 30. A slave girl is in trouble there. You will please take her with you. Help her to escape her slavery. You will know her by red paper flower pinned to her dress, left side."

The thirtieth arrived quickly. Lum Po and Man Sum stationed themselves at a distant vantage point long before "*Ah Mah*" was scheduled to show up. After a lengthy wait, they saw two men accompany the two women to the Clay Street location. One was the highbinder who had been escorting the women. The other was a newcomer, not dressed in highbinder garb.

The highbinder left the women in charge of this newcomer. Then he went to join his brothers in the third major Chi Sing-Suey Sing showdown.

Lum Po and Man Sum crept toward 325 Clay. They

prepared to make the final assault. They brought their tool chest with them. It consisted of a small sledge, some rope, and some pieces of cloth for gags.

They broke the glass portion of the door and entered the store. They found the doorway at the bottom of stairs inside. This door they found to be open. When they entered, they saw five women lying on cots, in various states of stupefaction. Attracted by the noise, the guard went out to the front of the building, whence he thought the noise had come. The rescuers followed, disarmed him, tied him up, gagged him.

Man Sum returned to the smoke-filled room.

"Hurry up and bring Ming Lee outside," Lum Po said. "I will keep watch. It's ten o'clock. The Suey Sings are at Waverly now. They will soon discover they have been duped."

Waverly Place was not far from the corner of Kearny and Clay. No point in Chinatown was very far away from any other.

Man Sum touched Ming Lee. She didn't respond, but he was overwhelmed by the sensation of touching her. He reached down and cupped her face, then he kissed her several times.

"Ming Lee, it is me, Sing Man Sum. I am taking you away from your life of slavery."

"Yes, Man Sum. Yes, I know you're here, Man Sum. I know it's you. I will go with you, anywhere you say, Man Sum." But she saw no difference between his real face and the face of her visions.

"Ming Lee, it is me, Man Sum, really me. I love you, Ming Lee," Man Sum said.

"Yes, Man Sum, my one only true love. I am ready to go with you. I am going with you now. We are going hand in hand to paradise."

"No, no, Ming Lee. Wake up. I am alive, real. We have to get out of here," Man Sum said, desperately shaking her.

Ming Lee wouldn't budge. "We will live together, all of us. In heaven together, in the Palace of Heavenly Peace."

"But we have to hurry, we have to leave right away. We can't stay here. The Suey Sing Tong men are on their way. If they find me trying to rescue you, they will kill us. Hurry, Ming Lee."

He looked into her eyes. She was looking back at him, talking to him, addressing him by name. But she was not talking to him at all. Her eyes were gazing past him. The sound of her voice was very far away. It was as though she were separated from him by an infinity of space, an eternity of time.

"We have to hurry, we have to leave right away. We can't stay here," she said, repeating Man Sum's exact words. But instead of making any effort to move, she put the pipe to the lamp's flame.

Man Sum tried to stop her, but it was too late. "No, Ming Lee, no more of that now!"

She breathed in the powerful fumes again. She settled down more deeply into the cushions.

"Oh, Man Sum," she sighed. "How very handsome you are. How wonderful to see you again, Man Sum. You have been in my thoughts many long hours, my love. You are here to stay."

"No we can't stay here!"

"There are trees, brooks, and beautiful little jade pagodas. So many places to worship in heaven. It is filled with the gods."

"Ming Lee, wake up!" he said, shaking her again.

Man Sum saw that Ming Lee was absolutely oblivious

to his presence. The other women were equally intoxicated. They had no idea that two strange men had just entered the opium den.

Man Sum shook her again, with even more urgency. "Ming Lee, I am not a phantom. I am real. I am really here. I am here because I love you. I have always loved you. It doesn't matter what's happened to you. We can still be husband and wife."

Then there were tears in Ming Lee's eyes. Suddenly, a very sober expression crossed her face. For the first time, she really did see him.

"Man Sum," she said.

As though she had forgotten something of the utmost importance, she took the jade ring off her index finger and handed it to Man Sum.

"I almost forgot," she said, "I wanted to give this to you. It's the ring of the jade emperor. It will make you wealthy, but you must be careful. You must not let the emperor see it on you. If he does, he will cut off your finger."

Man Sum accepted the gift, though he didn't understand its significance. "Thank you," he said simply.

Ming Lee had already sunk back into her reverie. Just then Lum Po burst into the room, his weapon drawn, shouting, "They're here! The Suey Sings are here!"

The ladies registered no reaction whatsoever.

Man Sum quickly pinned the red paper flower to Ming Lee's dress. "Ming Lee, this flower is for you. You must wear it. Wear it for me. Don't take it off."

"What a beautiful flower, Man Sum." Dreamily she tilted her head and looked at the flower.

Lum Po was nervously shaking Man Sum's shoulders. "The building is surrounded. We don't have a chance of getting out alive. The best shots in Chinatown are out there. They're going to get in the store. Grab Ming Lee. Bring her up there, up the stairs.''

"What?''

"What's wrong with you, you want to die? Are you that crazy?''

Suddenly Lum Po grabbed Ming Lee himself. He went up the stairs, carrying her in his arms. Man Sum followed.

Lum Po set Ming Lee down and tore the shades off the door. Light flooded the store, throwing weird shadows around the strewn debris. The Suey Sing highbinders were outside, on the street, about to enter. Lum Po held his gun to Ming Lee's temple.

He addressed the Suey Sings through the already broken window of the door. "I promise you, if you fire a shot or take another step, I will finish her.''

Lum Po's threat stopped the Suey Sings in their tracks. They were convinced by Lum Po's tone that the Chi Sing man was serious. They didn't want to lose one of the best singsong girls in their collection.

The stand-off lasted several minutes, but it was brought to an abrupt halt by the police. They arrived in squad cars and a paddy wagon. There were about twenty-five uniformed men in all.

"*Faan gwai ging chaat*, white devil policemen,'' the Suey Sings murmured.

The police held long-barreled shotguns and handcuffs.

"Drop your weapons and raise your hands!'' one of the officers said.

The Suey Sings reluctantly complied.

The highbinders were rounded up and forced to hand over their weapons. They were then herded into the paddy wagon.

Nobody paid any attention to Lum Po. He was screaming at the top of his lungs, "I will kill her! I will kill her!"

A large lady stepped out of one of the squad cars. She was Miss Sylvia Damon. Boldly she strode up to the store where Lum Po was still holding the gun to Ming Lee's head. She said to him, "Come along, young man, let that girl go, now. She doesn't belong to you, you know. She doesn't realize it yet, poor thing, but she belongs to our Lord Jesus Christ."

"*Jo mut yeh ahh?* What's going on?" Lum Po demanded.

"We all belong to our Lord," Sylvia Damon said.

Lum Po repeated, "*Mm ho yuk ah. Yuk yat bo, ngo da sey kui la,* don't move or I'll kill her."

Although the police and Miss Damon didn't know Chinese, they understood Lum Po quite well. They didn't move forward an inch. A stalemate had been reached.

There was only one person who could break it. That was Man Sum. He stood behind Lum Po. If Man Sum acted now, the consequences would be great. He would suddenly, with one gesture, become the enemy of Lum Po and his own father. The stakes were high, but he had to do it, even if it meant gambling with his life, and that of his love.

In one quick movement, Choy Wu's son grabbed the gun out of Lum Po's hand and directed it toward his friend.

"*Doy mm ji,* I am sorry," Man Sum said, "that I must do this thing. Please understand. I cannot let her be my father's slave!"

"You are a traitor!" Lum Po spat contemptuously.

"I am doing what I know is right. I tried reason. Now I must use action."

"You are already a dead man," Lum Po told him.

"When your father hears what you have done, he will empty the war chest to pay for your head on a pie plate."

"I will not be taken easily!" Man Sum asserted. He surprised himself with the strength of his own voice.

He then put his arm around Ming Lee's waist and led her gently toward the ample, welcoming bosom of Sylvia Damon.

Two burly officers easily subdued a stunned Lum Po. The expression of surprise and anger on Lum Po's face told Man Sum that their friendship was over. Man Sum would now be branded a traitor to the Chi Sing Tong. A price would indeed be put on his head, and Lum Po would probably be hired to kill him by Sing Choy Wu. The thought made him shudder. Man Sum had reasoned out the consequences of his action. But he couldn't escape inner conflict, guilt. He was, after all, a Chi Sing Tong man. And that part of him would not forgive.

News of his action would undoubtedly be sent back to his village in China.

"Sing Man Sum is a traitor to his father."

He would not be able to return to his own village. They would have no respect for him. He would be treated like a contaminated ghost. He would be assigned no tasks. Even the simple farmer's tasks would be denied him out of fear that he would do something destructive.

"An unfilial son is a broken plow. Useless."

Where would he go now? To whom would he turn? He was an outcast both in Chinatown and his native village.

The Suey Sing highbinders were all released on bail the following day. Lum Po had been in touch with Sing Choy Wu. He related the entire incident to him. Sing Choy Wu had the bail supplied to Lum Po through the lawyer, Porter.

Man Sum was now the only highbinder left in the county jail. No one supplied the bail money to get him out. He felt fairly sure his father, who would by now have heard what happened, would leave him in jail as a punishment. He also reasoned that Lum Po would probably be on his way back to Fresno soon. There he would make a full report of the incident.

He was right. The lawyer gave Lum Po a train ticket to Fresno. Sing Choy Wu met Lum Po at the train station. The two of them went to have tea at the only teahouse in Fresno's Chinatown, Gum Lung Cha Lau.

"I hear everything you say, Lum Po," Sing Choy Wu said after listening to Lum Po's recounting of what happened. "But it is still very hard for me to believe it."

"Your son has been acting strangely since he arrived in Gum San," Lum Po said.

"Yes, but to do this, hand Ming Lee over to that woman after disarming you. It is an act of the most blatant treason."

"My theory is that Man Sum is crazy," said Lum Po. "He was made crazy on the island because his coaching papers didn't help him to pass the interrogation. He has never recovered from that bruise on his soul."

"It is kind of you to call him crazy, Lum Po. But perhaps my son is simply a bad luck man."

"There is another explanation for your son's failure, sir."

"And what is that, Lum Po?"

"The woman."

"Yes. The woman. Surely," Choy Wu replied. "I am sorry he wanted her. He saw her first, after all. He perhaps should have been the one to have her. Then none of this would have happened. Father and son love one woman. No good can come of that."

"That is what has happened to him, I am sure of it. He has never forgotten the kindness of that woman, Ming Lee. And he imagines she loves him."

"True," Choy Wu nodded. "In this he suffers delusion."

Lum Po continued, "There is no reason to kill him, he is crazy. He will just destroy himself."

Choy Wu thought for a moment, then said, "Well, there is nothing I can do for him, if the boy has a sick soul. He is of no more use to us than dung on the path. He must be removed or we'll never get our cart through. We will post his bail. You will be waiting at the jail for him to be released. Follow him closely. When the opportunity presents itself, remove this obstacle from my life." Choy Wu's voice faltered as he choked back a sob.

Lum Po nodded. The order saddened him also. He had hoped the exalted master would not assign him to kill his friend. Now there was no choice. True, Man Sum had betrayed them, but Man Sum was just crazy. That was all there was to the matter.

"Yes, sir," Lum Po said. "I will do as you have commanded."

"And while you are at it, Lum Po, there is another piece of unfinished business to take care of."

"What is that, exalted master?"

"Chu Mae Pong. Let us not forget her. There is an account to settle with that traitor. She owes us a considerable debt."

"I will see that the payment is collected," Lum Po promised.

Chapter 17

In the back seat of the squad car, Kwan Ming Lee, sur-rounded by whites, began to cry, "*Faan gwai, faan gwai!*"

She was still under the influence of opium. It seemed to her she was on her way to hell itself. A strange, large woman tried to put a comforting arm around her. Ming Lee only saw a demon's hand reaching out to grasp her and pull her down to the hellish realms. The rescued singsong girl screamed.

Someone sitting next to her spoke to her in Chinese, saying, "You really have nothing to fear. That is your *Ah Mah*. She is not a devil. All she wants to do is help you and protect you."

She wished Madame Chu were here to protect her. Ming Lee had not seen her in such a long time. She had disappeared.

The car stopped on the steep Sacramento Street hill by a large brick building. Ming Lee had to be carried out of the car. Once they were inside the building, the large doors were bolted. All at once, Kwan Ming Lee was met by cheers and applause. The shiny faces of ten young Chinese women greeted her. They didn't look like reformed slave girls. They looked more like the daughters of some visiting Chinese dignitary.

"Who are these girls?" Ming Lee asked in Chinese.

"They are all singsong girls like you, Ming Lee," Sylvia Damon told her.

"We are singsong girls," one of the girls repeated. "And most of us have been pressed into the lowest service of them all, the 'cribs' of Sullivan's and Ross Alley."

If they bore any scars from their experience, one wouldn't know it to look at them now. They looked clean, well dressed, well fed. They looked prosperous!

After applauding Ming Lee, they all embraced their beloved *Ah Mah*. It was as though she were really their mother.

"*Ah Mah's* been successful again. She made another rescue."

"Another victory for Jesus!" yet another voice said.

"It's good to be back with my girls!" *Ah Mah* said. "And I thank the Lord, safe and sound. No scars, no wounds."

The girls all competed with one another for a second embrace from *Ah Mah*.

Seeing these shiny Chinese girls hug this big white devil turned Ming Lee's stomach. Her knees grew weak. She began to feel faint.

Ah Mah said, "She's tired and frightened. We'll take good care of her. See that she is washed and clothed. And then give her some soup. She looks starved, poor girl, and drugged as well. The food will help to speed up the wearing off of the opium."

The girls hustled and bustled to carry out *Ah Mah's* orders. They seemed to understand perfectly the meaning of her words. Each of the girls had apparently learned the barbarian tongue.

Ming Lee's first few days at the mission home were very pleasant. 910 Sacramento was not at all the place of torture the Tongs had led Ming Lee to believe. She was surrounded by cheerful and affectionate people. She actually felt more secure than she had at any other time since she'd left her family.

There were household duties to perform. The girls swept and mopped bathroom and kitchen floors. They did the cooking. They kept the hallway and living room carpets immaculately clean. They dusted everywhere. The work was shared by everybody, and the girls' spirit of cooperation made their tasks light. It was much easier than the work she did for her mother-in-law. There she had to do all the chores alone. Also, her mother-in-law had often lashed her with a cruel tongue. At the mission home, everybody spoke nicely. Everybody smiled. They were always so kind.

Then Ming Lee had the biggest surprise of all. At the mission home, she met the woman who'd first shown her Chinatown. It was the woman who'd gotten her started in the singsong girl's routine. It was Chu Mae Pong.

"Yes, Ming Lee," she said, "I have come to be a follower of our Lord Jesus Christ as *Ah Mah* has taught me."

"Chu Mae Pong! How good it is to see you again! You just disappeared. And nobody told me where you went," Ming Lee said.

"You see, the Suey Sing Tong had no use for me. They just turned me out on the streets. I was terrified that Sing Choy Wu had put a price on my head," Mae Pong said.

"Yes, he probably did," Kwan Ming Lee replied. "He will not forget your role in my abduction."

"There was nowhere I could be safe, except here,

with *Ah Mah*. I knew about the mission home. But I had always held it in contempt. So although I was terrified, I walked up to 910 Sacramento and asked to be admitted," Mae Pong said.

"And you were accepted without questions?" Ming Lee asked.

"They were very skeptical at first. I had a reputation as one of the most influential madams in Chinatown. But finally they admitted me," Mae Pong responded.

"Do you think they have accepted me also, Mae Pong?" Ming Lee inquired.

"The girls are so full of trust that it isn't difficult to earn acceptance. And then you find that this place becomes your home. These people become your family."

The mission home continued to puzzle Ming Lee. One day she asked Madame Chu, "We do very little work, each of us. We do housework and crochet. We are fed well and clothed. Is nothing else expected of us?"

Mae Pong gave her an understanding smile. "All that is expected is that we do our share of the chores around 910. And we must do our best to be helpful to one another. We are all expected to come to the aid of someone who is sick or grieved."

"I can't understand why people are so kind to me. What have I done to deserve it?" Ming Lee asked.

"We are also supposed to pay particular attention to first arrivals, such as yourself. They are in a delicate situation. Tongs have instilled in them a lot of fear regarding the mission home."

"Yes," Ming Lee admitted, "I heard plenty of terrible stories about it."

"But we all work together to cheer the newcomer up and make her feel at home, and she soon forgets those initial fears. That is what happened with you. You were terrified of everyone and everything here in the beginning. Now you feel all right about being here, don't you?"

"Yes, I feel all right now, I guess," Ming Lee said somewhat uncertainly.

Mae Pong put her hand on Ming Lee's shoulder affectionately. "You're doing fine, just fine. Some girls don't know how to get over their fear. Some of them leave and go back to their former life. When that happens we are all very saddened."

One afternoon a week later, there was suddenly a heavy knock on the door. Miss Damon opened it and was confronted by a policeman and a Chinese man. The Chinese man identified himself as Lam Wong.

The policeman said, "This man claims there is a Kwan Ming Lee staying here."

Miss Damon replied, "There is no such person living here."

"Well," the policeman said, "this Mr. Wong has a complaint. He says—"

"Kwan Ming Lee stole some money from the cash register of my store on Stockton," Lam Wong interrupted the policeman.

The policeman nodded. "Yes, we have to bring her down to the station for questioning."

"I just finished telling you," Miss Damon said, somewhat irately, "no one by that name lives here."

"I'm sorry, Miss Damon, but Mr. Wong insists that she is here. I have taken the trouble to obtain a warrant, so I'm afraid I'm going to have to search the premises."

Ming Lee did not hear the last part of this. She was immediately taken down to the basement by four girls. Two of the girls removed some barrels from the side of the wall, revealing a small secret panel in that wall. Ming Lee was shut up in the tiny space. It wasn't large enough to stand up in.

"You won't have to stay there long, Ming Lee," one of the girls told her, "but you better keep still. Don't move a muscle."

"We don't want you to be returned to your Tong master," another girl said. Then no one spoke.

After the panel door was slid shut, Ming Lee heard the barrels being replaced. She heard the shuffling of feet. Then silence.

No matter which way she sat in the tiny space, she was uncomfortable. Finally she bent her head over and placed it between her knees. She tried to remain as still as she could. Her legs quivered. The muscles in her back felt strained. The pain of holding that position was unbearable.

She was about to change position when she heard Lam Wong and the police officer in the basement, talking. They could not be more than five feet away. She had to stay hunched over, yet she felt that if they didn't leave soon, she would have to give herself away.

They said something to each other in English. Then they started removing the barrels. She could hear the barrels rolling and scraping along the basement floor. After that, the two men began drumming on the wall behind which she was hidden. They used their fists. Ming Lee's heart almost stopped.

After a while, the men discontinued the search. They mumbled angrily and their voices receded as they walked away.

Why hadn't they been able to find the hollow place in the wall? She wondered. The basement door shut, and she breathed a sigh of relief.

Soon her sisters returned and pried her out of her

hiding place. Immediately they began to massage her neck and her back.

"You must be prepared to go into hiding several times like that," Mae Pong said. "The tongs often take girls from the mission home to the county jail. Some false charge is brought against them, then the Tong supplies the bail money to take you out. Once they've got you out on bail, they've got you in their hands. You disappear quick."

"Disappear? What happens?"

"The girls who are 'bailed out' like that are never heard from again. Either they are watched more carefully so they cannot make an escape, or they are taken out of Chinatown altogether. Or maybe they're simply killed. You see why we were so careful to put you in a good hiding place?"

"Why couldn't they find the secret panel?" Ming Lee asked.

Mae Pong answered, "Except for that tiny space in which you sat, cramped, the wall is very solid. They did not happen to touch the hollow part."

Every Sunday morning, Wu Ting Lee led the Sunday school discussion group. The discussion group preceded the church services which were held in the chapel.

Wu Ting Lee was about thirty-five. She had been at the mission home longer than anyone else.

Now Wu Ting Lee was a leader of the girls, second in command to only *Ah Mah* herself. Ting Lee could speak Cantonese as well as Toisanese. She was appointed the task of missionary to the "daughters." She was the English instructor, too. On Sunday mornings, she made clear exactly what was expected of *Ah Mah's* daughters. They must become Christians. No images of the Chinese deities were allowed around the mission home. The girls weren't permitted to have any books written by China's great religious sages. Buddha, Lao Tze and Confucius were all wise, but misguided.

Every Sunday, Ting Lee repeated the Christian message. "The Holy Bible is the authority of Christianity. Chinese religious books were written by men. But the Holy Bible was written by God Himself. So the Bible is infallible. Nothing in the Bible can be disputed. Theologians disagree sometimes, but no Christians are in doubt as to its central message.

"That message states that human beings are utterly lost creatures. They are lost because of something called sin which every person in the world was born with. Sin came into the world through the first man and the first woman. They ate forbidden fruit from the tree of knowledge in God's own paradise, the Garden of Eden. When Adam and Eve disobeyed God, they were ordered to cover themselves and they were expelled from the Garden of Eden. They were sent into the cold world to make their way without God's help.

"Sin is any action taken contrary to God's laws. Prostitution is sin as is gambling, killing, and smoking opium. You singsong girls are guilty of sin, perhaps more than other people. You have violated the sacred uses of the body. You have done things God intended only for married couples. You made those sinful actions your daily life. So you have violated God's laws not once only, but again and again and again. For this you will be punished in hellfire.

"The worst sinners are punished more. They are made to suffer terrible torments. They're sent to a lower circle in hell. They're completely unredeemable. So they have to suffer excruciating torments throughout eternity, without relief. It is no use saying prayers for them.

"The Chinese religion teaches that one simply has to bury the body in the right place. At the funeral, priests try to deceive the evil spirits. This attitude is greatly mistaken. It dangerously assumes man has some power over God and the Devil. If some priests perform some tricks, everything will be okay. This is very far from the truth. God cannot be bribed or tricked. Red paper with holes in it to trap evil spirits will not help the sinner on his journey to the grave.

"It doesn't help to reform, either. You girls have left your way of life and have joined the mission home. You are no longer prostitutes, but that's not good enough. You can't make sins go away by promising God you will be good girls.

"The other day, Kwan Ming Lee was almost lost to the Tong a second time. If they had found her, she would have had to resume her sinful ways. That could happen to any of you. The Tongs are very clever. They use their legal trickery, and they get you back. What then? Unfortunately, sin committed under the direction of the Tongs is still sin.

"Is there a way out of this seemingly hopeless condition? Yes, there is a way out of the torment of hell. But that way is provided not by people, but by God Himself. God sent His only Son, Jesus Christ, down to earth. It was an act of great kindness. Sinful man, however, nailed Christ to a cross in Jerusalem. Through God's miracle, Christ bore in his death all the sins of humankind. This was God's great gift to humans.

" 'God so loved the world that He gave His only begotten Son.'

"You must believe that this is indeed true. God really has sent His Son to die for *your* sins. Then it is possible for you to be saved. Merely believe in Jesus Christ. Then the wonderful truth of His death on the Cross will transform you. And He himself will enter your black heart.''

While Kwan Ming Lee was listening to this Sunday school message, she noticed that the other girls were watching her. The reason was easy to guess. She was the most recent arrival at the mission home, and so far she was the only girl who had not committed herself to the Christian truth. She found the *faan gwai* religion interesting, but she was not ready to throw out all the deities she had known since she was a child.

What about her ancestors? Could she no longer pay them homage? She couldn't give up Kuan Yin, goddess of mercy. Who would listen to her tears? It would be impossible to make a commitment so soon to this new God. What did the Chinese deities think of Jesus Christ? She would ask them and find out. But, she realized, here at the mission home there was no opportunity to consult the gods. It was strictly forbidden to even mention them. So Ming Lee did not respond to this call for commitment.

Wu Ting Lee and all the other former singsong girls were disappointed.

Ting Lee would corner Kwan Ming Lee on occasion. ''Have you made your decision for Christ yet?'' she would ask Ming Lee.

''I'm still thinking about it,'' Ming Lee would reply, looking away or resuming some chore.

The others girls gently pressured Ming Lee, too. They would sometimes say, knowing Ming Lee was listening, ''Christ has certainly meant a lot to me. My life is different now. Since I allowed Christ to come into my heart, I haven't been the same.''

Ming Lee had to admit that the girls looked happy. They had obviously benefited from their new faith in the

Western God. Maybe, though, it was just the good food and the pleasant surroundings.

It also seemed that the girls were very similar to one another. They all expressed themselves in the same way. Evidently, the Christian vow was not quite enough. A convert also had to conform to some kind of unspoken code of behavior. These girls were cheerful all of the time. There were no exceptions.

But what were they cheerful about? They had no real freedoms. They could not go out. They were still pursued by their previous owners.

Sometimes Tong men would attack 910 Sacramento directly. Once, a stick of dynamite about to explode was found on the front steps of the mission home. Another time, a highbinder attempted to retrieve his Tong's stolen girl. He made an assault on the second story window. Fortunately, the windows were all barred and he couldn't get through.

The girls had a lot to worry about. Their lives, though better than they had been, were far from ideal. Yet they all manifested this consistent and unwavering cheerfulness. It seemed to be somewhat forced.

One night in November, the Tong struck the mission home with a death blow.

Ming Lee and Mae Pong were talking quietly after supper. The other girls were resting before their evening chores.

Suddenly they heard a woman's voice calling from outside, ''Mae Pong, Mae Pong!''

Several of the girls, including Mae Pong, went to the window.

''That voice, I recognize that voice!'' Mae Pong exclaimed. ''It is Shei Wai Tam!''

"Who is this Shei Wai Tam?" Ting Lee wanted to know.

"Shei Wai Tam is a singsong girl. She is also a friend. I managed the house where she worked. It was when I worked for the Chi Sing Tong," Mae Pong explained.

"Didn't you say the Chi Sings have a price on your head?" one of the girls asked.

"Mae Pong," the voice cried, "Mae Pong, I must speak with you. Please, come out!"

Ting Lee gingerly opened the drape a little. "Look across the street, Mae Pong. Do you recognize her? Is it she you spoke of?"

"It is she," Mae Pong said enthusiastically. "I must go to her. Probably she wants the help of the mission home."

Ting Lee said, "We'd better tell Miss Damon. *Ah Mah* will go out and speak to her."

"Mae Pong, please, come out! I must talk to you," the voice from the street called again. It sounded desperate, plaintive.

"Don't call Miss Damon," Mae Pong said. "I'll go. I want to have the honor of rescuing Wai Tam myself."

"Be careful," Ting Lee said. "Bring her inside the house right away. Tell her she has nothing to fear from us!"

Mae Pong opened the door and went outside. Ting Lee watched from the window with the other girls as Mae Pong crossed Sacramento Street.

Mae Pong approached the girl. Shei Wai Tam said something. Then a smile came over Mae Pong, and she embraced Wai Tam.

The two continued talking.

"Why don't they hurry and come inside?" Ting Lee said nervously.

Suddenly another shape emerged from the shadows. It was a man in an overcoat and a fedora hat.

Ting Lee lost no time. She ran to the door. "Mae Pong!" she screamed.

It was too late. There was a flash of steel, then Mae Pong fell. The shape took Shei Wai Tam's arm. She didn't look back. The singsong girl and the highbinder disappeared into the shadows and the fog.

"Mae Pong, Mae Pong!" Ming Lee cried. She tried to go outside, but one of the girls restrained her.

"Don't go out there, Ming Lee. There may be more highbinders."

Sylvia Damon was summoned. Ting Lee and Sylvia Damon went onto the street. They carried Mae Pong inside. They put sheets over the couch, then they laid her there. Blood drenched the sheets. Another of the girls called a doctor. Sylvia Damon listened to Mae Pong's heart.

"Nothing can be done," she said. "We've lost her."

For days, Ming Lee spoke to no one. She would not leave her room, remaining there to rock on her knees and weep. Over and over she called on the name of Kuan Yin. But heaven gave no answer, no reason for the death of her friend.

Ting Lee overheard Ming Lee praying, and this disturbed the Christian.

"Ming Lee, Ming Lee," she said. "Come join us. Join the other girls. Don't stay up here alone."

"This place is not safe!" Ming Lee said angrily. "We are not safe from Chinatown here. From the Tongs. You have lied to us. You and Sylvia Damon. We are not rescued, not saved. We are still slave girls. And we will always be nothing but dirty slave girls to you and to everyone else.''

"You are not dirty to Christ, Ming Lee. Christ loves you. And Christ loved Mae Pong, too. That's where Mae Pong is now, Ming Lee. Mae Pong is with our Lord. Why? Because, she believed in Him. She died as He did, attempting to save a sinner. Her death could not bring her more honor.''

That night, Ming Lee had a dream. She dreamt she was speaking with her mother-in-law. Her mother-in-law only shook her head. At that moment, Ming Lee realized that she was speaking to her mother-in-law from a prostrate position. Ming Lee was looking up from inside the coffin. She was the corpse. Now the lid was being nailed down by her mother-in-law, and as the nails went into the wood, Ming Lee felt nails pierce her own body.

She drummed on the coffin lid, but no one heard her. Her mother-in-law and the officiating priests were burying her alive. Long moments passed. Then a hideous demon's hands reached up from the ground and began fondling her. They were crude, inhuman touches, like those of her customers.

She heard voices calling out all around her, "Dirty, dirty, how dirty she is.'' But she continued to bang at the coffin lid with her fists.

Then she yelled out at the top of her lungs, "Jesus Christ, save me.''

All at once, the lid was torn off and a man was standing there. He had a beautiful, gentle face, flowing robes, and long hair. Ming Lee embraced him, and although she then woke up, she still felt his presence in the room. He was as real as the walls that surrounded her.

It was about three in the morning, but Ming Lee was too happy to contain herself. She went around the entire house waking up people and telling them that she had allowed the Lord Jesus Christ into her heart. She had decided to become a Christian.

About twenty-five sleepy women all put on their bathrobes. They were joined by *Ah Mah* herself. The missionary woman was so glad to hear the news that she wept. They all went downstairs to the main room. The rest of that evening they sang hymns together and joined hands in prayers of thanksgiving.

The district attorney, Matt Davis, reviewed the 325 Clay Street Tong battle. He noted that there were no murders. The Chinese only brandished their weapons briefly. Therefore, he recommended a dismissal of all the charges. This was preferable to a long, unsatisfying trial. Shyster lawyers, hired with Tong money, would be sure to win. They would obtain the release of the *boo how doy,* anyway.

The judge agreed. The sole prisoner left in county jail, Sing Man Sum, was released.

Man Sum did not know where to go, what to do. He knew a price would be placed on his head. His life wouldn't last much longer if he stayed in Chinatown. He had to leave, get out of Chinatown altogether. But where could he go?

As he left the jail, shots immediately rang out. They were aimed at him. He didn't know who was firing at him, but he didn't wait to find out. He ran with all the strength his legs could summon. Footsteps clattered behind him. From Broadway and Columbus to Grant was only a few yards. Man Sum headed for Grant, then the nearest alley, Sullivan's. He managed to elude his attacker in the darkness of the network of intersecting alleyways.

But he realized he would not be safe anywhere in Chinatown. Evidently, the Tongs were ganging up on him, so while it was still dark, he made his way to Market Street. Then he fled south of Market to Townsend and the railroad tracks. A freight train was at rest on the tracks. Man Sum got into one of the cars. He waited for a long time on a heap of straw that smelled of manure. At last the train lurched forward.

He was leaving San Francisco now. He was throwing himself and his fortunes to the winds. The next time he returned to San Francisco, it would be for one reason and one reason only. That would be to claim Kwan Ming Lee as his bride. Until then, he felt confident that the mission home would take care of her. She would be temporarily secure from the greedy hands of the warring Tongs.

He was unaware, though, that his father was conceiving a plan to get Ming Lee back. It was a plan, according to the lawyer, Porter, that could not help but succeed.

Chapter 18

It was a windy Sunday afternoon and the girls were making themselves ready for a picnic. They had all behaved so well the previous week that it was decided they should have the opportunity to visit the beautiful Golden Gate Park. Volunteers from the Cumberland Presbyterian Church would accompany the ladies. Two burly Irish policemen were also invited to come along to act as bodyguards. Miss Damon feared a repetition of the Chu Mae Pong killing.

The doorbell rang a half-hour earlier than the chaperones were due. But one of the girls was eager to welcome their guests from the outside world. She swung the door wide open without hesitation. It was very reckless of her, considering the dangers beyond that door.

A lone, slightly stooped gentleman stood on the doorstep. He was embarrassed to behold a living room full of young ladies, and he nervously adjusted his tie.

The girls thought his appearance was pleasant enough. He looked like he could easily be a Christian. His jacket was pressed like a Christian's. And his tie was maroon.

Kwan Ming Lee was in the kitchen. She was diligently arranging *dim sum*, an early brunch, delicacies for the picnic basket. One of the girls nonchalantly pranced up to her.

The girl said, "Yuk Wing Ling is asking for you in the parlor, Ming Lee."

Ming Lee blanched. "That's not possible."

"What's wrong, Ming Lee?" the girl asked.

The expression on Ming Lee's face was one of utter terror. "Yuk Wing Ling was my husband."

"Well," the girl giggled, "he says he still is your husband. I told him I thought you were in the kitchen, and that I would go and see if I could find you. I didn't know that you were married, Ming Lee. You never mentioned you had a husband."

Ming Lee was standing at the counter, staring at the picnic things, trembling uncontrollably.

"What's the matter, Ming Lee, what's the matter?"

"I don't want to see him. He's not my husband. My husband is dead. My husband died four years ago. Go into that parlor, please, and tell that man that my husband died four years ago and that it is not possible for him to be who he says he is."

But it was too late for Ming Lee to avoid a confrontation with this ghost, for he was now standing before her—a total stranger. What kind of trick was this, and who was playing it? she asked herself. To the specter she said simply, "I don't know you."

"Yes, you do, Ming Lee. I am Yuk Wing Ling. Yes, I heard what you said about me, that I was dead. But that isn't true. Yes, many people thought I had died. They thought I had been murdered by Tong men over a debt."

"You are not Yuk Wing Ling," she said.

He took a few steps closer to her. She could not meet his gaze. She stood with her back against the counter, frozen in fear.

"I myself caused that rumor. I wanted them to think I had died. I had other creditors, many creditors. I had gambling debts. I had to get rid of creditors."

"I don't know why you're telling me all this," Ming Lee said.

"They wanted money I didn't have. I let them think I was the one who died in the alley that night. While I myself fled the city."

"Why are you telling these lies? Who are you?" Ming Lee demanded angrily.

"It is me, my darling, it is Yuk Wing Ling. I am not a ghost."

"Get out," she said, her voice almost inaudible. By now she was breathing very hard and perspiring.

"I am your husband. Come to me, let me embrace you. I've missed you so much. How I've longed for the tender embraces we have known." He moved closer.

"No!" Ming Lee hissed, backing away in disgust.

The young man said, "We were together in China for such a short time. It was too short. I wanted to meet you when you arrived in this country. I couldn't. My creditors were highbinder Tongs. They would have killed me had I stayed."

"We were never together in China. What are you talking about?" Ming Lee said.

"Has my appearance changed so much that you still don't recognize me? Your appearance has greatly altered too, you know. I might easily have failed to recognize you. But my touch, if just once you would let me touch you, then you will see that all that is familiar about your husband will come back to you, Ming Lee. Please, let me touch you once." He reached for her.

"No. Don't!" she cried out. "Please, please leave

this place. I don't know you. Maybe I look like someone you know, but I am not the same person."

"We've really become like strangers to one another. But you will see, all that will change when you come to live with me."

"Live with you?"

"You see, I was in Virginia City, Nevada, at the silver mines. I was a miner there. I made a good wage, and I had some good luck at the fan-tan tables too. So I have made good my debts and now have nothing to fear from the Tong. I have made a home. Yes, there is a home for you. It will be our home. Come home, Ming Lee. Come home to your husband."

Ming Lee suddenly lost control. She began by crying softly. But the cry became a scream of anger. The feeling inside was similar to the first time Sing Choy Wu had made love to her. Violently, she struck out at the man. She was pulled back by the other girls. Then she reached for a knife and managed to throw it. It missed the man and instead struck the floor of the hallway that passed by the kitchen.

She screamed, "Get out, get out!" over and over until the man who claimed he was Yuk Wing Ling finally started to leave.

Before he went out the door, he blared, "I want you, Ming Lee. I want my wife back. I will have her back. She is mine. She is my wife!"

It took a long time before Ming Lee's quivering sobs subsided. When they finally did, she had no more appetite for a picnic in Golden Gate Park. Wearily, she dragged herself upstairs to her bed. She spent a sleepless, anxious afternoon gazing out her window at the sloping roofs of the buildings in the Chinatown she despised.

Sylvia Damon and the mission home's lawyer, Emmanuel Shepard, together with Kwan Ming Lee, sought the guidance of Christ in prayer. Then they got down to the business of preparing Ming Lee for the upcoming trial. Her alleged husband was trying to make good his claim in a court of law.

"Now," Shepard began, "you are absolutely sure the person you saw at the mission home was not your husband?"

"I am positive," Ming Lee said. "This was not the same man. There is no resemblance whatsoever to the man I married in China."

"Couldn't his appearance have drastically altered?" Shepard asked.

Ming Lee shook her head. "It could not have changed so drastically over a few years. This man's an impostor. I will have nothing to do with him! Why would someone make a claim of that kind? A total stranger. What does he want with me?"

"I very much suspect it is a Tong trick," Sylvia Damon said. "Her being returned to her husband would mean going back to one of her previous owners."

"I had heard that the Chi Sings were more or less eliminated. Wasn't there a battle which the Suey Sings won overwhelmingly around the Chinese New Year?" Emmanuel Shepard asked.

"There were one or two who survived," Sylvia Damon replied. "Their leader, Sing Choy Wu, wasn't killed. That's enough for a Tong to rebuild, provided they haven't lost all their money. The Tongs usually have enough illegal business enterprises to keep them supplied with funds indefinitely."

Sylvia Damon's knowledge of Tong affairs surprised Ming Lee. The missionary woman seemed to know as much about them as Chinese people.

"It doesn't matter," Damon went on, "who is behind this phony husband scheme. Surely one can predict their next move. This 'husband' will pursue the matter in court. There's no question of that. There is also no question that he will retain some of the best legal counsel in the city. He will be backed by Tong money and will be able to afford a good lawyer. If we lose this case, we'll lose Kwan Ming Lee.''

"Then we must prove that this man is a phony by showing that the real Yuk Wing Ling is a dead man. I have already checked the records and have been unable to find any record of him, dead or alive.''

"That's not surprising. As often as not, when the Tongs eliminate someone, there is no identification on the dead man, and he is simply labeled 'dead Chinese' and is so labeled in the morgue,'' Sylvia pointed out.

Now Emmanuel Shepard addressed Ming Lee directly. "Ming Lee,'' he said gently, "our only line of defense is your testimony. The Tongs will produce witnesses to attest to the validity of this man's masquerade, but no matter what happens in that courtroom, you must not indicate that there is the slightest doubt in your mind whatsoever that he is not your husband. Don't waver from that point, and you'll maintain your freedom.''

Jeremy W. Porter stood facing the jury. He had a confident smile on his face. With one hand, he held his lapel. With the other he gestured forcefully. Occasionally, he spoke in a soft voice and gripped both lapels. Sometimes he used both hands, gesturing wildly.

"Sylvia Damon,'' he began, "has created a camp of Christian slaves. That is what the mission home is about. She systematically remakes minds. Sylvia Damon is one of a breed of overzealous Christian missionaries who will stop at nothing to gain a soul for Christ, even if it means sacrificing a human being's intelligence, sensitivity and memory.''

Porter paused after the word "memory." It was the key word in his argument. "She demands nothing less than total obedience from her converts. They must forsake friends and relatives, children and husbands. The techniques she employs are like those used by hypnotists. The personalities of the victims are made over in the name of an extreme Christian viewpoint."

Porter's eyes briefly met Sylvia Damon's. The missionary woman was scowling at him. This encouraged him to hit harder.

"To please Miss Damon, the girls try to rescue as many so-called lost souls as they can. One such rescue attempt ended in the death of one Chu Mae Pong.

Sylvia Damon could not contain herself. She spoke up, interrupting Porter. "The Tongs killed her! Your employers, Mr. Porter!"

"Order in the court," said the judge, banging his gavel.

Porter, ignoring Sylvia Damon's outburst, continued, "Miss Damon is an unmarried woman. She has turned down offers of marriage on occasion. She has done so on the grounds that her missionary duties were more important than a husband or family. She is a frustrated woman. She takes her frustrations out on hapless Chinese girls."

Shepard stood up and said, "Your Honor, I object to this obvious defamation of the character of my client."

"There will be order in the courtroom," the judge commanded. "Please continue, Mr. Porter."

"Thank you, Your Honor. Having forsworn normal relationships between a man and a woman, she substituted an abnormal, fanatic relationship to her religion. She enforced her viewpoint in the environment of the mission home. Therefore, the mission home, instead of providing a refuge for the slave girl, became the worst kind of mental bondage imaginable. Sylvia Damon took advantage of the young prostitutes' vulnerability.''

Now Porter looked at Kwan Ming Lee and pointed at her.

"It is easy to convince these girls that in God's moral assessment they are worthless dregs. They have to repent their past mistakes. And once they repent, they have to erase their sordid past from their memories. That's so they can make room for a glorious future with Jesus.''

Porter paced slowly to the table where Yuk Wing Ling was seated and pointed to the alleged husband.

"It is no wonder poor Kwan Ming Lee cannot recognize her own husband. But I will produce a number of witnesses, friends and associates of Yuk Wing Ling, who will tell you that this man is who he says he is.''

Porter stopped, paused, then took his seat next to Yuk Wing Ling.

Emmanuel Shepard stood before the courtroom. He seemed more ill at ease than his opponent. "I will prove conclusively,'' he said, "that the man who calls himself Yuk Wing Ling is, in reality, a dummy of the Chi Sing Tong. He claims Kwan Ming Lee is his wife. This claim is a ruse, a Tong trick. The Chi Sings invested a lot of money in their singsong girl, so naturally they want her back. They want to return her to the degenerate occupation of enslaved prostitution. They are using this 'lost husband' scheme to get her out of the mission home.''

Porter stood and said, "Now who is defaming whom? I object to this defamation of *my* client's character!''

"Mr. Porter, sit down," the judge said.

"I object to the use of the term 'dummy,' " Porter said.

"Why object? Mr. Yuk doesn't understand it anyway," the judge said sarcastically. "Continue, Mr. Shepard."

"Thank you, Your Honor. Kwan Ming Lee is not a hypnotized zombie as my opponent has claimed. She is a happy and free young woman, thanks to Sylvia Damon. She is learning English, housekeeping, and skills such as sewing, cooking and knitting. The training she is receiving at the mission home will make her a contributing citizen of her adopted country."

Now Shepard raised his voice. It almost squeaked with rage. "My opponent's charge that Sylvia Damon is against the institution of matrimony is totally false. Although Miss Damon is not married herself, she rejoices when one of her reformed 'daughters of joy' finds the bliss of marriage with a suitable, constant partner. Miss Damon does not consider the mission home a substitute for the normal family of husband and children. On the contrary, the entire program at the mission home is designed to help the girls find good homes of their own. Miss Damon does have certain requirements for future husbands: they must be Christian, and they must have the financial means to support their wife. These minimal requirements help make happy families, as witnesses will testify."

As Emmanual Shepard had predicted, the trial was shaping up as a draw between the two lawyers. The alleged husband seemed on all accounts sincere and believable. Porter called a score of witnesses, who claimed they had no doubts the claimant was indeed Yuk Wing Ling. People knew him from his earliest arrival in Chinatown to his departure from the quarter. There were friends from Virginia City, where he claimed he had been for the last three years. He produced documents proving he was Yuk Wing Ling. Among these was a Chinese birth certificate. He even conjured a marriage certificate with Ming Lee's signature clearly affixed. His credentials seemed impeccable.

Porter also called to the stand women who had been at the Sylvia Damon home, but who had been reclaimed by their previous owners through writs of habeas corpus or other such schemes. These witnesses were back in the trade again. Their owners forced them on numerous occasions to give derogatory testimony regarding the mission home. But Porter had cleverly coached these women so that their stories met the needs of his arguments.

There were no wild fantasies about torture chambers in the mission home. There were no demons wielding red-hot pokers and drooling blue blood out of toothless mouths. The women presented facts true to their recollection, but they exaggerated greatly the pressure to adopt Christianity. They made it appear that Sylvia Damon was mesmerizing her captives. The witnesses pointed to the missionary's highly magnetic and charismatic personality, by which, they said, she had the power to cast spells over young women.

Yes, Porter presented the case very well. The jury was indeed leaning toward the theory that Kwan Ming Lee's mind might have undergone some alteration, and therefore could not recognize her husband.

As inevitable as the coming tide, the time for Kwan Ming Lee's testimony drew nearer.

"You must not give in to Porter," Shepard reminded her. "Hold true to what you know. Don't let him cause you to doubt your eyes and ears."

"Don't worry," she said. "I know what is real and what isn't. That man is not my husband. No matter what happens, I will stick to that fact."

In the beginning, she did very well, her lawyer and

Sylvia Damon agreed. Her first day of testimony went smoothly.

Emmanuel Shepard asked her several questions about her relationship to her husband. Ming Lee related how Yuk Wing Ling had bought her from her parents, then brought her to live with his family fifty miles away.

"He left three weeks later, promising to send for me after making certain arrangements. He didn't explain to me what these arrangements were, though," she testified.

"What did you think they were?" Emmanuel Shepard asked.

"I assumed he meant living arrangements. It wasn't until later that I realized he meant selling me to the Chi Sing Tong."

"How did you find out that he had sold you?"

"Sing Choy Wu told me. He is the exalted master of the Chi Sing Tong," Ming Lee said.

"And for what purpose did the Chi Sing Tong wish to buy you?" Shepard asked.

"They wanted to use me as a prostitute, here, in Chinatown."

"And so, posing as your husband, Yuk Wing Ling was in reality a slave broker. Is that right?"

Ming Lee answered, "That's right. There were several other wives in his life, I found out since. He brought them all over to the United States and sold them to one of the Tong organizations. I found out that he was killed by the Chi Sing Tong because he overcharged them for me, and then refused to return the difference."

Ming Lee's testimony occurred at the end of the day. It would be resumed the following day with cross-examination by Jeremy Porter.

Emmanuel Shepard turned to her after her testimony. He shook her hand and said, "Congratulations. That was very calm and careful testimony. If you behave that way tomorrow, we'll surely win. Just keep giving definite, forthright answers.''

"That's right," Sylvia Damon put in, "and you'll spare yourself the agony of once again being forced into slavery to the Tongs."

Ming Lee said, "I noticed two or three men. I recognize them. They're Chi Sing Tong men."

Her attorney said, "It's good you didn't let their presence disturb your concentration. After your first day on the stand, you can be confident you will defeat this plot against you."

What Ming Lee didn't notice was that one of those Tong men had dropped something in her purse while she was talking briefly with her attorney and Miss Damon.

That evening, before dinner, Ming Lee was left alone to rest and collect her thoughts.

Back in her room, she opened her purse to take out her comb. Then she saw it, a piece of red paper tied with a red string. When she undid the string, what she saw caused her body to freeze with numb fear. She brought her hand up to her mouth, afraid she would be sick. It was a human finger, and on it was a jade ring. In a moment she had calmed herself, and she noted the jade was not of high quality. It was not the same ring she had received from Choy Wu and then had given to Man Sum. It was not Man Sum's finger. But the message was clear.

Skillful calligraphy made the point. "Your testimony tomorrow in the devil's court will confirm that Yuk Wing Ling is your husband. Such verification must issue from your lovely throat. If not, the fate of Sing Man Sum will be the same as the poor servant of the Ming emperor's favored concubine."

What was Ming Lee to do? According to this note, either way she would lose Sing Man Sum. If she denied Yuk Wing Ling, they'd kill Man Sum. If she said yes to Yuk Wing Ling, she would again be enslaved.

The letter went on, "His death will come quickly also if you reveal *any* of the contents of this letter to your religious cohorts. I know that you gave the treasured ring to the traitor. You I will forgive, provided that the song you sing tomorrow is pleasing to my ears. As for the gift of the ring to Man Sum, you did not know what you were doing. You were in the dream that often deceives users of the pipe. He, however, I will never forgive. He knew precisely what he was stealing and from whom.

"We know where he is, and we are more than willing to dispose of him. Only you can save him.

"Save yourself, too, the experience of receiving another present like this one.

"You are ever one with my thoughts. Sing Choy Wu."

She took the severed human finger encircled by the imitation jade and wrapped it in the red paper. Then she threw the entire packet out of the window into an alley below. She steeled her nerves and went down to dinner.

The girls applauded her as she sat down to dinner. Only Wu Ting Lee noticed that Ming Lee was pre-occupied.

"What's wrong, Ming Lee?" she asked.

"Nothing," Kwan Ming Lee replied.

"But how do you *know* Yuk Wing Ling, your husband, was selling you to the Chi Sing Tong?" Porter asked her in court the following day.

She was his witness now. Emmanuel Shepard had finished interrogating her. In order to make Ming Lee feel ill at ease, Porter brought his face on a level with hers. He moved in very close. He never took his eyes off her.

"I know he sold me because I was informed of this fact by Mr. Sing Choy Wu. I said that yesterday."

"But did your husband ever tell you that he sold you into slavery?"

"No. He died."

"How do you know that he died?"

"Sing Man Sum told me."

"How did he know?"

"He received a message from Chinatown telling him that my husband had been killed. Later, his father confirmed it."

"Did you ever see the body? Did you ever identify the body of your dead husband?"

"No."

"So again, we have only secondhand reporting. One, he sold you into slavery, and two, he was murdered by Tongs. But in neither case were you able to verify these allegations firsthand."

"That's true."

"Now we move to a matter that is somewhat more complicated. I am referring to the current Mr. Yuk Wing Ling. You see Mr. Yuk Wing Ling sitting there at the table with my assistant. Let me ask you to tell the court now, is that, or is that not, the Yuk Wing Ling you married in 1909 in your village in China?"

There was a deafening pause.

Why wasn't she responding? Sylvia Damon and Emmanuel Shepard were both asking themselves. What's wrong with her?

"Please, will the witness answer the question." Judge Willard B. Clark turned toward her sternly. The interpreter whispered what the judge had said.

"I don't understand the question," Ming Lee said in English.

"You don't? The question was quite simple. Let me ask you this, Miss Kwan. What does your present state of confusion come from? The hypnotic spell these Presbyterians have put you under? I repeat, are you or are you not presently under a trance?"

"Objection. Leading the witness."

"Objection overruled."

"Let us assume, for the sake of argument, that Kwan Ming Lee is indeed under a hypnotic trance induced at the mission home. This trance is preventing her from saying what her better mind knows. Namely, the gentleman sitting there is her husband, whom she knows and loves, and with whom she longs to be reunited."

Porter walked over to Ming Lee. He put his hand under her chin and pointed her face toward the jury.

"I ask the court to behold the pallor of the witness. She is white with fear. If she says the truth, she will offend her good Christian keepers. She will earn theirs and God's and Christ's disapprobation and rejection. She imagines she will land in hell, to suffer torture for an eternity."

"No, no," Ming Lee said. "I am not afraid of Sylvia Damon. I am not afraid of the mission home. They would never harm me."

Porter pointed to her and said, "I direct your attention also to the tone in which she speaks. Her voice completely lacks inflection. She is demonstrating for you now all the symptoms of a hypnotically induced trance. Therefore, quite literally, her mind is not her own."

Shepard turned to Sylvia Damon and asked, "What's wrong with her? Why doesn't she speak?"

"I don't know," Sylvia Damon replied. "But Wu Ting Lee said she looked disturbed about something last night."

"I wish we knew what it was," Shepard said.

Porter continued, "Accordingly, I have taken the liberty of bringing with me to the courtroom today a hypnotist of some reputation. Will Dr. Spengles please come forward and be sworn in? I beg the court's indulgence, but in order to discover the truth of this matter, the state of the witness's mind must be determined, whether in fact it is her own or it belongs to others."

"Ojection, this is highly irregu—"

"Overruled."

"We will ask Dr. Spengles to put the witness into a trance. If the witness is not susceptible to hypnotism, my theory goes out the window. If she can be hypnotized, however, Dr. Spengles will ask her to show her true mind."

Emmanuel Shepard objected again. "This violates all courtroom procedures of the past one hundred fifty years, and it sets a dangerous precedent. The validity and value of hypnotism has yet to be established by the scientific community."

"Overruled. Mr. Shepard, we must grant these scientific disciplines their due in our courts of law. Otherwise our judicial system runs the risk of becoming antiquated. The sciences are as yet very young disciplines. We must help them along as best we can. I for one welcome Mr. Porter's innovation here today. You may proceed, Mr. Porter."

Ming Lee found herself being told to look at a shiny, gold disk that was moving in front of her eyes. Ming Lee obliged. She watched the disk move back and forth like a pendulum. She was unaware of the man holding the chain from which the disk was suspended. She just watched it move back and forth. Back and forth. She began to feel more relaxed. The images that had been sweeping before her subsided.

The hypnotist was talking to her. He was asking her to tell him about the man sitting at the table, Yuk Wing Ling. Was he her husband? The hypnotist was telling her to concentrate on the man's face. Didn't she remember that face?

In her relaxed state, she was able to see everything clearly. If she told the truth, the highbinders would kill Man Sum. They'd cut off his finger. It would be the finger on which she had placed the jade ring. Choy Wu would send her the finger, and she would know Man Sum had been killed.

She knew what she must do. She must save her lover's life. There was no other alternative. She would not let Man Sum end up like the lover in the story of the Ming emperor's concubine. No, that must not be.

She then said, "Yes, yes. You are my husband."

"That is your husband?" Porter asked as the murmuring in the courtroom grew louder.

"He is my husband." She pointed to the stranger sitting at the table. "There is no other."

As she said this, she grew more dizzy. The room spun, and with it, the faces of jurors, judges, lawyers, Christians, Tongs, gods and lovers. She tried to stand up with the others. The judge had said something and brought down his gavel. Everybody was moving around. The faces of Emmanuel Shepard and Sylvia Damon were downcast. They weren't even looking at her.

The man posing as Yuk Wing Ling had already stood up. He was shaking hands with the man called Porter. The room was slanted. Ming Lee couldn't stand in a room such as that. The sickness was down in the pit of her stomach. She couldn't keep it down there anymore. It wanted to come out. Before she could stop herself, it welled up from within her and issued from her mouth in a stream of mucus, bile and hatred.

Two very strong arms lifted her from the floor. She was led out of the courtroom to a waiting taxicab. She didn't know who was going to clean up the mess. But somehow it didn't matter to her. It didn't matter whether anybody would ever clean it up or not. Nothing mattered now. She was to be a slave again, but even that didn't matter, as long as she had saved her lover's life.

"They must not hurt Sing Man Sum. Other than that, nothing matters."

This was what Kwan Ming Lee kept saying to herself as she was led into the brick building on Clay Street, the residence of the Chi Sing Tong's exalted master.

Chapter 19

The *mui jai* had prepared a sumptuous meal. But Kwan Ming Lee didn't touch her food. Sing Choy Wu ate ravenously. He also drank copious amounts of rice wine.

After the meal, he looked at her for a long time without saying anything. In his drunken state, he thought his boasts might make an impression on her.

"I'm in a much better position to deal with the Suey Sings now," he said. "I have made some good bets, and they paid off handsomely. I've been able to recruit some fighting talent, that's right. I've got some new immigrants in my army. Paper sons, all. They prefer the soldier's salary I offer them to the going rate for cooks, kitchen helpers and houseboys."

Ming Lee didn't look at him. "You ordered Chu Mae Pong killed."

"That's right," he said. "She betrayed me. She abducted you."

"That was not Chu Mae Pong. It was Yuk Dai Gong's brother masquerading as Chu Mae Pong," Ming Lee said. "You should not have taken her life. She meant you no harm."

"How I conduct war is my business," Choy Wu said calmly. "How you make love is yours."

"I have no reason to make love," Ming Lee said bitterly.

"No? How about Sing Man Sum's life? How about that for a good reason?"

"You would take your own son's life? What kind of man are you?" she spat.

"I am the man to head the army to retake Chinatown," he told her. "Lum Po is quickly becoming the most renowned and feared of highbinders. In the last week, he has eaten mince pie—killed three of the toughest Suey Sing men. They didn't know what hit them. The Suey Sings paid the price for the New Year's massacre. They have been in the forefront of Chinatown politics long enough. It is time a real man took over."

That real man was none other that Sing Choy Wu. Yes, his son had disappeared, but he would be back. The girl would draw him back. Then Lum Po would get another shot at him. Meanwhile, the girl would be his to do with as he wished. Marry her? No, not after she had betrayed him. She was tainted with the smell of the white devil. She was like a whore who had been enjoyed by a white man. Afterward, no Chinese would have her. That was why she would have to go to the cribs. It was the only place left for a woman so tainted.

Before he would turn her over to the alleyway for resumption of her trade, he would enjoy her one more time. But she hardly looked in the right condition for love play. She needed a good pipe.

"It's time for a little opium, Ming Lee. It will relax you."

Choy Wu snapped his fingers, and the *mui jai* appeared with the pipe already lit.

"I will not touch that," Ming Lee said.

"You will. I command it."

Ming Lee reluctantly complied. She had no choice.

Soon she was reclining on his bed. The tension in her face gave away to an expression of inner peace. There was a painting on Choy Wu's wall. It was a painting of the ocean, the sun, and a wide, white beach. Ming Lee's eyes fixed on it.

When he was quite sure she was beyond the reach of disquieting thoughts, he promptly and unceremoniously disrobed her. He grasped her breasts, then her buttocks. He examined them as if to determine whether any part of her had been visibly damaged. She was indeed intact. He took off his own clothes and administered some sweet-smelling jasmine oil to her body. He worked it thoroughly into her genital region to insure the easy passage of his member.

Massaging her naked body aroused him sufficiently. Without so much as looking at her, he climbed on top of her and inserted himself. It didn't matter to him whether she noticed or not.

And it certainly didn't matter to her what he was doing. She was in another world, the world of the opium dream. The painting. Ocean. The sun. It shone so brightly. A beautiful day. The shining sun, the beach. She was there, on the beach, holding Sing Man Sum's hand. On one of his fingers he wore the jade ring she had given him. She wanted to take that ring back. It would cost him his life.

But there would be time enough for that later. Now they were together. They were alone together at last. Look. He is sitting over there. He's just sitting looking at her.

"Look at your own finger, Ming Lee," he is saying.

A bright gold wedding ring adorns it. This is our wedding day, she thinks to herself. He is my husband. She looked over at him again. How handsome his face was.

"You are my wife," he says to her. "No one can take you away from me now. I have made you the gift of a ring of gold in exchange for the gift you bestowed on me. We are married now."

"Yes. Oh, Man Sum, we have always been married. We have been partners in other lives. Always together, like the immortals."

Still he sat there, looking at her, smiling.

"Am I truly your husband?" he asked her. "Does your acceptance of the gold ring mean you are truly mine? I know that a man can say to a woman, 'You are my wife.' But that isn't enough. She can even say, 'I am your wife. You are my husband,' and that isn't enough either. People can wake up like after a dream. They can look at each other and wonder what they are doing together in the same room. They have been under some kind of trance. They may be married, but they are not really husband and wife. Something essential is missing between them, and not all the tokens of the wealthiest of emperors can make up for what is missing."

"The only thing that could be missing," she told him, "would be you. If you were gone or if you died."

She looked at the jade ring on his finger and thought of the horrible story his father had told her. She said suddenly, "I had better take that ring back. You said yourself that tokens were unimportant."

"Even death could not separate us now, Ming Lee. We are on a beautiful beach. The sun is shining brightly. How beautiful you are, Ming Lee, your lovely long black hair shining with so much light as the sun strikes it. Was long black hair ever that beautiful? Has the bright sun ever danced like that on black hair? Never. It is the dance of opposites. The yin is your hair, the yang is the sun. Finally, I understand the meaning of the dance of the opposites.''

"Oh, Sing Man Sum, your mind, your thoughts, they are so special to me, but oh, you must be careful, oh, there are those who want to kill you, my darling husband, and yes, your death *can* take this happiness away from me. Don't let it happen, dearest husband. The ring.''

He simply sat there looking back at her. Then she began to feel dizzy. The beach was spinning, the sun itself was rocking back and forth, back and forth.

Sing Choy Wu enjoyed himself. After resting for a time, he mounted her again and again. Having had his fill of her at last, he covered her with a sheet and blanket, took her into another room and deposited her into the bed. He went back to his own bed, climbed into the covers and enjoyed a deep, dreamless sleep.

For the next week, the ritual was the same. Ming Lee resisted until forced to smoke opium. She was thankful for the opium on one account. It caused her not to feel Choy Wu's embrace.

After the week was over, Choy Wu summoned one of his highbinders to his house.

"Take her to the cribs,'' he told his henchman.

He would not to speak to her or see her again. His revenge was complete.

"See to it she is guarded, day and night,'' he told the henchman. "I don't want any missionaries coming around there, trying to bail her out.''

She wasn't theirs, after all, she was his. He'd paid good money for her, hadn't he?

As she left his house, Choy Wu turned to her and said, "Wait until you've had a taste of the cribs for a while. Your parlor will look like an empress's sitting room.''

Ming Lee didn't answer.

Suddenly Choy Wu's expression softened. ''I wouldn't send you there if I had my own way. But I have to, you see?''

''I don't understand,'' Ming Lee said, avoiding his eyes.

''All of Chinatown knows you have been in the mission home. I could not marry you without losing much face. But if I had my own way, I would marry you. I still love you. How I wish we could marry. How I wish you could bear my sons,'' Choy Wu said earnestly.

''There is only one man I wish to marry, Choy Wu. That is your son. Man Sum is the only man I want to have children with,'' Ming Lee stated bravely.

''I understand,'' he murmured, lowering his eyes. Then he whispered bitterly between his teeth, ''That traitor!'' He paused. Then, looking at Ming Lee again, he said, ''You will marry a dead man.''

Ming Lee said nothing. Her hatred needed no words.

Ming Lee had walked by the infamous Bartlett Alley before. Not in her worst nightmares did she imagine she would work here. The cribs were like prison cells. The women peered out through the small, barred windows. Men of every variety and station were shopping there. They were shopping for flesh. But it seemed to her that the men weren't very impressed with what they saw. As they looked through windows, they wore lethargic expressions.

In the middle of the alley, one of the henchmen escorting her stopped, took out a key and opened a door. Ming Lee was firmly led into a tiny room. Then the highbinders exited and closed the door behind them. They didn't go far. Ming Lee could see them standing on the other side of the street.

The cell was plain and dingy. Years of opium smoking had stained the ceilings. Ming Lee shared the space with two other women. Both of them were considerably older than she. Both wore haggard expressions. But they were obviously pleased to see Ming Lee join their crib.

"What a pretty one," one of them said. "She's got real class, doesn't she?"

"Yeah," the other one said. "Put her at the window. Business will pick up. We can take on the ones who are waiting for her."

"Hello, honey," the first one addressed her. Then she started walking toward her.

Ming Lee backed off.

"Hey, don't be so frightened," the woman scolded. "I'm not that ugly, am I? I'm Polly. That's my American name. That's Mary over there. And your name?"

"Ming Lee," Ming Lee answered.

"Oh, Ming Lee, that's very nice." Polly tried to touch Ming Lee, but Ming Lee pulled her arm away.

"Don't you want to be my friend?"

"Stop it, Polly," Mary said. "Can't you see? She's a parlor girl. A girl that good-looking doesn't work the cribs."

"She's so pretty," Polly said. "It's all right. If I can't touch her, I'll just look at her. I could look at her all day and not get tired."

"Don't mind Polly," Mary said, trying to put Ming Lee at ease. "She doesn't mean you any harm, really. She's just trying to be friendly."

"That's right," Polly agreed.

Mary asked Ming Lee, "What happened, dear? How

did you get thrown into this dump? What'd you do, kick a highbinder in the crotch?''

"I tried to run away," Ming Lee said. "I went to the mission home."

"Oh," Polly said. "Ouch, they don't like that, the big boys. They frown on missionaries." Then she added, "But someone pretty as you, you'd think they'd give you a second chance."

Ming Lee sighed deeply and didn't answer.

"Cheer up, dear," Mary said. "We look out for one another in the cribs. Believe me, you have friends here. It won't be so bad. I have a pipe if you care for a smoke. That makes things go a little easier. You have a little pipe, now."

Ming Lee accepted the already lit pipe. She took a deep draw on it and felt better.

"All right, Ming Lee," Polly said. "How about going to the window, see who's out there? You stand at the window for a little while. It won't be long. I promise you."

Polly was right. Almost as soon as Ming Lee's beautiful face appeared at the small barred window, a crowd of men started to gather. Bills were shoved toward the window. Cries of "Me first!" and "Look, a new one!" and "She's beautiful!" were heard.

The crowd began to become disorderly, so the highbinders assisted. They took the customers' money and sent them in.

"You just have to wait," the highbinders told the customers. "She's not used to the cribs, and we're giving her a lot of rest between callers. She's not a machine, you know."

*　　*　　*

When Man Sum left the railroad yard in Sacramento, he wasn't sure where he was going, and he didn't have the slightest idea where his next meal would be coming from. He had nothing. There was the jade ring on his finger. He could cash it in and make a lot of money from the sale. That would feed him for a while and it would help him get started in some business venture. But no, he couldn't do that. It was Ming Lee's gift to him. He was right back where he started. He didn't know what he was going to do.

Maybe he could sell, be a peddler. All he needed were some wares. But what wares? He was sure he could sell anything. He could make another person feel there was value in an apparently useless item.

He began in the garbage heaps that adjoined the railroad yard. There he found discarded garments, and out of them he was able to salvage buttons, ribbons, and material for patches. He also gathered rubber bands, mirrors and boxes that could be fixed. He picked up pins, needles, shoes that needed work and bottles that needed cleaning out. He also found an old packing frame, which would come in handy as both a way to carry his merchandise and a way to display it.

He now had a portable retail store. He counted on the frugal ways of the Chinese to make his business go. If there was an item at the local five and dime that sold for eight cents, he would offer it for five. His item might show a little wear, but a saving of three cents was hard to turn down. And because time was money, at least another penny or so would be saved by the purchaser because the customer would not have to walk to the store.

A nickel or so a day could be counted on in the beginning. It was enough to purchase a bowl of rice or even some noodles. If he wanted to add a little meat or fish to his bowl, he offered an item from his wares as barter. There had to be something in that heap which would be of interest to just about anybody. His present occupation also had the advantage of keeping the highbinder off his track. For one thing, he always walked around with his head down, stooped under his load. For another thing, he was not idle. Idleness identified the *boo how doy*. Somebody just standing on a street corner doing nothing was likely to be a soldier, active or retired. Man Sum didn't appear to be one of these.

As time went on, he blended in with Sacramento's Chinatown. He was as much a fixture as the pagoda on Avenue C. White tourists liked to photograph him because he looked like something out of the streets of ancient China. He didn't mind this notoriety. In fact, he even enjoyed it.

When the children came chasing after him, calling him a "rag man," it gave him distinct pleasure. He genuinely liked children. He would try to sell them lollipops. Then he would set his load down and play with them.

He never ate more than a single bowl of rice a day, regardless of the amount of money he made through peddling. In this way, he managed to build up a little capital, which he invested in a few finer items to sell. He chose these items carefully from used clothing stores. Tirelessly he would bargain the proprietor down to a minimal price. He went after clothing that would get him the best return on his investment, usually items that would interest women, such as hose, corsets, nightgowns and blouses. For the home, he had dishtowels and washcloths. For baby, he had miscellaneous toys, shoes, shoelaces and bonnets.

He thought of Kwan Ming Lee daily. He had heard that his father had won her back through a lawsuit. In Sacramento, while peddling his wares, he overheard Chi

Sing highbinders gossiping on the street corner. He could not have been mistaken. It was she they were speaking of. Yes, undoubtedly, she would either be married to his father, or Sing Choy Wu would press her into the trade again, or both. All Man Sum's efforts at freeing her had been in vain.

He had to do something. This peddler's outfit had fooled the Sacramento hatchet men. Why wouldn't it work in San Francisco? His current occupation could function as a disguise. He would return to San Francisco, find Ming Lee and rescue her. They would go to the train station and take the train to Sacramento. If he was fast enough, it might work.

He had enough saved for a ticket. The following morning, he hoisted all his goods on a train bound for San Francisco.

Three hours later, he was back in San Francisco's Chinatown. He wore a red kerchief around his head. The tight kerchief made his hair stand up. This further distorted his appearance. As he walked with his merchandise, he stooped and affected an eccentric walk like that of an old man. Also, his skin was darker from spending days in the sun. The disguise worked. He walked through Chi Sing haunts such as Sullivan's Alley, and no one noticed him. Now to find Ming Lee.

That part wasn't hard. All of Chinatown had ears. He just had to put himself within earshot of the gossip of the local *boo how doy*. News of Sing Choy Wu and the beautiful "daughter of joy" was on everyone's mind.

"That will serve her right," Man Sum overheard a highbinder say. "She belongs in the cribs."

"Does she? Sing Choy Wu wanted to marry her, didn't he?"

"The *faan gwai* missionaries must have performed the

operation they are famous for. They must have fixed her so she can't have babies.''

"That's the real reason Choy Wu got rid of her,'' the other highbinder said. "He wants sons.''

The cribs, Man Sum thought, the lowest, most degrading place for a human being in Chinatown. They were worse than the dankest and most rat-infested of the opium dens. He had to get Ming Lee out at all costs.

He had all the information he was looking for. He trudged over to Bartlett Alley. He knew that was the main crib area operated by the Chi Sing Tong. Now it was a question of going from tiny window to tiny window in search of his beloved.

"Hey, peddler,'' one of the girls said. "Come on in and take a look. It won't cost much, and it'll be fun. You'll like it.''

Man Sum promptly went to the window. The woman who addressed him was thin and bent. Her eyes were bloodshot.

"I am looking for a certain woman,'' Man Sum said, affecting a hoarse voice.

"I wouldn't be too particular if I were you, old man,'' the prostitute responded haughtily.

"No, you don't understand,'' Man Sum said. "It is somebody I know. Her name is Kwan Ming Lee. Please, tell me which door is her crib. I have important news for her.''

"I bet you do,'' the scarecrow of a woman said. "Not a few of you beggars have information for that little bird.''

"Please, tell me where she can be found,'' Man Sum pleaded.

"All right, you just go to about the middle of Bartlett Alley. You will see a line of men. Stand in line. In a couple of days, you will see Ming Lee.'' With that, the woman clapped shut the little shutter of the crib window. Apparently, Man Sum had offended her by asking for another woman.

The woman was exaggerating the length of the line at Ming Lee's crib window. It wouldn't take him two days. There were five men ahead of him. It would be fifty minutes to an hour he would have to wait. He tried to keep his mind off what was happening in there. It was useless. He thought of her with all of them. His brain reeled and his stomach turned, but he must control himself. Soon, he would free her from this hell.

The wait seemed interminable. He averted his eyes from the customers who were leaving Ming Lee. He didn't want to see their faces.

Finally, his turn came. He looked through the tiny window and saw not her but another woman.

"Ming Lee?" he asked. Her name caught in his throat.

"Not here," was the response.

"But they said she was working here," Man Sum protested.

"*Yau sik*, she's resting."

"Please, let me talk to her," he insisted. "I'm a friend of hers."

"What's wrong with me, honey?" the woman said, holding her large breasts toward him for his inspection and moving seductively from side to side.

"Yes, yes, you're fine," Man Sum said, "just fine."

Polly opened the door of the crib and admitted him.

"Pay me first. That will be a dollar for ten minutes. If you want longer, it'll go up to two for fifteen minutes, and—"

Man Sum's voice interrupted her. "Ming Lee, Ming Lee!" he called out.

Polly grabbed him by the arm. "Hey, you! I said she was resting. Now you pay me or I will call somebody over here who will make you pay, peddler man!"

Man Sum wasn't listening to her. He called, "Ming Lee, Ming Lee!"

He heard an answering voice in the back room. "Man Sum!" Ming Lee had recognized his voice.

Man Sum threw aside the flimsy yellow curtain, revealing a short dank hallway and then another curtain. When he parted this second curtain, he found Ming Lee. She was nude, lying on a filthy mattress on the floor.

"Ming Lee," Man Sum said, "I'm taking you out of here. Get dressed right away."

"You can't," Ming Lee said desperately. "Get out of here, Man Sum. Get out of here."

It was already too late for an escape. Polly had called two highbinders to the crib. They both charged in, weapons drawn.

"There's someone after Ming Lee," Polly said. "She called him 'Man Sum.' "

The two highbinders looked at each other. "Man Sum? Mince pie!"

"Big price on his head. Get him!"

But Ming Lee had the presence of mind to push Man Sum into a secret passageway behind an old dresser. This passageway was where Tong men hid their singsong girls from police and missionaries. Many of the cribs had them.

The highbinders reached the room just as Ming Lee had finished replacing the dresser.

The men immediately began to move the dresser and open up the passageway, but Ming Lee slid in front of them. She writhed in a sensual manner.

"Wait a minute," she purred. "What do you want with him when you can have me, both of you? I'll take you both on. Don't you get lonely for a woman, standing out there all day?"

Her delaying tactic was enough to give Man Sum a head start. "Ross Alley," one of the men said. "Ross Alley, that's where the passage leads."

As the two men left the crib, the one who had just spoken turned to Ming Lee and said, "Choy Wu will hear about this."

The next day, when Ming Lee asked if Man Sum had been caught, the highbinders refused to answer her. She did not know whether his escape had been successful or not. She did not know if Man Sum was alive or not.

If he was alive, she wished he would not try to rescue her again. It was futile. There was no way out.

Now, Ming Lee needed more than ever to deaden herself. She was able to contact the dealer who had served the Palace of Heavenly Peace. Ming Lee was able to buy from her and also do some selling on the side as she had before. She was able to resume her opium business without much trouble.

Two months passed. By now, Ming Lee had grown used to the routine of the cribs. Even Polly's licentious stares and remarks no longer bothered her. Opium took the edge off everything, including the doubt in her mind as to whether Man Sum was alive or dead. But there was something else. Some change was occurring in Kwan Ming Lee's body. She was pregnant.

Mary had become her friend, and Ming Lee confided in her.

"There are doctors who can take of this for you," Mary said, "but it's much too risky. Girls have been known to lose their lives under rusty knives. It's not for you, my dear."

"Then I must go ahead and have this baby?"

"Unfortunately, the Tongs will do nothing to help. They don't want babies around. Babies get in the way of business," Mary said.

"So if I have this baby, what will become of it?" Ming Lee asked.

"There is only one thing that could be done. The baby has to be given away. Some Tong men, for a price, get rid of babies. But you will never know to whom your child is sold. This is the rule. Best thing to do is not worry. A couple of months after it's over, it won't matter anymore. It's too bad. You probably don't know who the father is."

"Yes, I know who the father is," Ming Lee said. "At least, I am fairly sure."

"Would he help you in some way?" Mary asked.

"I doubt it. The father is Sing Choy Wu, the exalted master of the Chi Sing Tong."

"Oh, I understand," Mary said. "Well, there are midwives who take care of pregnant singsong girls. They are very understanding. You pay her only what you can afford. The money you pay goes into a fund to help other pregnant 'daughters.' "

"I had never heard of the midwives before," Ming Lee said.

"No, it is a secret organization. It is secret because the Tong men want nothing to do with pregnant women. The worst thing you can do is cry to the Tong about your condition. They don't care. They would just as soon kill you for it."

Chapter 20

A woman named Yuen Pui Yen became Ming Lee's midwife. She would assist Ming Lee in the delivery of her baby.

The woman came one morning to Ming Lee's "crib" on Bartlett Alley. Ming Lee had been pregnant for four months.

"First of all," Pui Yen said, "I have good news for you. Contact has been made with a highbinder who will see to it your baby has a home."

"What is his name?" Ming Lee asked.

"Lem Choy," Pui Yen announced.

Ming Lee was distrustful when she heard the name. After all, Lem Choy had engineered her abduction and her subsequent servitude to the Suey Sings. But she really didn't have a choice. Lem Choy was the only one willing to do the necessary footwork in search of a buyer.

"All right," Ming Lee said. "If it must be Lem Choy, then that's who it must be."

"I'm sure he'll find a good home. He will try to find a merchant who can afford to buy a baby at a good price."

Then Pui Yen felt Ming Lee's abdomen. Her sensitive hands found the place where the baby lay growing.

The midwife smiled. "It feels to me as though the baby is progressing normally. I think it's going to be very healthy. It would be best if you stayed away from opium for a while."

Ming Lee agreed. "Yes, if the goddess of mercy didn't see fit to bestow great fortune on me, at least I can make it possible for my child to live a good life, even though I may never know him."

As Pui Yen was about to leave, she turned and said, "Oh, by the way, I have news for you. You are not alone in your pregnancy. A friend of yours has stumbled on the same road. Her name is Yan Chui Lee. As a matter of fact, I am assigned to oversee her pregnancy also. She is due around the same time as you."

"Yes, I know Yan Chui Lee very well," Ming Lee said. "She was the one who introduced me to the pipe. She told me that smoking opium was a good defense against finding myself in the shape I'm now in. Either I haven't been taking enough of it, or it's just a fairy tale."

"I have heard it said that opium would prevent the seed from taking root, but I have never seen evidence of it," Pui Yen said, smiling.

As the months wore on, Ming Lee grew despondent. She liked Pui Yen and felt that she could trust her, but the impending birth filled her with anxiety. Going through all that struggle only to give the baby over to Lem Choy, that bothered her. Lem Choy would betray someone in a minute if he was paid enough. Still more disturbing was never seeing the child again after its delivery. That thought made Ming Lee feel as though all life was just a losing battle against pain and misfortune.

Ming Lee was in her eighth month when Pui Yen brought news about an adoptive parent. "You can put your mind at ease, Ming Lee," she said. "Lem Choy has found a very responsible merchant who will be glad to take your child. He is, in fact, willing to accept not just one, but two babies! So Lem Choy will place both Yan Chui Lee's child and yours with this merchant."

"Please, might I know this merchant's name?"

"I'm sorry," Pui Yen answered, "I couldn't give you that information if I wanted to. Lem Choy wouldn't tell any of the women. He is keeping the information strictly to himself. The only thing he would tell me about the merchant was that he did not reside in San Francisco. That means he will have to travel some distance to deliver them."

"Some distance? But where?" Ming Lee asked anxiously.

"You must try not to bother yourself about that. It is out of your control. You must try to remain as relaxed as you possibly can. Eat well, and above all, don't try to exercise influence where you know it is impossible. I must ask you soon for money to pay Lem Choy his commission. He wants at least fifteen hundred."

"I don't have fifteen hundred," Ming Lee said, then added, "but a new shipment of opium has just arrived from China. I can pay Lem Choy in opium. It is the highest quality. Will he accept that kind of payment?"

"Don't worry. I will speak to him this evening. I'm sure something can be worked out. Can you put some paste in a jar so that he can try it? I happen to know he likes a good smoke, so I have no doubt your offer will be of interest to him."

Ming Lee kept her opium equipment on the wooden packing crate next to her crude bunk. She took the lid off the tin pillbox and scooped out some of the paste with a spoon. This she deposited in a small glass jar, on which she put a lid. She gave the jar to Pui Yen.

"Have you been smoking?" Pui Yen asked, having noticed that Ming Lee had an empty pillbox handy.

"Only a little," Ming Lee replied.

"That was very unwise. It might affect the baby's health."

"I am so anxious all the time, I can't stop thinking horrible thoughts. This is all that seems to help."

Pui Yen shook her head. There really was nothing she could say. She had seen the same pattern occur with other pregnant women of the cribs. Their existence was so brutal that they had to partake of the opiate even though it endangered the fetus. Pui Yen took a white packet out of her bag.

"Here," she said. "Here are some herbs that will help counteract unhealthy influences that are occurring or are likely to occur. Boil these herbs in water, one and a half cups down to one. Then drink the tea. It will be very bitter to the taste. But it will be good for the baby's health and yours, too."

In the late afternoon on May 5, 1917, Ming Lee began to feel a slight aching. It came and went, about fifteen or twenty minutes apart. She contacted Yuen Pui Yen. The midwife informed her that her friend, Yan Chui Lee, was having important sensations too.

Pui Yen said, "Lem Choy has arranged everything for the placement of the babies. He has also arranged for a room in the Gin Kong Tong headquarters where both you women can deliver."

Ming Lee was relieved. "It really would be much more comfortable and convenient than the crib would be," she said, "if only I am allowed."

When Ming Lee asked permission of the Chi Sing *boo how doy* whose beat was Bartlett Alley, the gunman shrugged his shoulders indifferently and said, "Sure, what do I care?"

Nothing seemed to evoke feelings of indifference in the Tongs more than the women's giving birth. It was a matter to be gotten over quickly and expeditiously, so the girl could return to her trade. How they got through it or who was involved didn't matter much.

The Chi Sings posted a man by the delivery room to make sure no one would steal Ming Lee after she had her baby. Yan Chui Lee and Kwan Ming Lee belonged to rival Tongs. That meant a Suey Sing man had to be stationed at the same post. Actually, the two enemy highbinders got along famously. They cracked jokes and exchanged stories while the women within suffered with their ever more frequent contractions.

Chui Lee's child, a boy, came after only two hours of labor, but Ming Lee's work went on for much longer, until in the middle of the night she was finally far enough along to begin pushing. Every push, however, racked her with pain.

"Breathe with the pain, breathe deeply," Pui Yen said.

"Lost control!" Ming Lee said. "Can't do anything about it."

Her shallow breathing caused her to begin to hyperventilate. This in turn made matters worse. She seemed to be spinning around the room in a vortex of unbearable agony.

But there it was. There, held in the arms of a smiling midwife, was the loveliest sight she had ever seen. Her child. The midwife handed the baby to Ming Lee. The little boy clung tightly to the reassuring warmth of its mother's swelled breasts. They rested now, mother and child. It was the most peaceful feeling Ming Lee had ever known, after the most painful experience she had ever had.

The two new mothers were too excited to sleep, even though they were both exhausted. They talked animatedly to each other. They compared the features of their two babies. They exchanged feelings about the marvelous and terrible ordeal they had both been through. And as a result, they grew much closer as friends. In the intimacy of their sharing they both forgot their little boys would soon be taken away from them.

The mothers rested in the little makeshift hospital of the Gin Kong Tong headquarters for a full two days. Lem Choy hadn't gotten around to attending to the responsibility for which he had been paid in full. The young mothers were not in a hurry to part with their babies. They were growing fonder of them as each moment passed.

Pui Yen taught the women how to breast-feed their infants, and before long, the little mouths were *sik yan nai*, eating people's milk, as though they had been doing so for months.

Lem Choy was late because he had been sampling the opium Ming Lee had given him as payment. But very early this morning he realized his duty was long overdue. He had to move the babies in the early hours so he could be certain he would not be followed by some highbinder. A rival Tong might try to rob him of the eight thousand dollars he expected to receive for the infants. He had to take the ferry to Oakland.

His customer was a laundryman living in that East Bay city. The ferry didn't leave until eight in the morning. That meant Lem Choy had to sit around pier thirty-seven waiting for the boat to leave. He would have two babies with him in straw baskets. He would have to be very careful to keep them warm. It would be very easy for them to die of exposure in the chilly, fog-laden morning.

Lem Choy entered the improvised delivery room just before dawn. As he had hoped, the highbinders guarding their respective properties were asleep. He brought the straw baskets with him. They both had strong handles so he could carry them. He also had an ample supply of little baby blankets. Pui Yen had left diapers and secondhand baby clothing the night before.

It was time for the mothers to say good-bye. Lem Choy stood by and waited patiently for the emotional scene to end. He had been witness to such scenes before, and he knew from experience that it was better to let the feelings be vented before taking the babies away. Once, he had tried prematurely to take the newborn from its mother, and despite her having paid him to dispose of it, she mauled him with her fingernails, etching long, bloody scratches on his face and arms. Since that occasion, he had always proceeded much more gingerly. It was a delicate business, severing the bonds nature had fought so long to tie.

Finally, when all the wailing and mourning had subsided, Lem Choy gently took each infant in turn and dressed it. Each mother lent a helping hand in the dressing. This took a long time. Each buttoning and securing of pins had to be accompanied by tearful hugs and fondlings.

Then the babies were carefully tucked into their portable beds. Different colored blankets were used so Lem Choy would know which one was which. Chui Lee's baby had a blue blanket, Ming Lee's a brown one.

The infants wailed. Their eyes reflected the terror of

being stuffed into a strange container away from their mothers.

When all the packing had been done, Lem Choy quickly grabbed the parcels and left without another word. Before the women knew what was happening, their newborn babies were gone. Lem Choy made sure he got out fast, before the women manifested the primitive impulse to hold on to their babies. He didn't want two irate women screaming after him down the street.

Kwan Ming Lee and Yan Chui Lee turned to each other for comfort. With their babies gone, they suddenly had no one but each other.

Lem Choy sat on the pier waiting for the ferry. Beside him were the two bundles. This task was not an unusual one for him. He had done it before, except today was going to be double money.

He had brought a pipe with him in his bag. A little of the dry ball was left in the bottom of the bowl, and he could do with a smoke. It'd cut some of the annoying chill out of the morning air. Ming Lee had been right. It was excellent opium.

As he smoked, he enjoyed the sound of the lapping of the bay's water against the piles that supported the pier. He totally forgot the infants who were in his care. Hadn't he taken enough precautions against the elements by carefully wrapping the newborns in warm blankets? He thought so. If there was any further safety in checking on them from time to time, he just skipped over that. He was enjoying himself too much with his pipe. He relished the shapes of pleasure and power that the smoke lazily conjured in the billowing fog.

Before his dreams were ended, the ferryboat was

receiving passengers. Lem Choy walked up the plank and got on board.

Forty-five minutes later, he was at the port of Oakland. He heard an infant's cry. Only one cried, the one wrapped in the brown blanket, Ming Lee's newborn. The other was still alseep. He took the trolley and got off in Oakland's small Chinatown. He walked to 231 Fourteenth Street, where a sign advertised Gum's Laundry.

Gum Sung Tom was the laundryman's name. He was about forty-five and had a very wiry build. He spoke very quickly, and at times rather loudly, precariously keeping hold of the cigarette dangling from his mouth.

He had no idea of what it meant to raise children, but he had the cash to buy a few. He was desperately lonely and needed the companionship of a family, but owing to immigration law, it was impossible to bring his wife over from China. In the back of his mind, he was also thinking that the children could eventually be his workers. They could assist him at the wash house, and he would not have to pay them.

Lem Choy knocked on the door. Sung Tom, who was still in the middle of working, didn't hear him at first. Sung Tom called out in English, "Open, not yet."

Lem Choy responded in Chinese, "*Hai ngaw, loh.* It's me. Please, open the door."

Sung Tom finally shuffled to the door and opened it. His eyes were red and bleary. They had deep shadows under them. He had been up all night working. His face was pale and sweaty. It was like a steam room inside the place. The stench of cigarette smoke was everywhere.

"Why don't you open a window?" Lem Choy asked.

The laundryman answered, "I don't want customers coming in yet."

Lem Choy quipped, "Your customers come in through the window?"

"Window open, they think, I'm open," Sung Tom said.

Lem Choy shrugged. "I don't have much time. I have to get back to San Francisco for business. So if you don't mind, I'll take my eight thousand."

"Beautiful babies. Both boys. That is very good. That is very good. Strong, too. I like strong boys," Sung Tom said admiringly.

"Yes, well, their mothers are strong, healthy young women. You are getting a very good deal for only eight thousand. Now, if you don't mind, I really am very busy."

Sung Tom put his ear to the two baskets. "What a noise this one in the brown blanket makes, while this one in the blue is pretty quiet."

"That one is still asleep," Lem Choy said impatiently.

"Yes, of course." Sung Tom hurried to the back of the store and disappeared into another room.

Lem Choy was trying to keep the one baby quiet by sticking his finger in its mouth and letting it suck. The baby was temporarily satisfied.

Finally, Sung Tom re-entered with an envelope full of cash. "Here is your payment," he said, handing the money to Lem Choy.

Lem Choy replied, "I'd better count it just to be sure. Oh, while I'm counting, why don't you find some milk or something to feed this baby."

"Yes, I bought a baby bottle and milk from a wet nurse. I'll go get it." Sung Tom ran excitedly to his kitchen.

"Make sure you have enough for both boys!" he called after Sung Tom. "The other one will wake up any minute now." Lem Choy quickly counted the money. He nodded, satisfied. Sixteen five-hundred-dollar bills.

Sung Tom returned with the bottle and was holding it to the lips of the crying baby, who upon receiving the nipple began sucking voraciously. "He likes it! He likes it!" Sung Tom said, beaming delightedly.

Lem Choy said, "Well, *joi gin*. See you next time."

"*Joi gin*," Sung Tom answered, still feeding the youngster.

Lem Choy let himself out and hurried down the street. He had almost reached the trolley stop when he heard footsteps running behind him. It was Sung Tom carrying one of the straw baskets, the one with the blue blanket.

When he reached Lem Choy, out of breath, he said, "What are you trying to do? What do you think you're trying to do to me? Will you look at this baby?"

Lem Choy looked at the sleeping baby. He couldn't figure out what Sung Tom was so angry about.

"Give me back four thousand," Sung Tom demanded. "This baby is dead."

Lem Choy complied with Sung Tom's request for half the money. The highbinder cursed under his breath. He knew it was his own neglect that had killed the child. It must have been that morning cold, he thought to himself.

"But which child is this who died?" he asked himself aloud. "It must be Ming Lee's. The one who is alive is Yan Chui Lee's."

"Yan Chui Lee?" Sung Tom repeated. "That is the real mother's name?"

"Yes . . . yes," Lem Choy responded.

But Lem Choy was confused, and he had assigned the wrong name to the blue-colored blanket.

"Yes, your child's real mother is the Suey Sing slave

girl, Yan Chui Lee,'' Lem Choy said. ''The dead child is
Ming Lee's. I think.''

"Poor little boy," Sung Tom murmured.

Lem Choy said, "I must take the child's body back to
San Francisco, back to its mother. I will give her
an opportunity to send the child's body back to China for
burial. I will bear the expense myself. This day started out
to be very lucky indeed. Now it has become most unlucky.''

Without another word, Sung Tom turned and went
back to his laundry. While walking, he counted the money
Lem Choy had returned to him. He wanted to be certain the
highbinder wasn't cheating him.

Lem Choy sullenly pulled the blue blanket over the
baby's lifeless form. Clutching the basket to himself, he
boarded the ferry and returned to San Francisco. Soon he
was standing in Bartlett Alley before Ming Lee's crib.

He breathed a heavy sigh and entered the crib. He
ignored the half-naked women who were beckoning to him
with lewd proposals.

"Where's Ming Lee?" he asked.

Polly pouted and answered, "In the back."

Lem Choy entered the tiny back bedroom. Ming Lee
was resting on a flimsy straw mat that lay stretched along a
splintered wooden floor. She was awake, just lying there,
staring at the cobwebs on the ceiling. Lem Choy stood
silently above her, holding the straw basket. She looked at
him. His face told her all. Ming Lee turned her head away.
A long pause followed. Neither one moved or spoke.

Ming Lee broke the silence. "What is it, Lem Choy?
Is he dead, Lem Choy?"

Lem Choy nodded.

Ming Lee looked up at the ceiling again.

"I will return all the opium that I accepted as

payment," Lem Choy told her. "I will pay for what I already smoked."

"I should not have paid you in opium."

"I will pay for the shipping and the burial," Lem Choy offered.

"Thank you," Ming Lee said without emotion.

Lem Choy felt flustered. "He . . . he must have . . . he must have been sick. I was very careful, really. I tried to . . . I tried to be careful."

"You were smoking, though, weren't you, Lem Choy? Weren't you having a pipe?" she accused bitterly.

Lem Choy stared at the floor and said nothing.

"It's all right, Lem Choy," Ming Lee said. "It's all right."

Another empty silence filled the room.

"Why don't you leave, Lem Choy? Just leave." Ming Lee's gaze remained fixed on the ceiling. "In fact, leave and take the body with you. Dispose of it any way you like. I just want to forget my son ever lived. I just want to forget, do you understand?"

"Yes," Lem Choy responded. "Yes . . . but I want you to know, I'm shipping the body back home for a decent funeral. I'll pay for everything." He paused. "Good-bye, Ming Lee."

"Good-bye." Ming Lee closed her eyes and Lem Choy started out the door.

As he passed through the door, his back was toward her and she saw the blanket, a corner of which cleared the rim of the basket.

"Stop! Stop!" she cried.

Startled, Lem Choy stopped and turned around. "What is it?"

Then she saw it clearly. The blanket was blue.

"Let me see the infant," Ming Lee said.

He could have switched the blankets, she thought for a moment, but then she saw the lifeless face. When she saw it, she began to weep. Yan Chui Lee's beautiful baby was dead! Poor Yan Chui Lee.

She said to Lem Choy, "That is Yan Chui Lee's baby, not mine. You wrapped mine in a brown blanket. Hers was wrapped in a blue blanket."

Lem Choy shook his head and blinked his eyes. "How could I have made such a foolish error?" Now he had to go to Suey Sing territory on Sullivan's Alley. He must find Yan Chui Lee and repeat the whole agonizing confession over again. Perhaps she would believe his story, that the child was sick to begin with and would have died in any case.

"I will go to Yan Chui Lee now. I will tell her that—"

"Wait." Ming Lee stopped him from leaving. "Why do that? What will it accomplish? Wouldn't it be better to let her be ignorant? Let her imagine her child is alive. If she will never see him again anyway, at least let her think he lives. She never has to know."

"You don't think I should tell her?" Lem Choy asked.

"I know what I felt just then when you told me that my child had died. That news would have broken my heart if it were true. Our lives as slaves of the Tongs do not have very many bright spots. The one bright spot was the birth of those two beautiful boys."

"And I am responsible for that little boy's death!" Lem Choy said sorrowfully.

"It is a tragedy that Yan Chui Lee's child has died, but the truth can be hidden from her. She does not have to experience yet another tragedy in her life. Please, please, will you keep this a secret from her?"

"I can agree to keep this sad news a secret. But if I do that, what will I do about the baby? The body must have a proper funeral. I don't want the soul to be grabbed up by evil spirits and taken to the domain of Yen Lo."

I will take it upon myself to be the custodian of the little coffin. We will bury the child temporarily here, in Gum San. When Chui Lee dies, if we survive her, we will dig up the child's coffin again and send it back with her."

"Back to our homeland, back to China," Lem Choy nodded.

Chapter 21

Lem Choy still had four thousand dollars on his person when he had the misfortune of encountering the Chi Sings' foremost new assassin, Lum Po. Lem Choy was no match for the younger and tougher *boo how doy.* Lum Po approached Lem Choy from behind, disarmed him, collared him and pushed him into the dark recesses of Stoppford Alley. This tiny niche between apartment buildings wasn't wide enough for cars. It was a dark dead end.

"Lem Choy, 'The Trick,' " Lum Po snarled. "I thought you had left Chinatown. Haven't seen you around."

"Oh, I've been around," Lem Choy said nervously. "I have no reason to fear anyone. I haven't done anyone harm. I have no enemies."

"No?" Lum Po asked. "That's good. That's good. It's best to remain neutral. Everybody's a good friend. You don't hate anybody."

"That's right," Lem Choy said, rubbing his neck, which hurt from having been collared and dragged into the alley. "I don't know why you attack me like that, Lum Po. I'm a friend of the Chi Sings. I helped the Chi Sings in the war."

"It was good of you to put us in touch with the

'invisible one' so we could conclude that business deal,'' Lum Po said in a flat tone. "Yes, you have done us favors."

"The money was good," Lem Choy said. "So why have you pushed me down this alley?"

"You don't live here?"

"No, I don't live here. I was on my way home. This isn't my home, Lum Po. You know that. Now please, let me go on my way. It was unkind of you to push me around like that."

"*Doy mm ji*, I'm sorry." Lum Po bowed gracefully. "I'm sorry if I have to put a hole in you. Or perhaps several holes." He pulled out his revolver. "The full price of the New Year's massacre has not been paid. You are a part of that blood debt. I have to balance the ledger. I'm the treasurer." Lum Po cocked the gun.

"Just a moment. I have money here. A lot of money. Four thousand dollars. That's a lot! Here. Take it!" Lem Choy reached in his pocket and dumped the wad of bills out of the envelope onto the pavement. Lum Po looked down at the money, and during this momentary distraction, Lem Choy broke into a run. But he didn't count on Lum Po's skill. Lum Po was able to reach down, pick up the money, then turn and fire. Lem Choy was caught in the temple a second before he turned the corner.

Lum Po ran over to the body and dragged Lem Choy back to the end of the alley.

"I am amazed," Lum Po said with an icy calm. "I expected you to give an account of yourself. Instead, you admit your guilt by throwing money in my face. For shame. We did not even need a trial. Only the execution."

The day before the New Year, Lam Wong, master of the Suey Sings, was murdered by Chi Sing highbinders as he sat in a barber's chair having his hair cut. The death of Lam Wong did not sit very well with the San Francisco Police Department. Lam Wong had spoken English. He had been one of the few who really got along well with the police. He had a few shady operations like everyone else in the quarter, but Lam Wong had always been outgoing, friendly, and had a great sense of humor, even when one of his establishments was being busted.

He made payoffs to the police and various civic leaders. He also threw banquets for them. He introduced the subtleties of Cantonese cuisine to barbarian palates. He even contributed liberally to various charity organizations, and he made sure everyone knew about it. Therefore, when the police learned of his assassination, they were outraged.

Murphy and his cronies Price and Cook met at Mooney's Irish Pub in North Beach. There they launched a plan of attack.

"This plan would make Kearny's sand-lotters proud, I'll tell you," Murphy said. "At last the final blow will be dealt to the Tongs. They won't soon recover from this one."

"The citizens are up in arms over the latest murder," Price said. "The time is right. Lam Wong's murder is the last straw."

Cook added, "Yes, now the city has to listen. The city wouldn't listen to the complaints of the merchants. The extortions have been going on for years. Only now that there's this murder, they'll listen. It's time to wipe out their headquarters."

"Axes, sledgehammers," Murphy hissed as he drummed his pint down on the table. "That's what we need, along with a few good men. Men that aren't afraid of sweat. And never mind your Oriental art collectors."

"We don't save nothing," Price said.

Cook added, "Crowbars. Don't forget your crowbars."

So Murphy and his band of axe-wielding comrades charged the Chi Sing headquarters. They reduced the ebony table to splinters. They crippled the high-backed chairs and destroyed ancient Chinese carpets. They threw precious Ming and Han vases out the windows.

When they were satisfied that the Chi Sings' rugs, furniture, artwork and altars were nothing but fragments, they moved on and repeated the procedure at the Suey Sing headquarters, the Gin Kong, the Kwong Duck, the Hip Yee. Virtually every statuette of every major and minor deity was shattered. Every Tong meeting chamber and joss temple was decimated.

News of the destruction traveled like lightning throughout Chinatown. *Chun Hungs* were pasted on every brick wall. They read, "Look out for Mo Fay and his men. They are dressed like peacocks and are coming to desecrate our sacred temples."

In every headquarters, Murphy, Price and Cook, decked out in blue uniforms, brought brushes and buckets of black paint with them. They ripped the fine oak wainscoting from the walls, then scribbled profanities in crude black letters. Anglo-Saxon curses, snarling and sloppy, dripped and dribbled over the intricate characters. Calligraphers had spent months carving them in fine wood or marble, or carefully brushing them on fine linen scrolls. Ritual vestments were shredded, stained or set aflame. Incense sticks were cracked, crumpled and ground under heavy boots.

Sometimes, a highbinder or two were caught inside the headquarters when the raid started. It was ascertained whether the highbinder had gainful employment, which he usually didn't. Then he was arrested for vagrancy and sent to the county jail.

The chief of police stated, "I will end highbinderism

in San Francisco." And he dispatched other police wearing blue to "raze the Canton of the West."

This unprecedented crackdown opened the door for newer, tougher officers for the Chinatown squad in the Murphy, Price and Cook mold. It spelled the beginning of the end for large-scale prostitution in Chinatown.

The biggest raid came in the autumn of that year. It was early September, around the time San Francisco was hit by Indian summer. For a couple of weeks, a very stubborn high pressure system sat on the state. The usual chilly fog was kept from oozing its way across the hills. San Francisco suddenly felt like the middle of the tropics. The temperature rose to the high eighties and stayed there even in the evening.

The new rabble-rousers took the opportunity to guzzle liquor, and they used their drunkenness as an excuse to release hostility. A squad of off-duty police was pulled together.

The mob marched on the cribs, and one by one the dark alleyways were brightened by torches. The highbinder guards scattered. One by one, the Irish lawmen stormed the cribs, pulling naked customers off their pleasure slaves, pummeling them, sending them onto the street and throwing their clothing after them. They hauled the women to the county jail and crammed them into cells. And then they ransacked the cribs.

Sing Choy Wu felt helpless during the crackdown. His highbinders had run from the *faan gwai*, and local merchants were leaving his organization by the droves. He lost himself in opium and in his art collection. But as he sat dreamily admiring his beautiful ceramic glazed horse from the T'ang Dynasty, he felt a pounding flash of pain in his chest. The pain was so sharp that it felt like a gun had gone off inside his body. The blow sent him writhing to the floor. He struggled to regain his breath. The *mui jai* struggled to get him into his bed. A half-hour later he was breathing normally, but he was exhausted and greatly weakened.

Lum Po found Choy Wu too weak to get out of bed. The heart attack had taken its toll on his life.

"My boy. I want to see my boy," Choy Wu said.

"We've got to get you to a doctor," Lum Po said.

"No." Choy Wu shook his head weakly. "It's no good. My wife, Ming Lee. My baby son, Man Sum. I want my wife and my baby."

Lum Po said, "I'll get your son. He's in the East Bay."

"Kill him! Kill him!" Choy Wu said deliriously.

"I will, sir."

"I didn't want to leave China," Choy Wu murmured. "I didn't want to leave her. She had a boy. I never saw my boy. I had to leave my family. We would have starved if I'd stayed. I didn't want to live among the barbarians. I wanted to live with my family. . . ."

Sing Choy Wu's tear-filled eyes closed for the last time.

After the cribs were raided, Kwan Ming Lee and Yan Chui Lee found themselves in the same jail cell.

"Where will you go, Chui Lee, when you are released from this cell?"

"I will probably go back to the cribs. This raid does not mean the end of slavery. The highbinders will reopen the cribs the day after tomorrow, and everything will be as it was."

"Don't go back there, Chui Lee. Join me. I am going to the mission home. You will like it there. Come with me. You will be free there."

"Free? I don't think so. Maybe for a few days, but the Tongs know how to get you back. They were successful in your case, weren't they? You lasted there only a couple of weeks."

"This time it will be different," Ming Lee said. "The Tongs are getting weaker and weaker. You've seen the *Chun Hung* warn of the raids of the peacocks. There have been many more raids recently on gambling, prostitution. And even the Tong headquarters themselves."

"The Tongs will just have to pay the police more money," Chui Lee said.

"It is said that these new police don't accept bribes or protection money. This policeman called Mo Fay who I remember from Angel Island is giving assistance to Sylvia Damon. And together, they are rescuing more and more slave girls. The highbinders can do nothing."

"Highbinders can do nothing but kill you," Chui Lee said.

"Highbinders are arrested for nothing more than standing around or meeting together. Everything has changed since the death of Lam Wong. Already the merchants are refusing to pay protection money."

Chui Lee pointed out, "They can't refuse for long."

"Chui Lee, where will the Tongs get the funds for their war chests if all these sources of revenue are taken from them? I think it won't be long before the Tongs will not be able to enforce their ownership of us. They will not be able to collect."

The expression on Chui Lee's face showed that she was not receiving this news with any hope or relief. What Ming Lee was saying seemed to have the opposite effect.

"I don't know. I don't really want to go to the mission home. I have no desire to become a Christian. I understand they put a lot of pressure on you to join that barbarian cult.''

"There is nothing wrong with Christianity. It is not a bad religion. It preaches that there is a God who loves humanity. You might even find that it would make a difference in your life if you believed,'' Ming Lee said.

"If I didn't know you any better, I would say you are trying to convert me. No, Ming Lee, I won't be joining you. I am sure my business will be thriving as usual in the next couple of days. If I didn't do this, I don't know what else I would do.''

"You could marry. You could marry and have a home of your own. That's what I intend to do,'' Ming Lee said. "I don't want to stay in that place forever. I want to raise a family.''

"Yes, that's easy for you to say, Ming Lee. You have your lover, Sing Man Sum. But I have no one. And besides, who would want me? Nobody wants a woman who has been soiled by a thousand hands. Nobody.''

"If you come to the mission home, you will meet someone kind, decent—''

"Anyway, I already have a family. I have my son, wherever he may be. One day, my son will find me. I think he will come to Chinatown to look for me one day, and then I will see him. I will see my son for the first time since he was born. I look forward to that moment. It is the one moment in my future I look forward to the most.''

Kwan Ming Lee saw that she could not persuade her friend, and that filled her with sadness. When the morning of their release arrived, the two women embraced and went their separate ways. Chui Lee went back to the life of a daughter of joy. Kwan Ming Lee went back to the mission home and the always welcoming, warm arms of Sylvia Damon.

*　　*　　*

The funeral of Lam Wong had been a lavish affair. It was attended by many highbinders and merchants, as well as Caucasian politicians. A lesser funeral for Choy Wu would mean loss of face. To provide Choy Wu with a respectable funeral meant emptying the last of the war chest. But Lum Po decided he had to do it. He added the four thousand dollars Lem Choy had given him.

He bought an oaken casket. It was covered with broadcloth. Choy Wu was laid in state in the funeral parlor at Jackson and Powell. The exalted master's body was dressed in fine Chinese burial raiment. He wore a cap with a gold ball on it, like the nobility of old China.

Lum Po hired mourners. They wore headdresses abundant with white flowers. White was the color of mourning for Chinese. The mourners kept up a continual wailing throughout the ceremony. Priests were retained to accompany the laments with clanging cymbals and incantations.

At the cemetery, the mourners knelt on a mat before the casket. Their foreheads on the ground, they rocked to and fro as they wailed, "*Ai-yah, ai-yah, yah.*"

Several priests wearing octagon-shaped hats beat gongs and lit sandalwood incense. The priests then droned Buddhist prayers. And while one of them rang a little bell, the others lowered Choy Wu's casket into the grave. They continued droning as they covered the body with dirt and stones. A simple slab with the characters of his name inscribed was set in the fresh dirt. Cooked funeral meats were placed on a platform next to the slab. There were roast pigs, sheep and chickens. And there were many bowls of rice.

A replica of Choy Wu's house was set on the platform. Red paper slips representing his possessions were put into the house. The entire house was ignited. This ritual was performed so that evil spirits would not rob Choy Wu's things in the beyond.

The funeral over, the spectators feasted on the funeral meats. When the feasting was done, they looted the plates and bowls.

Police waited for the completion of the ceremony before they picked up Lum Po. He was arraigned for the murder of Lem Choy and implicated in the murder of Lam Wong. Highbinders had talked to save their own skins. Lum Po was convicted and sentenced to life imprisonment. They took him to San Quentin.

Chapter 22

In March, Man Sum had left Sacramento and followed the dragon boat festival south, where he sold red paper and firecrackers, along with the usual items, to the festival's participants.

After the festival, he went to the town of Locke in the Sacramento River delta area. Locke was an unusual place. It was a town populated exclusively by Chinese. Man Sum fell in love with it. He decided he would stay in Locke rather than return to crowded, dusty Sacramento. There were plenty of customers here. When he needed to replenish his merchandise, he could always go back to Sacramento for a day or two.

All the residents of Locke lived in a tiny, four-block area, behind which stretched a large field to some railroad tracks. The field wasn't owned by anyone special, as far as anybody knew. So it belonged to the town. Each person had a plot of ground on which he could grow vegetables. That field was a colorful place indeed. The people grew a great variety of plants: all kinds of squash, melons and gourds were grown there. Trellises were built to grow peas and tomatoes.

There were small Chinese communities to the south in

nearby Walnut Grove and Isleton. These communities furnished markets for surplus food grown in Locke's fields. There were buyers, too, for the items decking Man Sum's pack. Man Sum would often trade his retail merchandise for produce, which he'd then sell at a profit in another town.

Locke had a simply decorated yet very appealing joss house. Man Sum, at the close of each day, would go there and light incense to the gods and meditate. He found the country air and the people of Locke a refreshing change from the other Chinatowns, particularly San Francisco's. There he had only known the stench of death and the sorrow of disappointed love.

One hot summer afternoon, Man Sum hauled a quantity of gourds into a grocery and general merchandise store in Walnut Grove. The proprietor was Tsui Pang Fai, a veteran of the "coolie" era in the delta. At that time, thousands of Chinese were retained for criminally slight wages to build huge levees. These levees opened substantial tracts of land for farming.

Man Sum's entrance into his store bearing wares on his back made Pang Fai smile.

"Well, look at you, young man," Pang Fai said. "You're doing just what I did many years ago."

The two men started talking. Man Sum told Pang Fai how he started his little business.

"I carry fast turnover items, and I count on the convenience of being there when the need arises," Man Sum said.

"Yes," Pang Fai nodded, "but you seem like an intelligent fellow, far too intelligent to be wasting your time carrying around loads of merchandise on your back."

"I like being outdoors," Man Sum told the proprietor. "But you're right. It's not a very stimulating life."

"Let me make you a proposition, young man," Pang Fai offered. "I will give you a job as my assistant. I'll give you a decent living, and you can set that pack frame of yours down for good."

Man Sum immediately took a liking to Pang Fai. "All right," Man Sum agreed. "I'll accept your offer, Mr. Tsui."

Pang Fai smiled. "Good. It will be good to have young energy around the store again. You see, my son went to join the American forces in Europe. He fought in the Great War. He died."

"I'm sorry to hear that," Man Sum said.

"He died for a good cause, though. He died for his country," Pang Fai said proudly.

"His country?" Man Sum seemed puzzled.

"The United States, son. His country."

"Oh." Man Sum was somewhat dumfounded. A Chinese considering the United States *his* country? That seemed like an altogether novel idea.

For the study of retail merchandising, Man Sum had found the right teacher.

"Foresight and courage," Pang Fai would say, "will always be the chief stock in trade of successful retailing, no matter what goods are on the shelves."

"What is meant by foresight and courage, Pang Fai?"

"Foresight to see the opportunity. Not when it is fully upon one, but when it is still a faint, approaching glimmer. Courage, not only to grasp the opportunity, but more important still, to be prepared to grasp it fully."

"What kinds of goods do you stock mostly, Pang Fai?"

"Well, when I opened my grocery stand, I never stocked items farmers could grow themselves. They all had gardens. They could grow their own vegetables. They could catch their own fish out of the delta. So I supplied meat they couldn't get elsewhere.''

"I see."

"I included items needed for farming. Everything from shears to gloves.''

"So you cater to the farmers mostly?'' Man Sum asked.

"Now, yes. But the future's what I'm concerned about. I have big ambitions.'' Pang Fai winked at the younger man.

Man Sum worked for a while at the store. Pang Fai respected Man Sum's energy and eagerness. There was an unspoken trust between the two men. A profound friendship was beginning.

Pang Fai began to confide in his assistant. "You, perhaps, will have a share in the future of the business,'' he told Man Sum one day. "I want to create an entire chain of retail establishments. I want to compete with Caucasians in nothing less than the retail department store.''

"Now that's foresight and courage,'' Man Sum laughed, clapping his hands.

"I'm talking about the single price system,'' Pang Fai continued. "None of this bargaining with the seller, trying to get the price down.''

"Fixed prices?'' Man Sum asked. Another new idea.

"Yes. That way, the experienced and inexperienced buyer are both treated fairly. I'm also talking about delivery service, full-page advertising, making refunds for unsatisfactory purchases—''

"Sounds very modern,'' Man Sum said, "and ambitious.''

"I'm talking about doing an annual volume in excess of a million dollars,'' Pang Fai said.

"A million dollars?" Man Sum exclaimed in surprise. "That may be a little too ambitious for a country store."

"Do you think I am just dreaming? I can tell you are a dreamer too."

"I suppose I am," Man Sum said.

"Dreamers are ordinarily not of much use. But if they have foresight and courage, there is very little that can stop a dreamer," Pang Fai said, and winked.

An annual volume in excess of a million dollars, Man Sum thought. What a war chest a department store owner would have.

Pang Fai continued, "I'll tell you who I admire. Then you tell me if you agree or not. The White House store in San Francisco was established in 1854 when San Francisco was a gold mining town. It was, of course, a small shop when its owners hired Raphael Weill, a young French boy of eighteen. The store became a great department store and Raphael became a great citizen and philanthropist."

"Raphael Weill. Must have been a dreamer like you and me."

"The earthquake of 1906 really separated those who had courage and foresight from those who did not. The greatest of all was this Raphael Weill, then nearing seventy. Why, he started plans for rebuilding while the ashes were still hot."

"Are you sure he wasn't Chinese?"

"He lived to be eighty-four. The White House claims to have run the first full-page ad ever run by any store. It closes on only two holidays. One is February twelfth, Lincoln's birthday, and the other is September ninth, the date California was admitted to the Union."

Before Man Sum could register admiration, the wizened dreamer launched into another story. "San Francisco is full of such men. That's what makes it a challenge to a

Chinese businessman. Macy's is another fine old store that started business in 1854 just after the gold strike."

"Ah, Macy's. Very famous. Union Square."

"Destroyed by the earthquake and fire of '06. They also showed great courage in arranging temporary quarters, in immediately buying new stocks of merchandise and laying down plans for a new building.

"Then there's the City of Paris. It dates from 1850 when a Frenchman named Felix Verdier sailed into San Francisco Bay with a chartered ship bearing silks, laces, fine wines and other products from France. He sold them from the decks of the vessel. Then he moved ashore, started a store called the City of Paris. He had the foresight and courage to create a unique wine department. It is kept supplied by the many vintners operating out of Napa and surrounding areas. So there you have it.

"But what you don't have yet is a great, courageous, forward-looking Chinese department store in California. That's where you and I come in, son."

When Pang Fai called him "son," Man Sum honestly felt he had found a father at last.

"All right, Pang Fai. I'm with you. Let's do it."

Man Sum certainly couldn't complain about the way he was being treated as an employee of Tsui's store. He was entrusted with more and more of the business, and this included contact with Caucasian customers. His English improved steadily, though slowly. He was given living quarters in the rear of the store, a room of his own! His salary was good enough to live on with some luxuries. And now Tsui was planning to make Man Sum a full partner in the business.

A headline in the *San Francisco Chronicle* for September 13, 1918, caught his attention: POLICE CRACKDOWN ON

TONGS. With his present level of English, he could not make out the rest of the story, but his partner translated it for him. The cribs of Chinatown were completely routed. Prostitution in San Francisco's Chinatown had come to an end.

And there was another item in the paper as well. His father, Sing Choy Wu, had died.

His father was dead and he had not been the kind of son his father had wanted. He felt little emotion at the news. He had never been close to his father. Lum Po had been more like a son to Sing Choy Wu than Man Sum. It might have been different if he'd known his father better. He'd known his father only as "the exalted master." He thought of how Choy Wu had treated him after the New Year battle. That was the closest he had ever come to knowing Choy Wu as a father.

He had an old photograph of his father. He put it on the wall of his small apartment. He placed a stick of incense on the table. The incense smoke rose and curled about the picture. Man Sum prayed for his father's departed spirit. Without question, his father would join Man Sum's ancestral tablet. Man Sum would venerate him with devotion. He would be filial in that regard, far more than he ever could have been to the living man.

But where was Kwan Ming Lee? He had to find her. He still loved her. That meant returning again to San Francisco, despite all the dangers of doing so. San Francisco. Twice he had barely escaped that town with his life. Crackdown on the Tongs. What did that mean? Were the highbinders all in jail? And if they were, would the *faan gwai* courts make the charges stick? Or would the slick white lawyers come to the Tongs' aid as they always had in the past?

* * *

Sing Man Sum was lost in thought as he sat in a seat in a passenger car of the Southern Pacific Railroad train bound for San Francisco. Traveling this way was a little more comfortable than riding the freight train, he mused, smiling. The view was better, too. He was dressed in a sport coat, a tie and a white shirt. That way he looked like an American.

He reasoned that if Ming Lee wasn't in jail and the cribs were indeed no more, there was a chance she had found her way back to the mission home. He had read about her court case in the Chinese papers, of course, and saw immediately that his father was behind the scheme. Because of that episode, he thought it might be a problem getting her out of the mission home again. Miss Damon might not let any strange Chinese see her.

He arrived in Chinatown in the morning. It was immediately obvious that things had changed drastically. The quarter looked like an armed camp. Street corners where highbinders used to stand around talking and smoking were now occupied by San Francisco police. They were dressed in blue and held large billy clubs. They regarded everyone who passed with suspicion. There were no highbinders anywhere, nor was there any sign of highbinderism. The flags that had topped the various Tong headquarters were gone. The windows were completely boarded up in the Chi Sing Tong headquarters. The sign with the characters for victory, union and Tong had been torn down. Only a few months ago, Man Sum wouldn't have dared to walk the streets of Chinatown. Now he felt safe. Safe but strange, as if instead of real *boo how doy*, their ghosts walked these labyrinths.

As he approached Sacramento Street, another fear took hold. Suppose Kwan Ming Lee wanted to have nothing more to do with him? It had been years since they vowed to love each other. The meeting in the opium den didn't count. On that occasion, she was possessed by the drug. She didn't really know what she was saying or doing. He touched the jade ring on his hand. Would she remember that she had given it to him? By the time he reached 910 Sacramento, the imposing red brick structure, his hands were sweating and he felt his fingers trembling.

Wu Ting Lee, Sylvia Damon's most trusted reformed daughter of joy, answered the door. She was wary. Man Sum's nervousness made her ill at ease. "Yes?" she asked.

"I have come to see Miss Kwan. Kwan Ming Lee," he said timidly.

Wu Ting Lee now grew very suspicious. "I am sorry, but Miss Kwan Ming Lee is not here."

Man Sum felt his heart sink. "Not here? But does she reside here? I mean, does she live here?"

"Well, what is your business with Miss Kwan, sir?"

That was a difficult one to answer. If he merely said he was her friend, that might look like he was lying, like he had something else he was covering for. On the other hand, he was not her husband yet, though he intended to be. He decided to tell the truth.

"I am her husband . . . to be. I am not her husband yet. I have come to ask her to be my wife, if she will accept."

"I am sorry, sir, but Miss Kwan is not available. She is not here. She doesn't want to see anybody from the past. Especially husband. She has come here to make a new beginning, as we all have. Undoubtedly, you were one of her customers and have taken a fancy to her."

"No, no," Man Sum protested. "I was not a customer." Now he was growing angry. "Let me in. I must see her."

"No. No one by that name lives here, sir. Please,

now, leave this place or we will have to call the police. You are mistaken. The woman you wish to see was here, but she is no longer. Now, please leave."

It was a crestfallen Man Sum who left the front steps of the Presbyterian Mission Home on Sacramento Street. From what Wu Ting Lee had told him, he had no idea what had happened to Kwan Ming Lee. After the raid, had she gone back to the mission home? Or had she returned to the cribs? Perhaps she had been killed or hurt. She might be in the hospital. He had heard of a case in which Tongs, rather than give up their property intact to authorities, had disfigured a singsong girl. They had cut up her face with a knife so she would no longer be beautiful. Maybe Ming Lee had been disfigured.

Sing Man Sum had no place to go. There was nowhere in San Francisco he could stay. He would just have to return to Walnut Grove. But it was unthinkable for him to have come all this way for nothing. If he loitered, he'd be picked up soon enough by the police. He'd be arrested, accused of highbinderism. Perhaps they'd find out he was a paper son. He'd be deported.

He didn't need that.

So Man Sum walked. He thought of the good shoe leather he was wasting, but he walked anyway. He walked as if he were engaged in some important business. He walked briskly and with purpose. Then he thought he heard footsteps behind him. He turned right at the corner of California and Leavenworth, and as he walked, he listened for the footsteps. He heard them again, only this time they were running. He ran, too. Had he been discovered by his former brethren? He didn't look back. When he reached the top of the hill, he let his legs carry him down, drawn by gravity, fast as he could go. Still, he heard the running footsteps to his rear, clapping against the pavement.

Then he heard his name being called. "Man Sum, Man Sum!" The breathless voice calling out his name was a woman's.

He turned before reaching the bottom of the hill.

It was Kwan Ming Lee!

He fell and slid a few feet down the hill, but he got up again and ran in the direction he had heard the footsteps. By the time he reached Kwan Ming Lee near the corner of Leavenworth and Jackson, he was out of breath and could not speak.

She was also out of breath.

They did not embrace or even smile at each other.

Ming Lee felt embarrassed and unladylike for having chased him, and she was suddenly ashamed of her forwardness.

Man Sum, in turn, felt like a fool for having panicked and run away from a woman's footsteps. He should have known by the sound of the feet falling on the pavement that it was a woman, not a man following him. Having tripped and fallen on that hill also made him feel like a bit of a fool. He gazed at Ming Lee's face. It had not been disfigured. It was as beautiful as he remembered it from Angel Island so long ago.

Ming Lee finally broke the silence and said, "I have to go back to the mission home. It is almost dinner time."

"I will walk with you. I had hoped we would have more time together to talk."

"We say prayers before we sit down to dinner. If we miss the prayers, we can't have dinner. We have to go to our room."

"The person I spoke to said you did not live there."

"She was just trying to protect me. I had just come

downstairs when you were about to leave. I recognized your voice, Man Sum.''

"I live in the town of Walnut Grove. I work in a general merchandise store with Tsui Pang Fai. We have become business partners. We have big plans to expand the general merchandise business.''

Ming Lee remarked, without apparent enthusiasm, "I am glad you are happy.''

They were nearing Sacramento and Powell Streets. They were only a block from the mission home. Man Sum didn't have much time to say what had been on his mind.

"I said that I was in business. I want you to know that I now have the financial capability to begin a family. It would be a modest start, but Pang Fai knows a lot about retailing. He has given me a lot of good advice, and he has been generous with his time. Soon we will prosper.''

By this time, they had reached 910. Ming Lee said, "I'm glad. I'm very glad you have the financial capability to start a family. I think if you feel that way, you should start one.''

Man Sum prevented her from opening the door. "It is with you that I want to start this family, Ming Lee. I want you to be my wife.''

Ming Lee's hand tightened on the doorknob. "I am sorry. I cannot marry you, Man Sum. I cannot marry anyone who is not a Christian.''

If she felt this way about him, why had she run after him? he wondered. Why hadn't she just let him go?

He wanted to ask her this, but instead he said, "No, that is true, I am not a Christian.'' Then he looked away from her.

She felt divided. Man Sum was the one she truly loved, but she feared her love was wrong because Man Sum wasn't a Christian. If she married such a person, it would mean she would be betraying the Lord. She feared that her love for Man Sum, the non-Christian, was merely the temptation of the flesh. Satan himself was probably sending this person to her, the one person she loved so much. And he was sending him to tempt her away from the path of Christianity. She was trying very hard to follow the path this time.

She had already backslid once. When she had returned to the trade, she had forsaken her Lord totally. The world had overwhelmed her. She had even gone as far as reverting back to her opium habit and her old pagan beliefs. Now the world, in the form of Sing Man Sum, was threatening to take her away from her Lord again. She wished she had the courage to simply tell Man Sum to go away.

Miss Damon was so strong in Jesus. She had turned down marriage twice to men she'd loved in order to continue her missionary work. Why didn't Ming Lee have that courage also? She didn't have it because, as Wu Ting Lee had said, she was still too young in the Lord.

Now Man Sum spoke in an unusually loud voice. "Just because I am not yet a Christian does not mean I cannot become one. In fact, I *will* become a Christian. I will renounce all my beliefs in Lao Tze, Confucius, Buddha. I will put all that aside and follow you and follow the *faan gwai* . . . I mean, the Christian religion."

"No, Man Sum, you cannot do that just to please me so that we can be married. If you are going to become a Christian, you must do so because the grace of God has touched your heart."

"Good. How do I get this grace to touch my heart?"

"You must fully believe that Jesus Christ has died on the Cross for our sins."

"Yes, yes," Man Sum insisted. "That is all very

possible for me to believe. I just need to read about it, study it, that's all, read and study.''

"It's not as simple as that!''

Suddenly the door opened. Wu Ting Lee stood there. She said, "Ming Lee, it is late. You'd better come in to supper now!''

With that, she drew Ming Lee into the house and closed the door on Man Sum. He knocked on the door several times, but no one answered.

Ming Lee, like Man Sum, was not pleased with the way their meeting had gone. His attitude confused her greatly. How could she know, once he adopted Christianity, that he was truly sincere? What if he said he was a Christian, then renounced the faith after they married? She knew that she was very weak spiritually. If she married Man Sum and he renounced Christianity, she would not be able to maintain her faith. She would bend to the pressure around her. That was what had happened the last time.

Wu Ting Lee and Sylvia Damon had both been very critical of Ming Lee for abandoning her faith after Choy Wu had gotten her back. She had done herself great harm. She had also given the mission home a bad name. People thought that if Ming Lee was so weak-willed, the mission home must not really reform its girls. Once they left and were reunited with the Tongs, it was as if nothing had happened to them at the home.

So Ming Lee had been asked to perform a kind of penance. On the evenings it was her turn to serve in the kitchen, Miss Damon always found some extra tasks for her to perform, such as cleaning the stove or the ice box.

When Wu Ting Lee reported to Miss Damon that Ming Lee had run after some strange man, the missionary was, to put it mildly, concerned. A hasty conference was called.

"Now, Ming Lee," Sylvia Damon said, "I understand you have been chasing a young man."

Ming Lee blushed. "A friend visited me the other day," she explained. "He was sent away. I wanted him to know I was alive and well. I didn't want my friend to worry."

"You won't be alive and well for long if you run onto the street like that. You remember what happened to Chu Mae Pong," Sylvia Damon reminded her.

"Yes," Ming Lee said. "I cannot forget that."

"Who is this 'friend,' Ming Lee?"

"He is Sing Man Sum. I knew him on Angel Island. We met there. For a while, he was a highbinder with the Chi Sing Tong."

"A highbinder? A Tong hatchet man, you say?" Miss Damon asked, shocked.

"But he isn't a highbinder anymore, *Ah Mah*," Ming Lee said.

"My dear," Miss Damon remarked, "many highbinders have 'reformed' recently, since the crackdown, rather than face stiff prison sentences. But that doesn't make him any less of a criminal. You must never see him again. Do you hear?"

"Yes, *Ah Mah*," Ming Lee said.

Sylvia Damon made it quite clear where matters stood on the question of relationships with the opposite sex. She said, "We must exercise great care and discipline. We are fallen creatures in the eyes of God, sinners one and all. Those of us who have been so abused and exploited by men must take special care."

"I told him I wouldn't marry him unless he became a Christian, *Ah Mah*," Ming Lee said.

"We are accustomed to this abuse, it is familiar to us.

Therefore, it is very easy to fall into a similar situation again. Human beings only repeat themselves. It is only God who is able to change man. Man is hopeless, and cannot change himself.''

"But perhaps Sing Man Sum will change, if he becomes a Christian," Ming Lee said.

The missionary leaned forward, frowning. "Ming Lee, the young man is a paid killer and assassin of one of the Tongs!"

"I must protest, *Ah Mah*. That is not true."

"Is it not?"

"Man Sum is no longer a highbinder. More than that, when he was a highbinder, and there was a war with the Suey Sings, Man Sum didn't fire a shot. Man Sum is a scholar and a poet. That's what he really is. I have some of his poems here, poems that he wrote to me on Angel Island."

Sylvia Damon merely shook her head. "We all want to love and be loved. That is our nature. There is nothing wrong with that. It is in a woman's nature to give herself to a man, to become a wife to him, to serve him always, to bear his children. We are not opposed to marriage and family here."

"I don't want to marry him unless he chooses the Lord," Ming Lee protested.

"However, the marriage must be made by God. Man cannot make a marriage. If you marry this man, you will be in the gravest danger of repeating yourself. He is a Tong man, and Tong men do not keep the ones they marry. They sell them."

"No, no. Man Sum would never sell me again into slavery. Never."

"Only the strongest, most rigorous and disciplined

belief in our Lord Jesus can save you from the hell of your previous life. I am worried about you, Ming Lee. I have seen you reach the heights of faith. And then you fell just as deeply into unbelief and despair.''

"Yes, I know that, *Ah Mah*. But this time my faith is really strong," Ming Lee assured her.

"Then I see you going out into the street and chasing a highbinder around the block, throwing yourself into his embrace.''

"I didn't embrace him. I didn't.''

"No?"

"I have accepted the Lord Jesus as my savior. I have admitted my sin!'' Ming Lee insisted.

"But He has yet to work a change in your heart. You must abstain from meeting this man or any other man until the Lord has done His work in you. Will you promise me that you will not see him again?"

"Yes, *Ah Mah*, I promise.'' Ming Lee said, weeping.

"There, there, that's my good girl.''

Miss Damon took the young woman into her arms and comforted her. "You will see. The right gentleman will come along with God's intercession. You will find happiness. He will be a gentleman of means and he will be a Christian. I know that such a man exists in your future, Ming Lee.''

"I pray it will happen, *Ah Mah*. I so deeply want to be married and have a family.''

Ah Mah patted her and said, "I know. I am praying that it will happen, too.''

When Man Sum began working at the store again, his friend and partner noticed that something was wrong.

"As always, you are doing an excellent job, Man

Sum. But what's on your mind? Come. A grain of sand can hide a mountain. You are concealing a mountain of thoughts with your usual cheerful manner. Tell me. I am your friend.''

Man Sum decided to tell Pang Fai.

After concluding his explanation, Man Sum added, "In my opinion, it is a lost cause."

Pang Fai laughed. "We shall remove this obstacle from the road as one kicks dried ox dung aside."

"How is it possible to do that, Pang Fai?"

"Foresight and courage. One of the principles of courage in the business world is this rule: always go to the top. Don't deal with underlings, assistants. Go to the top. Now, the top of the mission home is the missionary. This woman they call *Ah Mah*, well, she is the one we must deal with."

"I fear I already have a bad name with her. I was one of the trained soldiers in my father's army. Ming Lee must have told them about me. One of them looked at me like I was trying to take Ming Lee back to the cribs."

"Weren't you responsible for getting her into the mission home?" Pang Fai asked.

Man Sum nodded. "If only Sylvia Damon would believe it. I was the one who wrote the note asking her to rescue Ming Lee. But I don't think she would believe me."

"There is a Presbyterian Church in the town of Isleton. We will introduce ourselves to the minister. We will tell the minister that we believe in the tenets of Christianity, and then we will join his church."

"Us? Chinese? Join a church full of whites?"

"We will become exemplary churchgoers. We will go out of our way to say hello to the minister every Sunday."

"But we're Chinese!"

"Undoubtedly, we will be the only Chinese members of the congregation. That's good. It shows we have foresight and courage. It will be a compliment to his ministry. It will show that the power of his delivery of the 'message' is strong enough to reach to even the hardened souls of 'the heathen.' "

Man Sum was quick to grasp the meaning of his partner's strategy. "Then I will tell him I want to marry a Christian girl who resides in the mission home in Chinatown."

"That's right. That's right. You will request that not you or I, but he himself, go and talk to Sylvia Damon. He will tell Miss Damon that you are a good Christian with economic credentials as well."

"You're a genius, Pang Fai!" Man Sum said delightedly.

"*Koi wui gai siu ney la*, he can introduce you. His recommendation will do the trick!"

"Yes, yes, you're right. Go to the top. Never mind what's below. Just deal with the top."

"It is a very important lesson in getting what you want out of life, whether it be in the world of business, or in the world of love," Tsui Pang Fai said, smiling.

So Man Sum and Pang Fai became members of the First Presbyterian Church of Isleton. Dr. Mayfield, the minister, welcomed the two Oriental converts to his church with excitement. That heathens had come to his church for salvation flattered his ego. He in turn was most cordial to the Chinese men. He shook their hands after the Sunday morning service.

Man Sum was lost. He always had to follow Pang

Fai's lead as to what to do next. The homily in particular baffled him.

"Did you understand any of that sermon?" he asked his partner.

"About half," was the reply.

"Can you explain it to me?" Man Sum challenged.

"He was talking about love. Love everybody, that kind of thing."

Being asked to explain the sermon made Pang Fai somewhat uncomfortable. He didn't like sermons, he liked action. So his explanations of what Dr. Mayfield had said were always very brief.

But he would always say to Dr. Mayfield, "You speak very good today, Doctor, very good. Even I, my English not very good, I can understand."

This pleased the pastor no end.

One afternoon, the two Chinese men requested counseling. Dr. Mayfield was more than happy to oblige them. He bade them sit in the leather chairs around his walnut-topped desk.

Pang Fai appointed himself spokesman. "We very trouble. Need you help us," he said.

"Anything I can do to help, I will," Dr. Mayfield promised.

With occasional asides in Chinese from Man Sum, Pang Fai outlined the problem his partner had.

"Man Sum want to marry San Francisco girl. She Christian. Man Sum talk to her before, but Christian mission mother, she say Man Sum is bad."

"Man Sum is bad?" Dr. Mayfield said. He was making sure he understood.

"He is not bad. I know he good, good man, good

worker, good Christian man. Better you go talk to mission mother Damon.''

"You would like me to talk to her, is that it?'' Dr. Mayfield asked.

Pang Fai nodded. "Tell her Man Sum, he is good Christian, good man. Let Man Sum marry Christian girl. Long time ago, Man Sum, he is Tong. But he no like Tong. He get out quick.''

"Tong? Man Sum was a highbinder, you mean?''

"He no like Tong. You very good tell mission mother, Man Sum no like Tong, get out quick. Now he work for me. He very good worker. He Christian, pray to God. All the time, he pray to God. He want marry Kwan Ming Lee. He love her.''

Dr. Mayfield agreed to help them.

A meeting was arranged with Sylvia Damon by telephone for the following day. The minister rode the train down to San Francisco early in the morning. He took a cab to 910 Sacramento Street. Sylvia Damon was very impressed with the minister's presentation.

"But,'' she said, "it remains for me to be fully convinced that the young man in question has reformed. I offer a compromise. Sing Man Sum is not to see or call Kwan Ming Lee for at least one year. If after a year's time, Man Sum is still actively involved in the church and is still a good citizen of Walnut Grove, I would give permission for the two to be married, but it must be a Christian wedding.''

"I assure you,'' Dr. Mayfield said, "it will definitely be a Christian wedding. It will be a Presbyterian wedding. I will undertake to marry the young people in my church in Isleton.''

Man Sum, upon hearing this news, gave an uncharacteristic yell for joy.

*   *   *

During the following year, Man Sum worked hard at the store and even harder learning the difficult and complex English language. He stumbled and slurred over all its syntactical vagaries and its slippery vowels and consonants. He had an opportunity to talk to the people in the church. They were always willing to help him with his English. But mostly he enjoyed practicing with American children because they laughed so easily.

At the close of a year, to the day, Man Sum appeared at the mission house with a little box, inside which an engagement ring was enclosed.

This time, Wu Ting Lee was all smiles when she opened the door. Sylvia Damon and Ming Lee were seated at the couch in the living room. They were dressed in bright cotton dresses, carefully pressed. Ming Lee smiled demurely. One of the other girls served tea and cookies.

"Please sit down, Mr. Sing," Sylvia Damon said.

"Thank you very much," Man Sum replied in his best English.

"How are you today, Man Sum?" Ming Lee asked, also in English.

Man Sum looked at her for a minute. He struggled for the right answer. "I am fine, thank you. And you?"

"Just fine."

"My, my, Mr. Sing," Sylvia Damon said, "you speak English quite well."

Man Sum looked at her uncomprehendingly.

"*Ney gong ho ho. Kui wa ney gong ho ho,*" Ming Lee whispered to her perspiring suitor.

"No Chinese, please!" Miss Damon requested, holding up a forefinger in warning.

"Thank you very much." Man Sum said.

"Now, Mr. Sing," Sylvia Damon began. "What is your business with us here today?"

"I business on Walnut Grove," Man Sum said.

"No," Miss Damon said, shaking her head. "Today, today. Why are you here today? What do you want?"

"I want to marry Kwan Ming Lee," Man Sum said to *Ah Mah*.

"Very good, Mr. Sing. Now tell her."

"*Ngo ho—*"

"In English, please!"

"I want to marry you, Ming Lee." Then he held the box out toward her. "You give this ring . . . to you."

Kwan Ming Lee was considered very lucky to have the prospect of marrying such a good and handsome Christian man.

Man Sum thought to himself that it wouldn't be long before he would make Ming Lee return to the religion and customs of her own race. All it would take, he reasoned, was getting her away from *Ah Mah* and the mission home. Thanks to his partner, he had succeeded in doing just that.

The wedding ceremony was held at the First Presbyterian Church of Isleton.

When the priest performing the service asked "Do you take this woman to be your lawful, wedded wife?" Man Sum needed a little coaching from his partner and friend, who was now his best man.

Loud whispers in Cantonese were heard throughout the ceremony.

Sylvia Damon herself, together with Wu Ting Lee and a few other girls, attended the service. Miss Damon wept as if she were giving away a daughter. Some of Man Sum's friends from Locke and Walnut Grove were also on hand. While the service was decidedly Christian, the wedding banquet took on the flavor of the Orient completely. It was a sumptuous feast consisting of many of the fine, fresh vegetables grown in Locke, and fresh fish caught in the delta. In the streets of Walnut Grove, where the banquet was held, the guests exploded firecrackers. Someone donned a lion's head and began to dance.

PART IV
THE FAMILY
AND THE ORPHAN

"What are the things which people consider good? Kindness of the father, filial duty of the son; gentleness of the elder brother, and obedience of the younger brother; righteousness of the husband, and submission of the wife; kindness of the elders, and deference of the juniors; benevolence of the ruler, and loyalty of the minister. These ten are the things which people consider good."

—Confucius, The Li Ki

Chapter 23

Both Man Sum and Ming Lee had lived in quarters that were more cramped than those they were now going to occupy. A small kitchen adjoined an equally small living room, which had been converted into Man Sum's bedroom. The bed had been wide enough for Man Sum, but it was somewhat narrow for both of them. For now, though, it would suffice.

Despite their cramped quarters they felt very lucky because they had a good stove. The stove had been built in the Chinese fashion. All of the sides were exactly the same, neither too thick nor too thin. If one hit any side of the stove, a pleasing tone could be heard. The sound was the same for each side struck. The opening for the wood was exactly in the center. That way, all sides of the stove gave off the same amount of heat. Above the stove, Man Sum had placed the traditional god of the kitchen and a scroll on which was written in Chinese, "May our rice never burn."

A little *ting*, a small copper caldron, sat on a table by the stove. In it, incense sticks could be lit to pay homage to the god of the kitchen, and inspiration for good cooking would be dispensed. When they entered their little apartment together for the first time, they saw that Pang Fai had covered the bed with evergreen branches and pecan nuts.

A note was left for them which said, "May the union always be fresh as the evergreen and as prosperous, and may many children bless this household."

Ming Lee made some sage tea and sweetened it with sugar. This drink was a talisman calling on the gods to make the couple's destiny sweet and happy, not bitter. The bed was the only place in the living room to sit. They first had to clean all the evergreen branches and pecan nuts off it. Then they sat down together, but they could think of nothing to say.

Finally, Ming Lee looked at the jade ring on Man Sum's finger, the one she had given him. It was believed that jade was a kind of barometer of health. When one was feeling fine, the jade would shine. But if one was sick, then the jade would reflect that state by looking dull.

Ming Lee said simply, "The jade is bright."

Man Sum looked in her eyes. "I am happy," he said. They embraced.

"Are you sure you're happy, Man Sum? I was watching you during the banquet. You looked, well, you looked worried," Ming Lee said.

"I was a little worried, that's true."

"Is it my past, Man Sum? That's it, isn't it? My past and all those men. And your father, also."

"Well," Man Sum said hesitating, "I was concerned that, after all those experiences, you would be—"

"I would be what?"

"You would be different. Changed."

"I am changed, my dear. I am different. But one thing has remained the same."

"What is that, Ming Lee?"

"I have always loved you, my darling." Tears came to her eyes.

Man Sum thought he had never seen anything so lovely as those tear-filled eyes.

Ardently, he held her face between his hands. "I too have held to that love. It held me, and never let me go. What is this miracle? I have you."

"Yes, yes, Man Sum, you do."

"After all these months, years, disappointed dreams, nightmares, at last, at last, oh, Ming Lee, my Ming Lee."

"Man Sum, my darling. My darling."

As he touched her, her body quivered with pleasure. How different this was, she thought. This, this was how God meant it to be. How great God was to give human beings this means for pleasure. It had never been pleasurable before. Always, before, she tightened and withheld her body as men took it for their own satisfaction.

But this was her husband giving her pleasure, and she let herself go. It wasn't as difficult as she had thought it would be. He was so tender with her, so gentle and caring.

Yes, she had heard of a woman's sexual climax. The singsong girls spoke of it. Some of them had experienced it with customers. Ming Lee, however, had not even come close. But in Man Sum's arms, how the sensations in her body were growing, growing. Something so large and powerful was happening. Was this what those singsong girls were referring to? Was it going to happen to her now, on her wedding night?

Man Sum, too. He was feeling so much pleasure. Love for her was giving him this pleasure. How he looked at her. How full of love his eyes were. Love for her, and no other. Love for Ming Lee.

Yes. Yes. Yes.

"I love you, Ming Lee."

"I love you, Man Sum."

And when it was finished, they clung to each other for a long, long moment.

Ming Lee finally broke that deep silence. "Are you smiling, my love?"

"Yes, I am. Are you?"

"Yes."

"Let's see," Man Sum said.

The man and woman, wife and husband, looked at each other. And they continued to smile at each other that night. And the night after that, and the night after that.

Working in Tsui Pang Fai's general merchandise store made Man Sum feel somewhat restless. For all of Pang Fai's ambitions and ideas, he didn't, to Man Sum's mind, conduct his business very efficiently. There was too much stock that never sold. The turnover occurred with the foodstuffs that Pang Fai obtained locally. The store was more like a grocery store than a general merchandise store. Large quantities of dry goods and hardware lay on the shelves without being touched for months.

A relatively small section of the store was reserved for the groceries. These goods sold fairly quickly.

"Let's conduct an inventory of all the goods in stock," Man Sum suggested one day.

"The time to run inventory isn't for another two months yet," Pang Fai argued.

"We don't know what we have anymore," Man Sum said.

"If we do an inventory, we'll have to close the shop for a couple of days. Means we'll lose some business. So, I'd rather postpone the inventory," Pang Fai said.

But Man Sum insisted. "All right," he said. "I'll do

it myself. I'll do it in my own time, after the store closes. I'll work every evening until it's accomplished."

Pang Fai relented. "Since you're being so stubborn about it, I'll help you."

Man Sum discovered that, for every item on the shelves, ten items were hidden away in various drawers or chests. These items seemed to be mostly for farmers: feed, gloves, shears, pails, fencing, shovels, hoes. There were overalls, boots, hats, rugged shirts, and so on. At present, the clientele of the store consisted mostly of the Chinese from Locke or Walnut Grove. Very few *sai yan*, Westerners, patronized the store.

Man Sum said, "The display of the items is so haphazard. How can the farmers know the store has what they're looking for?"

And, Man Sum asked himself, what about all the other people living in the various communities in the area who were not farmers? And what about the needs of the wives of the farmers and the wives of the other workers? Man Sum had noticed that it was the women, not the men, who did most of the shopping. These American women did not shop necessarily knowing what they wanted, but often they would be led to buy by a pleasant-appearing package clearly visible on the shelf.

Man Sum encountered another difficulty. He could not tell how long an item had been in stock.

"What can we do about that?" Pang Fai asked.

"I suggest we mark everything that has been in the store for more than one year with an 'XX.' If it has been in the store for between six months and a year, mark it with 'X.' 'X' and 'XX' items must be sold quickly to make room for the items that move faster."

"Yes, we have too much old stock in this store," Pang Fai noted.

"Maybe we need to conduct a clearance sale to clean out this old inventory," Man Sum suggested. The longer the item has been on the shelf, the more unpopular it is."

"You are right," his partner acknowledged. "Look at these heavy gloves. I guessed that I would be able to sell a lot of them, but it was a poor guess. I think I only sold one pair."

"If a customer refuses to buy it," Man Sum said, "why will he not refuse to buy it in the coming season? Reason tells you that, if he has been refusing it for many months, he will continue to refuse it, indefinitely and forever."

Pang Fai nodded. "Unless we radically change the conditions under which we offer it."

Man Sum said, "That's why I suggest holding a *maaih pehng*, a sale, for this old stock."

Man Sum's enthusiasm and insight impressed Pang Fai and inspired him. The partners worked together to make long lists of everything in the store. As Man Sum suggested, they put an "XX" on items over a year old.

To learn more about the business, Pang Fai and Man Sum spent the summer studying the major department and chain stores in Sacramento. They looked at prices and displays. They waded through advertising that was difficult for them to understand. They carefully monitored the sales results of their own store. They worked very hard to establish a basic stock list designed to cut down the inventory substantially while increasing the salability of the stock. Now came the hard part: clearing out the "XX" items.

Pang Fai protested that he had paid good money for that merchandise. It must be worth at least as much as he paid for it if not more. And why shouldn't he make a few dollars on each of those items? But they remained on the shelf even though the partners advertised a clearance sale and slashed prices.

Man Sum would say, "If we keep the item and it won't sell, it continues to depreciate. The original investment just continues to dwindle!"

"That's easy for you to say. It came out of my pocket, not yours," Pang Fai would argue.

Then they would get rid of the item by cutting the price to next to nothing. The two of them were beginning to learn that the value of their goods lay only in what people were willing to pay for them. An item, no matter how much it cost the store, was valueless until it was sold. It just took up room.

We've got to face the merchandise. Face it. Look at it." Man Sum was forever going into the basement and the attic and the back room where stock was kept. He would pull everything out and look it over. He would check it against the basic stock list and the inventory list.

After a couple of well-advertised clearance sales, there were still some "XX" items not moving, so Man Sum borrowed a truck and carted the stuff to the Sacramento city dump. Pang Fai didn't speak to him for a week. But with the money and space freed up, they began to stock their store with what they learned were fast turnover items. Man Sum determined that the item must be the right style, the right price, have a wide appeal, have a good value, and a colorful package. The store began to attract more customers, especially Americans, and profits increased.

Man Sum still wasn't satisfied. "This store has too many hiding places for our merchandise, corners where items go to sleep. There, that long, plain oak counter might be comfortable to lean on, but we are throwing space away. That counter could be used to display merchandise. When we throw away space like that, we throw away dollars, too.''

He carefully listed every bit of shelving and drawer space that stood in the way of the merchandise being openly and prominently displayed. Then for days he made designs on paper of a new store layout, with sections devoted to separate departments. It was as if he were creating a small department store here, in Walnut Grove. For the smaller items, he designed and built tables divided into bins. He used glass divider strips, just as he had seen in the Macy's and Mayfair bargain basements in Sacramento. He asked himself, How does my layout compare with the soundly developed standard layouts of the chains? The chain stores maximize sales return for every square foot of floor space.

The partners closed the store for a week and remodeled it from the top down. When they reopened, the place was very different. It had more light and everything was in plain view. And now hardware and men's durable clothes were replaced by hosiery, towels, underwear, lingerie, blankets, apron frocks, paring knives, electric toasters, costume jewelry, handbags and soap. They fixed the prices, always ready to change them, but never with the customer present. No bargaining was permitted. The prices stayed fixed until the proprietors determined that the price was too high or low.

They bought a stenciling outfit and price tags for all purposes in the store: a tiny bin ticket size, the window item size, the five and half by seven-inch size, and the seven by eleven-inch size. A filing system was adapted for price tickets and cards. No item was displayed without a price.

Though Man Sum was preoccupied by the dry goods business, he was virtually the only person with whom

Ming Lee communicated. She could have gone out shopping or visiting in Locke, but she was still frightened to leave the tiny apartment or the store. There were still the Tongs. They had greatly diminished in power since the police had begun their crackdown, but they were not gone completely.

She enjoyed helping in the store. Dealing with the American customers made her feel that her English was improving. The other place she felt at home was Dr. Mayfield's Presbyterian Church in Isleton. Although she didn't understand all the words, the church was comfortably similar to the mission home, which she greatly missed.

Man Sum, on the other hand, no longer attended church. He didn't read the Chinese translation of the Bible either. His excuse was that he was concerned with getting the dry goods business to show a decent profit. That meant revamping the entire operation. He had no time for the foreign religion, as he put it. It was beginning to be as Ming Lee feared; Man Sum was losing interest in Christianity.

One time, the couple had a discussion about it which almost became an argument. This discussion occurred when Ming Lee wanted to put a picture of Jesus Christ on the wall of their tiny dwelling.

"That picture looks out of place on the wall, Ming Lee," he said. "It is too large and it doesn't fit with those Chinese landscapes."

Ming Lee replied, "I know that it doesn't fit. But it is important for us to be reminded that Jesus is present here since we are both Christians—though we seem to be too busy to observe our faith."

"One doesn't need to do anything to observe one's faith, Ming Lee. It is enough just to have the faith."

"Do you still have faith in Jesus, Man Sum? Are you

still a Christian? This is something I am not altogether sure about. We never talk about it. I never see you pray. You no longer attend the church in Isleton.''

Man Sum attempted to duck the question. ''There are some things about this Western religion which I believe in very strongly. 'Do unto others as you would have others do unto you.' That idea is very good for personal relations and also business relations, so I heartily subscribe to it. I am in doubt, however, about the Christian attitude toward humanity. Why does it consider humanity to be so bad, so full of 'sin,' as the Christians put it?''

Ming Lee frowned and said, ''It is true, isn't it? I know I am a terrible sinner. I can't begin to count the number of terrible things I did.''

''You were forced to do those things, Ming Lee. It was just like being forced to remain at Angel Island. You were imprisoned. There was nothing you could do. There was no way out. To say that it is your fault is to put too much blame on yourself. You just make yourself feel very bad. Therefore, you can do nothing about your condition.''

''Jesus can do something about my problem.''

''Too many people wait for a Jesus or some other god to come along and solve their problems. But the world just doesn't work that way. You solved your problem by escaping from the Tongs and by marrying me. It wasn't Jesus who got you out of Chinatown's bagnios, but me, Sing Man Sum, your husband.''

''Jesus was working through you. Jesus works through others even though they might not know it.''

''I agree, Jesus helped and so did the other gods, the god of heaven, the god of fortune. Yes, the gods have been good to us.''

Ming Lee spoke somewhat angrily. ''No, we have to

forget about those Chinese deities. There is only one God, and Jesus is His only Son.''

"I am sorry, Ming Lee, but that is another aspect of Christianity I disagree with. I simply do not agree that Christianity is the only true religion or that the Christian deities are the only ones which exist. I am not willing to believe that the highest place in heaven is so sparsely populated. The Chinese have enough trouble getting established in American society without getting rejected from heaven as well.''

Ming Lee was close to tears. "But I promised. I promised Sylvia Damon and Wu Ting Lee. I promised God and Jesus. I promised I would worship no other gods. I must hold on to my faith, I must.''

"I am not forbidding you to believe in Christianity, Ming Lee. I only insist we don't throw away all those good lessons from our heritage. They are true, too. I do not insist we light incense sticks everyday to the kitchen god or Kuan Yin. But I think we need to follow the tenets of Confucius very carefully if we want to have a successful family and business.''

Ming Lee did not answer. Although she loved Man Sum, she found herself wishing she were back in the mission home. If Miss Damon knew that Man Sum felt this way, Ming Lee would never have been permitted to marry him. Far from being a sincere Christian, it was obvious that Man Sum had simply joined the church in order to satisfy Sylvia Damon and thereby marry Ming Lee. This was trickery. And now she was trapped being the wife of a heathen, an unrepentant sinner. How would she learn to adapt herself to this marriage? She was so confused. She resolved to keep her Christian ideas to herself. She would pray to Jesus when she was alone.

The discussion helped them in some ways. Ming Lee no longer expected Man Sum to go to church with her or to join her in prayer. Therefore, she saved herself the experience of being continually disappointed. On the other hand, Man Sum was perfectly content to allow Ming Lee to follow her Christian teachings, certain in his mind that eventually she would "get over it."

One Sunday, after church, Man Sum took her fishing. They borrowed a rowboat from a fisherman living in Locke, and they set off on a beautiful summer's day. Lazily they floated from one of the channels to another. There was hardly a breeze. All was still except for the insects and the soft sounds of the current brushing against the little boat. All was peaceful.

As he cast the line over the side of the boat, he recited a poem. "A fisherman throws his nets out from a motionless boat. The net breaks the surface of the water. His thoughts are at home with his wife. He will return to her, bearing food, like a swallow to its mate."

She reached for his hand.

Six weeks later, Ming Lee began to suspect that her body was undergoing a familiar change. After a visit to a Chinese doctor in Locke who performed a modern test, her suspicions were confirmed.

"Man Sum," she told her husband later, "I am going to be a mother."

He was overjoyed. "I must tell Tsui. We will have a celebration."

Ming Lee thought about her son, whom she had been forced to give up, and felt deeply saddened. Where was he? Where was her little boy? Was he still alive? But now she would have a chance to give birth to another child, and nothing would take this child away from her. Not floods, earthquakes, or Tongs.

Tsui's Dry Goods was beginning to enjoy a fine reputation. There, the housewives from the neighboring communities of Isleton, Locke, Ryde and Walnut Grove could usually find what they were looking for at a price comparable to the chains in Sacramento or San Francisco. Why travel all that distance when you could get the same merchandise right here in the delta? they reasoned.

Man Sum painted the front of the store bright pink with blue trim. He painted the sign to reflect the bargains within. "Tsui's Dollar Store," it began to be called. Then, after that, simply, "The Dollar Store." As their profits mounted, they began to contemplate investing in another store in Oakland.

The Dollar Store in Oakland was located at 2321 East Fourteenth Street, on the edge of Oakland's Chinatown. Man Sum would manage the Oakland store while Pang Fai would remain in Walnut Grove. Although Man Sum in some ways hated to leave the delta, he very much wanted to move for two reasons. First of all, his ambition was leading him to create a chain store such as he had seen in Sacramento. He had visions of The Dollar Store being located in every major city in California. Why not? The store was designed to meet the needs of lower and middle income families. These families shopped in the bargain basements of the high-priced department stores. The Dollar Store would consist exclusively of discount items. Moreover, its items would appeal more to women than to men. Man Sum had observed women constituted the overwhelming majority of shoppers. The other reason for leaving Walnut Grove was simply that, with the baby coming, Man Sum and his family would need larger living quarters.

Above the new store, there was a flat where the Sing family would live. The flat was spacious compared to the tiny rooms Man Sum and Ming Lee had occupied in the back of the Tsui's store in Walnut Grove. There were two bedrooms, as well as a large kitchen, and there was a sizable living room, too.

Chapter 24

Ming Lee's first child was harbored only nineteen blocks away, at 231 Fourteenth Street. Gum Sung Tom had named his adopted son Bo Mat, or "valuable treasure."

At three years of age, Bo Mat had busied himself with his toys in a safe corner of the laundry shop. His favorite toy was a cow that would go "moo" when he tilted it. But even though his son was so young, Sung Tom was already putting the boy to work. Bo Mat certainly didn't do much. He mostly went to get things for his father: the receipt book, a box of soap, an empty laundry basket.

By age six, however, he was beginning to do some hand ironing, and by ten years of age, he was expected to carry the workload of a mature adult. He was permitted to play with his friends an hour a day and half a day Sunday, but the rest of the time was spent in his father's shop. He didn't know what it was like not to be always wiping his brow. His friends called him Hon Gum, "sweaty" Gum, because the humidity from the steam in the shop caused him to perspire constantly. Moreover, the boy was continually burning himself from touching the hot iron.

Rather than take pity on the youngster for burning himself this way, Sung Tom would scold him roundly for his carelessness. "What's the matter with you, Bo Mat? Are you crazy? Watch where you put your hands."

"I can't work this fast. I just can't, Father."

"You have to learn to work fast without burning yourself. That's what this business is about. We are already one day behind in our orders. If you can't work fast, you get further and further behind."

"But it hurts!"

Still, Sung Tom did not do anything about the boy's burned hands. Instead, he said, "Keep working even though it hurts. Work will keep your mind off it. Before you know it, the pain will be gone."

He was right. The pain went away eventually. But it always came back. Working so quickly, Bo Mat was sure to burn himself again and again. He sometimes burned himself five or six times in one day. Before he collapsed from exhaustion each night, he wept from the pain caused by the burns and had to stifle his tears so that Sung Tom could not hear him. The older man would fly into a rage if he heard the boy crying.

"The only thing that destroys efficiency worse than complaining is crying. Don't let me hear you cry or you'll feel my slap."

One summer day, the temperature rose to above one hundred degrees Fahrenheit. It was the hottest day in the shop Bo Mat could remember. The steam and the heat made him extremely uncomfortable. He felt like he was suffocating. Each time he took a breath, it was a struggle. Moreover, the pile of clothes he took from the drier was particularly difficult to press. It consisted of several men's shirts, some of which had ruffles, and women's dresses with pleats.

After Bo Mat pressed a few of these garments, Sung Tom came over to inspect the boy's work. "What are these clothes doing on the 'finished' pile?" he grumbled.

"I have already ironed them," Bo Mat replied in a timid tone.

"You call these ironed? Look at these wrinkles."

Bo Mat honestly could not see them. He asked innocently, "What wrinkles?"

"These wrinkles!" Sung Tom's voice shook as he shoved the shirts into his son's face. "And these wrinkles. And these wrinkles."

Close up, Bo Mat could see where he'd missed a couple of spots.

"Do them over. All of them. Do them over. If you have to work all day today and all night tonight, you will get these clothes pressed perfectly. What will the customer think if he puts on this shirt and looks in the mirror. He will never come back to my shop again, I will tell you that. Because of your careless work, I lose customers. They don't complain, they just don't come back. They tell each other, 'Don't go to Sung Tom's laundry unless you want wrinkled shirts!' I don't know. I have to do all the washing plus the flat work on the big press, two hundred sheets today alone. I can't always be watching you. I would have no time for my own work if I had to keep my eye on your ironing. I have to trust you to do a good job."

"You can trust me, Father." Bo Mat said this to stop his father from complaining more than anything else.

"No, I can't. That's the trouble. You cost me customers. I lose customers because of you, your carelessness."

The suffocating heat and the emotional exhaustion were too much for Bo Mat. Angrily, he yanked the iron's cord, pulling the plug out of the wall. He threw the iron across the room and stalked toward the door. "Then don't trust me, Father. Get somebody else."

Sung Tom intercepted him before he could reach the door. "Where are you going? You can't leave the shop. I didn't give you permission to leave, did I? What are you doing, trying to destroy me? Pick up that iron. That's valuable equipment, irreplaceable. What do you mean by throwing it around the shop?" He pushed the boy back from the door. Bo Mat looked at the iron leaning on its side. Reluctantly he walked over and picked it up.

"Bring it here. Show it to me. Hurry. We can't afford this much time away from our work! Already we're at least two days behind in our orders."

Bo Mat brought him the iron. Sung Tom held the iron by the handle and turned it in all directions. He switched the temperature regulator back and forth. Carefully he examined the whole length of the cord and the plug.

"You should never unplug any electrical equipment the way you did. You could injure the plug. It would result in a fire. Then, because of you, I would be ruined."

He plugged the iron back in. Bo Mat knew that his father would not punish him for his outburst, not during working hours. Punishment took too much time away from the job. But after the day's work was completed, he could expect a whipping.

The whipping came at exactly ten o'clock that evening. Sung Tom used a length of rope hardened with starch. The boy was forced to lie face down on the spot the iron had landed when he threw it. After each stroke of the rope, he was made to apologize. His father coached him on what to say.

"The wrinkles." And then the whip cracked on his back.

"I am sorry about the wrinkles," Bo Mat said.

"Pulling out the plug by the cord." Again the whip sounded.

"I am sorry about pulling out the plug by the cord," Bo Mat repeated.

"Throwing the iron." Again the boy felt his father's whip.

"I am sorry I threw the iron."

"Trying to walk out on the job." This time the whip made an especially loud sound as it crossed the boy's back.

"I am sorry I tried to walk out on the job," Bo Mat grunted through gritted teeth.

Sung Tom brought the whip down on the boy's back with extra vehemence. "It was not just the job you were trying to walk away from, but your family as well. That is the most serious offense of all. I have trained you from a baby in this business so that you could work side by side with your father, and together, we could make a family business that would be profitable and give us esteem in the community. That was my hope in training you, my son, in this business. I didn't put in all that time and energy training you only to have you leave the business and abandon the family. You will one day take over this business. Then you will train your own sons. That is the Chinese way. A man's sons are the most important investments he can have."

Bo Mat didn't really know what being Chinese meant. All his questions about China and his father's background were dismissed with the statement, "You don't want to hear about that. It's not a pretty story." Or his father would respond after much pestering from Bo Mat, "I'll tell you what China is like in one word: misery. Maybe you will visit China someday. Then you will know what I mean, and you will be very glad you were born here, in the United States, as far from that wretched place as you can get.''

"But what do you mean, Father? What is China like?" Bo Mat asked.

Sung Tom leaned forward, pointing with his chopstick for emphasis. "Let me tell you something. If you think working in this laundry is hard, you should know what it's like to work twice as hard in the fields and have all your crops taken by the landlord or a creditor, leaving you close to starvation all the time. All right. There you have it. That's what China is like. Now, stop asking me questions about it. I'd like to forget I was born there."

"All right, Father, I won't ask you about China anymore, but what about my mother? Where is she? Is she still in China?"

"Don't talk about your mother."

"But Father . . ."

"Don't ask me any more of your stupid questions."

Bo Mat didn't ask his father any more questions about China, or about his mother, but questions continued to plague the boy's mind. Who was his mother? What was she like? Was she dead or alive? His father's avoidance of these questions infuriated the boy.

An opportunity to learn a few more answers came a year later. Sung Tom had a large press, which he'd bought with a good part of his savings. This press was able to handle large quantities of flat laundry. The laundry would be placed on a ribbon feed and introduced into the ironer. After that, it would be handled by a system of padded rolls and finally a rectangular metal chamber heated from within by steam. The heat plus the pressure smoothed the linens as they were passed through the machine. The machine could move quite fast, some eighty feet per minute, but Sung Tom had to adjust the machine to its lowest speed setting, for he alone had to feed the machine and run to receive the pressed result at the other end.

Today, a deafening clanking sound came from the machine, followed by a loud hissing. Steam was leaking everywhere, and the clanking was growing louder. Sung Tom quickly turned off the apparatus. Rather than suffer an expensive repair bill, he preferred to take the entire machine apart, find the defective part and take it to the manufacturer's representative in San Francisco. After an elaborate, painstaking session with the machine, he found what he thought to be the problem, a broken seal in the steam cylinder. The following day, he borrowed a friend's car and took the cylinder to the city.

"I'll be gone much of the day," he told Bo Mat. "I want you to work just as hard as if I were here. To make sure that you will not get into any trouble, I have carefully counted the number of items that need ironing. It should take you the entire day to finish the work. If there is work that has not been done, then I will know that you have been loafing. Don't make it necessary for me to arrive at this conclusion." With that, his father turned, hoisted the broken cylinder on his shoulders and left the shop.

Bo Mat took the rare opportunity of his father's absence to rummage through the shop and their living quarters for clues about his mother's identity and his own origins. The more his father had avoided this issue, the more whetted Bo Mat's appetite for truth had become. He began at Sung Tom's desk, on which the ever-present abacus rested. He pushed the abacus aside, then opened the top drawer. Carefully, he spread the contents of the drawer on top of the desk in the order that he took them out. That way, he could replace them in the same order, and his detective work would not be discovered. In the top drawer, he found nothing but receipts and other documents pertaining to the business. When he reached the bottom drawer of the desk, he discovered a box in which letters were kept, but they were in Chinese, and he couldn't read a word of Chinese.

He went from the desk to the closet, hoping some clue might be discovered there, some photo or object that would shed light on the matter. Nothing. Bo Mat was so disappointed at coming away from his search empty-handed that he just walked out of the store.

He walked down the street and all the way to downtown Oakland. He looked at the shop windows, with their expensive dresses on display. For many blocks he walked down Fourteenth Street, not knowing where he was going. But the act of walking away from the shop helped him to release pent-up feelings and frustration. As he walked, he sobbed. And as he sobbed, he cursed his father, the laundry, and the world that held him as a slave of ignorance about who or what he was.

Without thinking about what he was doing, he entered a place called The Dollar Store, a discount merchandise store. Discount, he thought. It didn't matter that it was a discount store, for he had no money to pay for anything. His father had never let him have any money. Only after pleading could he get a few cents to go out and buy candy. Here, there was a wealth of candy and toys. It was all out in the open within a hand's grasp.

He watched a boy his own age reach for a nice-looking toy car and take it up to the cash register and hand the cashier a quarter and a dime, thirty-five cents. Bo Mat had never had thirty-five cents to spend. Why should that boy have the car, and why should Bo Mat have to settle for no car? No toys? No candy? Then he saw another boy with his mother. His mother held him by the hand. His mother picked out a shirt for the boy in the boy's apparel section of the store. Bo Mat had on his sweaty blue workshirt. He never wore nice clothes. Why? Why did the other boys have mothers who picked out their shirts for them when he didn't have a mother at all? He didn't even have a chance to go to the store. He was supposed to be back in the laundry at this moment. If he was discovered away from the laundry, his father would whip him. Why did the other boys have mothers and thirty-five cents while he had whippings?

Something at that moment told Bo Mat that he was as deserving of good things as all the other boys. Suddenly he didn't care that he didn't have thirty-five cents. He was going to have that car anyway. His hand reached out for it, and his fingers held the smooth metal sides of the toy. The muscles in his stomach tightened around a yawning pit of fear that suddenly gripped him with a force he didn't expect. He was scared, very scared. What if he was caught?

"May I help you?" A Chinese lady, about thirty-six years old, was standing by him, watching every move he made.

Does she suspect me? Does she know that I am about to steal the toy? "Yes, I . . . I want to buy this toy," he said, trying to control the trembling in his fingers and trying to look as calm as he could. The lady seemed quite friendly. She was smiling at him. She must not know that he was a common thief.

"That's a very pretty car, isn't it? We have sold a lot of them lately. It's an exact replica of a Studs Bobcat, which is a very popular car these days for grownups. I have a son who is somewhat younger than you are, and he seems to enjoy playing with it."

Why is she talking to me? Doesn't she have anything better to do? "Yes, I like your store. I will certainly come here again." Her stare made him feel very uncomfortable.

"What is your name?" she asked.

"My name is . . . is Douglas Fairbanks." This was the first alias that crossed his mind. He regretted using it.

"I am Mrs. Martin Sing. My husband is the owner of this store. Do you live near here, Douglas?"

"No. No, I'm from out of town. I'm from the East. I'm just visiting the bay area. Now, I am in a hurry. I have to go. Let me pay for this car." He was going to reach in his pocket and then act surprised not to find any money there. Then he was going to return the car to the shelf.

"Just pay the cashier, Douglas. There, at the front of the store," she said.

This was his chance to have the car after all. As he walked, he could feel her eyes still on him and the metal of the toy sliding against the sweat of his palm. He reached the cashier, did a slight turn toward the register, then ran as fast as he could out of the store and down the street. He could hear the voice of the lady he had been talking with behind him, calling out his alias, "Douglas, Douglas!"

Bo Mat turned down a side street, ran onto East Fifteenth Street for a while, turned down another side street, and ended up on East Sixteenth Street. At last he could no longer hear her voice. He grabbed a paper bag from the gutter and stuck his brand-new Studs Bobcat in it. He knew he had done something wrong in stealing the toy, but he felt very happy with the car. No one had ordered him to do it. Moreover, he now had something that was completely his own. He was possessed by an exhilarating sense of freedom. He had to get back to the shop in a hurry so he could hide his newly acquired treasure.

When he opened the door of the laundry, he realized that he had lost track of the time. It was already five o'clock. He had gone to the store near closing time, and that was why the owner's wife had been there. She was probably going to lock up for the night. Sung Tom was already home. He was just finishing reassembling the large press. When Bo Mat saw his father, his instincts told him to run away as fast as he could, but for some reason, his feet would not move. He just stood there in the doorway. Sung Tom turned and saw his adopted son holding a paper bag and looking terrified.

"Come in and close the door behind you," Sung Tom said.

Bo Mat obeyed.

His father stood by the machine holding the wrench he was using to bolt the parts of the press back together. "What's in the paper bag?" he asked, his voice full of suspicion and menace.

"I want to go to school," was Bo Mat's reply. "Other kids go to school, public school. Why can't I go to school?"

"I already explained all that to you. School would be a waste of time for you. You're going to take over this business. Everything you need to know you will learn right here in this shop. Besides, I can't afford to send you to school, you know that."

"Public school in America is free."

"Time isn't free. Every second, time passes away. Time and money are lost if you are not working. I have invested too much already to make a worker out of you." Then his voice rose, pushed by the force of some bitterness his son didn't comprehend. "The barbarian school will teach you nothing but the barbarian's ways. It is bad enough to live in the barbarian's country and have to suffer his abuses, without also getting mixed up by his ideas. You are Chinese—"

"What does that mean, I am Chinese? What does that mean? You won't tell me. You won't explain to me anything about my origin. I can't just be Chinese because you tell me so. I have to find out what it is to be Chinese. And who are these barbarians you speak of?''

Now Sung Tom moved closer to Bo Mat, and he was pointing the wrench at him. "Let's see what you have in that paper bag," he said.

"No, it's mine," Bo Mat hissed.

"Son of a whore, give it to me."

"What did you call me?"

"Bastard," Sung Tom cursed, striking at Bo Mat with the wrench. Bo Mat dodged the blow.

"Are you drunk, Father? Why are you calling me that?"

Sung Tom was suddenly calm. "The press is back in good working condition. By taking the broken part to the manufacturer, I saved almost fifty dollars over what it would have cost if they sent a repairman here to the shop. I would have been charged for dismantling the equipment, a task I was able to do myself. I haven't started up the big press yet, but I'm sure it's going to work just fine, just fine.''

"Why did you call me a son of a whore? You have never said anything like that to me before.''

"What's in the paper bag, son?" Sung Tom asked quietly.

"A toy car," Bo Mat said simply.

"Where were you all day? You didn't iron one of the shirts that were set aside for you as your day's chore. I counted them when I got home. That was the first thing I did. Not one of the shirts has been touched, nor has the iron been heated. It is in the same position it was in yesterday. It is still cold.''

"I want to go to school. I don't want to work in this shop all day. I want to learn. I want to learn about cars.''

Sung Tom moved a step closer to Bo Mat. He was

still grasping the wrench. This time, Bo Mat was cornered between the wall and the big press which was perpendicular to the wall. "Let me see the toy." Sung Tom extended his left hand toward the paper bag, while in his right hand he held the wrench.

With foolhardy bravado, Bo Mat pulled the brand-new Studs Bobcat out of the paper bag. "Here it is. It is mine."

"Where did you get it?" Sung Tom asked, moving a little closer.

"I got it at the store, The Dollar Store, which is up the street," Bo Mat answered.

"How did you pay for it?"

"I didn't," the boy replied. "I took it because I wanted it."

"Very good," his father said. "Now that you have had a chance to play with it, let's you and I go back to The Dollar Store and return it with my apologies."

"Why your apologies?"

"A son's misdeeds are always the result of bad training. Therefore it is the parent who is ultimately responsible. I have done a poor job of raising you, evidently. You have turned out bad. I might have had better luck with the other one. Who knows? If I had both of you to raise, perhaps one of you would have turned out all right. As it is, I have thrown away good money on rotten fruit. Let's take the toy back to the store."

"We can't. The store has already closed. It's past five. Anyway, I don't intend to take this car back. I want it," Bo Mat said firmly.

"Give me the car." Sung Tom reached for the car, but Bo Mat jerked it away from him. Sung Tom followed with a swipe of the wrench, which connected with Bo Mat's shoulder, sending the boy sprawling to the floor, writing with pain. Bo Mat still held the car, but Sung Tom kicked the hand that held it, and the boy released his grip. The laundryman picked up the car, looked at it, then threw it forcefully against the brick wall. In his anger, he forgot that the car hadn't been paid for. The metal made an ugly sound as it struck the wall.

He yelled, "You will never, never leave this shop again! Your privileges are revoked forever. You will work extra hours. Your Sunday free time is canceled. You will work until we can pay for that car out of your extra hours. But it won't stop there. You must be punished for your bad behavior and taught that it doesn't pay to be a thief. No one else will teach you, so I must do it. Now get up, go to the ironing board and begin the ironing. You must finish those clothes before you go to bed this evening. I don't care if it takes all night to finish. You are very far behind, so get started."

Instead of doing as his father requested, Bo Mat crawled toward the car. His tears made it difficult for him to see the damage that had been done. He wiped his eyes and looked the car over. The front end was badly scratched and crunched.

"I have to fix my car first," Bo Mat said stubbornly.

Sung Tom picked up the wrench and threw it at his adopted son. The boy managed to duck, and the wrench collided with the wall. "I paid good money for you. Therefore, you have to work."

It was starting to sink in. Paid good money for him, Bo Mat thought. "You mean, you're not my real father?"

"I am your master. You are my slave. I *own* you. I bought you for four thousand dollars. Your mother is a prostitute in San Francisco whom I never knew. Yan Chui Lee is the name of the dirty bitch whose whoring is responsible for your birth on a dirty bed. There was another little mutt born at the same time. I had purchased the two of you, but the other one turned out to be dead on delivery. Now you have turned out to be worse than dead. You've become a criminal. I can see where you're headed. You are lucky I saved you from a fate worse than death. If it wasn't for me, you would have been raised in a brothel.''

An infuriated Bo Mat, clutching the broken car, stood up as tall as his four feet eight inches would make him. ''I would rather have been raised in a brothel than this hot hell.'' He stood there for a second. ''You're not my father,'' he said. Then he quickly picked up the wrench and threw it, with all the force his thin arm could muster, against the big press Sung Tom had just repaired. ''I don't have a father.'' He turned, and as fast as his feet could carry him, he ran out of the store and down the block. Sung Tom was too worried about the big press to chase after the boy. Bo Mat had proven to be an investment too costly to maintain, and too difficult to repair.

As he ran, Bo Mat thought of the name of his mother, Yan Chui Lee, a prostitute. He was the son of a prostitute, and he didn't even know what a prostitute really was. All he knew was that the friends he occasionally played with always said the word ''whore'' or ''prostitute'' with a snicker, as though even speaking the word was bad. So a prostitute must be a bad woman, an evil woman of some kind, Bo Mat decided. He was determined to find his mother, whether she was a prostitute or not. He would go to San Francisco's Chinatown and find her. At least he would try.

As he ran, he looked back and saw that the man he had thought was his father wasn't even following him. So he relaxed his stride and started to walk.

It then occurred to him that he had no money. He would need the fare to get across the bay and into San

Francisco. And what about the evening's bowl of rice? What about tomorrow evening's bowl of rice? Shelter from the evening chill, which was already biting at him? He didn't have a jacket. In fact, he didn't have anything. Not a thing.

He remembered how easy it had been to walk into The Dollar Store and walk away with a toy worth thirty-five cents. If he could walk away with a toy that cost thirty-five cents, why couldn't he just take the thirty-five cents? Or thirty-five dollars? He was fast on his feet. He could run. He could turn a sharp corner. He had gotten away with the toy car. He could get away with another theft. Perhaps he would be caught. They'd send him to jail. They would hang him. It would be better to be hanged than to do laundry work for another minute, he thought. He wouldn't even mind if his shirt was wrinkled. People would look on while they hanged him. His false father would watch and be glad. Perhaps they would find his mother. She would watch him hang, too, but she would cry, "I never knew him."

There was a coffee shop on the corner of East Fifteenth and McArthur. It had a long counter. He could see the cash register right next to the counter. He walked into the coffee shop and sat at the counter on the stool nearest the cash register. He thought, The next time the waitress opens the register, I will reach over and take whatever is there. He tried to stay calm, but his stomach muscles tightened. His fingers shook, and his palms sweated. He was hungry, too. It was dinner time. He ordered a steak with baked potato and corn on the cob. He ate hurriedly. It was delicious.

He was halfway finished with his meal when an elderly man walked to the register to pay. The waitress opened the register. Bo Mat's hand was there in the interval of the time between the collection of the man's cash and its placement in the register. But the waitress was fast, too. Her hand gripped the boy's tightly before he could make his escape. Without thinking, he applied his teeth to the waitress's hand. It loosened. He was out of the restaurant and running. A man was chasing him. Bo Mat turned a corner and slipped into a thin alleyway between two buildings. The man ran past. Bo Mat stayed hidden in the little space until dark. He was excited and happy. He opened his still-quivering fingers to find five twenty-dollar bills. One hundred dollars.

The red light district of Chinatown wasn't frequented by very many eleven-year-olds. Bo Mat felt self-conscious and conspicuous in Sullivan's Alley. Women's faces appeared at the tiny windows of the small apartments that lined the streets. He went up to one of the windows. The heavily made-up face of the singsong girl peered down at him.

"Do you know where I can find Yan Chui Lee?" he asked.

The girl looked at him with a cold expression in her eyes. "Give up, little boy. If you find her, you won't like what you find."

He simply walked to the next window. There he asked the same question and was met with, "Go away, kid." None of the girls said they didn't know her. None of them said "I don't know" or "Never heard of her."

After trying at four or five of the slits in the doorways of the women, Bo Mat became aware of two very sinister-looking men following him. Before he could reach the next door, one of the men was blocking his path.

"Nieh ni do yau mut yeh si?" the man asked him in Cantonese. "What is your business here?"

"I'm looking for my mother," Bo Mat said.

"There are no mothers here. If you're lost, you'd better go to the police station. Your mother's not around here, that's for sure."

At that point, Bo Mat remembered how the laundry-man, his ex-master, had dealt with the building inspector. The building inspector, Mr. Peterson, had told Sung Tom that the laundry's ventilation system was seriously inadequate, a health hazard, in violation of the city's building code. Sung Tom slipped him fifty dollars. Without a word, the building inspector tore up the citation, stuffed the pieces into his overcoat and left the building.

A spunky Bo Mat looked the highbinder in the eye, and he produced from his pocket two crumpled bills. "Here's forty dollars," he said, "if you'll tell me where my mother, Yan Chui Lee, can be found."

The hatchet man raised his eyebrows. "Where did you get that money?"

"Never mind where I got it. Do you want the money or not?" he asked, purposely ignoring the fact that the highbinder simply could have taken it from him and left.

The highbinder seemed impressed. "Okay, kid, I can take you to her. She's not too far from here. But I warn you, you're not going to like what you see. She's pretty sick."

"I don't care if she's sick or not. I must see her."

"Follow me, then."

"Aren't you going to take the forty dollars?" Bo Mat asked.

The *boo how doy* smiled back over his shoulder at the boy. "Never mind that. Keep your money."

They turned a corner off Sullivan's Alley and were soon walking up another alley that was completely deserted. Although it was daytime, this place was dark. The buildings seemed to curve inward upon it, blocking out any light. The narrow street was dank and pitted. A chubby rat lumbered along the gutter, stopping and sniffing at each speck of garbage. The highbinder creaked open a battered door. As he did, Bo Mat began to hear the moans. They were faint at first, but grew steadily louder as the man and boy crept down the hallway. The hallway was so dark that Bo Mat had to feel along the walls to determine that he was going straight, and the walls were wet and smelled of urine. When they reached the tiny room at the end of this hallway, Bo Mat understood why the women of Sullivan's Alley had been reluctant to direct the boy to this place. There were three women lying on straw mats. Each had an old, thin blanket to cover her, but it wasn't enough. The room was chilly. The windows were made of oil paper rather than glass, and more cold air than light came through them. All three of the women were awake, but listless. Their faces were expressions of agonizing misery.

"What's wrong with them?" Bo Mat asked.

"They're dying," was the highbinder's disinterested reply.

Chapter 25

"Mother?" Bo Mat said to no one in particular. There was no response from any of the three women. "Yan Chui Lee?" Still no one responded. "You've taken me to the wrong place," the boy said to the highbinder.

"This is the right place." The highbinder nodded slowly. "The woman you're looking for is that one, in the corner. She's too sick to answer you."

Bo Mat looked at the small form huddled in the corner. All he could see was the back of her head. She was propping her head up with her arm and murmuring something to the wall.

The highbinder started to leave. "Listen, kid, this place makes me feel uncomfortable. When you're finished talking to her, I'll be outside waiting for you."

"Why are you going to wait for me? I can find my way around by myself."

"I have some business to discuss with you." With that, the highbinder turned and parted, stooping so his head would not hit the low ceiling of the hallway.

Bo Mat reached out and touched the shoulder of the woman facing the wall. "Yan Chui Lee?"

"Yes," she said in a faint, hoarse voice without turning around.

"I'm . . . I'm your son."

"My son," she repeated flatly, without the slightest hint of emotion. There was a pause in which neither of them spoke. Then, slowly and painfully, the sick woman turned to face her visitor. She studied his face for a long time, as though searching for something. There was despair in her eyes. Whatever she was looking for could not be found in the face of the boy.

"Your son," Bo Mat said, trying to convince her. She was so thin, and her skin so tightly drawn, that her pallid face looked like a skull. Her eyes, on the other hand, were large and vibrant, desperately looking for something. "Gum Sung Tom told me your name. He said he purchased me. There was another baby also, but that baby died. I found this out only yesterday. The laundryman had been keeping this secret from me my entire life. Gum Sung Tom, the laundryman, said my mother was Yan Chui Lee . . . a . . . a prostitute. So I came to San Francisco to find you."

"There are many women of easy virtue in San Francisco," she said. "There must be well over three thousand. Out of that number, there are a few, perhaps, who have the same name I do."

"I am eleven years old. Did you have a child eleven years ago? And after you had the child, did you sell him? And is it true that you have never seen him since? If all that is true, then you are, in fact, my mother."

"Everything you say is true about me," she admitted.

"Then you are my mother."

"What do you want with me?" Her eyes still looked desperate and searching.

"I just wanted to meet my mother. I was hoping—"

"What were you hoping?"

"I was hoping perhaps we could be together, since you are my mother and I am your son."

"It would be nice for a mother to be with her son. It is a nice thought. Now, perhaps you'd better go." She started to turn toward the wall again, but Bo Mat stopped her by placing his hand on her shoulder.

"You are very sick. Let me do something for you. I will go and find a doctor for you, or I will take you to the Chinese hospital."

She laughed. "It's too late for that, way too late. If I were well, I would still be useless to them. I am too old. And I still owe them thousands."

"Who do you owe money to?"

"Tongs. They left me here to die. This is the end of the road." Her head sank down and she lay against her filthy straw mat.

"I'll pay the Tongs and I'll pay for a doctor too. I know how to get money, lots of money."

"Do you?"

"Yes, look at this." He showed her the money he had left. "You take this. It's yours. I can get more of it. I can get twice as much in five minutes."

"I don't want somebody else's money," she said without looking at it.

"But I want to help you, Mother."

"I am not your mother," she said in a bitter and irritated tone. "Therefore, I don't want your help. I had one hope in life, and that hope has just died. I have nothing more to live for. Please, leave me to die in peace."

"You are. You are my mother! Gum Sung Tom told me your name. The highbinder took me here, pointed you out to me. And you admitted you gave birth to a son eleven years ago."

"I have studied your face, listened to your voice. All it would have taken is one gesture or sound I could recognize, anything that came from my blood in you." Her eyes filled with tears. "If you were the baby I knew, grown to boyhood, you would have brought me back to life. I would have embraced you, showered you with kisses. I would have walked out of this place and into the sun. You would have cured me, because that baby was the one hope I had left. It was a hope that was dimly alive within me like a single, glowing red coal under a heap of grey ashes. It was the hope of seeing my son again. He would come to me, and he would save me. I would live with his family. I would have the honored position of *Ah Mah*. His wife and children would respect me, and my wasted past would be wiped clean. Now I know that baby died. Yes, he died eleven years ago. You're the son of the other one. You're Kwan Ming Lee's baby. Kwan Ming Lee is your mother, not I. My little one died in the cold on the ferry. They all lied to me. She said her baby died and my baby lived. That's not true. They gave me false hope. They gave me a dream that would never be realized. I know that now. I see you, and I know who you are."

"I'm sorry," the boy stammered. "I didn't know."

"You didn't know. Of course not. How could you know?" Her voice rasped bitterly, then turned into a paroxysm of coughing. Her frame shook violently, and she threw herself back down onto the bed, still coughing. "Opium," she wheezed. "Opium."

She pointed to the small table near the papered window. On the table was a bamboo pipe with an earthenware bowl. Bo Mat picked up the pipe.

"That's it. Bring it here to me." He brought the pipe to her, and she quickly put the stem to her mouth, then said, "Light it, light it." He saw some matches by her mat, picked them up, and lit the pipe as she requested. She drew the smoke deep into her lungs. "Now, leave me," she said. "There is nothing you or anyone else can do for me. Let me die in peace."

Bo Mat gently lay the frayed blanket over her and left.

The boy learned that the highbinder's name was "Snake." Snake told him that the Suey Sing Tong he worked for had some jobs for kids Bo Mat's age, stealing jobs. Snake said that he was impressed by the way the young man handled himself.

"You don't have to worry about the police," he told the boy. "If you get arrested, you can count on the Tong to get you out. We take care of the police," he chuckled, "the way you tried to take care of me with your forty dollars."

Bo Mat accepted. He really had no other choice, no other place to go.

His life now consisted of many acts of petty crime, from shoplifting grocery stores to snatching purses. The proceeds of these robberies always went to Snake. In exchange for Bo Mat's quick-fingered work, he was given lodging and meals. He was also given a moderate allowance so that he could buy candy or toys or whatever else he wanted, and he was given plenty of free time day and night to wander about and do anything he wished. He spent much of his time at the various bagnios inquiring about Kwan Ming Lee, who, it now appeared, was his real mother. He finally talked with an older prostitute in Ross Alley who informed him that Kwan Ming Lee used to work there, but had since left. No one knew where she went. He went around to a few other brothels, but only halfheartedly. The prostitutes only shook their heads when he mentioned her name. After that, he called off the search and devoted himself exclusively to perfecting his skills as a petty thief.

He lived in the basement of the Tong headquarters, relocated now in an old, abandoned building, with five other boys who were also discarded sons of prostitutes. He became a close friend of a tough kid who knew Chinatown's streets very well. His name was Lop Pun. But he liked to call himself Daih Lop Sop, or "big garbage."

Bo Mat, however, liked calling his friend Sop Sop, and Lop Pun himself thought he liked Sop Sop better, so he adopted the new name. Sop Sop and Bo Mat became an indomitable team in Chinatown's streets. They enjoyed picking the pockets of numerous tourists. Sop Sop would play the obsequious Oriental boy. He would go to the tourist, bowing profusely, and offer his services as luggage carrier or guide or whatever came to mind. Of course, the tourist would usually refuse this service, but the tactic was to continue to badger the tourist until he or she became irritated and off guard. Then Bo Mat would swoop down on the tourist, lift a wallet, a purse, or a piece of luggage. Sop Sop would become outraged at this act of a fellow Chinese. He would tell the tourist that he, Sop Sop, would catch the thief and bring back the stolen article. Then he would run after Bo Mat, and the two would return to the Tong headquarters basement to examine and share the excitement of the loot.

One late afternoon, it was particularly foggy. Sop Sop and Bo Mat were sitting around the steps of the Tong hall feeling lazy and bored.

"I'm tired of the usual stuff," Sop Sop said. "I want to do a big job. This stuff we're doing is for kids. I want to hit Lim's Jewelry on Grant."

"You're crazy," Bo Mat replied.

"Why? Why am I crazy? I need a watch. Jewelry is lots of money. You can hide it easy, put it away for the future. Cash it in or gamble with it. We keep most of it ourselves."

"Keep what?"

"Jewels, watches, diamonds. You name it. Big stuff. Who wants to fool around with people's baggage, purses, wallets?"

"For a job like that you need a gun."

"Well?"

"We don't have guns, Sop Sop."

"If you can get a wallet from a tourist, you can pick a gun off a hatchet man."

That night, the two boys crept into the room in the headquarters occupied by Snake and two other highbinders. It was two o'clock in the morning, and the toughs were fast asleep. The boys slipped their skilled, deft fingers into the holsters that were slung over the chairs near the sleeping hatchet men. The guns were kept close to the sleepers so that at a moment's notice they could be deployed for a bite of "pie" or a larger war. The boys knew exactly where to go. But as Bo Mat slid the Colt .45 out of Snake's holster, the boy misjudged the pistol's weight. He had never handled one before. The gun fell from his grasp and careened to the floor.

Snake bolted upright and hissed, "Who's there?"

Bo Mat stood there, paralyzed with fear, not knowing what to do. Sop Sop grabbed him by the shirt and the two youngsters ran out of the room, down the stairs and out of the building.

"It's the kids," they could hear Snake screaming from upstairs.

But the two youths turned into one alley, then another,

until a labyrinth of alleyways and a blanket of dense fog separated them from the Tong men who were pursuing them. They scaled a narrow wooden fence that connected two buildings and hid themselves in the pinched space. Sop Sop huddled next to Bo Mat and admired his newly acquired Colt .45.

Suddenly, Sop Sop pointed the gun at Bo Mat, cocking it. "I'm going to splatter your guts all over these walls."

"Hey, be careful. It could go off," Bo Mat said.

"You tried to get us caught, get us killed. What'd you mean, waking up Snake like that? You might as well have poured water on his face," Sop Sop said while recklessly pushing the muzzle of the gun against Bo Mat's chest.

"Look, Sop Sop, it was a mistake. It just slipped out of my hands, that's all. I wasn't trying to wake anybody up. Now, would you be careful with that thing?"

"Shut up!" Sop Sop could hear footsteps coming closer. He looked through a slight opening in the slats of the fence. All he could see were shadows of two large men in the fog. "It could be them."

The heavy-sounding footsteps passing by gave no hint as to who the shapes were. "We have to stay here until morning," Sop Sop said. "Then we'll take care of the jewelry store. Don't try anying, Bo Mat. You and me are going to go through with this job. You're my Tong brother. We're Tong brothers, you and me. Remember our oath."

Bo Mat was relieved when Sop Sop placed the gun on the concrete and wedged himself in the corner made by the fence and the building.

"My father was a Tong who got killed," Sop Sop said. "My mother told me my father was a Chi Sing. He was killed on a New Year's day on a roof. My mother had a lot of paying customers, but only her true lover, she said, could be my father. She told me I look like him. He was the bravest Tong man in Chinatown. Everybody stood aside when he walked down the street. They ambushed him on New Year's day. That was bad luck, my mother said. It meant that year was going to be full of bad luck, death. She died before the year was out, my mother. You know who your father is?''

"No," Bo Mat answered. "I haven't met my mother yet. No one knows where she can be found. As for my father, I haven't really thought about him. I suppose I'll find out who he is someday if my mother knows who he is."

Bo Mat looked over at Sop Sop. He was already asleep. Bo Mat tried to sleep, but he couldn't get himself into a comfortable enough position. Finally, as the mist around him began to illumine with the daylight, Bo Mat's head sank to his knees.

He was awakened by the sound of Sop Sop rummaging through the garbage. Sop Sop finally found what he wanted: an old, torn shirt. He took the shirt and used it to wrap up the gun. He grabbed some paper bags, emptied the garbage out of them, folded them and carried them with him. Then the two of them went to Uncle's Café on Clay Street and ordered a big breakfast of eggs, toast, hash browns, sausage and milk. They sneaked out of Uncle's Café in a hurry, though, when they saw Snake and the other *boo how doy*, the owner of the stolen gun, enter and sit at the counter.

They spent the day watching Lim's Jewelry Store, which was on Grant Avenue near Washington Street. They tried to look as inconspicuous as possible by walking up and down Grant Avenue, blending in with the tourists and the shoppers.

"What are we wating for? Let's move on the store, Sop Sop," Bo Mat said.

"Not yet. Too many customers in there," Sop Sop replied.

All in all, it was the worst day Bo Mat could remember, a lot harder than working double shift at Gum's Laundry. His palms were sweaty and his heart was constantly fluttering.

"Don't worry," Sop Sop comforted. "I'm the one who has the gun. I'll keep the proprietor quiet. You just fill these paper bags with everything you can get your hands on. It's almost five-thirty. That means it's closing time. Time for us to make our move."

Sop Sop was right. Lim, the proprietor, was soon alone in the shop except for one or two customers. The boys entered the store. Lim said, "I'm sorry, boys. I'm just now closing."

Sop Sop said, "But it's my mother's birthday, and I really must find a nice locket for her. I will just be a couple of minutes, Mr. Lim."

"All right, but hurry. I must close up."

By that time, the last customer, hearing Lim was closing up, left the store.

For a while, the merchant busied himself with his abacus and didn't pay attention to the two boys in his store. While Sop Sop pretended to be looking over the lockets, Bo Mat just stood in the center of the store, holding the paper bags and looking nervous. Both boys' inexperience showed through their self-conscious behavior, and they were lucky the merchant wasn't watching them.

Sop Sop suddenly turned around and started to unwind the torn shirt to expose the gun, but just at that moment, his eye caught something in the window, and whatever he saw startled him. Bo Mat turned. It was a police officer. The officer said and did nothing, just looked at the two boys, from one to the other. He was holding a nightstick behind his back with both hands. Then he took the nightstick and tapped on the glass door. Sop Sop quickly tightened the shirt around the revolver. Bo Mat stood trembling. Lim looked up from the abacus and nodded to the policeman. The policeman smiled and nodded back. Then the policeman hurried on.

"Cops!" Sop Sop dropped the gun to the floor and ran out the door. The muzzle of the weapon was showing through the shirt.

Bo Mat dashed over and reached for the gun, but at the same time Lim ran to the door.

"Hold it," Bo Mat commanded, trying to unravel the shirt. It seemed to be tied in a knot around the gun.

But the proprietor was now out on the street and yelling for the officer.

A police whistle sounded as Bo Mat finally freed the gun from the shirt.

"Hold it right there," the boy called. Lim saw the gun and raised his hands over his head.

"Come in here," Bo Mat ordered.

The jeweler came back inside.

Bo Mat got behind the counter. Now there was no time to think about sweaty palms or rapid heartbeat. "Get rid of the cops," he directed Lim. "Tell them everything's all right. Tell them you made a mistake. Tell them anything, but get rid of them. If you don't, *da sey ney*, I'll kill you."

Five Caucasian policemen appeared at the doorway. Bo Mat was hidden from view. He had left the paper bags in the center of the floor. Lim just stood there.

"What's going on, Lim?" one of the officers asked.

"Nothing, officer. There was a robber, but he didn't

take anything. He ran away, after Mulligan came to the door.''

Without Bo Mat knowing it, the jeweler was darting his eyes about wildly to signal to the police that something was indeed amiss.

"What's on the floor there?" the officer asked.

"They're just paper bags," Lim responded. "The thief dropped them when he ran out."

"Let's have a look at those," the officer said. He came into the store slowly, then reached down and picked up the paper bags. Bo Mat remained crouched behind the counter, still as a stone.

"Yeah, they're just paper bags. Pretty smelly, though. Must have picked them out of the garbage, whoever it was." Then the policeman pushed the merchant out of the store and simultaneously drew his revolver.

Bo Mat could not tell what was happening. As he crouched down on the floor behind the counter, he kept thinking what a fool he had been to go along with this scheme of Sop Sop's. They had been perfectly successful stealing from an occasional tourist. Why did they have to take on something this big when they were both still a couple of kids with no experience in this kind of thing. Neither of them even knew what it was like to fire a gun.

Bo Mat nervously rubbed his finger along the trigger of the revolver and waited for the all-clear signal. He was sure the jeweler was going to tell him that the police were gone and it was safe to come out from behind the counter. It never occurred to him that the jeweler would do anything but cooperate with his demands. Everything was going to be all right. There was nothing to be afraid of. Bo Mat would just walk out and forget the whole thing had happened. He would apologize to the jeweler for having caused him this great inconvenience. Then he would bring the gun back to the highbinder and apologize for having taken it. The highbinder would laugh it off. They always laughed things off when you thought they were going to get mad. Just when you thought they'd surely kill you for something, they'd turn to you and slap you on the back and have a good laugh about it.

"All right, come out from behind there."

A gun fired, not the policeman's gun, but his own. He had been so startled by the sound of the gruff voice that he had pulled the hair trigger he had been nervously fingering. The bullet struck the wainscoting in the far wall, missing a calendar by a quarter of an inch, putting an ugly black gash into the wood.

He heard the policeman scramble for cover. "Give up! Give up! You don't have a chance!"

The boy heard more police whistles, more running feet, sirens, hushed voices. He heard the movement of heavy shoes in the room in back of the store. More police, he concluded. They were all over the place. It was all because he had that gun. The little gun had made them call out practically the entire police force to deal with him. Yes, they were afraid of him, as he had been afraid of Sung Tom, his "father." How the laundryman had made him tremble, just by frowning at him. When Sung Tom raised his voice in one of his rages, Bo Mat thought the old man would kill him, and was terrified. Now the tables were turned. Now he had the authority, thanks to the highbinder's weapon. He had fired a shot. He had proven that not even a regiment of police could cow him into submission.

"No," he heard himself saying. "No, I won't give myself up."

He then heard the sound of urgent voices and began to feel strangely giddy with his newly found power.

"Listen, kid, give yourself up. We'll give you a break. It won't go as hard for you as you think. You still have a chance to get a break from the law if you give up now. If you keep this up, it'll be harder. It'll get harder and harder, the longer you keep this up. Do you want to spend the rest of your life in prison? Young guy like you throwing away your whole life?"

"I'm not giving up. Not until I get paid," Bo Mat said.

"What do you want?" the officer asked.

"I want my freedom, and I want jewelry. Jewelry and cash."

"I think something can be arranged, son," the officer responded. "Just give up the gun and we'll talk it over."

"Don't call me that. I'm nobody's son."

"You an orphan?"

"Nobody calls me son."

Then there was silence. The officers were talking among themselves. He could hear a crowd gathering in the street. There was silence because he had the highbinder's weapon and could command silence. He was telling himself that he was invulnerable, that he had power, that there was nothing they could do to him as long as he hung on to the weapon. But on the other hand, he felt increasingly nervous and frightened. What would be the outcome of all this? He had certainly gone too far. He had indulged in a dream of being as smart and tough as the highbinders. But he knew what would happen. He would never get out of there without being caught or killed. He wanted so much to command others, to get back at all of them for having made him a slave all his life. Holding that gun, for these moments, had made him feel like he had that command.

The silence was broken by the voice of a different sort of man, a very kindly man. "Young man, young man," the voice said, "I know you must be feeling very upset right now. I want you to know that, whatever your feeling, whatever that torment is, you have a friendly ear here, willing to listen to your troubles."

"I don't want to talk. I have nothing to say to you!" Bo Mat yelled out. "I don't know who you are."

"Well, I am Dr. Steven Roberts. I'm a missionary, and I work with Chinese boys without parents. There are a lot of orphans like you in Chinatown. I run a home for orphans. I'd like to invite you to join us there, join our little Christian family. I can promise you, it will be a place you'll grow to like."

"What is it?" Bo Mat asked. "Some kind of factory?"

"It's not a factory, son."

"Why does everybody insist on calling me son? I'm not anybody's son. I've had bad experiences with families. Listen, I don't want to be somebody's slave. I don't want to work fifteen hours a day in somebody's factory."

"What's your name, young man?"

"Bo Mat. I don't have a family name."

"Bo Mat, the home is no factory, but I can't promise you it will be a free ride, either."

"I won't work for anybody!"

"Well, you'd have to study pretty hard, Bo Mat."

"You mean, it's a school?"

"Education is the major part of our business."

Bo Mat thought for a long time about this offer. A school. School was a luxury to him. He had always envied those who could go to school. There was so much to learn about. In school, he could learn about China. And when he knew enough about China, someday he would go there. Then he would learn what it meant to be Chinese.

"Yes, all right," Bo Mat said. "I'm going to give

myself up. Tell me how I do it. How do I give myself up?''

The officer said, ''Throw the gun over the counter, count to five, then come out with your hands over your head.''

Bo Mat did as the officer asked. As soon as he threw the gun away, three police officers were at his side. He didn't even have time to stand up.

''Put your hands on the counter,'' they demanded. Bo Mat had no choice but to comply. Dr. Roberts was trying to say something to one of the officers. They seemed to be arguing, but Bo Mat couldn't understand what they were saying. Suddenly, handcuffs were being put on him. He was placed in a squad car. Dr. Roberts was nowhere to be seen.

''But what about the orphan home, the school?''

No one would answer his questions. He was taken to the county jail on Broadway and Columbus. His fingers were drummed onto a black ink pad and roughly pressed against a card on which his name was typed, and his address, which was ''no address.'' He was thrown in a tiny, dark cell. He shook his head and thought, No one really had to comply with any promises made once he had given up his gun. He should have used the gun. At least he would have died belonging to himself and to no one else.

After he had spent a lengthy time lying on the cot in the dark, unable to sleep or think very clearly, his guard opened the cell and nodded him out. Handcuffs were placed on him, and he was led to a small room where sat a police officer and a man in a grey suit with a neatly trimmed beard. The bearded man did all the talking.

''Bo Mat, I am Detective Wigfield Doogin, juvenile division, and this is Sergeant Bromley. Please be seated. Now, Bo Mat, Dr. Roberts, of the Mission Orphan Home on Lombard Street, has stated that he will accept you into his organization. We would be more than willing to allow you to enter Dr. Roberts' home, but we also have obligations to the city of San Francisco and the safety of its citizens. Unfortunately, you were carrying a gun and used it to fire at a police officer.''

"I didn't fire at the officer," Bo Mat protested. "The gun went off by mistake, because I was nervous."

"Well," the officer shrugged, "that might be true. But then, you have to look at how a jury will view that particular point. The fact that you were even carrying a gun makes your offense much more serious. Whether you fired it or not, you carried the gun, and that makes you a threat to the lives of the citizens of the city and county of San Francisco. Therefore, we have little choice but to send you to the California Youth Authority maximum security facility in Chico."

"But Dr. Roberts promised I would be admitted to the orphan home!"

"Dr. Roberts is a missionary. He's not a judge. He may or may not be familiar with the state laws. He should be, if he deals with juveniles. In any case, he can't offer you a place in the home until you fulfill your obligation to the citizens of the city and county."

"How long would I have to be kept in Chico?"

"That would be for the judge to decide. But I would guess you could expect to be out in about four years, if your behavior stands up well to a thorough examination."

"Four years!"

"At least that. And you can consider yourself fortunate that you probably won't be charged with attempted murder."

Bo Mat buried his head in his hands.

"But," the detective put in, "there is a way to

shorten and perhaps even eliminate the sentence. That again would be for a judge to decide. You would have to cooperate with the juvenile division in the identification of other juveniles involved in crime in Chinatown. Now, our understanding from talking to the jeweler, Lim, is that there was another youth involved in the holdup. Is that true?''

Bo Mat did not reply.

"Come now, Bo Mat, you appear to be a smart enough lad. You don't want to go to Youth Authority, you really don't. You want to join Dr. Roberts' school for oprhans, don't you? Well, I can't make any assurances, but I *am* fairly certain your case will be given the highest consideration if you name your accomplice in this matter."

Bo Mat thought of Sop Sop. Why had his friend run out on him? Sop Sop had made no effort to tell Bo Mat that he wanted to run. He was thinking only of himself. So hadn't Sop Sop betrayed him? If Bo Mat gave the detective Sop Sop's name, it would be what Sop Sop deserved. Sop Sop would get a light sentence. And then Bo Mat would be able to go to the orphan home. Bo Mat was about to give the authorities Sop Sop's name, but then he shook his head. The name wouldn't come out. He just couldn't do it. He didn't know why. But he knew he would have four years to think about it.

"Too bad." The detective shrugged and gestured to the guard, who removed Bo Mat and returned the boy to the tiny cell.

A week later he stood before the judge for sentencing. The judge told him much the same thing as the detective had. It was the gun that made all the difference.

They came for him the following morning, armed guards with handcuffs. The drive to Chico was long and dreary.

Chapter 26

The executive offices of The Dollar Store were located in a series of suites above the company's San Francisco branch at 823 Market Street. The suites took up the entire floor. The partners who had founded the company, Martin Sing and Peter Tsui, were still its executive directors.

Man Sum and Pang Fai had decided to change their names because they had to deal with many Westerners. Caucasian businessmen had constantly tripped over the Chinese names. So one day Man Sum started calling Pang Fai "Peter." Then Pang Fai called Man Sum "Martin." Man Sum insisted, however, that his wife be referred to as Ming Lee. He didn't want her to have an American name. Her place, according to him, was in the family, not the business community.

The Dollar Store had come a very long way since the Walnut Grove days. In jest, Martin Sing called them the days "when everything was hidden under the counter."

It was February, 1929, and business couldn't have been better. The company's assets were approaching the two-million-dollar mark, and they were growing by leaps and bounds. They had fifty stores up and down the West Coast, from San Diego in the south to Seattle in the north, and they had expansion plans which included other Western states such as Colorado, Nevada, Utah and Arizona. Their extraordinary growth stemmed from Martin Sing's avid playing of the stock market, which he called the sure-fire fan-tan game he'd always been looking for. Of their two million or so in assets, they kept only the thinnest margin for their working capital. This gave their buyer a constant case of bad nerves, but it freed the rest of their capital for investment in stocks.

They dealt with a brokerage house on Montgomery Street run by Dick Tully, a slow-speaking but extremely effective stockbroker. From their one and three-quarter million in assets, The Dollar Store partners were able to invest seven and a half million in stocks. Business was booming, and stockbrokers themselves were making millions. An investor could deposit twenty percent of the stock's value with the brokerage firm, and the firm would lend the investor the remaining eighty percent. Martin Sing constantly bought "on margin" so the company usually owned five times as much stock as it could pay for. As the prices of these stocks advanced and Tully sold them, the partners made five times as much profit. They paid interest on the loan from the broker, but all the dividends from the stocks were theirs. Peter Tsui had registered concern when Tully's brokerage raised their loan rate from ten to twenty percent, but that didn't bother Martin. "It will take some of the weaker investors out of the market, which will add to its health," he said.

Today, however, February 7, something in the paper caused the more cautious Peter some concern.

"Did you read this?" he asked Martin.

Martin had just talked to his broker and was, in fact, jubilant. "Listen to this first. I just talked to Tully. He says our stock in Radio Corporation has risen ten points in

New York. Ten points! I told you we should stay in there, didn't I? I told you we should hold on to that stock.''

Martin's enthusiasm over the Radio stock didn't diminish Peter's concern. ''But Martin, it says here that the Federal Reserve has issued a warning to brokerage firms who extend loans to speculators. Listen. 'The Federal Reserve Board has issued a forthright statement to the effect that too much of the country's bank credit was being absorbed by speculation.' ''

''What is 'speculation' supposed to mean?''

''You know, gambling on the stock market.''

''What we are doing is not gambling, Peter, even though I make that joke about fan-tan. You know, you shouldn't take what I say so seriously. We are investing in the economy of this nation. We are Americans now, citizens. It is our duty to help our new country grow. That's what we are doing. Investing.''

''Yes, but I'm afraid this warning may mean the Federal Reserve will raise the interest rate. They raised it last year from three and a half to five percent. Luckily, the market held up, but what if the rates are raised again? Other people are reading this, thinking the same thing. It could mean a downward trend in stock prices, Martin. I mean, the Federal Reserve has never made a statement like this. It looks like a whole new change of attitude, and that means tighter money is down the road.''

Martin Sing lit a cigarette and leaned back in his chair. ''Tully says he doesn't think the Federal Reserve Board has the power to affect the market. According to him, the power lies with the banks in New York, controlled by wealth. They more or less dictate to the Federal Reserve what it should do. No, I'll believe it when it happens, I mean, when they raise interest rates sufficiently to affect the market.''

Peter threw up his hands in a gesture of exasperation. "By that time, it might be too late, Martin. Values could dip so far that we'd lose a couple of million dollars or more."

"Well, Peter," Martin said, "why don't you sit down there and make a recommendation."

"I think we should sell off a good portion of our stock and put the proceeds into our own business."

"The dividends allow us to expand."

"We could expand even more if we—"

"Expand more? Where? Death Valley?"

"Will you let me finish?" Peter implored.

Martin lit another cigarette with the one he had just smoked. He extinguished the first cigarette in an antique porcelain bowl he was using as an ashtray. "Finish," he said with a shrug.

"I think the capital we're using to replenish the inventory is too small. Every month we just squeak by."

"But we're making it," Martin said. "You'll have to admit that. Wasn't I right about keeping the inventory moving? Whatever you can say about inventory, you can say about capital. Money that sits around chokes a business just like goods that gather cobwebs on shelves."

"Martin, you know I agree with you, but I think we're putting too much faith in the stock market, that's all I'm saying. What about bonds?"

"Bonds?" Martin winced with contempt.

"The secretary of the treasury, Andrew Mellon, is advising investors to buy bonds. He points out their relatively low prices and high rate of return."

Martin leaned foward and blew a long stream of smoke over his desk. "Peter, there is nothing *exciting* about buying bonds. The market is exciting. It's better than the lottery. It's better than mahjong. I like the stock market. *Ho mm ho ah*? All right?''

Martin smiled. He appreciated Tsui's sense of caution, and although he didn't admit it to Tsui, the statement by the Federal Reserve Board and the advice to buy bonds by the secretary of the treasury caused him to worry a little bit. What if there were to be a downtrend in the economy? But, of course, if stocks failed, there were still the stores. Even in the worst of times, the stores would still do business because they sold all items at a discount. People whose salaries were cut would come to The Dollar Store instead of Macy's. Therefore, in bad times, they would do even more business than they were doing now.

After working until nine or sometimes ten at night, Martin went home to his modern, stucco house on the Washington Street hill just above Mason Street. He had tried to buy a house in the city's upper-class neighborhoods and even in the middle-class neighborhoods around Richmond and the Sunset, but realtors refused to sell to him. He dismissed racial prejudice as a product of small minds, and resolutely refused to let it bother him. The home on Washington Street, he reasoned, suited his needs and those of his family quite well.

In addition to Jack, born in 1920, the Sings had four other children: Laura Mei, Cynthia, Thomas, and little Ronald. When Martin arrived home, he usually found his wife sewing clothes or working in the kitchen. It infuriated him. They had the money to hire a servant girl to do that kind of work, but his wife refused help. She always said she needed to do something with her hands while her husband was away at work and her children were at school or asleep.

But he often found her weary when he came home at

night, and that was the time he always most wanted to talk to her. This evening, however, she was less tired than usual, and she greeted him with a radiant smile. He seated himself at the kitchen table while she warmed up the rice.

"Are you okay?" he asked as he settled into his seat.

"Everything's fine with me," she replied, but he detected something in her tone that indicated to him there was something she was keeping from him.

"And the children?" he asked.

She did not answer. She took the pork, chicken and vegetables left over from the evening meal and put them in the wok, a large Chinese frying pan, with a little water. The wok hissed from the high flame, and the steam swirled to the ceiling.

"Didn't you hear me?" he asked.

"Yes," she said. "You asked about the children. They're all fine."

"They're asleep?"

"Yes, they're all asleep. All except for Jack."

"I noticed the light was on in his room," Martin said. "I hope he's studying his Chinese. The last time I checked, he was way behind his class at the Chinese school."

Ming Lee dished up the rice, then placed the chicken, pork and vegetables in a separate bowl and set everything on the table for Martin to help himself.

"You know, it isn't easy for Jack to go to two hours of Chinese school after a full day of private school. Vallejo School is difficult. He gets homework from both, and that's why he has to stay up so late." Martin paused, putting some rice in the small bowl set before him. He added pieces of meat and vegetables. "Any complaints?"

"What do you mean complaints, Man Sum?" she asked.

"Does he complain to you about all the homework he has to do?" he asked as he ate his meal.

She seated herself opposite him and straightened her long black hair. "No, he doesn't complain. You know him better than that. He's like his father that way. If something is very difficult for him, he prefers to suffer in silence. He knows he only has himself to rely on. No one else. He knows he has to get the job done, and so he pushes himself until it's completed."

"Is there anything wrong in that?" Martin asked, neatly placing the chopsticks over the bowl, a sign that he had finished eating.

She began to clear the dishes off the kitchen table. "Sometimes I think Jack works too hard. He's only nine years old."

"I think you're too soft on him, Ming Lee."

"Too soft?" She frowned.

"Yes, nine years old isn't too young to learn about discipline. When I was nine, I didn't do anything but work. It made a man out of me. It will do the same for him. He must be strong. His race puts him at a disadvantage in a hostile world."

"Other children his age," she argued, "especially Caucasian children, have time to play with their friends. Jack is always studying. That's why other boys don't ask Jack to play with them. They know he'll say he's too busy."

"They don't ask him out to play because he's Chinese," the father said with a certain bitterness in his tone.

"I don't think that's the reason."

"It's better that he plays with only Chinese children anyway. The *faan gwai* are unjust."

"I haven't heard you use that expression in a long time."

"What expression? *Faan gwai*? No, I have never forgiven them for permitting the Tongs to rule Chinatown through the corrupt court system."

"That court system saved you from going to prison."

"That court system was responsible for making my wife miserable in the past!" he said, making a fist.

"You shouldn't talk about the past. You don't want the children to know about it, do you?" she whispered.

"The heavens forbid. They would lose all respect for their parents, and our family structure would quickly disintegrate. Children must be able to look up to their parents and respect them. We must be examples of virtue they can follow. If not, they'll turn out badly." He paused, looked at her, and felt a sudden warmth toward her. "I'm sorry." He placed his hand on hers. "I love you, no matter what. You know that, don't you?"

She brushed away a tear. "I know. I know, dear. But sometimes I think there are just too many ghosts from the past. I wish we didn't have to live so close to Chinatown."

She was thinking of her other child, the one she had when she was a prostitute. Man Sum must never know about that child, she thought. If he ever found out, she was certain he would throw her out or kill her. She had felt a great affection for that little one. Perhaps she felt so strongly because he had been taken from her. She had never been able to get him out of her thoughts. At the same time she wondered about him, she dreaded the possibility of his finding her. But that would be impossible. If he searched for his mother, he would find Yan Chui Lee, not Kwan Ming Lee.

He noticed her brooding. "You're concerned about something," he said. "I can always tell when you are concerned about something because you look at the mountain.'' Smiling, he indicated with a nod the Chinese painting on the wall of the mountains of Chungshan.

She could not tell him her true thoughts, so she chose this moment to tell him something else she had been putting off. ''It concerns Jack. I thought of keeping this from you, but it is the wife's duty to tell her husband everything and keep nothing from him.''

He nodded. ''What is it you have to tell me?''

''I received this note from his Chinese teacher.''

He read the note aloud. It was written in Chinese. ''Your son Jack Sing, I am sad to report, is not doing well in his Chinese studies. I consider it a serious enough problem to write you this note so that, as his father, you may command the proper obedience. Yesterday, I found him reading an American comic book. The comic book was hidden inside his Chinese textbook. I hope, after your talk with the boy, this kind of behavior will not be repeated in my class.''

''An American comic book?'' Martin stared at the note in disbelief. ''I will have a talk with the boy.'' He rose from the kitchen table.

''Man Sum.'' Ming Lee placed a hand on his arm as he was about to leave the kitchen. ''Don't be too hard on Jack. The boy has really been working very hard at Vallejo. All his grades are excellent there.''

''But Ming Lee, it is important that he know who he is, that he is Chinese. If he can't read or write his own language, then who is he? He isn't white. He isn't Chinese. He's nothing. No. His performance in the Chinese school is just as important as his work at Vallejo. I really must talk to him.''

He left her looking anxiously after him.

He entered Jack's room without knocking. Jack looked

up from his long desk, on which were textbooks, pencils and notebooks, all neatly piled according to subject.

Around his children, Martin assumed a slightly formal, authoritarian manner. He pulled up a chair and sat rigidly facing his son. Jack turned his chair to face his father.

Martin spoke solemnly. "Jack, there is a matter that has come to my attention that I feel I must speak to you about."

"All right, Father," Jack replied deferentially.

"It concerns this note that the family has received from your Chinese teacher. He states that you are lagging behind in your Chinese studies. Now, Jack, I want you to explain to me why you think you are not doing well in Chinese."

Jack sat stiffly in the chair, bowing his head to avoid his father's eyes. He said somewhat mechanically, "I will make every effort to improve, Father. The Chinese characters are difficult for me to remember, but that is only because I am not intelligent enough. Therefore, I must study harder than the brighter students. This I will do, Father. I promise."

"Your answer does not entirely satisfy me, Jack. Simply follow the teacher's instructions. Copy the character over ten times as he says, review it regularly, and you will learn it. Do what the teacher tells you to. Respect his wisdom, and he will guide you to learn. Your problem is not intelligence, but obedience. Do you do everything the teacher tells you to do?"

Jack knew about the note his Chinese teacher had sent home because his mother had already shown it to him. He had been expecting his father to come into his room. He had been apprehensive all evening, and now he dreaded his father's reprimand.

"I try to do everything the teacher tells me, but once I didn't do what I was supposed to do in class."

"Once?"

"I am speaking of the note my teacher sent to you and Mother. The teacher told you about the comic book I was reading."

"The American comic book."

"Well, it wasn't just a comic book. I mean, the stories in it weren't funny. They were true stories. They were stories about the Great War."

Martin held out his hand. "May I have the comic book, please?"

Jack reached into the drawer of his desk and pulled out the comic book. "If you look at it, Father, you will see that there are no funny stories. They are serious tales about war heroes. They explain how American young men fought with great bravery in Europe, all different kinds of Americans—Negroes, whites and Chinese—all fighting side by side for freedom and democracy."

Martin took the book. "Chinese may live in America, speak English and go to American schools, but Chinese are not Americans, and they will never be Americans. You will never fit into this society. You are Chinese. Because of the color of your skin, you will be denied homes, jobs, and even reservations at restaurants and hotels."

"I still feel that I am an American, Father," Jack said.

Martin, in his vehemence, was beginning to shake the magazine at his son, but he caught himself and brought it down to his side. "If you had relatives in China, though you might be an American citizen, you would not be able to bring your relatives here to live with you. Husbands are separated from wives, parents are separated from their children. If this country really offered equality to all its citizens, regardless of their racial backgrounds, this kind of discrimination would not exist. You are young, and so you have not seen what I have seen. But you don't need to. You will take my word unquestioningly, without argument. You may not fully understand this, but China is your true homeland. You must learn Chinese because the time may come when China will be great and wealthy and you will be able to go back to your home, and never live as a stranger in a foreigner's land the way I have had to.''

"But Father, this country has been good to you, hasn't it? Look how successful you are in the department store business.''

"I have not been successful because this country gave me anything. Every step of the way, I have had to use my own brains.''

"But in another country, you couldn't start with nothing and build such a large and successful business.''

"That is only because this country enjoys such wealth. I have worked hard. America was called the golden hill for a reason. I have applied my pickaxe to the rock and hit a good vein. I have been lucky in addition to swinging my axe very hard. It doesn't go so well for others. And I do not let my success in this land make me forget that I am Chinese first.''

Jack felt confused. What his father was saying was the exact opposite of what his teachers at Vallejo had been telling him. Every morning, at the beginning of the school day, Jack's first period teacher would lead the students in the Pledge of Allegiance: ". . . one nation, under God, indivisible, with liberty and justice for all.'' His history teacher constantly reminded the students how fortunate they were to live in this land, a land where everyone, no matter where he came from, had equal opportunity. America, his teacher had said, was a country of immigrants. Immigrants founded the country, and immigrants continued to flow into the country, providing it with its lifeblood.

After a pause, Jack decided he would try to explain his feelings to his father, but he was not very hopeful he would be understood. "Father, I was born in America. I have been going to American schools and my teachers have all said that no matter what race we belong to, we are all Americans first. The soldiers in the Great War were fighting for America, not China or Africa. I don't feel like a stranger here. This country is my home."

His father answered him with a disapproving stare as he said, "In a Chinese home, you do not offer your opinion. You accept the judgment of your elders. We who have had experience of the world know more than you do. It would be futile to try to explain everything, all the whys and wherefores of the judgments we make. Your position is not to question us, but to obey and agree."

"Yes, Father," Jack replied meekly and returned his gaze to the floor.

"Now, this is my rule. Since the difficulty of the Chinese characters seems to be a problem for you, you will copy out the characters exactly twice the number of times the teacher tells you to. That's right, twice as many times. You will show the results of your copying to me after each evening's homework."

"Yes, Father," Jack murmured.

Suddenly there was a cry from the next bedroom. The conversation between father and son had been loud, and little Laura Mei, three years old, had woken up.

"Daddy, Daddy!" she cried.

Martin's expression softened, as it always did for

Laura Mei. For her, he would stop being the stern disciplinarian. Instead, he would start rolling around with Laura Mei on the floor, roughhousing and giggling. Jack couldn't help but feel jealousy and resentment toward the younger children. It seemed to him that, by virtue of being the oldest, he was given the strictest treatment and the least affection.

"My baby, my sweet baby," Martin said as he went into his youngest daughter's room. Jack could hear, through the wall, his father speaking to Laura Mei in tones of endearment. He could hear his father humming her back to sleep.

That was the last time Jack saw his Great War comic book.

On the following Tuesday morning, about eleven o'clock, there was a knock on the door.

A woman in her mid-forties stood before Ming Lee. She vaguely recognized the visitor, but could not place her. The woman was dressed in a maroon, padded Chinese jacket. Despite her plain appearance, her eyebrows were plucked and she smelled of cheap perfume. Ming Lee suspected she was a prostitute. Not wishing the children to be exposed to such a person, she stepped outside with the woman and asked in a rather cold tone, "What is your business?"

"You don't recognize me, Kwan Ming Lee? I am the midwife who delivered your first child. I am Yuen Pui Yen."

Ming Lee was startled and her heart began to race. The child she could not forget. Her boy, the helpless little boy they took from her. Had the midwife heard any news of him?

"What . . . what do you want?" she asked hesitantly.

"Well, you know how news gets around Chinatown. This news may just be rumor and may not have anything to do with the truth."

"Go on."

"Ming Lee, if you remember, you told me that should I hear any news about the child, I should tell you. At that time, I said I had to keep all such information secret from the singsong girl mothers, as we couldn't have them imposing on their children's new homes."

"Yes, please continue."

"Well, I have some information about that child now that I am able to give you."

"Please, tell me what news you have."

"Ming Lee, this is very embarrassing, but I am . . . no longer young. Therefore, it is not as easy for me to profit from my trade. The Tong takes everything, and I am quite poor. You, on the other hand, seem to have been blessed by the gods of fortune."

"I understand," she said. "Please, wait here." Ming Lee went to her dresser. From the top drawer, with trembling fingers, she lifted out a lacquered box. She pulled a twenty-dollar bill from the box. She brought the money outside and gave it to the midwife.

The midwife accepted the cash with a nod of gratitude. "The rumor is that Yan Chui Lee was visited by the boy recently."

"She was?"

"But if you want to learn more about that visit, you will have to talk to her personally. I know nothing more. If you want to hear what she says about the boy, you must hurry. Yan Chui Lee is close to death."

"Where can she be found?"

"I am sorry to have to name that place. Perhaps I

shall not have to name it, and you can guess. It is the pit
of hell every woman enslaved to the Tong fears most.''

The midwife did not have to name the place. Ming
Lee knew it well. After the midwife left, Ming Lee resolved to visit Yan Chui Lee. They had not seen each
other since the day they had gone their separate ways. It
would be unpleasant indeed to visit her old friend in what
was known as ''the hospital,'' but for news of her boy, she
would go there.

Twenty minutes later, Ming Lee felt she was again
Kwan Ming Lee, the prized slave girl of Chinatown's
bagnios. It seemed like she had traveled back in time ten
or fifteen years. As she entered Sullivan's Alley, she saw
it had not changed much in all these years. She was
suddenly aware of a Tong man eyeing her, and realized it
was quite dangerous for her to be here. The Chi Sings no
doubt still considered her debt to them unpaid. The Tongs
might kidnap her then and there, force her into slavery in
another place, or take vengeance on her by disfiguring her
or even killing her. These thoughts increased her anxiety as
she turned into the dead end alley where the ''hospital'' was
located, but she heard no footsteps following her, heard no
one calling out her name gruffly, mixing it with profanities.
She knelt at the mat of straw where the invalid, her old
friend, lay. As Yan Chui Lee turned toward her, Ming Lee
saw in her what she herself could have become: a discarded,
worn-out piece of property, a cast-off slave.

Chui Lee recognized her immediately. ''You have
come to find out about the boy.''

The suddenness of her statement embarrassed Ming
Lee. ''That, yes, but also, Chui Lee, to help you. You
should not be here. You should be in a real hospital.''

''I want to be here,'' Chui Lee said. ''I don't want to

be patched up and sent out to do battle with animals again. I want to say good-bye to the whole rotten business. That's why I'm here. I'm here for my health, you might say.'' Her laughter turned into a fit of coughing.

"You were recently visited by your son. It must have been wonderful to see the one you brought into the world.''

An ironic smile crossed Chui Lee's moist, pale face. "Am I to believe you braved the dangers of these streets to inquire about *my* son?''

"Of course," Ming Lee said nervously. "Was he not born under the same star as mine, who died? The birth of the two children was a very special moment for me, Chui Lee. That my child died gave me great sorrow, but that yours lived was my compensation.''

Unexpectedly, Chui Lee's bitterness softened and she extended her hand to her fortunate friend. "You have chosen well. The path out of slavery and Chinatown was the correct path. It led you through the gates of fortune, and I think, by the looks of you, toward longevity, too. I should have followed you to the house of the barbarian Christians. I know you lied to me. Now, for the first time, I realize you lied to me out of love for me. Your lie gave me hope when I was in despair. Although the hope was false from the beginning, it still sustained me through many desperate and unbearable times. And so, though I should hate you for lying to me, I thank you. I thank your loving heart. I could tell that the boy was not mine by looking into his eyes, for when I looked there, I saw his mother.''

Ming Lee stammered, "Chui Lee, I . . . I . . .''

"Don't speak, don't apologize, don't be ashamed to have come here. You want to know what has become of your first-born. I know what has become of him. The walls of Chinatown are ears, so I have listened with them and heard everything. First, Ming Lee, I told him the name of his real mother. I gave him your name.''

This news frightened Ming Lee. If the boy should come to her home, then her husband would learn the secret, and her children would know her past. That would be disastrous.

"You mean, he will seek me out?"

"You needn't be afraid of that," Chui Lee soothed, reading her friend's thoughts. "He is in reform school, locked up for armed robbery."

Ming Lee's stomach muscles flinched involuntarily. "No!" she cried. "What prison?"

"California Youth Authority. It's located in Chico. You can visit him there, and you needn't be afraid that he will interfere with your prosperous life."

"Chui Lee," Ming Lee said, "I want to thank you for telling me all this. You're right. I have been concerned about my first-born. He has been constantly on my mind." It surprised her that she managed to blurt all this out with such candor.

"Ming Lee, one question. How was the body of my darling one disposed of?" Yan Chui Lee asked.

"Lem Choy and I buried the infant in the Chinese cemetery. We had planned to unearth the remains upon your death, if we survived you, and send both your remains back to the homeland."

"That is not necessary," Chui Lee told her. "Only, I do wish to be buried next to the grave of my little one. That is all I wish."

"It shall be done," Ming Lee agreed.

"We'll stay here, on the hill of gold, my son and I." Chui Lee smiled slightly and closed her eyes.

"Yes, Chui Lee. Don't worry about anything. I will take care of it."

But then Ming Lee saw she was no longer speaking to Yan Chui Lee. Her old friend had gone away to find peace at last.

Ming Lee arranged, in secret, to have her friend, Yan Chui Lee, buried next to the body of her infant. It was done just as she had promised.

Chapter 27

On Monday morning, October 21, Martin Sing arrived at his office late. He found his business partner, Peter Tsui, talking on the phone. Peter seemed to be agitated.

As Martin walked in, Peter spoke into the phone, "Wait, Dick, Martin is here. You should talk to him directly, and tell him what you told me." Peter handed the phone to Martin. "There's trouble," he muttered.

Martin took the phone. "Hello, Dick. What's the trouble?"

The voice on the other end of the line did not speak with its customary calm. "Martin, have you been following the market the last couple of weeks?"

"Yes, there's a lot of selling going on."

"I should say there's a lot of selling going on."

"And I know there's been a general decline of stock prices in the last month. The 'bears' are taking advantage of the decline. Their are a lot of people selling short. They borrow stocks, sell them, then buy them back at a lower price. They make a profit from the dip in values, and they help create the decline. These are the people that are ruining the market."

Dick said, "Those are the people that seem to understand the market the best. They're finding the stocks that are vulnerable, the ones that are already weak. It's the weakness of the market itself that's giving the 'bears' a heyday, selling short.''

"This sort of thing has gone on before in the market," Martin replied. "Every time the market rallies, these 'bears' are squeezed out. They still have to buy back the stock they borrowed. They have to buy it back for more than they sold it. They end up losing money. Then this kind of thing stops."

"Do you really think it's temporary?" Dick asked.

"I'l be glad when the hard realities of the market break these 'bears' and they find something else to do with their time," Martin said.

"I'm not sure it is a temporary setback in the market," Dick said anxiously. "We may be in for a more serious downtrend. The boom the economy has had for the last six years may finally be at an end. There has been too much speculation. The market has been seriously overbought. There's no place for it to go but down. The young 'bears' may be more realistic than the overly optimistic, bullish speculators. A lot of the wealthy are selling their stocks and moving into bonds, which are more secure."

"You're the expert, Dick, not me. I'm a Chinese philosopher. The *I Ching*, the great book of Chinese philosophy, says that in times of adversity it is important to be strong within and sparing of actions. One must dwell within a maelstrom of difficulties as if they didn't exist. The market will come back up. If the prices now dip low, the next rally will bring the values back up higher than they were before they began to dip. This is the way the market has behaved over the last six years."

Dick was not about to be convinced by Chinese philosophy. "In August the Federal Reserve Board raised the interest rate they charge bankers from five to six percent. The Fed did this to tighten up credit extended to brokers, like me, who let their customers carry a lot of stock on a thin margin. What this phone call is about is simply this: I have to ask you to pay off your loan. The bank is pressuring me. I can't borrow any more from them, and I'm caught in a bind.''

"But Dick, I don't see how we can do that now. We'd have to sell four of our stores to come up with the seven and a half million.''

"My position is this: unless I get the balance of your loan, I'll have to throw your stock on the market. It'll sell at the lower price, and you'll lose quite a bundle. If you want to hold on to your stock in the hopes that the market will rally and regain its strength, then you have to make good on your loan. I don't like to do this to you fellows, but I've got to survive, too.''

There was a pause at the other end of the phone while Martin considered what Dick was saying.

Peter was on another line listening. Martin covered the mouthpiece of his phone and whispered to him, "Can we get buyers for those stores?''

"We would take a terrible beating if we did that, Martin.''

"Well, let's see if we can raise three million from selling **half** as many stores,'' Martin suggested.

Peter shrugged. "What choice do we have?''

Martin returned to the phone and said to Dick, "Listen, will you settle for fifty percent of margin, Dick?''

"All right. I want to keep you fellows as customers. I'll hold on to your stocks at fifty percent. But I can't promise to give you margin forever. If the market gets much worse, I'm going to have to call in that fifty percent, too, or sell at any price.''

"Okay, give us a couple of days to turn this thing over. It won't be easy. We're not that liquid. You know how it is," Martin explained.

"Sure," Dick replied, trying to sound friendly. "You fellows are doing the best you can. We're trying to work together. That's what this is all about. Working together. We'll weather this thing, I'm sure."

After the phone call, Peter Tsui and Martin Sing sat down in Martin's office to talk things over.

"I'm not sure things are going to get much better," Peter said. "Wouldn't it be better to sell off some of our stock? There are a lot of indications we're in for a downward slide in stock values. Europe, for instance, is already going through hard times."

"No," Martin replied adamantly. "This is just a temporary setback."

Peter didn't say anything. He just sighed and looked worried.

"It's not as serious as the expression on your face," Martin insisted. "We'll put three of the stores up for sale and borrow from the bank against the sale. Dick gets his three million in a couple of days. The stores will sell inside of a couple of months, and until then we pay the interest at six percent. But six percent for a couple of months isn't bad. Everything is going to be all right."

"I hope so." Peter could not keep the doubt out of his voice.

As promised, Dick Tully was hand-delivered a check for three million dollars in two days. It was Wednesday, the twenty-third. Tully was hardly paying attention when he received the check. He was following the line of ticker tape that announced the stocks' price changes. During the morning of the twenty-third, a sudden weakness in automobile accessory shares was followed by a general recession in prices that quickly accelerated. By early afternoon, something had snapped, and an epidemic of selling was ravaging Wall Street. Two and a half million shares changed hands in the last hour of trading. When the market closed, most of the stocks were at their lowest point in the long autumn decline. It was a major bear market in stocks after a major bull market with the unprecedented duration of almost six years.

Martin and Peter were also following the developments on the big board at the stock exchange on Montgomery Street. They were greatly disappointed that not even a moderate rally had materialized. They took consolation from the evening paper, in which renowned economists were quoted saying the worst was over, and pointing to several factors that would bring the market back up. They claimed that investment trusts were waiting for bargain prices, and now that these were available, there would be a powerful upsurge of buying. They said that the market had been reacting naturally to the abnormally heightened activity of earlier months, and that soon a balance would be restored as the market "righted itself."

On Thursday, October 24, neither Peter nor Martin could be found at their offices on Market Street. They were at the stock exchange on Montgomery Street, closely following the events that were happening in New York. They were not alone. The building was thronged with investors looking fearful and jittery. The stock exchange opened its doors at eight, and it was already crowded by eight-fifteen.

Transactions were numerous. Customers the night before had told their brokers to buy stocks, often at prices below the preceding day's close, but many more had placed with their brokers "stop-loss" orders. This meant that the broker was instructed to sell a given stock as it reached a price below a previous market value. In that way, the investor was able to hold the line against further loss. Martin and Peter had placed no such "stop-loss" orders with Tully, so their stocks lost more and more value. American Telephone and Telegraph, Radio Corporation of America, Westinghouse, and even U.S. Steel, were losing two, then four, then eight, then ten points. The downward slide seemed endless. All around Martin and Peter there were shouts of "Sell at the market!" and investors frantically fighting for telephones to reach their brokers in an attempt to unburden themselves of the losing stocks.

Still, Martin insisted they do nothing, though the two men were literally watching millions disappear before their eyes. The business they had painstakingly built up over the years was rapidly getting eaten up by the selling panic spree now taking over the stock market.

Why? Why had Martin tied so much of their earnings up in stocks in the first place? Why, thought Peter, was he manifesting this strange calm when all around him men and women were tearing at their hair?

"We have to sell now, Martin. Look, everyone is selling. We might still salvage something, but if we let this go on, I am afraid we will lose everything."

Martin observed the turmoil on the floor with a philosophical detachment. "There is no reason to fear. Those stocks have real value and deserve higher prices. It is simply this American mentality that is the problem. Americans are always either wildly pessimistic or wildly optimistic, but they never know the reality of what they are looking at. They are living in illusion, and each one feeds illusions to the next one. They do not follow their inner natures; they follow the crowd. But I, for one, refuse to follow this barbarian mob in its orgy of self-destruction."

Then Martin began to do something very strange. In the middle of the floor of the Western branch of the stock exchange, while hundreds were losing their life's savings, he danced. His dance traced the slow and meditative movements of T'ai Chi, which he had learned as a boy in China.

"Are you out of your mind?" Peter cried out.

He might have asked the others on the floor of the exchange the same question, for although Martin was doing something quite unusual, the panicky investors totally ignored him. They were too busy trying to rescue lost fortunes and savings to observe the antics of the "heathen Chinaman."

Various New York bankers that day bought some of the declining stocks in order to support the market. They were trying to use their influence to reassure the public and to stop the panic. They knew that a prolonged panic could ultimately result in the erosion of the country's strongest financial institutions, so they had to act quickly. The bankers favored some of the stocks that recovered somewhat from the tumble they had taken earlier in the day. Convinced that the bankers had saved the day and that the worst was over, Martin and Peter breathed sighs of relief and returned to their homes.

Martin called Dick Tully that evening and found him still in his office.

"Well, Dick, what is your opinion now?"

"The bankers, I think, saved the market. Your stocks lost considerably, but they are on their way up again, Martin."

"Then you would advise me to hang on to them and not sell."

"Yes, I think the worst of the selling trend is over. But I need more margin from you fellows. You're one of my biggest accounts, and I'm afraid I just can't carry three million. One and half million, maybe, but three million is too much for me at this time. I'm being squeezed out by these new interest rates and lower stock prices."

"I understand," Martin said cheerfully. "I'll talk to Peter tomorrow, and we'll see what we can do."

Friday morning of October 25 confirmed Martin's philosophical point of view and his "wait and see" attitude. The opening prices of several stocks in New York were higher than at Thursday's close. The partners made arrangements for the sale of four more of their locations to close their margin account with Tully. They reasoned it was better to buy their stocks outright rather than continue borrowing money from Tully.

"Why owe Tully even one and a half million? Why not just settle our debt?" Martin suggested, and Peter nodded.

They would now own their stocks outright. That meant that when they sold their stocks at a higher price, all the profit would go to them. It was a comforting thought.

The fear that had possessed stockholders the day before was absent today. Less than half the number of transactions occurred.

Saturday's market was also calm. The lower prices at the close of trading could be explained. Dick Tully and other brokers were still selling accounts belonging to those who could not make their loan payments on their margins. Unfortunately, there were many left who could not pay. Brokers' staffs were working overtime to try to settle all those outstanding accounts.

Sunday, everyone rested. Martin felt good now that he and Peter owned their stocks outright. Monday, surely, the recovery would begin. It would be a slow recovery, Martin predicted, because the market had taken quite a fall, especially on Wednesday. If all went well this next week, however, there was nothing more to fear. They could begin to use their dividends to buy back some of the facilities they had to let go in order to close their margins.

But the worst was yet to come.

Again, side by side with The Dollar Store partners, several hundred anxious speculators gathered at Montgomery Street. Those who could not get inside had to wait outside and get the news by word of mouth. The most important sign, the one which would bring the most reassurance, was stability. If the prices held to Saturday's level, then the panic could be expected to reverse itself. But the hoped-for stability was not reflected on the ticker tape. U.S. Steel, the most important stock, the one considered the prime indicator, along with International Telephone and Telegraph and General Electric, and in fact all of the blue-chip stocks the bankers had supported, had gone down. They were the very stocks the two partners owned.

Many stop-loss orders had been placed with brokers. These orders fixed the selling price just below Saturday's closing. So once the market opened with prices off, a sudden flood of selling engulfed it.

In the first half-hour of trading, many stocks lost five, then ten points. Before anyone realized what was happening, U.S. Steel had dipped below two hundred. The panic that had been so great on Wednesday came back this Monday morning, only it was twice as intense. The word "sell" was on everyone's lips.

Peter's terrified eyes met Martin's. The calm had gone. The philosophical point of view had evaporated. Martin's eyes mirrored Peter's own horror. They were ruined.

"What will we do, Martin? What will we do?"

Martin's face was streaming with tears. "Sell," he said.

Martin had a life insurance policy worth one hundred fifty thousand dollars. All he thought about was that his death would feed his children. For the first time since the old days, he walked the streets of Chinatown without a bodyguard. Wasn't there still a price on his head? Somebody better put a bullet through him, or he would do it himself. No Tongs stalked him. No one so much as glanced in his direction. No one brushed against him. There was just the thick, cold fog. Although he paced the darkest alleyways, there were no gunmen waiting to settle debts from the past.

For the next week he walked around Chinatown or locked himself in a room in his house. He spoke to no one, not even his wife or children. He couldn't bear to look at them, he was so ashamed. Why hadn't he seen the crash coming? Why hadn't he listened to the warnings of his partner? Of Dick Tully? Of the newspapers? He turned over every alternative to suicide. Was there a way out other than taking his own life? Visions of his future looked blacker by far than death. Ming Lee was still beautiful. She could start working the streets again. He and the children would feed off the sale of his wife's body. By comparison with that possibility, suicide looked like a blessing.

Then, one evening of the following week, he went to the closet in the bedroom. In the bottom of that closet was a wooden box filled with old clothes, an abacus, pictures, books and souvenirs. It must still be there, he thought. He hadn't looked at it for years, the Colt .45. It was wrapped in a piece of cotton cloth and white paper, and wound up with string. He hadn't needed it since he had first hired a bodyguard several years ago. Now, of course, he would no longer be able to keep a bodyguard.

Without a word to anyone, he took up the package and left the house. His destination was Portsmith Square. There were trees there. It was as good a place as any. He sat down on the bench, and without a pause began to unwrap the package. There it was, the gun Duk Fong had so patiently taught him how to fire, the gun he had never used on another human being. He would be its first victim, and he would need no marksmanship skills to hit his target.

As he lifted the weapon to his temple, he suddenly felt a woman's hand on his shoulder. It was his wife, Ming Lee. She had seen him leave the house and had followed him.

She was standing behind the bench, and now came around and sat down next to him.

"Don't try to stop me," he said in a cold, detached voice. "Go back to the house and take care of the children."

"No," she replied in an irritated tone. "I will stay right here until you stop this foolishness."

"There is nothing left for me to live for. I have nothing. I am nothing. Only my death is worth something. Only my death means something."

"Nonsense," she barked. "You had nothing before. You were an immigrant with no money, no knowledge of the language and no job, but look what you did, what you built. You started with nothing once. Certainly you could do it again."

"This is different. I had success, I was lucky. I had status and respect in this community and in my family. Now, no one can respect me because I don't respect myself. I have acted foolishly, stupidly, and out of selfishness and greed. I have behaved like a reckless gambler and my reward is that I have lost everything.''

''Your family has not lost respect for you,'' Ming Lee said.

Martin looked at his wife. ''The gods of the beneficent heavens grant a man, if he's lucky, one chance to make a fortune in his life. If he fails that one chance, he is not given a second. Furthermore, I have lost face. I cannot make the proper sacrifices to my ancestors. I cannot even bow before them without feeling I am profaning them. I cannot look you or the children in the eye again.''

''Man Sum, give me that gun at once.'' Ming Lee's voice was quiet and firm.

''No, I cannot. I must do this.''

''Money does not matter,'' she said. ''One million, ten million, none of it means anything. It is just paper. You have your life. You have your body, your hands. As long as you're alive, you can do something. And your children need you alive.''

Her words reminded him of what he'd said to Lum Po so long ago at Angel Island.

''It will be hard, going on,'' he said quietly. ''It will be hard.''

Swiftly she snatched the gun out of his hand, then carefully put the cloth and paper and twine around it. ''It will be hard, but we will go on,'' she said.

''Our real fortune is not money. It is our lives together and our love for each other.''

The Sings sold their house for five thousand dollars. They moved to a run-down apartment house on Powell Street. The apartment had two rooms, a sink and a stove. The sluggish toilet was down the hall. The four families on the same floor shared it.

Ming Lee began doing piecework in a sewing factory,

and Martin found work as a waiter at Dung Ho's Restaurant on Washington Street after waiting in a line for the job with two hundred other men. The children, of course, could no longer go to a private school, and were enrolled in Commodore Stockton School on Washington Street, one block from Dung Ho's Restaurant.

The Sings adjusted to their new, modest life. They managed to get by. Their life was not different from most Chinese families living in Chinatown. The jobs paid poorly and the hours were long, but at least they had rice and vegetables to eat. Martin eventually learned to cook. It paid a little better than waiting on tables, but it also meant standing long hours in front of a hot, fiery stove. The oil from the wok often spattered in his face. But at least the work was honest, and he made a salary of fifteen dollars a week. They would not starve.

Lum Po's parole from San Quentin occurred on the morning of April 14, 1933. He had served thirteen years of his twenty-three-year sentence, but his behavior in prison had been nothing short of exemplary. On the evening of the fourteenth, he showed up at the Chi Sing Tong headquarters. The last person the men there wanted to see was a highbinder.

"We're not a fighting Tong anymore, Lum Po," he was told by a merchant who recognized him. "This is just a peace-loving organization. All we want to do is help people the best we can through this depression. We don't have any war chest, and we're out of the rackets."

"That's okay with me," Lum Po said. "I don't carry a hatchet or a knife, and I probably never will again. I just want to find an honest job. I figured since I made an oath in blood to this organization, you would at least let a brother put a bed down until he got himself some work."

The merchants looked at one another and nodded. During these depression years, the Chi Sings had often given lodging to their Tong brethren who came through San Francisco. There were many men traveling from town to town, picking up odd jobs here and there. But it made the members somewhat uncomfortable to extend hospitality to a former professional killer.

"All right, Lum Po," the merchant finally said. "But remember, we don't want any trouble."

"I promise you I won't give you any." Lum Po smiled. "My parole officer wouldn't like it, and I don't particularly relish the idea of returning to that prison."

"Well, up those stairs there's an empty space. Room across the hall."

Lum Po stood at the door for a moment before going up. The merchants were eyeing him warily over their mahjong tiles.

"Any food?" Lum Po asked.

"Yes," the merchant who had been talking to him replied. "There's a little rice available in the evening in the community dining hall. If you have three cents to contribute to the meal, that would be appreciated. If not, you can still eat there, and then pay us back after you get some work, if you get some work."

"Thanks, brother." Nothing like making me feel welcome, he thought sarcastically. His eyes fell on the gashes in the wall, scars of the police attack that had broken the spirit of the Tongs. That spirit will never die in me, he promised himself, leaving the frightened merchants to their game.

Coincidentally, the room assigned to Lum Po was the same one that he and Man Sum had shared twenty-three years before when they both had first started their *boo how doy* training with Chinatown's top hatchet men. Sing Man

Sum, he thought, was the arch traitor of his Tong, the unfilial son of Sing Choy Wu; twice unfilial to his father, by blood and by oath. Lum Po thought of his own father, brutally murdered by the Suey Sings. He closed his eyes.

Sing Man Sum would have to die. And also his whore. Treason was unforgivable. Times had changed, he could see that. The *boo how doy* tradition was dead. He saw some of the bodyguards of the bagnios in Sullivan's Alley. Punks, he sputtered, kids who couldn't shoot to hit a block-wide brick wall. Yes, the glory of the Tong was gone, but he, Tom Lum Po, would bring it back. He was still a skilled fighter. He would start his own Tong, train his own men in the skills he had learned so well from Duk Fong. But first, business had to be taken care of. A score had to be settled.

"Is it still true," he asked the man sitting opposite him at dinner in the small dining hall, "that Chinatown's walls have ears?"

A few chuckles went around the ordinarily somber assembly of diners. The question was addressed by Lum Po to a man that looked to be about his same age and build. Maybe he carries a hatchet, Lum Po thought.

"I wouldn't know about San Francisco, but it's certainly true of New York Chinatown," the man replied.

A man in his sixties sitting on Lum Po's left said, "San Francisco Chinatown's walls have more ears, because there are fewer Chinese to gossip about. Who in particular did you want to know about?"

"Sing Man Sum."

"Oh, that's a story. Did you know that he became quite wealthy? One of the wealthiest men in Chinatown. A fat cat, I should say. Then the crash hit, and he lost everything." The man laughed. "So did I, as a matter of fact." Then he frowned. "Sing Man Sum, though, was a millionaire. Discount department store business. It's defunct now. They had a store on Market Street. It's all boarded up. They can't get rid of it. Oh, yes, Sing Man Sum. He's a cook now. Just an average cook. Works at Dung Ho.''

"Dung Ho Restaurant on Washington Street?"

"That's right," the man answered. "What a tumble. Oh, that crash! They say his wife saved him from committing suicide. He has five children. Three boys and two girls. They live in a place on Powell Street. The Dollar Store, that was the name of his business. Started from a tiny general merchandise store in Walnut Grove, but he played the market! And lost. So did I. I lost my life's savings." He laughed. "I shouldn't gamble, but I can't help it. I love to gamble. There's fan-tan on Ross Alley. You fellows interested? We play with halfpennies. Slips of paper you buy from the bank represent halfpennies."

"Not tonight, friend. But thank you for the information about Sing Man Sum."

"He a friend of yours?" the man asked.

"You might say I owe him a favor," Lum Po replied.

The man sitting opposite Lum Po said, "I'm Szeto. Szeto Lim Wing. My friends in New York call me Larry."

"I've heard of you. The Chi Sing-Gin Kong war on the East Coast. September, 1923."

"I'm one of the survivors, yes," he said with characteristic Oriental modesty. The Larry Szeto he had heard about was more than a survivor.

"I'm Lum Po."

"Yes, I've heard of you. It would be about time for them to grant you a parole." The New York highbinder smiled and nodded.

"Then we've already met, through reputation, at least," Lum Po suggested. He was thinking that between the two of them, they could run both coasts: singsong girls, drugs, gambling. The old life, the good life.

"We have a lot to talk about," Larry Szeto said. "Come on. I have a few pennies. I'll buy you a cup of coffee to celebrate your parole."

Over coffee, Lum Po explained to Larry Szeto the history of Sing Man Sum's treason to his Tong. Larry agreed the offense was serious. Lum Po told of the vow he had made to his exalted master. It was a vow that couldn't be broken. Otherwise, Kwan Kung, the god of war, would take revenge. Larry agreed.

"There is no Tong organization on the East or West Coast anymore. The depression wiped out the war chests," Larry said. "And the organizations have turned soft. They're mostly old men without teeth. They don't want *boo how doy* around because they're afraid of trouble. So a man can't make any money anymore."

"We could form our own Tong," Lum Po said excitedly.

"Why not? All right, it's done!" Larry Szeto said. "I've been waiting years for someone to come along with whom I could go into business." Then Larry grew more serious. "This Sing? What's his name?"

"Sing Man Sum."

"Yes, it seems that's the first item of business we have to attend to," Larry said.

"Yes," Lum Po agreed, "and the sooner the better."

The two highbinders went into the rest room of the coffee shop. It was nothing like the "barracks" of old, but it would have to serve. There they tucked their bull-nosed .45-caliber handguns under their belts and closed their jackets. They were ready to eat pie.

It was ten o'clock. Dung Ho's had closed at nine-thirty. The cooking staff was cleaning up and preparing for the following day's lunch. The *boo how doy* stationed themselves across the street from the restaurant in the shadows of the buildings.

As soon as Sing Man Sum left work, he was aware of something amiss. Someone was in the shadows watching him. He had never forgotten that a price was still on his head. And now, finally, someone was gunning for him. There was a thin alleyway that ran from Dung Ho's to Jackson Street. He took it. Then he knew who it was that was after him because he heard his name being called.

"Sing Man Sum!"

It was Lum Po.

"You're dead!"

The gunshot rang in the dark alleyway, but Man Sum had already turned the corner and was running up Jackson Street. Lum Po's second attempt on his life had failed, but he knew Lum Po would keep trying until he succeeded.

Martin burst through the door of the apartment. Ming Lee awoke with a start, which in turn woke little Laura Mei and Ronald, who were sleeping next to their mother. Martin fastened the door latch. Jack was at the desk studying. He turned and saw that his father was extremely agitated.

"The gun," Martin said. "I need the gun."

Laura Mei clung to her mother and cried, "Daddy. Daddy."

Ming Lee had hidden the gun after Martin had tried to commit suicide. Thinking this was an attempt to repeat that incident, Ming Lee shook her head and said, "No, I will not give it to you."

"You must! They are coming," Martin said, his face white with terror.

Now Ronald began to cry. "Mommy, Mommy! I'm scared."

Martin knelt by the bed and calmed him. "I'll protect you, children. I won't let them in here."

Jack piped up, "I'll help you, Dad. I'll fight them too."

"Is it the Tong?" Ming Lee asked, trying to mask her own fear.

"Yes," Martin confirmed. "It's Lum Po."

"Does he know where to find us?"

Ronald and Laura Mei were disturbed by their mother's anxiety and let out howls that awoke both Cynthia and Thomas. Now the whole family was awake.

"We'd better call the police," Ming Lee said.

"No." Martin shook his head. "This matter is between Lum Po and me. I have to settle it my own way. Get me the gun."

"What's going on?" little Thomas asked.

"Dad's going to a gun battle with a Tong man. And I'm going, too. It's a Tong war," Jack answered.

"That's enough, Jack, Thomas, all of you children. There is nothing to be frightened of. There are some bad men out there, and I'm just going to protect you from them. You can help me by remaining very still, very calm. Do you hear me Laura Mei? Ronald?"

"Yes, Daddy." Laura Mei was trying very hard to control her tears.

Meanwhile, Ming Lee had taken a look out the window. "They're there," she said.

Martin looked out the window, too. He could see two men standing against the building across the street, looking up toward their apartment.

"I'm going to the kitchen for a minute and I'll be right back," Ming Lee told the children. "Mommy and Daddy want all of you to be very brave. Try as hard as you can to be extra-specially quiet. And pray to God and Jesus that everything will be all right.''

"Hurry, Ming Lee,'' Martin whispered.

Ming Lee went into the kitchen and Martin followed her. The children lay down in their beds and tried to obey. But Jack, unbeknownst to his parents, followed Ming Lee and Martin into the kitchen. He watched as Ming Lee stood on a chair and reached to open the top cupboard. There, under some pans, she found the white package with the twine around it. Without saying anything, she handed the package to Martin. Wide-eyed, Jack watched as Martin quickly cut the string with the kitchen knife and pulled out the .45-caliber gun. His own father had a gun, he thought excitedly. His own father was a highbinder, a Tong man. Jack had played games with his friends in which Tongs fought one another in bloody combat. He knew vaguely that his own father had been involved with the Tongs and proudly bragged about it to his friends. But here was direct proof and here a real Tong battle was about to take place. And he would be right in the middle of it.

Martin turned and saw his son watching him. "Jack, go back in the other room.''

"I want to help you kill them, Daddy. I want to be a highbinder like you.''

"I'm not a highbinder, Jack. I'm a cook, and I'm a family man. I'm just trying to protect my home from criminals.''

"Jack, go to bed,'' Ming Lee demanded.

"Do I have to?'' Jack pleaded.

"Yes, you do,'' Jack answered impatiently. "Go to bed immediately. Go in there with the other children.''

Jack obeyed.

Martin turned to his wife. "It has happened, that which we feared the most. They have come to collect the price on my head. If there was any other way out of this thing, I would take it.'' He placed his hand on her cheek.

''I just wish that all these Chinatown ghosts would go away and let us live our lives. We have everything to be happy about. We have beautiful children. Why don't these evil people leave us alone?''

''We can't be happy until the ghosts are destroyed,'' he said. ''I have to destroy them. They're my ghosts. If I don't show that I'm strong enough to deal with them, the underworld will send more to haunt us. More and more will keep coming until our lives become unlivable. Hungry ghosts are not satisfied until they devour completely everything that is alive. I must show that I am strong, but I am not sure if I am strong enough.'' He embraced her. ''You have your Christian God and I my Chinese philosophy and deities. Now I need the strength of both, because I am afraid. I am as afraid of those two men out there as I have been afraid of anything in my life.''

''My darling,'' she said, ''I will pray to Christ for you. And the children are already praying. There, now. All the spirits of goodness are behind you.''

''Most of all, I need you,'' he said.

Her eyes were filled with tears. ''You have me.''

He touched her hand, and then released it. ''Now, I must go.'' And with that, he turned and left the door to the kitchen.

Ming Lee looked out the window, hoping the two highbinders would no longer be there, but they had not moved.

Martin checked the gun to make certain bullets were loaded in all the chambers. Then, holding the pistol at his side, he slowly descended the stairs. Sweat broke out on his forehead. His heartbeat thumped loud in his chest, and both his hands trembled. He was out of shape, he knew.

His *boo how doy* skills were rusty. Cold as ice, that was the motto of the professional soldier of the street. He recalled the squirrel whose left eye was caught by Lum Po's sharp bullet at fifty yards. Now Lum Po, his old friend, would be aiming for him.

Martin entered the street, his weapon drawn.

"Wait, wait," Lum Po called to him. "Put that thing away, Man Sum. I don't want to fight." Lum Po and the other man were crossing the street toward him. Martin did not put the weapon away.

"Look, you see? We're unarmed." Lum Po pulled his jacket to one side and showed Martin that there was no handgun in his belt. The other highbinder did the same.

"We don't want to fight," the man with Lum Po said. "We just want to talk. Have a friendly conversation."

"This is Larry," Lum Po said, still watching Martin carefully. "Larry's from New York, looking for work here. Isn't that right, Larry?"

"That's right," Larry agreed. He was also looking at Martin, sizing him up.

Martin put his gun in his belt.

"I hear you've got a family," Lum Po went on. "Sons?"

"Three sons," Martin answered warily.

"He's got three sons," Lum Po nodded toward Larry.

"I heard him," Larry mumbled.

"No, Man Sum, you've got the wrong idea. It's true there was once a price on your head, but times have changed, haven't they? Nobody has a war chest to pay the kind of price a head like yours should bring." Lum Po laughed heartily at his own joke. "Anyway, like the *faan gwai* say, it's all water under the bridge. Forget it. You're my friend."

Lum Po's apparent friendliness caused Martin to drop

his guard for a moment. A serious error. Larry took advantage of that split second to charge Martin and disarm him in one swift, deft movement. It all took place so close to the doorway of Martin's apartment that Ming Lee could not see it happen.

"We're going for a short drive," Lum Po said. "The car is over on Clay Street."

Larry had put the gun in the pocket of his jacket, but he was still holding on to it.

"Where?" Martin asked.

"Let's go. It's getting late." Lary motioned with his head.

Martin was made to walk ahead of them to their car on Clay Street. Larry got behind the wheel while Martin and Lum Po hopped in the back seat.

The car turned right and went through the long Stockton Street tunnel that separated Chinatown from downtown San Francisco. Then they turned right on Geary.

"Sorry I neglected to answer your question back there," Lum Po said. "You asked where we were going. We're going to pay a visit to your father. We're going to the Chinese cemetery."

"I see," Martin said. "I heard that he was buried there."

"It's too bad you were too busy to attend his funeral."

Martin said nothing in reply.

"He's buried there only temporarily. I promised him I would send his bones back to China to be buried in his village graveyard. He wants to be laid to rest in his homeland. We thought maybe you could help us, since you are his son."

"Help you?" Martin asked.

"It's bad luck for strangers to touch a man's bones. It's best if the bones are handled only by the man's nearest kin. You happen to be his son, and we happen to be going to the cemetery. So it would be convenient if you could help us out.''

Larry showed Martin the shovel and a medium-sized lacquered box in which the bones would be placed. "This is the box we'll use to ship his bones back to China."

They turned through the rickety gates and followed a twisting road that wound up a hill. Wind whipping off the ocean whistled through the trees, and crickets made a racket in the lengthy yellow grass. They stopped the car and turned off the headlights.

"This is it," Lum Po said. "His grave is on that hillside, through those trees."

They walked past several gravestones with Chinese inscriptions, honoring beloved ones who had passed on. Finally, they reached his father's grave. Martin was handed the shovel and was told to begin digging. He complied. Lum Po relieved him from time to time. Larry held onto the metal weapon in his pocket. Once in a while he walked partway down the hill to make sure no one was coming up.

The work was exhausting. Martin had already put in a rough day in front of a hot stove at Dung Ho's. The digging was starting to get to him. Lum Po noticed the strain on Martin's face.

"Not much more," he said. "Anyway, you ought to feel good about doing this work, Man Sum. It is the work of a filial son. If you couldn't obey him as you should when he was alive, this act of obedience is a small restitution."

Finally, they reached the coffin, which was now in splinters. Larry lowered a kerosene lamp to Martin. "When you find the bones, I'll give you the box to put them in," Larry said.

"All right, now," Lum Po ordered, "find your father's bones."

"Even with the light, it's hard to see down here," Martin answered. "It'd be much easier to find bones in the daytime."

But after looking awhile, Martin found shreds of bone that were already somewhat decomposed. "All right, I've got something. Hand down the box to me."

Larry handed down the box, and Martin carefully began putting the pieces of bone inside. This is all of what was left of his own father, he thought. Just this pile of bones. Sing Choy Wu, the exalted master. When Martin had finished gathering the bones into the black box, he handed the box up to Lum Po. Then he started to crawl out of the grave himself.

"Just a minute," Lum Po said. "Are you sure you got all the pieces? You better dig around a little more to make sure you haven't overlooked anything. That could be very serious for your father's spirit, if some of him got back to China, but some of him remained here in the country of the barbarians."

Martin shone the kerosene lamp on the dark soil once again and ran his fingers through it. All he came up with were what seemed to be rocks, although in this light he could have easily mistaken rocks for bones. "There are just rocks," he said. "I don't think my father would like to be buried next to rocks from America, unless they were gold rocks."

Lum Po laughed. So Martin began to climb out of the grave.

"Stay there," Lum Po ordered. He pulled a weapon from his jacket. Larry also aimed his handgun at Martin. "He wanted his bones sent back to China, but that was only half of his request. The other half was that his son be buried in his vacated grave.'' With that, Lum Po kicked some of the removed dirt back into the grave and onto Martin.

"Lum Po, this will put you back in prison. This time on death row. Is that what you want?'' Martin knew there was no hope of coming out of this situation alive, but for his family's sake, he engaged in the futile exercise of trying to talk himself out of it.

"I don't have any choice, do I, Man Sum? An oath is an oath. I would be dead if I failed to live up to my oath one way or the other. The secret society works in mysterious ways, but it always works. Its laws are inexorable.''

Larry was getting anxious. "Come on, Lum Po. Let's get this over with.''

"No, I have been waiting ten years for this moment,'' Lum Po said, looking Man Sum straight in the eye. "I have been planning it and thinking about it. This moment when, before the bones of Man Sum's father, I could become his son. That's what it means. You see, Man Sum, by eliminating you, his flesh and blood, I take your place. I become his son. He took my father's place, you see that? He was a father to me, and I loved him much more than you did. What did you do? You loved that little whore better than your own father! And she turned out that way because of you. If she'd stayed with her rightful husband, Sing Choy Wu, then she would have turned out all right. She would have been somebody. But you destroyed her, sent her to the Christian *faan gwai*, and that hastened his death. That is why I must punish you.''

Suddenly there were voices in the shadows of the trees. "All right, drop those guns!'' someone shouted in the dark.

It was the police. Lum Po turned and fired at the

shadows, and the shadows burst with exploding return fire. Lum Po and Larry fell to the ground and lay in the soft dirt that surrounded the grave of Sing Choy Wu.

A policeman walked out of the trees, approached Martin and offered to help him out of the grave.

"It's all right, I can get out myself," Martin said.

He pulled himself out of the ditch he had dug. "Thank you, officer," he said. Then he picked up the black box and walked down the hill.

He carried the black box containing the bones of his father to the ocean. He sat on the beach with the black box between his knees for a long time. Across the ocean was the great continent of China, that land of immense history and poverty, ignorance and brilliance, superstition and knowledge. He held the black box aloft and said to his father, "It will be all right now. You are going home."

He returned to the apartment on Powell early in the morning. He was disheveled and his clothes were torn. Ming Lee opened the door.

"Martin, thank God," she said, reaching out and embracing him.

After a moment, he pulled away from her and placed the box outside the door to the kitchen. He draped an old, worn tablecloth over it.

"We have to send this to China as soon as possible." He turned to his wife. "How did the police happen to be there at the cemetery?"

"I called them as soon as you walked out the door, Man Sum. I was so afraid."

"You called the police?"

"Yes," she said.

"They must have seen me being taken to the car. They must have followed us to the cemetery." Man Sum reached out and took his wife's hand. "Once again, Ming Lee, you have saved your husband's life."

Chapter 28

Bo Mat was released from the California Youth Authority's care on June 30, 1933. He served the full sentence allowed by law for a juvenile attempting armed robbery. Dr. Steven Roberts had petitioned several times over the years for Bo Mat's parole, but every time Bo Mat's case was reviewed, more blemishes were discovered on the youngster's behavior record. It seemed he was unable to stay out of fistfights with other boys at the institution. He couldn't abide racial slurs of any kind. He was proud of being Chinese, even though he himself didn't know what being Chinese really meant. Often white or black youths would call Bo Mat a "Chink" or a "slanty-eyed banana." Bo Mat would not pretend to ignore these insults and would attack the perpetrators, even those larger than himself. Although he was small, he was a scrappy, muscular youngster, apt as not to lay his adversary in the dust of the prison yard.

The other boys learned quickly how to make him angry, and in the long, boring days at the reform school, a good brawl was one of the few available ways to break the monotony. Accordingly, Bo Mat continually found himself battling other youths. When his four years were up, the

Youth Authority was more than glad to let Steven Roberts take him off its hands.

When Bo Mat was at last delivered to the orphanage, the director had reason to regret it. Bo Mat was extremely jittery and defensive. The other boys at the orphanage were afraid of him and avoided him. This made matters worse. The third day he was there, sixteen-year-old Bo Mat, for an imagined slight, beat up eleven-year-old Lam Kwok. Little Lam Kwok was so severely injured that he had to be hospitalized. Steven Roberts began to realize he was stuck with a difficult behavior problem. Some of his staff, in fact, urged Dr. Roberts to return the unruly youngster to the stricter reformatory for delinquents.

"We don't have the facilities or training to deal with him, Dr. Roberts," Mary Parker said. Mary was one of the teachers on the staff.

"All right, all right, Mary. Tell you what. Ask him to come to my office tomorrow at the beginning of class. I'll have a talk with him."

The following day, Bo Mat came bursting into Dr. Roberts' office. The boy was upset. "What do you want with me?" he snarled at the director. "What did I do? I didn't do anything. It's them. They all call me names behind my back. They whisper to each other, then they giggle. But you don't believe me, do you? Nobody believes me." With that, he slammed his fist against an oak chair.

Roberts didn't argue. He simply said, "It must be very painful to feel that everybody is talking about you behind your back."

"I know you don't want me here, and I don't much like it here. I'm not being helped. And I'll tell you another thing. Unless I get some help, I'm going to leave, just walk out. You'll see."

"Where would you go if you left us, Bo Mat?"

"I don't know. I don't know where I would go."

"Back to the Tongs?" Dr. Roberts asked.

"You'd like that, wouldn't you? Yes, then you could say, 'I told you so.' Yes. You'll enjoy watching me get into trouble, watching me get caught. Read all about it in the papers. Well, I don't plan to get caught. I have friends out there. I learned how to handle myself. I won't make any more mistakes. Nobody who's smart gets caught. Only the stupid get caught, and I'm not stupid. Oh, I know the white bitch teacher thinks I'm stupid. She complained about me, huh? Don't think I don't know. I know." Bo Mat expected to get slapped down for his cheek.

But Roberts only said, "Bo Mat, there's the door. You can leave any time you like, but I'll tell you something you might not believe. I don't want you to leave. And I'll tell you why. I think you are sincere in your desire to change."

Bo Mat lowered his head. He said, "Nobody can help me." But he knew that Dr. Roberts had come to the heart of the matter.

"It won't be easy, Bo Mat. That chip on your shoulder seems to be bolted in place. It's there for a reason. I think we need to talk about that chip you're carrying. So I suggest we have some talks. Yes. Every day, instead of going to Miss Parker's class, you'll come here. We'll have some jasmine tea and talk about whatever you'd like to discuss."

"All right," Bo Mat said. Then he added vaguely, "I know what you're trying to do: get more confessions out of me. Think you'll get me to confess to more crimes so you can have me sent away again. I can talk all you want. It doesn't matter. I'm a good talker. I'll talk about everything and nothing. But that doesn't mean you'll find out anything. You're wasting your time."

During the following weeks, the sessions between Dr. Roberts and Bo Mat consisted largely of drawn-out pauses punctuated by short questions and answers.

"Tell me about the laundryman," Dr. Roberts asked.

"What do you want to know?"

"Was he kind?"

"No."

"What did he do to you?"

"A lot of things."

"Did he beat you?"

"Yes."

Roberts never complained about the dribbling information the troubled youngster provided. Little by little, even through this slow process, a picture began to emerge, and as time went on, Bo Mat began to trust Dr. Roberts.

It soon became apparent that something painful was causing Bo Mat to demonstrate such hostile feelings. Dr. Roberts' suspicion was confirmed when Bo Mat one morning suddenly put his hands to his face and wept, but when the director asked him why, Bo Mat responded with stiff silence.

"Life can treat a person pretty badly," Dr. Roberts told him. "It's not wrong to get angry. You can get angry without punching somebody in the jaw. Just blow up, yell, let off the steam. On the other hand, you can't fight everybody that calls you a Chink. If you did, you wouldn't have time to do anything else. And you can't hit the laundryman back for beating you either. He's not here. Besides, hitting him back probably wouldn't remove the pain he caused you. Heck, it'd just remind you of it. I get sad sometimes, too. It's a very human thing. And that's not bad. In fact, when you can feel that sadness, that's a really good sign."

"Is it?" This puzzled Bo Mat.

"It shows you've got some guts.

Bo Mat shook his head. "Guts is the last thing it shows."

"Nope. Anybody can put up his fists and hit another kid. It certainly doesn't take much to knock a kid five years younger than yourself to the ground.'

"Now wait a minute," Bo Mat said agitatedly

Roberts stopped him. "It takes a lot more courage to confess that you're hurting inside and that you're willing to show it to someone else."

It wasn't until the following week that Bo Mat was able to return to the subject that filled his eyes with tears. The interim sessions with Dr. Roberts were marked with Bo Mat's angry outbursts at everyone who thought he was inferior.

Finally, he poured out his frustrations "She was sick. Really sick. There was no one to take care of her They left her there to die."

"Who, Bo Mat, who?"

"Yan Chui Lee was her name She had powder on her face, rouge, lipstick, like the others in Sullivan's Alley. Only Yan Chui Lee said I was not her son. I belonged to one of the others out there. Kwan Ming Lee."

"Your mother?"

"My mother is Kwan Ming Lee. I don't want to see her. I don't want to know her. She's one of them. They call out to men from the little windows. The men go in there. I saw them. They go in there for ten minutes. Anybody can go in there if they've got a few dollars My mother is one of them. This Kwan Ming Lee who had to get rid of me because I would have been in her way while she had men in there. Word must have gotten to this whore, my mother. My mother, the whore!"

"Go on, Bo Mat, word must have—"

"Word must have gotten to her I had been looking for my mother, thinking it was Yan Chui Lee. So this whore, Kwan Ming Lee, tried to visit me at Youth Authority. Came up there to Chico. This guard, smirk on his face and everything, came to my cell and said, 'Lady who says she's your mother is out there.' I could tell by the smirk on his face, she was probably worn-out looking, with powder, rouge, and plucked, penciled eyebrows." Bo Mat stopped abruptly.

"Continue, Bo Mat."

"I can't talk about this. I can't."

"You can, Bo Mat. You must."

"Besides, she was probably hustling business with the guards while she was waiting for me. I said, 'No, I don't want to see her.' Just like that. My own mother, whom I'd been looking for. So the guard just shrugged and didn't try to talk me into seeing her. He was probably glad because now he didn't have to wait till the end of our interview to go with her somewhere in the prison. I said again, 'I will not see her. I want nothing. Do you hear me? I want nothing to do with her. The guard left. That afternoon, he walked by my cell on his rounds, and he said. 'That lady stayed around a long time. She couldn't believe you didn't want to see her. She kept telling me you were her son. Anyway this sad woman just left.' "

Bo Mat sat for a long time in the oak chair in Dr. Roberts' office. There was an anguished expression on his face, but he didn't say anything. Then, unexpectedly, he pulled a rumpled piece of paper out of his pants pocket. He showed the piece of paper to Dr. Roberts.

Dr. Roberts asked, "Is this the phone and address of your mother, Kwan Ming Lee?"

Bo Mat nodded.

"She lives here in San Francisco, in Chinatown. Powell Street. Do you want to see her, Bo Mat?"

"I don't know."

"Well, you're sixteen years old. You can see her if you want to. Certainly, it's your choice, but I'll tell you what I think." Dr. Roberts paused, then continued. "I think you should definitely see her, but not now."

Bo Mat started to say something, but Dr. Roberts interrupted. "No, not now. You're not ready for that yet. Seeing her won't solve your problems. But you took a big step in the right direction today, you know that? You let go of some of that pain you've been holding on to, and you admitted to yourself that she's important to you. You can't just dismiss her. What do you think? I don't like to tell people what to think or what to do. It's just not my way. And I don't think it helps young men or women to grow up if adults are always making decisions for them. So that's why I'm asking what *you* want to do."

Bo Mat thought for a long time after Dr. Roberts had spoken. Finally, he said, "I think you're right."

Roberts reached out and the young man shook his hand. "Tell you what, young fellow. Maybe you'd better give me that phone and address for safekeeping. If you keep carrying it around like that, I think it wouldn't be long before it fell apart altogether."

After that session, Bo Mat decided he would rather attend class than come to these discussions. Suddenly he felt a thirst for knowledge that he had suppressed since his laundry days, when he had not been allowed to attend school with other children his age.

Over the next few weeks, Mary Parker noted marked improvement in Bo Mat's behavior. Once he started to apply himself to his studies, Bo Mat quickly excelled. He became an avid reader and writer. He enjoyed writing essays and expressed himself on a wide range of topics. But, she supposed, the most dramatic symbol of the change in his behavior was that he volunteered to help the slower students. With sympathetic patience, he would go over and over grammatical sentence structures. He was equally proficient in math, and could often be found in the classroom with other students, helping to explain to them math problems on the blackboard.

Within a year, however, Bo Mat's mood grew restless again His mind began to wander in school, and Mary Parker started to worry. She felt that since Bo Mat had come such a long way in the last year, it would be all right if she asked him herself what the trouble was.

His answer was very simple and to the point. "I want to learn Chinese," he said.

Miss Parker immediately consulted Dr. Roberts and Bo Mat was called to his office the next day

"All right, Bo Mat, you can learn Chinese," Dr Roberts nodded "But I think you should also attend high school You can, of course, continue to board here, but as for your studies, you would be offered a much wider range in public high school. We're going to send you to the best high school in the city academically, Lowell High. Then, after school is out, you can pursue your study of the Chinese language."

For the next year, Bo Mat went to Lowell High. He also attended classes in Chinese held at three-thirty every day in Cumberland Presbyterian Church at the corner of Powell and Jackson.

Finally, in his studies of the strange calligraphy and sounds of the Chinese language, Bo Mat found another interest that was all-consuming. brush painting

During Bo Mat's senior year in high school, Dr. Roberts called him into his office

"Bo Mat," Roberts said in an encouraging tone, "I think you're ready now."

Bo Mat knew immediately what Dr. Roberts was referring to. "I know I am."

Steven Roberts handed Bo Mat the piece of paper on which his mother's address and phone number were written. Bo Mat sighed. This was going to be a rough one, he thought, but it had to be done.

It was February 20, 1936. The Sings had recently celebrated Chinese New Year. It had been a happy celebration. The New Year's day was a time for the family to come together over good food, and for all the children to receive red envelopes with lucky money inside. But the family harmony that marked the Sings' New Year's festivities came to an abrupt halt that evening.

It all started when Jack announced: "I'm trying out for the baseball team."

This was greeted with cold silence. Each member of the family knew Jack was acting in defiance of his father. Baseball practice was held after school, the same time as Chinese class.

Martin said firmly, "You're *not* trying out for the baseball team. You will continue your Chinese studies. Your work has consistently been mediocre, and I want you to make up for it in the few years that remain before you go to college."

"I'm quitting Chinese school," Jack replied.

"You're what?"

"Sir, I'm quitting Chinese school."

Now the atmosphere was charged and tense. This was the first time any of the children had openly defied a direct command from the head of the family.

"I have to quit Chinese studies, because otherwise, I wouldn't be able to attend baseball practice," Jack said.

Martin glared at his son. It was a great disappointment for him to hear this, but he had been expecting it. The *faan gwai* schools, he thought, were to blame for spreading teachings that undermined the order and integrity of the family.

There was suppressed anger in Martin's voice when he said, "It is bad luck to begin the new year on a note of disharmony This argument will cease. You will obey me, Jack."

"No," Jack responded.

Ming Lee, deeply distressed that the tension between Jack and her husband had finally come to this open conflict, spoke quickly to the other children. "Ronnie, Cindy, Tom, Laura Mei, go into the other room. Your father and Jack are having a private discussion. Go do your homework."

The other children obeyed instantly, but while in the other room, they all huddled against the door to the kitchen and listened, fascinated by the battle which was taking place as their mother cleared the dinner dishes.

"The coach, Mr. Smith, has been watching me play during gym period. He told me I was a pretty good shortstop, and I ought to try out for the team."

"Yes, Mr. Smith. You told me about him," Martin said. "He's the one who calls you 'China boy,' isn't he?"

"So what?" Jack asked.

"Do you think he calls you 'China boy' out of respect for you or your ancestry?" Martin raised his eyebrows inquiringly.

"Dad, in America, people respect you for what you can do, for what you accomplish. They don't care who you are."

"Mr. Smith is spitting on your people. And if I were

you, I would step out of the way. That spit is poisonous. It robs a man of his blood, and after his blood is gone, he becomes good for nothing.''

"First of all, Dad,'' Jack said, "I don't take the coach seriously. He just doesn't bother to learn people's names, that's all. He uses tags for people so he can identify them. He doesn't mean anything by it. He deals with a lot of kids in gym class. Calls kids by all sorts of names. When a boy has acne, he calls him 'Pimples.' He doesn't mean anything by it.''

"Well, your name is Jack Sing,'' Martin said. "Tell him to learn it, or somebody will come to your school and teach it to him, namely, me. Jack Sing is your name.''

"Be careful, Martin,'' Ming Lee interjected.

"Why should I be careful?''

"You're starting to sound like a *boo how doy*.'' The words got out before Ming Lee realized what she had said.

"*Boo how doy*? What's that?'' Jack asked.

"Never mind what that is,'' Martin muttered defensively.

Jack had already guessed correctly that the term had something to do with Tongs and violence. He already knew that his father had had some involvement with that violence, and that this was why he still kept the gun hidden in the cupboard. Jack knew something of the Tong gangsters, and he remembered very well his father going out one night to confront two of them, pistol in hand. But since that event, his parents have never discussed Tongs, or gangsters, or even what had transpired that late evening. Who were those gangsters and what did they want from his father? Jack had never learned. There were many mysteries connected with his parents. What were they hiding? he wondered.

"It doesn't matter whether the coach calls you 'China boy' or not. You will do nothing about it. If you must submit to that kind of treatment in gym class, you must, but you need not suffer further humiliation of that kind by joining the baseball team.''

"Perhaps if I join the baseball team," Jack argued, "Mr. Smith will begin to call me by my real name. He won't call me 'China boy' any longer because he will see that I intend to become a serious athlete."

"You are not going to become an athlete," Martin insisted.

"I want to play baseball professionally," Jack countered.

Martin shook his head. "Nonsense. You know very well what my plans for your future are. You shall have a college education. You will study to become a practical businessman or an engineer. They are fields in which it is reasonable to suppose a Chinese can succeed in this country. You're not going to take any chances with your future security."

"I'm not interested in security."

"You're crazy. Is that the kind of ambition your school fills you with? An athlete? That's the most ridiculous thing I have ever heard. Who ever heard of a Chinese athlete, playing with white boys on American teams. That is just plain silly." Martin laughed out loud.

"It's better than being a cook," Jack threw in.

This remark brought Martin to his feet. "I brought honor to my parents. At sixteen, I was a boy, a child. I knew nothing of the world. I did not make decisions for myself. I listened to my father, I knew that what he wanted for me was best, and I obeyed without question. Without question!" At this point, Martin turned and met Ming Lee's eyes. Both knew, of course, he was lying, but it was necessary to set an example of obedience to one's parents. It was necessary, even if it meant telling lies about the past.

"No! This is America, Father. I am an American, and making your own choices is what this country stands for. That's freedom."

"I am Chinese."

"I am American, Father." Jack stood up. They faced each other without speaking. Then Jack burst out, "I hate being a Chink. I hate my slanted eyes and yellow skin. I hate all your secrets and your ancestors and your chopsticks. I hate all of it! I'm an American and I want to play baseball. I want to drink beer and chew gum and read comics. I don't care if I never see another grain of polished white rice in my life. I'll eat hot dogs."

"Eat hot dogs and die. You're already dead to me, Jack. Dead."

"Your head is full of dead ideas. Obedience. Obedience. Don't think. Just obey. It's that kind of dead idea that has made China what it is, a country full of slaves, a country that has not progressed beyond the Middle Ages. I like America because Americans have new ideas. Americans are not afraid to think for themselves."

"New ideas are never good ideas."

"In American families, children are encouraged to think for themselves. In high school, the teachers encourage you to think for yourself. I come home, my father tells me, 'Don't think for yourself. Obey, obey, obey. Don't question, don't think.' When I go to Chinese school, it's the same thing. Repeat. Repeat. Repeat."

"That is the way to learn something important," Martin said.

"Baseball's not like that. You're alone out there. The ball comes to the shortstop, he's got twenty million choices how he'll play that ball. What is he going to do, ask the coach? You ought to watch baseball, Father. Then you'll see what I'm talking about. You have to make your own choices.''

"I'm not talking to my son Jack, Ming Lee," Martin stormed. "I'm not talking to him. He is my eldest boy, and he should provide the example to the younger ones. He has failed, failed utterly in his duty.''

"I don't have to provide an example to them. They can think for themselves. They don't need me. Just like I don't need you to make my decisions for me," Jack shot back at his father.

"I'm not talking to him. He has slandered and cursed his own people. He has spat upon us all and spread blood poison throughout our house. He has desecrated his own ancestors and become an evil ghost. Such is the strange power baseball has over the son of a man." Martin sat down and wearily shook his head.

"Jack," Ming Lee said, "you should not talk back to your father.''

"But Mom, I have to express myself.''

Martin turned to his wife and said, "Tell Jack, my dead son, to stop talking.''

"Jack, stop talking." Ming Lee responded automatically to her husband's command.

Martin growled, "It is fortunate I have other sons.''

Chapter 29

Of the thirty or so Chinese students at Lowell, Jack Sing was one of five who showed up for the baseball team tryouts. About fifty boys in all turned out for the handful of positions open. One of these was catcher, and the other was shortstop. There were three positions open on the second-string team. These were shortstop, right field and second base.

When Jack Sing was invited by Coach Smith to try out, he hadn't realized there would be so many vying for so few openings. He felt he had no chance at all.

For an interminably long time, the hopefuls were made to stand in a line while the varsity worked out. The varsity players looked like real professionals. How the ball would whiz around from baseman to baseman!

Finally, Coach Smith started to call candidates onto the field. Jack began getting butterflies. How far down the list was he? He had no idea. Coach Smith just called the boys at random. The team's best hitters would bat sizzling grounders to those boys trying out for shortstop. The ball would have to be skillfully fielded and thrown to first for the out. Each boy was given three tries at fielding the speeding bouncers. Several disappointed candidates couldn't stop one.

"China boy," Coach Smith's deep voice boomed out of his barrel chest. Jack's heart started to pound as he adjusted his cap and made for the position. "Not you." Coach Smith shook his head. "Him!" The coach pointed to another Chinese boy. They were all "China boy" to the coach. Jack noted that nobody had yet been able to field all three ground balls.

The Chinese youngster who was called fumbled badly the first two and barely made a play on the third try. He caught the third hit all right, but threw wide to first. The other players shook their heads and smirked at one another. He knew what they were thinking: a China boy's place is in the kitchen or the laundry, not the playing field.

Still, no one had been able to turn in that perfect performance when Jack's turn finally came, near the bottom of the heap.

"China boy," the coach bellowed, nodding straight at Jack.

The first hit in Jack's direction caught the edge of the bat and sent an easy dribbler well within his range to the left. He charged the roller, scooped it and made an easy, firm throw to first. No one was impressed.

"That was a cinch."

"Doesn't prove a thing. Give the China boy a ball that can hurt him," said the red-headed kid playing third.

A high-bouncing ball careened toward Jack. He reached down, but the ball shot upward and leapt over his head. But he was quick. He reached up with his glove and snagged the ball. The throw to first was mere child's play.

"Wow," was the involuntary reaction of the third baseman.

The left fielder who had been backing Jack up called, "Two in a row. Pretty good."

The third ball was supposed to be a liner, but Jack sensed the batter was going to swing late and pull the ball toward third. Jack was on his way. He stretched his mitt, leaping at the same time, and sent the red-haired third baseman sprawling. The ball smacked into his glove and held. His movement to his feet and his throw to first were accomplished in one swift, coherent, coordinated play. The first baseman didn't have to move. Jack was the first to succeed all three times. He now knew he had nothing to worry about. His confidence was back. The coach narrowed the number of candidates down to eight and told the rest that, though they had all made outstanding attempts, this was not the year for them to join the team.

The eight remaining boys took turns at bat against the team's best pitcher, Ace Ludwig, who was also something of a school hero. Ace had a deadly fastball and enjoyed making a mean face before streaking it across the plate.

Ace struck out four of the candidates before Jack's turn at bat came. Tipped fouls were the only contacts the hopefuls' bats had made with Ace's speedy pitches. Then Jack stood ready at the diamond. Ace looked mean. The windup and the throw across the plate all occurred while Jack just looked on. The pitch was a strike. Jack realized he'd better put his bat out over the plate the next time.

He did. He hit the ball hard, and it managed to find the blind spot over second base and lined strongly to center, bouncing before the center fielder could catch it on the fly. Jack happily sauntered to first and stood there proudly with one foot on the bag.

Later, Coach Smith took him aside. "China boy," he said, "you're pretty good. I'm putting you on the team. But not at shortstop. You'll be a catcher."

Jack was puzzled, but still pleased to have made the team.

Every afternoon at baseball practice, Jack patiently bore the inconvenience of putting on the catcher's equipment: mask, chest protector and shin guards.

After about a week, the coached asked, "What's your name, China boy?" ,

"Jack Sing."

"Okay," the coach said. "We'll call you Jack Singer from now on. Jack Singer. Remember."

"All right, coach, but why?"

"Why? Well, ah, it's easier to remember. More American."

Jack suddenly realized why he was playing catcher. The mask on his face would make it impossible for anyone to know he was Chinese. The coach wanted to cover up the fact that he had recruited a Chinese boy on his team. Why? Because the overriding opinion was that the Chinese weren't athletes.

Later that week, the coach said at practice, "Singer, you keep catching. Keep that mask on and stay behind the plate. You won't be going to bat for us."

That's when Jack began to have second thoughts. He had hit well against Ace and the other pitchers in practice. He was picking up the position of catcher well, although initially it had been unfamiliar to him. He could not understand why he wouldn't be allowed to go to bat. Everybody believed that the Chinese weren't athletes, but couldn't there be an exception that would change everybody's mind? Or maybe it was the case that once everybody's mind was made up, nobody wanted anything to change.

Jack was beginning to see his father's point. Perhaps it was not possible to belong to the country he'd been born in. But neither did he feel the least bit like a Chinese. The customs and traditions his parents engaged in seemed totally foreign to him. Even the Cantonese tongue, with which he was familiar, felt awkward and strange as he spoke it. The Chinese class had bored him. He had always daydreamed about sports, sports that were characteristically American. These sports formed much of American tradition and folklore. The coach had made him fit in by changing his name, so it would sound Caucasian. That made him more a part of the team, yet he was still excluded from full participation

Confused, Jack consulted his parents, and confessed what had happened. His father, of course, seized the opportunity to gloat.

"They want to disguise that you are Chinese by putting you in a catcher's costume. Perhaps that suggests a career for you. Welders wear masks, too. You could become a welder."

Ming Lee scolded her husband. "This is not something to joke about," she cautioned.

"I agree," Martin said. "I agree. One cannot go through one's whole life wearing a mask. It is as though you were ashamed of being what you are. Is that any way to live? To walk around ashamed of being Chinese? I don't think so. I seem to have the crazy notion that being Chinese is actually something to be proud of!"

Jack felt miserable. "It looks as if I was wrong. I said that Americans respect talent more than anything. It wasn't who you were that mattered, it was what you could do. But this experience has shown otherwise. It appears that you have to have skin that looks like milk." Jack lowered his head.

"What are you going to do about it, Jack?" his father

queried. "I'll ask you, since you were so insistent the other night that you be allowed to think for yourself."

"Dad," Jack said, "I am sorry I was disobedient."

"You will return to Chinese school?"

"Yes, I will."

It was Friday evening. Jack resolved to quit the baseball team the following Monday. But something happened on Saturday to change everything and confuse matters even more.

Ronald was at the YMCA, and Tom and Laura Mei were at the Chinese playground on Sacramento Street. Cynthia and Jack were home studying. Martin was at work. Ming Lee was wrapping ground pork in square wonton for the evening meal. There was a knock on the door.

"Jack, answer that, will you?"

When Jack opened the door, a young Chinese man stood there. He looked familiar to Jack. Jack thought he had seen him around Lowell.

"Kwan Ming Lee?" the stranger asked.

"What?" Jack didn't recognize the name.

"Kwan Ming Lee *hai mm hai do ah*?" Bo Mat had asked if Ming Lee was there.

Ming Lee was completely taken by surprise. She burst out of the kitchen and stood facing the stranger. "I am Ming Lee," she said.

"I am Bo Mat," the lad said. "I am—" He was about to say he was her son, but Ming Lee interrupted him."

"I know," she said. "Please, come in."

She turned to Jack and Cynthia. "Children, I want to speak to this young man privately. You can come in later, and I'll introduce you. You see, he is from China, a distant relative."

Jack shook his head. More secrets, he thought to

himself He was very tired of secrets. His family seemed to thrive on them. He couldn't stand being left out, so he decided to put his ear against the kitchen door and hear as much of this conversation as he could. Cynthia, ignoring him, busied herself with her studies

Ming Lee invited the young man into the kitchen. She poured him some tea, then sat down opposite him and poured a cup for herself

"I didn't think I would ever see you," she said, not looking at him. "Are you well?"

"I'm fine," Bo Mat said.

"My son, my own first-born." Ming Lee reached her hand toward his, but he withdrew from her touch. There was an embarrassing pause.

"I am doing very well. I have been living at the Chinese boys' orphanage. They've given me a lot of help I'm going to high school now, and Chinese school. This is my last year at Lowell."

"That's the same school my oldest boy, I mean, my next oldest boy goes to," Ming Lee told him. She was desperately searching for the feeling in herself that had been taken from her so long ago: the special love of a woman for her first-born child.

"Yes, I recognize him," Bo Mat said. "I have seen him in the hallways. I didn't know he was your son."

"I have four other children. Five children in all by my husband, Martin Sing. Two girls and three boys."

"That's nice." Bo Mat wasn't looking at her. He wished he hadn't come. He could think of nothing to say to this strange woman. There was a long, awkward silence.

Ming Lee finally spoke. "Bo Mat, why is it that when I came to the reformatory, you did not want to see me? I am your mother."

"Because I knew that you were a prostitute. I knew

that I was the son of a prostitute, and that meant my father
could be anybody off the street with a few coins in his
pocket. I had seen Sullivan's Alley, and the other place,
where the old ones are taken to die. I was sickened and
ashamed.'' Bo Mat tried to control his revulsion.

"Please, let us not speak of this loudly. My children
don't know about my past life, and I don't wish them to
know, not just yet.''

"I am sorry.''

"Would you like some rice? It's cold out today. A
little rice will warm you up.'' Ming Lee rose and went to
the stove.

"All right. That would be nice, thank you,'' Bo Mat
said.

As Ming Lee was dishing up the rice, she heard the
front door slam shut. She opened the kitchen door. Cynthia was in the far corner of the room, reading, but Jack
was nowhere to be found.

"Where's your brother?''

"I don't know, Mother,'' Cynthia replied. "He was
sitting by the kitchen door, then he just got up, grabbed his
jacket and ran out. I don't know where he went. I think he
was trying to eavesdrop on your conversation. I know I
shouldn't tell you that, but maybe he heard something that
upset him.''

"Well, there is nothing that can be done. If he went
out, he will be back. He is a big boy. He can take care of
himself.'' Jack knows, she thought to herself. The secret's
out, but it's just as well. It would have come out sooner or
later. They must all know about Bo Mat, and they must
receive him into our family. I will not lose him a second
time.

Bo Mat sat down to the rice. A plate of sliced chicken

and snow peas and a plate of chopped, sautéed vegetables were placed before him.

"This is good," he said. "The food that's served at the orphanage is nothing to brag about. It's nice to taste good, family cooking."

"I hope you may enjoy many good meals in this house, Bo Mat."

"I don't know. It's probably not good for me to come here. I should not come again. Already, my presence has upset your son Jack. I don't want to cause dissension in your family."

"Bo Mat," Ming Lee replied, "you mustn't say that. Don't say that you won't come back. My family will be made to understand, and they will accept you. I promise that."

"I am, after all, not your husband's son. I am another man's son. I am young, but I am old enough to realize that a man wants his own sons, not someone else's. And besides, you yourself don't know what kind of father I had. He could have been anybody."

Then Ming Lee said, almost whispering, "I know whose son you are."

Bo Mat stood up. His face showed great excitement. "You know who my true father is?"

"Yes," she said. "His name was Sing Choy Wu. He is dead now. He was my betrothed at one time, and he was the father of my husband."

"What kind of man was he, this Sing Choy Wu?" Bo Mat asked his mother.

"He was the leader of one of Chinatown's most powerful Tong organizations, the Chi Sing Tong. What kind of man was he? He was both very gentle and very cruel," she answered. "He loved me deeply and wanted to kill me for having betrayed him. He was a complex man.

"He died soon after you were born. He had defeated his enemies, the Suey Sing Tong, but the Chi Sings were in turn defeated by the San Francisco Police Department."

"Where is my father buried?" Bo Mat wanted to know

"Until recently, in the Chinese cemetery in the Richmond district. Then his bones were dug up and shipped to the village where he was born: Wing Tan Ho in Canton Province, southern China."

"Some day I will go there," Bo Mat said. "I will visit my father's grave."

"My son," Ming Lee smiled, "it is good to see you at long last."

"Mother," Bo Mat replied, "you know I would have come sooner, but I was very disturbed by Chico, and I felt too much hatred toward you for bringing me into the world and abandoning me. I realize now that I blamed you for all the bad things that had happened to me. I blamed you for allowing me to be sold into slavery to the laundryman in Oakland."

"You should blame me. You should. I should never have done such a thing. I hated to give you up. I hated to," she said.

"But you really had no choice. It took me a long time to find that out. It took a lot of soul-searching too," he said with deep emotion he could not conceal. "I had to get these feelings of hatred out of the way before I could come to you, don't you see? And I have, Mother, I have."

"You have become a man, Bo Mat, and you are ready to take your place as the eldest son of this family, and by example to show the younger ones the way to growth and maturity"

"I would be most glad to have that opportunity,

Mother.'' And as he said this, he bowed with reverential respect.

"Go now, Bo Mat, and come back in three days, Tuesday evening. At that time, you will meet my family, which will then become yours. In the meantime, I will talk to my husband and my children. I will explain everything to them. Everything will be in the open, and if we trust in God, everything will be forgiven. We will be together again, my own, dear first-born.''

There were tears in her eyes as he rose to go.

A little later, Jack came back.

"Where have you been?'' Ming Lee asked.

"Just walking around Chinatown, that's all,'' he said in an irritated tone.

"Jack, is there anything wrong?'' his mother asked.

"No. Nothing's wrong. I'm old enough to go out and walk around Chinatown, aren't I? Nothing wrong with that, is there?''

Ming Lee continued to probe. "You seem to be disturbed about something.''

"I'm just fine, Mother, just fine.'' He sat on the old overstuffed chair and sighed.

"Jack, were you listening at the kitchen door when I was talking to that young man?'' she asked.

"You mean my brother?'' he responded with bitterness.

"Then you *were* listening. You heard everything that was said?''

"Yes, I heard everything. I don't know what is better, to have secrets or to have the truth. I don't like either one very much.'' He started to fidget.

"Jack, I—'' Ming Lee started to say.

"There is one thing I cannot understand,'' Jack interrupted. "How could Dad have married you?''

"Your father loved me. As Jesus taught, when you love, you forgive. I beg you, Jack, if you love me, also forgive me. The past is past. It is dead. It is no more. I'm now a Christian. You understand enough about Christianity to realize that if you believe, the Lord wipes your soul clean."

"The past isn't dead at all, Mother. The past is alive and well. My so-called brother is the past."

"Bo Mat is good, Jack. He is a good person. You will see when you get to know each other. Soon you will become friends. Bo Mat is mature, he's—"

"Not like me, huh? The masked man," Jack said heatedly.

"Jack, please."

"I don't want to have anything to do with him."

"There's no reason to be jealous, Jack," Ming Lee said gently.

"Jealous? Of that bastard?"

"He's not . . . don't you ever call him that. Why must you have such a filthy tongue?" Ming Lee was growing angry.

Jack clammed up and wouldn't say another word. Ming Lee tried to talk to him further, but he still would not say anything to her. Finally she gave up and went into the kitchen to prepare the evening meal. It was five o'clock. Martin would be home from the restaurant soon. Saturday evening was one of three evenings he was permitted to leave the restaurant early in order to dine with his family.

As Martin was leaving the restaurant, he saw a familiar figure and face smiling broadly at him. It was none other than Tsui Pang Fai, Peter Tsui. There were patches on his pants and his shirt collar was frayed. Why in

heaven's name was his old friend and partner so happy?
Martin wondered.

"Martin, I've been looking for you," Peter said. "I
have to talk to you. Something has come up."

"Well, Peter, actually I was on my way home to have
dinner with my family. Would you like to join us?"
Martin offered.

"*Mm daak haan.* I don't have time, Martin. I have to
go back to my apartment and get out some papers from our
days at The Dollar Store," he said.

"What do you want those old papers for? I thought
you got rid of them a long time ago. They aren't worth
much, are they? Since the bankruptcy, I tried to forget we
ever had that business." Martin scratched his head. He
thought his friend was becoming a little loony.

They walked together up the Jackson Street hill. They
both had to keep moving to ward off the cold. Neither of
them was properly dressed for the chilly air of the Chinatown
winter, where the damp fog seemed to eat into one's
bones.

"Haven't you been reading the papers, Martin? It's
true we're still in the depression, but there are signs that
things are going to start to get better. There are a lot of
tensions in the international scene for one thing. There's a
dictator in Germany, Adolf Hitler. He has plans for
taking over Germany, and the Japanese are in China. The
Japanese are getting ready to take over China and all of
Asia. Martin, soon there will be more jobs and more
money in people's pockets as this country starts to gear up
for war. I haven't been talking to a fortune-teller. I have
been talking to Chinese merchants who know how to look
ahead. But I have bigger news than that. The Chinese
merchant companies remember us, remember what a contribution we made to the community in our business. I talked

to one of the merchants who is an important member of the Chinese merchant companies. They have put some capital together, and this merchant says he thinks we can get a low interest loan from them." Peter was practically bursting with enthusiasm.

"You mean, start up The Dollar Store again?"

"Yes, start from scratch. Right here in Chinatown. Start modestly, of course, but we know how to build a business, you and I. We would have to be a little more careful with the stock market, of course." Peter laughed and winked.

Martin laughed too. It was good to laugh at the mistakes of the past.

"This merchant says the Chinese merchant companies were impressed by the integrity with which we conducted our business. We didn't get into notorious and illegal stuff the Tongs were doing, though we had the capital to. The merchant companies considered us to be examples to the Chinese community that one could be successful without running clandestine, immoral enterprises."

"Don't they know I was once a Tong man?" Martin asked skeptically.

"They may know it, Martin, but your record of service in the business community has been impeccable since The Dollar Store. Okay, I'll see you soon, Martin. Next week we'll get a presentation together to give the merchant companies. I think we've got a great chance to make a comeback." Peter slapped Martin on the back.

Martin smiled. "Foresight and courage, as you once said."

"Foresight and courage!" Peter echoed, nodding, and went on his way.

Chapter 30

Martin was grinning from ear to ear when he sat down to dinner, but he decided he wouldn't report the conversation he had had with Peter until after the family had eaten. However, he began to sense a certain tension in the air. Silence during the meal was customary, but there was something more somber about this silence tonight.

At Ming Lee's request, everyone stayed at the kitchen table while she cleared the dishes. She told her family she had important business to discuss.

Jack was growing increasingly nervous as Ming Lee finished clearing the table. Then finally she sat down and looked at each family member in turn, until her eyes fell on her husband.

She started to speak, but Martin interrupted her. "Before you say what you have to say, I have some very good news I want to share with the family."

Ming Lee was relieved both that her announcement would be postponed, and that her husband seemed to be in a good mood.

"On the way home from the restaurant, I met Peter Tsui. You all remember him, he was my business partner. Well, Peter thinks we have a good chance of getting a loan from the Chinese merchant companies. They seem to think that putting us back in business again will help the Chinese business community. They have very good memories of The Dollar Store. I had hoped for a long time that something like this would happen. Well, you all are glad to hear this news, I hope? Jack, aren't you glad? You look a little concerned.''

Jack said, ''That is very good news, Father. But I am anxious for Mother to give her news, too.''

''Of course, of course, and I am sorry to interrupt, but I just wanted you all to know there is reason for hope, thanks, and excitement in the new year. Well, go on,'' he said as he turned to his wife.

''There is something I have to—'' She stopped, unable to continue. No, she *had* to continue. This had to work. Inwardly she prayed it would work. Please, make him be understanding and forgiving, God. Don't let him be angry. Put into his heart love for his new son.

''There is something I have to say.''

''Yes, dear, we are all waiting. What is it?'' Martin asked patiently.

''It has to do with our lives, Martin, before we were married,'' she said.

''We agreed we weren't going to discuss that. I see no reason to bring it up,'' he said with finality in his voice. ''Especially now that we're about to apply to the Chinese merchant companies for a loan. The companies must not know anything about our past.''

''There is a reason now why we must discuss this,'' Ming Lee said darkly.

''This is not for the younger children to hear.'' He was about to tell the younger children to leave the kitchen.

''No!'' Ming Lee cried. ''There have been too many closed doors between the truth and the ears who have every right to hear the truth. They must know, they must know now, and you also must know. The past has to be made an open book, Martin.''

''One's children have to learn respect for what is right and good,'' Martin said. ''They have to have parents whose conduct is exemplary so they have something of value upon which to pattern their own lives. If you speak of those things in the past which should be left buried in the past, you will raise filth and vermin, and you will infest my house. I now ask you to stop this conversation immediately before it goes any further,'' he insisted.

But Jack put in, ''It's pointless to try to hide behind masks. You said so just the other day, Father. I already know everything. The secret is already no longer a secret. But I think I might even know more than you do, Father, so you'd better listen to Mother. Listen to what Mother has to say.''

''Your mother has never kept secrets from me. Whatever her past, one thing is certain: there has always been complete honesty between us.''

''Go ahead, Mother,'' Jack urged.

''No,'' Martin protested.

''Listen to her!'' Jack exclaimed. Taken by surprise, Martin fell into silence.

''Please, understand me, and forgive me for not having told you all sooner, but I am a mother,'' she said.

Everyone laughed, except Ming Lee. It was quite apparent to all that she was a mother.

''I mean,'' she said, speaking over the laughter, ''I have another son. An eighteen-year-old son. None of you know about him, except for Jack, and Jack just heard about him today. His name is Bo Mat. I didn't want any of you to know this because Bo Mat is not your father's child. He is the child of another man. You see, after he was born, he was taken from me and sold to a laundryman in the East Bay. Today, I met him for the first time. He is a fine young man, strong and good. He has become that way after many difficult struggles. He has achieved this maturity on his own, with no help from parents, without the protection and love of a mother or a father."

There was silence until Martin said, "Impossible."

"It is not impossible. Dear God, let my husband hear me. It is not impossible. It is true."

"This is true?" Martin said after a pause.

Martin rose and went into the other room. Ming Lee followed him.

The other children were talking excitedly about what they had just heard. All but Jack had been taken with the idea of having a half brother. Jack sat silently while the commotion reeled around him. In his heart, mingled with the confusion this news awoke in him, there was a deep anger he could barely contain.

In the next room, all was quiet except for the children's voices filtering in from the kitchen.

"Martin, please."

"Don't talk to me."

"I hoped you would understand."

"He came and saw you today?" Martin asked.

"Yes, he did," Ming Lee replied.

"You must never see him again. Is that clear? Nor must anyone in this family see him again," Martin said bitterly.

"But he goes to Lowell High School. Jack can see him every day," Ming Lee argued.

"He must never be allowed to come near us. He will contaminate us. Ming Lee, we have an opportunity to begin again. If the merchant companies hear that illegitimate sons are coming around the Sing household, asking for favors—''

''He's not asking for favors,'' she interrupted irately.

''Well then, what the hell does he want from us?'' Martin hissed. Now the children had stopped talking in the kitchen and were listening to the argument taking place in the living room.

''He wants to be accepted into the circle of his kinsmen,'' she stated flatly. ''He wants to take his rightful place.''

''He has no rightful place.''

''He does,'' she insisted.

''What? The son of some Cantonese miner who bought you with a thimbleful of dust? He has a right in my house? How do you arrive at that conclusion, Ming Lee?''

''He is not the son of a Cantonese miner,'' Ming Lee grumbled.

''No? Then some other Chinese. I hope, at least, the father was Chinese.''

''Yes, he was,'' Ming Lee nodded.

''Hear me well, Ming Lee. I'll kill him if he comes near this place. I swear, I will kill him. You will have nothing more to do with him. Nothing. Do you hear?''

''You won't kill him, Martin. You will love him, as I do, because he is a part of me, Martin, my flesh and blood, as he is also your flesh and blood. He is your brother.'' Ming Lee couldn't stop herself from revealing the fact.

This statement stopped Martin cold. ''My . . .''

''Your brother.''

''You mean . . . ?''

''Sing Choy Wu, Martin. Sing Choy Wu.''

There was a silence. Martin sat and held his head in his hands.

"He's my son. Bo Mat is my son," Ming Lee appealed.

"He's not *my* son!" Martin brayed. "I have nothing to say. I cannot think. I don't understand this. I have never heard of such a thing. This has never happened before to anyone I know. All I know is that he is not my son, and I want to have nothing whatsoever to do with him! Is that clear?"

"I wish that you would reconsider for my sake and for the sake of our whole family."

"I have already stated my decision," Martin said evenly. "I must hold to it. I cannot change my mind. That is my decision, and you must all abide by it. All of you. This thing that has happened must not reach the ears of the Chinese merchant companies or anyone else in Chinatown. We must stop talking of this matter."

"I can't stop talking about it, Martin," Ming Lee said in an exasperated tone, "or thinking about it. I just can't."

"You must," Martin demanded. Then he got up out of his chair and swung open the door to the kitchen. Martin stood at the door and looked at his children. "Forget that this matter was ever spoken of. We will not receive this person into our house as a relative or as a guest. May I have that promise from each of you?"

"Yes, Father," each of the children said in turn, except for Jack.

"What about you, Jack? Can I count on your silence as well?" Martin asked.

"Yes, Father," Jack agreed.

It was not easy for Jack to avoid seeing Bo Mat. Jack knew that he would pass his half brother every day in the hallways of Lowell High. The following Monday, Jack tried his best to keep his eyes averted when he happened to glance at Bo Mat, but on Tuesday a confrontation was unavoidable. During lunch Bo Mat sat in the chair across from Jack in the cafeteria. Bo Mat didn't have a tray of food with him or anything to drink. He had taken that seat just so he could talk to his brother.

"Jack," Bo Mat said, "do you know who I am?"

"Yes, I know who you are."

"I haven't heard anything from my mother or any of the rest of you about tonight."

"Tonight?"

"Yes," Bo Mat said. "Mother invited me to come to your house for dinner tonight so I could meet the entire family."

"I don't know anything about it," Jack said without looking up.

"You mean, she didn't tell you?" Bo Mat asked.

"No." Jack was beginning to feel very uncomfortable under Bo Mat's scrutinizing gaze.

"I was supposed to come over tonight. That is, I think so," Bo Mat said. "Did Mother discuss me with your father at all? Did they talk about me?"

"I don't know," Jack replied evasively.

"Jack, you must know. That place where you're living is so small, you'd have to know what everyone is saying or doing."

"When they speak in Chinese, I don't understand them."

"What? You can't understand Chinese? Didn't you go to Chinese school?"

"Yes, I went, but it bored me. I couldn't stand it. And anyway, since I joined the baseball team, I have no time to learn Chinese."

"You made a mistake there. *Naahm pa yap chaw hong.*"

"What did you say?"

"I said, 'A man fears to enter the wrong trade.' "

"I don't understand any of that," Jack replied in an irritated tone.

"I don't understand how someone who is Chinese would be bored by his own language and culture," Bo Mat said pointedly.

"It's none of your business." Jack looked at his half brother for the first time. There was hatred in Jack's eyes.

"I want us to be friends, Jack. After all, we are brothers. I'm not trying to meddle in your business. I know that I, for one, worked hard to learn Chinese. I suppose I did it because all I knew about myself was that I was Chinese. In fact, when I graduate from college, I plan to go to China, stay there for a while, and learn what it's like to live there." As Bo Mat spoke of this, his eyes lit up.

"The sooner the better," Jack said under his breath.

"What?"

"Look, why don't you just let me alone? I don't like company. I want to sit here alone, do you mind?"

"But I still don't know about tonight," Bo Mat persisted anxiously.

"The deal is off!" Jack exclaimed. "Did you hear me? There has been a mistake."

Now Bo Mat started to get angry. "Mistake? What do you mean, mistake?"

"A case of mistaken identity," Jack said. "You're no relation to me, my father, or my mother."

"There has been no mistake," Bo Mat said slowly.

Jack drummed his fist down on his tray. The heads of other students turned in his direction.

Jack, aware of the eyes of others on him, lowered his voice. "What do you mean, coming to our house and telling some story about how you're my mother's long-lost son? You expect anyone to believe that? I spotted you for the impostor you were the moment you opened the door. Maybe you heard that my father was at one time a millionaire, and you hoped to pick up a little money to finance your junket to China."

Bo Mat was beginning to have those familiar feelings from the reformatory days. He thought he had licked those feelings, and didn't expect them to come back. But come back they did. "Nobody calls me an impostor," he said, narrowing his eyes

"You're not my brother. My mother wants to have nothing to do with you, and nobody else in our family does either So just get out, before you are thrown out."

Bo Mat reached across the table and grabbed Jack's arm in a viselike grip. "You're lying to me, Jack. Why don't you tell me the truth? Your dad didn't like the idea, isn't that it?"

Jack struggled to loosen his arm from Bo Mat's grip, but Bo Mat only tightened his hold.

Jack said in a loud voice, "Let go of me! I don't have to tell you a thing!"

"Don't you lie to me!" Bo Mat yelled. Everyone in the cafeteria was watching them now.

Jack jabbed his fork into Bo Mat's arm. Bo Mat recoiled in pain, releasing his grip on his half brother. But then Bo Mat jumped across the table and promptly threw himself on top of Jack.

Jack countered with a punch to the side of Bo Mat's face that was sufficiently powerful to knock Bo Mat from off the top of Jack's body.

The crowd was cheering wildly. The way was cleared

for the two boys as they rolled on top of each other. Jack connected with another blow to Bo Mat's midsection as they rolled along the cafeteria floor. This blow forced Bo Mat off his opponent again, and landed Bo Mat on his back, but Bo Mat managed to stand up quickly. Jack rose also, and now the two young men faced each other.

Just then, two male teachers began to push their way through the group watching the fight. One of them happened to be Mr. Smith, the baseball team coach. The two men were yelling, "Break it up, break it up!"

But the teachers were too late to stop the fists. Jack successfully defended himself against the first few punches, but the experience of the reformatory had made Bo Mat a hardened fighter. Jack had the fast reflexes and the strong muscles of an athlete, but he was no match for Bo Mat's street-born toughness. Soon, Jack was struggling just to ward off the blows that were coming faster and faster from Bo Mat's angry hands. As Bo Mat pummeled his half brother again and again, Jack weakened and went to his knees. Bo Mat had one or two cuts, but Jack's face was a mass of bruises. It finally took both teachers to contain Bo Mat.

When the fight was stopped Bo Mat was sobbing.

"I have no choice but to expel both of you from Lowell for one year," Principal Davis said. "I hope during this period, intelligent young men that you both are, you will see what it costs to allow your behavior to sink to the level that was evident in that cafeteria. You will also see that such behavior accomplishes nothing. I regret that the other students encouraged it rather than stepping in to put a stop to it. It just cannot be condoned at Lowell where our business is scholarship and college preparation. I have nothing more to say on this matter, boys."

*   *   *

Martin blamed the fight at Lowell High School on Bo Mat. "A kid with a record like that shouldn't have even been allowed in that school in the first place," he said.

Ming Lee said nothing, but inwardly she longed to see her son again. On the pretext of doing shopping in Chinatown, she walked toward the corner of Jackson and Powell and there caught a cable car. She got off at Union Street and transferred to a bus going west, toward the Presidio. She got off at Steiner and made her way to the orphanage. A boy directed her to Bo Mat's room, but she found it empty. She asked various boys about Bo Mat, but no one had seen him leave. Mystified, she knocked on the door of Dr. Roberts' office.

"Yes?" he said, opening the door. "Mrs. Sing, come in. I've been expecting you." He offered her a chair.

As she sat down, she said, "You've been expecting me?"

"Yes. And I suppose Bo Mat had been expecting you to come by here also."

"Bo Mat?" she said excitedly. "Then he's here after all?"

"No, Mrs. Sing, I'm afraid not. He left this morning, early, before anyone got up." Dr. Roberts' voice was sad. He had grown to feel very close to the young man.

"Where, then, did he go? Do you know?" she asked.

"Yes, I know. He left me a note explaining everything."

"Tell me where he is. Please, Dr. Roberts, I must see him."

"I'm afraid that's impossible, Mrs. Sing. And I don't think I should be the one to tell you of his plans. He intended to tell you himself. He left this for you." Dr.

Roberts pulled a letter out of his desk. It was sealed and addressed, "To my mother, Ming Lee."

Ming Lee quickly opened the letter and read it.

Dear Mother,

By the time you read this note, I will have joined the merchant marines. I hope to be on my way to China. I don't know how long it will take me to get there. I will have to earn my passage by doing very hard and dirty work. All I know is that I must go. China is all that I have left. I suppose China and the Chinese people are my true family. There is much that I can do there. China is in the midst of a struggle against a vastly superior Japanese army This army has already occupied Manchuria and now seeks no less than a complete takeover of the entire country. Mother, I am deeply sorry about what happened at the cafeteria at Lowell. It was my fault entirely. I was very foolish to think I could just barge in on your family after all those years and not upset everybody. But now I am going away, and I will not bother you again. I may die fighting for China, but that does not matter. If I can help make China victorious, perhaps your husband will accept me as a son, and Jack and your other children will accept me as a brother. If I can make you proud of me, then I feel my life will have been worthwhile.

                                        Bo Mat

After reading the letter, Ming Lee buried her face in her hands and sobbed, "My son, my son."

Steven Roberts said, "Perhaps it is better this way,

Mrs. Sing. Bo Mat didn't tell me what happened at your home, but the last few days his mood had completely changed. He had become unfriendly and withdrawn, just the way he was after leaving the reformatory, so I assumed it had to do with the reception your family gave him.''

"But he is going to China, where there is a war going on. I don't want my first-born son to die in a war, Dr. Roberts. I know what China is like. I don't want any of my children to go there. There is nothing there for them. *This* is their country. America. This is where they belong.''

"Perhaps," Dr. Roberts said, "the only way Bo Mat can find that out is by going back to China and in some way repeating the journey you and your husband took to the United States. When he comes back, he may appreciate what this country has to offer him much more.''

"Yes, what you say could be the virtuous result of all this . . . if he lives, Dr. Roberts, if he lives.''

Ming Lee could do nothing about the numbing pain she felt inside. Walking was a very poor remedy indeed, but it was the only one she had. She felt as bad as when the highbinder first took Bo Mat from her breast. As she was crossing Broadway, a smiling man came running toward her from the corner of Mason Street. It was Peter Tsui. He was jumping with joy, oblivious to the sadness which was apparent on Ming Lee's face.

"Ming Lee, Ming Lee!" he called out to her. Then he reached her, out of breath. "We got the loan, the Chinese merchant companies have granted us the loan!" he exclaimed.

She could think of no response to this news.

He could not understand why she wasn't more enthusiastic about this news. "Ming Lee, aren't you glad?"

"Yes, it's very good, Peter," she remarked without inflection.

"Very good? Martin and I have been waiting ten years for this. Ten years! Don't you realize what this means? Martin won't have to stand in front of a wok all day anymore, getting grease burns on his fingers, singeing his eyebrows. It means The Dollar Store is back in business, and it'll be better than ever. We've got the experience to make it better. It'll be bigger than it was before the depression, you'll see."

Ming Lee was glad when she finally reached her apartment. She turned quickly and coolly away from Peter, nodding good-bye to him. He looked after her, scratching his head.

What's the matter with her? he wondered.

That evening, after Ming Lee read Bo Mat's letter to Martin, Jack, and the others, there was a silence.

"I wish that fight had never happened," Jack said remorsefully. "I wish that I'd tried to understand him. I didn't dislike him. I thought he was a threat to our family. I don't know. I just wish he was here so I could tell him I'm sorry. After all, he's my brother. We shouldn't have fought each other."

"Perhaps he will not be hurt in the war," Ming Lee said hopefully.

"I wish him well," Martin said, somewhat sheepishly. "The poor kid."

Ming Lee was angered by her husband's sudden change in attitude toward Bo Mat. "*You* wish him well? You, who would have nothing to do with him! All you could think about was the embarrassment he might cause you, your loss of face. It didn't cross your mind that he was a fine young man, worth knowing, no matter how he happened to come into the world. Because you refused to see him, he has gone away to die in China. You have killed my boy. I don't know if I can ever forgive you for that.''

Ming Lee stood up from the table, took her coat and stalked out of the apartment.

Martin rushed to the door and called out to her as she walked briskly up Powell Street.

"Don't talk to me!" she yelled to him over her shoulder.

He threw a coat on and rushed out the door and eventually caught up to her as she was crossing Pacific Avenue.

"Ming Lee, Bo Mat's case is not hopeless," he told her as he rushed along beside her to keep up with her frenzied pace. "Once he gets there, he may see for himself how terrible the conditions are and decide to come back. He may realize that China is not his country and therefore not worth dying for. Any number of things might happen. I have relatives in Wing Tan Ho who are still alive. At least I think they are alive. I have never written to them. But I will write them now. There is a good chance that Bo Mat will go to that village, to visit the grave of our father. I will write a letter to Bo Mat and leave it with the relatives. In the letter I will apologize for our family's treatment of him, and I will tell him he has a family here that he can call his own.''

Ming Lee did not say a word and continued along in angry strides until she reached Columbus Avenue. Then she turned right. Without looking at Martin, she said, "You have come to your senses too late, Man Sum. You have shown me only that you are a prejudiced human being. You didn't even meet him. You didn't see him or talk to him, yet your prejudice told you he was no good. There were reasons why he got into trouble, but you would not listen to those reasons. You hate him because you hated your father. But Sing Choy Wu was no father to Bo Mat. He only planted the seed, then died. Bo Mat has not had a real father. The laundryman was a tyrant. Dr. Roberts was the closest Bo Mat ever came to having a father. You had the chance, Man Sum, of being a real father to Bo Mat, but you threw away that chance."

They continued on for a long, wordless stretch until they had reached the beach facing the bay. Ming Lee sat on some stone steps overlooking the water. Martin sat next to her. Looking out onto the bay, they could see the Golden Gate Bridge. The ocean was beyond. A single lighthouse stood on Alcatraz, the island prison. Farther out into the bay was another island, Angel Island, where they had met so many years ago. Chinese immigrants were still being processed and detained there, just as they had been when Kwan Ming Lee and Sing Man Sum first came.

They sat together in silence, both of them feeling the great pain of separation, one from the other. This was the most serious crisis their marriage had yet suffered. Martin longed to reach for her hand and hold it. He remembered when they were separated by the Tongs, how he had longed to touch her then. The long years that stretched from their meeting on Angel Island to their wedding seemed like an eternity. Then they had been married, and he had enjoyed the luxury of having her by his side ever since. During the worst times, she had been with him and they had remained close. But she was as far away from him now as she had ever been.

"Ming Lee, I beg your forgiveness."

Ming Lee sat silently a moment, then said, "If Bo Mat dies, how can I forgive you? Or even myself?"

"If you cannot forgive me, what then will you do? Leave me?"

"I could not do otherwise," she said with conviction.

"How about our children? Bo Mat isn't your only child," he protested.

"I don't know. I just don't know. But I feel you and I are strangers in the same house."

"It seems our marriage can survive only if Bo Mat stays alive. If he dies, our marriage dies with him," Martin sighed.

Ming Lee nodded. "It must be as you have said. There is no choice."

Chapter 31

Bo Mat stood on the dirt road just outside the village of Wing Tan Ho in Kwangtung Province. All about him, as far as the eye could see, was a large plain. A light haze covered it. The fields were empty and brown, dry and caked. There were sickly looking grey stalks. Wisps of dust lifted from the ground, swirled, then died. Wing Tan Ho was in unoccupied Kwangtung. The Japanese held the West and Pearl Rivers and their deltas. They also occupied the cities of Canton, Kowloon and Hong Kong. But the rural interior, scattered with tiny villages, didn't concern them. Neither did it concern the Japanese invaders that a serious rice famine was taking place.

Bo Mat paused before entering the tiny village. He had already seen so many poor and starving people on the road, and he dreaded to enter the place where the father whom he had never known was buried. But he had made up his mind that the pilgrimage was necessary, so he took up his pack and proceeded toward the little cluster of houses.

The village appeared deserted. There were only twelve houses clustered together. The windows and doors of the small adobe structures were boarded up for the most part, and the silence was overpowering. Only one or two people appeared at the doorways to eye the stranger curiously. Children with bloated bellies and dry, brittle hair ran up to Bo Mat with their hands extended palms up and their thin voices whining. Dogs barked.

One adult was making his way in rapid strides toward the visitor. He was a ruddy-complexioned peasant, short and wiry. He had the same indomitable smile Bo Mat had seen in so many of these people. The adult spoke to Bo Mat in Cantonese, but the sound of the language was rougher and less distinct than the Cantonese he had learned in school, so he had difficulty understanding the man. He had to ask him to repeat several times before he could understand. On the other hand, the peasant laughed at hearing Bo Mat's stilted, school-learned version of the tongue.

"You are Bo Mat?" the man asked loudly, to top the shrill pleas of the urchins.

Bo Mat was shocked at hearing his name mentioned. He had told no one he was coming to this village. "Yes, I am Bo Mat," he said.

"I am Sing Dong Tan, the second grandson of your father's youngest brother. Welcome to our little village. It's a very poor place, not worth visiting, but we are honored to receive a visitor from America. Follow me. Come this way, please."

Dong Tan lightly placed one hand on Bo Mat's back, and with the other gestured him toward one of the small adobe houses. Like the other places on the dusty street, this one looked yellowish, withered and crumbling, as though it had been battered by centuries of dust storms. The windows were made of paper that had been rubbed with grease.

Inside, Dong Tan set his wife and four children scampering about doing various cleaning and cooking chores to make their guest feel comfortable. When at last his host handed him a bowl of rice and a little pork, Bo Mat was taken aback with embarrassment. He saw that he was the only one eating. Dong Tan had deprived his entire family of its evening meal to properly welcome the visitor from America.

Bo Mat took a couple of bites, then rubbed his stomach. "I can't eat anymore. *Sik bau*. I am full."

"No, you aren't," his cousin said. "You must eat more. Eat."

Bo Mat was caught between taking food from the family's mouths and offending his host. He compromised. He ate a couple more mouthfuls, then handed the bowl back to his cousin. "I'm really full, now," he said.

Dong Tan reluctantly took the half-eaten bowl of rice back from his guest. But then, instead of feeding his family with the rest, he threw it in the bucket of garbage in the corner.

"How did you know who I was?" Bo Mat asked Dong Tan after the meal. "I told no one I was coming here."

"This came a few months ago." Dong Tan handed Bo Mat a letter. It was from Sing Man Sum. In the letter, Sing Man Sum was extending an apology for the poor welcome Bo Mat had received. Martin was also inviting Bo Mat to become a part of the family.

The peasant smilingly watched Bo Mat read the letter from far away. When he finished reading, Bo Mat crumpled the missive and stuffed it in his pocket.

"Everywhere I see people who are poor and hungry," Bo Mat said. "The Japanese must be stealing your food, but I see no Japanese in the countryside."

"Japanese do not steal our food," Dong Tan said.

"Only landowners steal our food. We must give the land-owner eighty percent of the harvest. If we starve to death, he doesn't care. He gets back the land, and then he can rent it to someone else."

"Is this true of all the farmers? Do all the landowners demand that much payment?"

Dong Tan smiled. "Oh, not all. Some demand ninety percent." The peasant let out a raucous belly laugh.

Bo Mat took the matter more seriously. "Something must be done, Dong Tan. You must send a letter of complaint to the Nationalist government. Everybody in the village must sign it. I will deliver it to Chiang Kai-shek myself. The government must step in and put a stop to this."

Dong Tan looked at Bo Mat. The peasant was grinning from ear to ear. "The government knows all about it. The landowners keep the government in power. If the peasants have anything to say, the Kuomintang would just disappear, like that."

"No," Bo Mat said, "Chiang Kai-shek is committed to the democratic principles outlined by Sun Yat-sen. The people's livelihood is one of those principles. The peasants must be treated fairly by the landowners. If you're being treated unfairly, you can't sit back and take it. You've got to complain."

"You don't understand. It doesn't do any good to complain to the government. They don't listen, they don't care. If they tried to do anything, the landowner would know exactly which officials of the government to bribe. That's all," Dong Tan chuckled.

The following day, Bo Mat's cousin took him to the place where Sing Choy Wu's bones were laid to rest. They followed a narrow path for about a half mile, then turned into a rice field.

"This is our land," Dong Tan said. "It's about two acres. And there is your father's grave."

Bo Mat looked at the center of the field. There were several large rocks, and around them a cleared area where the remains of joss sticks jutted from the ground. The shrine to Sing Choy Wu was huge!

"But the gravesite is too big! This land is for growing rice. You could grow a lot of rice where this grave stands. Aren't there graveyards?" Bo Mat asked.

His cousin smiled. "The public graveyard is only for the landowner's family and kinsmen."

"Look, Dong Tan, this is a nice grave for my father, but I think you should get rid of it. Take his bones and just feed them to the . . . just throw them out! You need this land for rice. Your family is starving."

"I'm sorry you don't like the shrine," Dong Tan said with a hurt look in his eyes. "But it must be this large. Sing Choy Wu was not just anyone. He made his village very proud. He was a *Gum San haak*, a Gold Hill guest. We still sing songs about his visits to the village and about his successes in the golden hills. You see all the incense sticks? That should tell you how much the people of this village care about your father. Of all the ancestors, he has the highest place of honor. The immortals have prepared a place in heaven for him. We must honor him as do the immortals themselves. To do any less would be to earn the disfavor of the gods. Unthinkable."

On their way back to the village, they came across a dog digging at something at the side of the path. Bo Mat looked more closely. The dog was uncovering a corpse. Bo Mat pointed it out to his cousin, but Dong Tan just shrugged. In the village, there was a vendor selling leaves and bark. A couple of people looking grey and thin were trying to eat withered roots.

"Has the Nationalist government begun any relief effort for the sufferers of the famine?" Bo Mat asked.

"No relief," was the reply.

"There must be grain in other parts of this country that could be sent here. This is an emergency. People are dying everywhere," Bo Mat said.

"I don't think they care about us in Chungking."

Bo Mat wasn't willing to take his cousin's word for it. He walked the four miles to the railway station to catch a train going west.

"The train only goes as far as Kweiyang," the station-master told him. "From there, you've got to take a bus. It's another six hundred miles from there to Chungking."

About a hundred peasants were sprawled about the train station waiting to escape from the hunger, hoping to travel west to where there was food. There was an over-whelming stench of sweat, urine and filth. Babies wrapped in dirty rags suckled at their mothers' breasts. Eyes black as coal and filled with infinite sadness scarred the faces of the unfortunates. A train stopped at the station. It was already full, yet many grabbed on to the outside of the train. The train sped forward, and those too weak to hold on fell into the railroad bed, then staggered back to the station.

Bo Mat waited. He didn't want to take the place of one of these peasants who were starving and needed relief, so he waited for a train with plenty of seats. But the peasants kept coming, so many of them. And always the trains slowed at the station but never stopped. They were always full.

A Caucasian man who was also waiting for a train west asked Bo Mat if he was a student

"No, I'm not. I'm American-born. I was in the merchant marines."

"American? So am I My name is David. David Bennet. I'm a missionary. I'm with the Presbyterians, and I'm from New York. I was watching you. I could tell you were new to Chinese trains '

"What am I doing wrong?" Bo Mat asked.

"You have to show your ticket. You bought a valid first-class ticket None of the rest of them have tickets. They have to take you first, they have to take ticket holders. Then anything that's left over they can give the peasants. Now the man you show the ticket to is that soldier standing between the cars. These trains don't have regular conductors. I was watching you, and I could tell you didn't know what person to show your ticket to."

When the next train going west pulled into the station, David Bennet led Bo Mat to the soldier, took Bo Mat's ticket from him, then gave it with his own to the soldier. The soldier nodded and went into the car, and at gunpoint forced two peasants out of their seats.

The peasants reluctantly got up and stood in the aisle while David Bennet and an embarrassed Bo Mat took their seats.

"I didn't realize we would be taking other people's seats," Bo Mat said.

"Well, lad," the missionary said sardonically, "this isn't the United States, the land of individual freedoms. Unfortunately, freedom here is enjoyed only by the few. If you didn't assert your prerogative, you could have remained at that station for the duration of the war."

Bo Mat asked the missionary about his work.

"It is a painfully slow process. Pagan traditions and

rituals have an uncanny hold on the minds of the people.
Christian ideas are just too foreign, but life here is pleasant.
My wife and I live in a nice house with servants near Sian.
The servants are Christians, and they are very inexpensive.''
He reached in his bag and pulled out two items wrapped in
foil. ''Fried chicken,'' he said. ''Want some?

Bo Mat declined.

As the missionary unwrapped the chicken and began
to eat, Bo Mat noticed that several peasants were following every movement of the food, from hand to mouth,
mouth to tongue, and the motion of David Bennet's throat
in the process of swallowing.

''Why did you come to Kwangtung?'' Bo Mat asked.

''I was dispatched by the Nationalist government's
relief agency to report to them the extent of the famine in
Kwangtung to determine what steps would be necessary to
aid the peasants,'' David Bennet replied.

''Well, you see how serious it is. People are dying of
starvation and deserting villages. I've even heard of inci-
dents of cannibalism,'' Bo Mat said.

''Yes, it's rather bad, but the government doesn't like
bad news. I have to be very careful not to overdramatize
the situation,'' the missionary told him somewhat guardedly.

''What do you mean?''

''You will find out yourself when you reach Chungking.
Chiang's ruling clique is very sensitive to anything that
can be interpreted as criticism. If you have bad news, you
have to temper it. If you call this an out-and-out famine,
you'll be laughed at and discredited. You have to be
diplomatic, otherwise these peasants will get no help at all.
So you say, 'Most of the peasants are doing fine, but the
pressures of Japanese occupation mean that relief will be
necessary for some of the villages, particularly the ones

bordering the occupied areas,' something like that,'' David Bennet nodded.

"But it's not the truth,'' Bo Mat put in. "The famine is completely widespread. People are dying everywhere. The situation is urgent. Unless huge relief efforts are instituted, thousands if not tens of thousands of people will die. I'm sure that if the Nationalist government appeals to the United States, and the extent of the problem is made known to our government, money will be sent for food and medical supplies.''

"But you see, Chiang Kai-shek will lose face if the famine is publicized. He feels he would be blamed for it. It would be his fault because he didn't institute agrarian reform as set out by the three principles. He's doing the best he can, but he's sensitive to the way his actions are viewed by others. If he feels he could be blamed for a problem, he doesn't want to admit it exists,'' the missionary said. Then he added, "Politics is somewhat complex in China.''

The train pulled into the city of Kweiyang in Kweichow Province. The missionary bade Bo Mat farewell.

"I'm going to spend a few days here at a villa of a colleague of mine,'' David Bennet said. "He invited me to stay with him in the event I passed through Kweiyang. I'm going to take him up on it. His wife's a wonderful cook.''

After a day's wait in a crowded, noisy bus station, Bo Mat took a bus, which stalled many times on the narrow, primitive road that wound ever higher toward the Szechwan uplands. Bo Mat feared he would never make it. The bus poured out dense clouds of black smoke as though it had no oil. He saw several trucks that had been abandoned on the road, and they appeared to have been stripped of all usable parts. Also along the road were many vendors of miscellany: auto parts, fans, clock radios, dolls, playing cards.

When he first saw the hilly streets of China's wartime capital, Chungking, Bo Mat was reminded of San Francisco. The dense winter fog that engulfed the streets was also reminiscent of the Gold Hill. And like San Francisco, Chungking had a strongly cosmopolitan flavor. All of the foreign embassies of necessity followed when the National-ist government moved here. Also, there were refugees from every part of China. In addition to native Szechwanese cooking, one could find Fukienese, Cantonese and Hunanese restaurants

"Foggy here, isn't it?" he said to a fellow passenger.

"Lucky," the passenger replied cryptically.

"Why lucky?" Bo Mat asked.

"Because the fog prevents the Japanese from bomb-ing the city. In late April, when the clear weather comes and the fog lifts, the bombers will be coming. We'll have six months of clear weather and six months of bombs. So enjoy the fog while the peacefulness lasts!" he explained.

A five-century-old wall encircled the city Eight of its nine gates faced the cliffs that rose above the rushing Yangtze, but the ninth gate opened onto solid land. This gate was called Tung Yuan Men, or "the gate that con-nects with faraway places." Bo Mat's bus rumbled through this gate.

Bo Mat got off the bus at the station, then didn't quite know where to go. Soon he found himself pierced to the bone by the cold, damp fog. Several times, he almost lost his footing on the street. It was covered with inches of thick mud, slick and slimy.

Bo Mat had limited funds, whatever he could salvage from his year's earnings on the ship. And he didn't know how long he would be staying in China, so he had to choose low-cost accommodations.

He soon left the clatter of contrasts in the thoroughfares and descended a steep hill into a labyrinth of alleyways, like San Francisco again, but these alleyways were much more narrow. It was impossible to avoid drippings from the roofs. The gutter was inundated with filth and garbage of every kind. He even witnessed a mother holding her child over the gutter so the baby could relieve himself.

This was the Szechwanese area of the city. This old, run-down section on the hillside had been occupied by poor Szechwan people long before the East Coast refugees came.

It was here that Bo Mat found an inexpensive hotel, but the hotel keeper was not friendly. He didn't even attempt to communicate with Bo Mat apart from one or two inarticulate grunts.

Bo Mat was tired from his long day and it was late. As night approached and engulfed the city, only meager dots of light occasionally broke the darkness, but hundreds of high-pitched human voices, laughing, singing or shrieking, penetrated to his dim room through paper-thin walls. He lay awake for a long time in the blackness, shivering with cold and listening to the strange cacophony. Then he heard the sound of marching soldiers. There must have been a lot of them, he thought. The regular steps sounded endlessly, past the point when Bo Mat fell asleep.

The next morning, Bo Mat was awakened by the sound of explosives.

The hotel keeper explained, "They're blasting deeper holes in the cliffs for air raid shelters. It's March. The bombing will begin later next month."

Bo Mat went to the nearest newspaper stand and began browsing among the Chinese and English language newspapers. They were filled with optimism about the war. VICTORY AFTER VICTORY, read one headline. There were many Chinese victories, and many more Japanese casualties than Chinese. But there was no mention of the disaster that was taking place in Kwangtung Province. This information must reach the newspapers, Bo Mat thought. Then if the Kuomintang fails to act, public pressure will force it to respond. Bo Mat asked for directions to the foreign newspaper offices.

The Chungking Press Hostel was two miles from the river, out at the other end of the city. When he reached the hostel, he found its offices were located in the Nationalist Party Ministry of Information. Bo Mat entered through a field fenced in with bamboo palings and fringed with banana trees. There were two wood and wicker dormitories with gaps in the walls. Below the walls were mounds of mud plaster, which had been blown down by bombings. The newspaper offices were across a courtyard from the dormitories. Bo Mat asked to speak to an American correspondent. He was directed to the office of Christopher Thompson. Bo Mat didn't walk into Thompson's office alone. A Chinese man followed him. Bo Mat assumed this man was also a reporter working with Thompson.

The stranger followed Bo Mat in and sat at another desk and began looking through some papers. Thompson looked up and designated a chair for Bo Mat next to his desk. He asked Bo Mat what he had on his mind.

"Sir," Bo Mat said, "there is a famine of major proportions in southern China, Kwangtung Province. There is no mention of this famine in either the American newspapers or the Chinese newspapers. Hundres and thousands are dying or close to death, and no one has been told."

Thompson placed his fingertips together, leaned back in his swivel chair and peered at Bo Mat over the arch of fingers. "Have you reported this information to the authorities?"

"No, I haven't," Bo Mat said.

"Why not? They're better equipped to deal with such things than newspaper offices."

"I felt that it is possible they would not listen to me. I am not a reporter. I'm just a visitor from America."

"That's no reason to assume the government wouldn't listen to you." The reporter glanced over at the Chinese man at the other desk. The man didn't look up. "The party is always open to receiving news from the countryside, particularly where the welfare of the people or the army is at stake. Sometimes communications get bogged down, and it is difficult to get news of provinces far from Chungking. The Japanese have a habit of cutting phone lines, scrambling radio signals."

Bo Mat was somewhat confused. He frowned. "I talked to a missionary on the train who said that he had been sent by the government to investigate rumors of a famine in Kwangtung. The missionary told me that he would probably have to greatly minimize the seriousness of it. He said that if he told the truth, the Kuomintang would interpret it as a criticism of Chiang Kai-shek's regime."

"I don't understand," the reporter said. "Why should a famine in Kwangtung imply any criticism of the Kuomintang? Surely, the Kuomintang would not be expected to predict the weather."

"I just thought that if there was any resistance to giving relief to the people of Kwangtung, a newspaper story would bring public pressure, that's all," Bo Mat insisted. "If they knew of it in America, they would send money to help the people of Kwangtung, I am sure of it."

The reporter leaned forward. "I see that you are

obviously a young and somewhat inexperienced fellow. You're new to China, and therefore apt to exaggerate what you see here. People go hungry here more often than they do in America. There are many more mouths to feed and less food to go around. Now what you saw could very well have been a setback in a particular region. A crop failure. But don't forget, there are three rice harvests a year. One crop failure doesn't mean thousands will die. It means some people may starve to death, yes, but the vast majority, who are smart enough to save some of the grain from the previous harvest, will survive. They always do. China's strength is in the earth."

"I saw people eating dirt and bark. I saw abandoned villages. I saw dogs digging up corpses in fields. I saw hundreds of starving people grabbing on to trains in the desperate hope they'd make it to the west where they could find relief," Bo Mat said.

"I'm sure you *thought* you saw a famine taking place in Kwangtung. I am only suggesting that you didn't know exactly what you saw, because you do not know this country. My advice to you, young man, is to forget it. You're a tourist. Enjoy your stay here. There are many things to see and do in Chungking, even during wartime," Thompson said calmly.

Bo Mat was becoming irritated. He couldn't make any sense out of the correspondent's refusal to believe the obvious fact. "Well, if you won't do anything, I'll talk to everyone I can think of in Chungking until I get some pressure put on this government for relief for those people. I see there must be some kind of censorship going on if you won't report this disaster. You only report good news. Victory after victory. I wonder if anything you write is the truth!"

With that, Bo Mat stalked out.

"Good luck," the correspondent called after him sarcastically.

Bo Mat began walking back to the center of town. He decided to take this matter to the universities. Students there would certainly listen to what he had to say, and they might be able to help him find a way to convince the Nationalist government that action must be taken to avert a tragedy in Kwangtung.

As Bo Mat was walking toward the river, he suddenly experienced a chilling sensation at the back of his neck. He didn't know exactly how he knew, but he was sure that he was being followed. He felt that he had better not look back to verify it. If his trackers were discovered, they might do something terrible to Bo Mat. But what might they do? What could they do? What, really, had Bo Mat done wrong? He had openly criticized the government. His trackers were government agents! The Kuomintang secret police!

But he was just an American trying to get relief for some peasants. He wasn't trying to undermine the government's policies. He turned one corner, then another. He heard footsteps behind him. They were growing closer. Bo Mat entered a crowded street, then zigzagged through the crowd quickly in an attempt to lose his trackers. He looked behind him. He saw two men pushing through the mass of people he had just passed. If he could just make it as far as the Szechwan sector where the alleyways meandered crazily down steep slopes, he might be all right.

There was a break in the crowd. Bo Mat started to run. He was already on the steps that descended down toward the ghetto. He darted to his left and into a dark alley enclosed by buildings so close together that their roofs practically touched. He charged down this alley, bumping into a man who was carrying two buckets of water, one on either end of a pole. The buckets spilled, and the man turned to curse at Bo Mat in the harsh, shrill, high-pitched tones of the Szechwanese dialect. The buckets rolled down the hill until they caught in the cobblestones.

Bo Mat turned into another narrow alley, dodging mounds of garbage as he ran. At last, he thought he had outrun his followers, so he started to walk. But as he turned another corner, two men pointed toward him and gave chase. These were not the two men who had originally been following him! The problem was his dress. He was obviously a Westerner. He had passed a marketplace earlier in the day. He decided he had to reach that marketplace and exchange his San Francisco clothes for a Szechwan turban, loose shirt and tubular, padded pants.

He turned down a street in the direction of the marketplace. He looked back. Now there were four secret police chasing him. He passed an alley to his right, and down the alley he could see an opening where stalls were set up. The marketplace. He dodged into the next alley, then ran down another that veered at an angle to the right. This time he was following the slope downward. It was the steepest descent yet. He slipped and rolled. When he reached the bottom, he was below the marketplace.

He looked around and couldn't see the secret police. His arms were bruised and scratched. He climbed the steps to the stalls. It was an excruciating climb. He was exhausted from running and stumbling.

Finally, he reached his destination. He looked around, but there was still no sign of the secret police that had been following him. The clothing vendor's dialect was undecipherable, but Bo Mat pointed to what he wanted. By the time the vendor was finished with him, he looked like a Szechwan peasant. He bought a cloth bag so that he could keep his original clothes. They were warmer than this Szechwanese outfit. He blended into the crowd. Now he saw his trackers searching for him.

He hurried out of the marketplace into another winding street. This one rose to a dizzying height. His new clothes were drafty. He was cold. He walked around as long as he could stand it, then resolved to return to his hotel.

When he reached the hotel, he wanted nothing more than to collapse in his bed. But what if the secret police were waiting for him in his room?

He asked the hotel keeper, "Did anyone ask for me?"

Without looking at him, the hotel keeper shook his head and grunted, "No."

"Nobody was here? Nobody at all?"

"Nobody."

Bo Mat assumed he was safe. He had managed to outrun and outwit the Kuomintang secret police. He was very pleased with himself. Still, he could not figure out why they would want to arrest him. He had just wanted to save a few peasants from starvation. He put the key in the lock. But before he turned the lock, he listened at the door for a couple of minutes to make sure he would not be running into the arms of the police. He heard nothing. He turned the key and paused again. Still he heard nothing. He opened the door a crack. If someone was in there, he would still be able to get away if he saw them in time. But through the crack in the door, he could see nothing in the room. He opened the door all the way. No, no one was there. Quickly, he entered and shut the door behind him. He latched it, then went to inspect the bathroom. He shot the bathroom door open. No one there. The closets were empty as well. He fell onto his bed, breathing a sigh of relief, and allowed his tense muscles to relax, letting his exhaustion take him over.

But as he began to doze, he heard a knock on his door.

"Who is it?" Bo Mat called out toward the door.

There was no answer.

"Who is it?" Bo Mat repeated.

Whoever it was knocked again.

Bo Mat threw his legs over the side of the bed and stood up, swaying slightly from tiredness. Again the knocking came, heavier this time. Bo Mat walked to the door. "Yes?" he said.

"Open up," a voice said.

"What do you want?" Bo Mat asked.

"You. I want you," the voice said.

"Who is it?"

"The newspaper. I'm with the newspaper."

Bo Mat breathed a sigh of relief. He opened the door.

It was the Chinese man whom he had seen at the American correspondent's office. "I'm with the newspaper," he said. He stood rigidly in the doorway, staring at Bo Mat.

"Yes, I recognize you now. Come in, come in."

The man entered the hotel room and closed the door behind him. He stood by the door with his hands behind his back.

Bo Mat sat on the bed. "You work for the American correspondent."

"Yes, I'm the translator," the man said, smiling broadly. "Thompson doesn't speak a word of Chinese. He can't read Chinese, either. But Thompson is a good journalist. One of the best. He's very objective. Not like some of the others."

"Do you know," Bo Mat said, "the Kuomintang

secret police have been following me? I wonder why they would want me. Do you have any idea?''

''How do you know it is the Kuomintang? The secret police? Perhaps it is thieves who are following you,'' the translator said.

''Thieves?''

''Chungking unfortunately has its share of undesirables, thieves, Communists.''

With a puzzled expression, Bo Mat regarded his visitor. ''What exactly is the reason for your visit?''

''I ought to be asking you the same question,'' the man said, smiling again.

''You mean, why am I in China? I am here because I am Chinese. I have no family in America. I never knew my father. I can never know him because he is dead. But I can know my country,'' Bo Mat said. ''The Chinese people are the only family I have.''

''Are you in contact with the Communist Party?'' The translator leaned forward.

''No, I have no knowledge of any Communists!'' Bo Mat said vehemently. It was obvious that this man was no translator.

''I must ask you to come with me,'' the man said.

''Why? I've done nothing.''

Then four men appeared at the door. They had apparently been waiting in the hall, listening to the interview. Bo Mat dimly recognized them. They were the men who had been pursuing him.

One of them took Bo Mat's wrists, pulled them together behind his back, and bound his wrists with rope. The translator just stood there, smiling. Two of the men then went through Bo Mat's bag, emptying the contents on the floor. They searched the closet and pulled all the drawers out of the dresser. They lifted the mattress off the bed and tossed it aside.

Then Bo Mat was taken downstairs and placed in the back seat of a car. Two men sat in the back seat on either side of him, while the other two sat in front. The translator with whom he had just been speaking disappeared.

"I'm an American citizen," Bo Mat stated. "I demand to be taken to the American Embassy."

The men ignored him.

"Where are you taking me?" he asked them.

No answer.

After a long ride through dark streets, the car approached a huge gate, guarded by men in uniform. One of the uniformed men nodded and the car passed through the gate. A huge concrete building loomed on the right. They got out of the car and entered the building. A lengthy staircase led to a dimly lit corridor. Bo Mat was taken down this corridor for a while. He could see no end to it. He was led, finally, into a brightly lit office. His captors shoved him inside, and he found himself standing in front of a large table. There were several more uniformed men seated at the table, and others were standing around looking at him. An officer at the table was writing in a book.

Bo Mat said to him, "I am Bo Mat. I'm an American citizen, a merchant marine. I have done nothing wrong. I demand to be put in touch with the American Embassy."

The man said nothing, but continued to write. One of the men untied Bo Mat's hands, and he was taken into another room that was empty. Here the light was even more glaring. Bo Mat was told to sit in the corner. He waited there for several long minutes.

Finally, a uniformed man came up to him with a pad and pencil. "Your name?"

"Bo Mat."

"The purpose of your visit?"

"I . . . wanted to see China, the birthplace of my father, who is deceased."

The man looked at Bo Mat for a moment with blank eyes, then continued, "How long have you been a member of the Communist Party?"

"I am not a Communist!" Bo Mat protested.

Three men he hadn't seen before entered the room and shut the door behind them. They wore heavy boots, and they carried sticks. The man with the pencil said, "We want you to give us the names of the Communists who have contacted you in Chungking."

"I know no Communists in Chungking," Bo Mat said, frightened.

"Do you know this man?" The interrogator showed Bo Mat a picture of a Chinese.

"I have never seen him before in my life," Bo Mat said.

"What about this man?" Another picture was presented to Bo Mat, and then another one. Each time, he denied knowing the individual in question.

"You're a Communist, aren't you?"

"No."

"Confess."

"No, I'm an American. An American."

The interrogator shoved a list of names in his face. "Read this list and point to the names of the people you know."

"I don't know anybody on that list."

The man with the pencil nodded to the others. "Take him away," he said.

Holding Bo Mat's arms, the men led him along the corridor, then down a stairway and into a vast, dark yard.

When they had crossed this yard, one of the men knocked on a metal door. It creaked open. A man inside mumbled something, then Bo Mat was led through the door and down a corridor. Another heavy door was opened, and Bo Mat was untied and shoved through it. No more words were spoken to him. He was left there, locked up in the darkness.

He didn't know how long he had slept when the door was opened, but late morning daylight from some window streamed into his cell as the guard told him to rise and follow him. Bo Mat was led the way he had come, though everything looked different in the daylight. He finally reached the room off the corridor with the long table and the officer writing something in a book. The officer looked up and saw Bo Mat standing there.

The officer smiled. "It appears we have indeed made a mistake," he said sheepishly, "but you see the problems we are up against. We couldn't take any chances. We have to follow up every lead. Every accusation has to be fully investigated."

Who had accused him? Bo Mat wondered.

Then Christopher Thompson, the American correspondent, entered the room. "Bo Mat," he said in a jovial tone, "it's good to see you. It's especially good to see that you're still alive."

"No thanks to you!" Bo Mat shot back angrily.

"I'm sorry about all this, but I must protest my innocence."

They left the prison together. Thompson took him by car to the central part of the city. At Thompson's insistence, they went into a restaurant so Thompson could buy lunch for Bo Mat.

"I'm not to blame for getting the secret police after you," Thompson told him after they'd been seated at a table. "It was Chan that had you followed and arrested."

"Chan?"

"Yes. He doesn't work for the newspaper. He works for the government's censorship arm. He comes to my office every so often and makes sure that what I report is complimentary to the Nationalists. Listen, Bo Mat, everything I said to you that day was a masquerade for his benefit. While I was telling you how naive you were, I was drinking up what you were saying about the famine in Kwangtung. But that Chan is a fanatic. He convinced himself you were a Communist agent, then put the secret police on your trail. I asked around, pulled a few strings of my own, and got you out. If I hadn't acted, there's no telling how long a time you would've ended up spending in that hole."

"Then I was right about the censorship," Bo Mat nodded.

"You sure were. Listen, I can't tell you how frustrating it is trying to get facts around here. I'm pretty new to the newspaper business myself, and I have to cover the whole political scene in Chungking as well as the war news. I'm working all day just to keep up, and I can't get anything in depth. I want to travel to the provinces to find out what's really happening in this war, but it's impossible for me to get away."

"But even if you write something truthful, you're liable to get censored, aren't you?" Bo Mat inquired.

"I wouldn't publish it here," Thompson said. "I'd have it smuggled out, get it to the American newspapers. Bo Mat, we have to get the truth out to people, in spite of the government."

"What about the famine in Kwangtung?"

"I've written up the information you gave me, and it's on its way to the States. I've sent copies of it to the Embassy. I'm hoping that as a result, we'll begin to see some American pressure brought on Chiang to bring some relief to that area. Pressure from the American government seems to be the only thing he responds to. But information is the key. Information and documentation."

"I want to help," Bo Mat said.

Thompson's face lit up. "That's what I was hoping you'd say. You have an eye for what's going on, and you're not afraid to look hard and long and say what you see. So I want to offer you a job. They pay me pretty generously, much more than I need to live on. I'm not married or anything, so I'd like to hire you out of my salary. I have a feeling you'd make a good newspaperman."

"When do I start?" Bo Mat asked.

With Peter Tsui at his side, Martin confessed to the Chinese merchant companies. He told them everything about his past and his wife's past.

"In spite of everything, I consider Bo Mat to be my son. He shall be accorded every respect a son of mine is due," Martin told them. "I realize that the Chinese merchant companies have high moral standards. I know that my confession may jeopardize our chances of obtaining a loan, but I believe it was necessary to be honest with you. You should know exactly who you are dealing with. That way, there will be no confusion or feelings of distrust if this information surfaces later."

The president of the merchant companies, Wu Jiu Fan, said, "We appreciate your honesty, Martin Sing. But your past as a successful businessman is much more interesting to us. We are sure neither you, your wife, nor your children are street criminals. You are upstanding members of our community. You have been for years. In any case, nobody is perfect."

There were a few outbursts of laughter when the president said this last sentence. Martin didn't know what the laughter signified.

"I am happy to announce that, this new information notwithstanding, the Chinese merchant companies overwhelmingly approve a low interest loan for you and Peter Tsui."

All applauded as Martin accepted the check.

"This will go a long way toward getting The Dollar Store operating again," Martin told them. "Peter and I are looking at a building on Powell, between Broadway and Vallejo."

"That's outside the present borders of Chinatown," the president pointed out.

"Yes, it's owned by Italian businessmen," Peter Tsui put in. "They want to move out of the city. So they're giving us a very good deal."

"You gentlemen have what it takes to give our community a new lift. Boom times are coming, and we want you to help us. We invite you to join the Chinese merchant companies. Sit in on our meetings. Vote on our resolutions. Give us the benefits of your skill and experience."

"Certainly," Martin said, speaking for himself and Peter. "We would be honored to accept your invitation to join the Chinese merchant companies."

The grand opening of The Dollar Store was held on June 14, 1938. Friends of Martin and Peter gave gifts of plants to wish the two businessmen good fortune. Red banners with good wishes written on them flew from stakes in the plants.

The new store was immensely successful. It was patronized by Chinese, Italians, and many other groups. There were bargains to be had in clothing, kitchenware and hardware. Martin's sons Ronald and Jack worked full-time at the store. Laura Mei, Thomas and Cynthia worked there after school.

When the store had been in operation for eight months, Peter Tsui approached Martin one evening.

"Martin, I am getting old," he said. "It is time for you to buy my share of the business."

"No, Peter," Martin replied, upset. "I can't imagine running this business without you. You don't have to wait on customers. I and the children will do that. But I need your guidance."

"I want to move back to Walnut Grove, and maybe open a little store like I had before. I'm too old. I don't feel so ambitious," Peter said, shaking his head.

"You want to forfeit your membership in the Chinese merchant companies?" Martin asked.

"Oh, Martin, I am tired of them. All they seem to think about is money. Also, as I grow old, I miss the delta. Everything is much slower there, much more relaxed."

Martin could see that it was useless to argue with Peter. Papers were drawn up, and Martin purchased Peter's half of the partnership.

"You and your wife and children must come to visit me in Walnut Grove sometime," Peter said the day he left.

"Of course, Peter," Martin assured him. "We'll come visit you often."

"Always remember what I told you, Martin. Foresight and courage!"

*   *   *

In June of 1940, Jack Sing, age twenty, and Ronald Sing, age eighteen, decided to enlist in the United States Army. Martin tried to talk them out of it, but his arguments fell on deaf ears.

Martin thought about Peter Tsui's son. He had lost his son in the Great War. Martin didn't want to lose his own sons in a war, but they were stubborn, like their mother.

Jack and Ronald left the following week. They began their basic training at Ford Ord, near Monterey, California.

Chapter 32

It was December 7, 1941. Chungking was delighted with the news: the Japanese had attacked Pearl Harbor. Crowds in the streets rejoiced. Rumors went around that Tokyo was in flames. Five hundred American planes had bombed Japan's capital. In fact, the Americans had a mere shell of an air force in the Philippines: thirty-five B-17s, of which seventeen were destroyed on the ground in the first day of action.

However, hope ran high in the offices of the Kuomintang. Everyone was convinced the Americans would take care of the Japanese for China.

America was poorly prepared for the war she was about to enter. The information that came out of China didn't paint a picture of Japanese superiority. Japanese military might was underplayed. And the courage and skill of the Chinese soldier was vastly exaggerated. It was said the Japanese were nearsighted. They wore tennis shoes to the battlefield. They had no understanding of sophisticated arms or equipment. Their aircraft were antiquated. American Intelligence had recorded the excellent maneuverability of the Japanese Zero, but Washington ignored the facts in favor of the stereotype.

*   *   *

Both Jack and Ronald wanted to follow their half brother, Bo Mat, to China, but the day they got their orders, they discovered to their dismay that they were to fight on opposite fronts. Jack was to be dispatched to Kunming in southern China, the capital of the province of Yunnan, which bordered Burma and Indochina. Ronald was on his way to London.

From the air, Jack could see a long blue lake to the south, and to the north a huge mountain cut by deep gorges. This mountain the American soldiers called "Old Baldy." Not far from the airport was the housing for American personnel. These were hostels. There were about fifteen of them. They accommodated altogether about thirty-five thousand American military personnel. The Chinese government set up these hostels, and they were palatial by Chinese standards.

Kunming was the terminal of the Burma Road. This road was of great strategic importance. It connected China with vital supply lines in the west by way of Rangoon in the Bay of Bengal, but the Burma Road was closed and in the hands of the Japanese.

But General Stilwell, head of all American forces in China, wanted to send troops into Burma and open up the blocked road. It was rumored that a joint Chinese and American campaign was in the offing; Chiang Kai-shek had only to be convinced of its importance. If a battle for the Burma Road was to materialize, only the best of the troops stationed at Kunming would be involved. Jack and the other enlisted men all hoped they would be selected.

The men were able to get a pass about once a week. Entertainment in Kunming was the local movie theater. Old movies were shown there. Then there were the bars, which served an array of Chinese whiskies. Chinese liquor was all that was available. The army could not afford to fly beer or American liquor over the Hump. American whiskey could be purchased on the black market for one hundred dollars a bottle and up. The soldiers, however, settled for the Chinese liquor. It sufficed for getting drunk.

Then there were the prostitutes, who could be found wherever there was a bar in Kunming that catered to American enlisted men. The prostitutes liked American money.

Jack Sing didn't like to get drunk, and he didn't like the spectacle of Chinese women of easy virtue fawning over inebriated white soldiers. He drank his *pai gar* slowly and found himself longing to be back in San Francisco.

While he was in the midst of this fit of homesickness, he became aware that a woman was sitting next to him, looking at him.

He returned her look. "Hello," he said in English. "Do you speak English?"

She frowned and shook her head and looked away.

Jack tried another tactic. "*Ney gong gwong jau wa ma?* Do you speak Cantonese?"

He'd guessed correctly. She turned to him and her face beamed.

"*Hai la.* Yes, I do," she acknowledged.

They carried on an animated though somewhat stumbling conversation. Jack's Cantonese was not the best, but she greeted his mistakes with delightful giggling. Jack was thoroughly charmed by her.

"I don't like American men, I like a Chinese man," she said. "Because I am Chinese."

"Well, you can't like me, then, because I am an American," Jack responded.

"You are Chinese," she insisted.

"All right, but I'm both. Or maybe I should say I am

neither. If one has to be one or the other, then I am neither.''

"That's all right. You can be both if you want to. I don't mind. I will like you anyway,'' she smiled.

Jack felt a tingling warmth pervade his body.

"I am Wei Tim Min,'' she said.

"I am Jack Sing,'' he replied. "I have a pass this Sunday. Would you like to go for a walk by the lake?''

"I will go anywhere,'' she said, giggling. "I will follow you.''

She appeared to be as excited by his presence as he was by hers.

"You don't speak a word of English,'' Jack said to her on their walk. "But you must deal with Americans as part of your profession.''

"Yes, that's right. I don't speak to them, though. There is never any talking. I don't like the sound of English. I never want to learn it. I hope I never need to learn it,'' she said.

Jack came right to the point of what was bothering him. "Why,'' he asked, "does a woman as fine as you are have to work as a prostitute?''

"I have never known anything else,'' she replied. "My family was starving. There was no food. What the landowners didn't take, the bandits took. There wasn't enough food for all of us children. I said I would leave. One less mouth to feed. I didn't know where I would go. I was thirteen years old at the time. My father wept. My mother wept. We were a loving and a close family. I came to Hong Kong. If I was to survive anywhere, it would have to be Hong Kong. There were no jobs, of course, only many sailors, of all nationalities, with money. I had no choice. Then I had to flee here to escape the Japanese.''

They saw each other every day for the next month. In each other's company, they found refuge from the tedium and the tension of the war.

One Sunday, on their walk by the lake, Jack said earnestly, "If I had my way, Tim Min, I would take you out of your profession. You would never have to use your body to survive again. You deserve better than that, far better." Jack realized that he was in love with this Cantonese woman, so in love that he would do anything for her, anything.

"I never thought I would ever be able to feel anything for a man," she said. "Never, never. But you're different. You're different from all of them, Jack. Please, you will not leave me. You will not die in the war, Jack."

"I will take you with me to America when I return. We will be married, Tim Min. I want you to be my wife. Never have I wanted anything so much. Tim Min, I love you."

"I love you, Jack," she returned. "I will not, cannot, touch another man. I will die of starvation before I touch another man."

"There is enough, enough from my soldier's wages to keep you. I want to keep you. You won't starve. You'll never belong to anyone but me. Me. My little salary will support us both. It must. If you can—"

"I can, I can," she said.

"After this war, I will take you back to America with me, Tim Min. And then we'll be married." He was trembling as he grasped her hand.

"Married? America?"

"But you won't have to worry. We will be together. In America, I can get a good job. We'll live very well, you'll see. My father was once a rich man, and he's going to be a rich man again. I can work for my father, and when he dies, that successful business will pass on to me. So you see, Tim Min, you will be a rich lady!"

"It doesn't matter," she said, "rich or poor, as long as I have you."

They both vowed not to go near the red-light district or the bars. They belonged to each other now. They didn't need Kunming's form of entertainment.

The next Monday, the base had a visitor. General Joseph W. Stilwell, "Uncle Joe." He was dressed as always, informally. He wore combat boots, fatigues and a rumpled sweater. Uncle Joe passed Jack in the mess hall and, surprisingly, remembered him from basic training at Ford Ord.

"Hello, Jack," he said.

Jack rose and saluted. "General Stilwell, sir."

"At ease, Jack, and keep up the good work."

Later in the day, Jack was called to a meeting. It took place in a conference room in one of the buildings of Jack's hostel. When he reached the room, he was surprised to see the building surrounded by MPs. One of them checked Jack's I.D. against a list before allowing Jack to proceed any farther. There were fifty soldiers there.

General Stilwell was seated in the front of the room, looking calm, but alert and expectant. The air was filled with excitement. The general rose slowly and sat on a table. He leaned forward and met the men's eyes as he spoke.

"Men, we're going through a rat hole to reach our objective. We're going through the worst jungles you can imagine. We'll start at Ledo in northwest Burma. Our goal: Myitkyina, the northernmost Japanese garrison and air base. We'll begin our march in December, and we'll reach and take Myitkyina by early May, before the monsoon begins. You men have been hand-picked by me to join our Twenty-second Division. You will be flown to India for training one week from Monday. Your base will be Imphal, about two hundred miles south of Ledo. Any questions?''

Jack rushed to the spot where he and Tim Min always met at the lake. He was about an hour early. Restlessly, he waited for Tim Min to appear. She was right on time. Jack had carefully weighed the words he would say to her, but when he began speaking, he found that he was unable to think clearly. His mind was a jumble of warring passions.

''What's wrong, Jack?''

''Tim Min, I must leave you, for a while.''

''No, don't leave me,'' she pleaded.

''I have been chosen for combat duty. I will go this Monday for training, but I will be back. I will not leave you forever.''

''I am so sad to hear this. I don't know what I will do.'' She started weeping.

''Tim Min, let's get married now.''

''Now?''

''There's no point to waiting. There's a chaplain at the hostel. We will go to him. He will marry us at once.''

They rode bicycles back to the compound. The chaplain gave an endless lecture about the necessity for caution in matters as serious as matrimony, but Jack stamped his feet impatiently to hurry the man on with his sermon. Jack had never been more certain of anything in his life. After the ceremony, the couple found a hotel in town.

They forgot the heat and the sordidness of the hotel room the moment they touched each other. How beautiful she was, he thought. From her long, black hair to her gentle breasts; from her slender thighs to her delicate feet.

She looked untouched, like a porcelain sculpture of a Chinese goddess. It was impossible to believe that she had been a prostitute. Impossible. He shut her past out of his mind as he gently stroked her face, her arms. Her past was forgiven. It was true. She had had no choice. How could she have? Thirteen years old, destitute.

With each light stroke of his fingertips over her naked body, she closed her eyes to savor the pleasure he was giving her.

All that afternoon was theirs. It would be over soon enough. He must not think about the afternoon being over. It was just beginning. He could imagine it going on forever, the sound of her sighs as she relished his touch.

"Oh, Jack." Her whole sweet form pressed against him, and he drank in her body, as if to say, *Never again will we be parted.*

It was not only pleasure they were feeling, not only their bodies pressing against each other; it was fuller than pleasure. It was a desire for her, to have her always. His mind throbbed with the thought of her as he held her, as he made love to her. There could be nothing else but her in his life, forever. There was nothing that had meant as much to him as this moment.

After they made love, they lay there, stretched out on the bed, shoulders touching, nuzzling like kittens. She giggled. How happy she was. Nothing could come between them now. Not the future, not Burma, not Stilwell, not the war. Not the past. Nothing could harm them now. They were together. They wanted only each other.

"You're leaving on Monday," she said. "And how long will you be gone?"

"It isn't certain. Although the general says the campaign is aimed to reach its objective before the monsoon, early May."

"It is now November. You won't come back until May? That's too long," she said. "I won't let you stay away from me for so long. I will come to wherever you are and visit you."

"I'll be in the jungles of Burma," he told her. He stroked her hair. "I wish you could come with me. It would be far less lonely if you were there. But you cannot."

"I will find you," she said. "I will fly over mountains and valleys until I see you. Then I will descend, and we'll make love in the jungle."

They both laughed.

But soon the afternoon came to an end. She went with him to the base, and for a long while they said nothing. It was, after all, time to say good-bye to each other.

"It isn't easy," she said, "to let you go."

"We leave each other as husband and wife," he murmured.

"Yes."

"When I come back, you will go with me to America."

"Hurry, hurry back," she cried.

"I will." He turned toward the base and left her looking after him.

It was the morning of June 26. The Y-force was closing in on Myitkyina from the east, and the Sixty-sixth Regiment was coming from the west. Jack's unit and a unit of Merrill's Marauders were holding the airstrip from dugout trenches that encircled the field. There was a jovial atmosphere among the hungry men. At last they could feel that this struggle was coming to an end.

Jack sat in his trench and reread the letter his wife had sent him a month earlier.

My dearest husband,

I hope this letter reaches you in Burma, my
darling. I have done little but think about you,
wishing you were in Kunming so that we could
walk by our lake. You must come home soon,
love, so that you will be able to greet our child
when it comes into the world. I am going to have
a baby. It is going to look just like its daddy if
it's a boy, and just like me if it's a girl. I want it
to be a boy so it will look just like you. I want to
have two of you. One is not enough! Do take
care of yourself, Jack. I try not to worry, but I
think of you and the war and all that killing, and
I cannot help but feel anguish. Our child is due
in August, and I want you to be here, in Kunming,
by its mother's bedside. Every night, I dream of
your smiling at me in bed, but I wake up and
your image breaks apart and scatters like falling
leaves. I miss you, my darling. . . .

A father, Jack thought. I will be the father of our
baby. We will be a family. Beloved Tim Min. How I want
to be with you now, hold you now. You are eight months
pregnant. Who is caring for you? Who is helping you up
the stairs? No one. I should be there. I should be by your
side. Now. Not here in this wet wasteland. What am I
doing here? Too many mountains separate us. After
Myitkyina, I pray they will let me go to you.

Suddenly, a vicious mortar attack was directed at
them. Jack huddled in the bottom of his trench. The attack
lasted close to thirty minutes. Then the machine-gun fire
started. The Japanese were in the jungle surrounding the
airstrip and firing at the defenders in the trenches. Jack
called out to his troops that they must hold their ground.

What was this? A last-ditch effort? Did they hope to succeed? It was an absurd offensive. Suicidal. The Japanese were defeated and they knew it, yet they seemed to be pouring everything into the retaking of the airstrip. Jack's men kept up a sustained fire at the periphery of the jungle. The Japanese held fast. A stalemate.

"We can cut them in half, sir. I know how." The voice was that of Liu On Jew, a Chinese enlisted man who had a particular hatred for the Japanese. His brother had been killed earlier in the campaign. "There's a gap in their encirclement, sir, through those trees. There's a swamp there. It runs about fifty yards, side to side. I can get into that swamp and start hitting the Japanese flank. We can set up a position on the side of the swamp, if the men can cover me."

"All right, Liu, if you think you can make it in."

"I want to give it a try." Liu beamed at Jack.

Jack was genuinely impressed with this soldier's courage. He nodded to Liu, who instantly made a zigzagging go for the swamp.

But Liu didn't make it. He was shot in the leg. He held up in some high grass, but couldn't move forward to the swamp's edge or back to the trenches on his own. It would only be a matter of time before the machine-gunner found his shape in the grass and finished the job.

Jack cursed himself. How dumb it was to let that kid take that chance. It was his own fault for letting the kid go. The Japanese gunners were everywhere, but Jack would have to get the kid back to the trenches.

By now, allied mortars were strafing the forest that rimmed the base. Jack could take advantage of the shelling to retrieve the kid. He ordered his men to cover for him, and leapt out of the trench. He reached Liu and lifted Liu's thin arm around his own shoulder. Then he ran, in spite of the weight of the soldier's body on his back.

He was five feet from safety when he was hit. He stumbled forward, falling into the trench. Liu fell to his side.

I'm hit, I'm wounded, Jack thought. Back. My back. But I'm still alive. They've got to get us to a medic. A hospital. Liu's hit worse. Mine? Just a flesh wound. God, how my back hurts. They'll get the bullets out. I'll be fine.

Someone was calling out, "They're here, the Y-force."

The Y-force is here, the Y-force, Jack thought. I was wondering when they would get here. Wish they had come ten minutes faster! The Japs are finished now. They can't hold on. They're pinned between us and the Y-force. Damn this wound.

Liu was looking at Jack with anxious eyes.

"Myitkyina is taken. Myitkyina is taken."

Jack felt himself being picked up, carried. They were placing him on a stretcher. There were no more mortars hitting the airfield. He was being carried to the center of the field. There was a DC-3 transport waiting. There were other men on stretchers. They were taking him to the hospital. He would be all right. He would see Tim Min again. He would see the birth of his first child. And then he'd go back to San Francisco. Chinatown. His parents. He'll bring his wife with him, and their child.

The big engines of the plane were roaring. Speed built up on the runway, then the plane lifted. Good-bye, Burma. Good-bye, Japs. God, how his back hurt. He felt like he was lying in a puddle. Could he have lost that much blood?

Then there was blackness.

*   *   *

Slowly, consciousness dawned. He was aware of pain, a dull pain pervading his back. Over and under him were clean white sheets. He was wearing a green shirt. There was a face above him. It was a friendly face, he thought, but he couldn't see the features clearly. Everything was blurred.

"Where am I?" he mumbled.

"Chungking," a familiar voice answered.

"Chungking? You mean the capital? But I thought they flew all the wounded to Ledo, at the India-Burmese border," Jack said.

"Yes, that's right. You were flown to Ledo, but your condition made it necessary for them to fly you to Chungking. You were given initial treatment in Ledo, a blood transfusion, and the bullets were removed," the voice said.

"What condition? What's wrong with me?" Jack asked in an urgent tone.

"You must try to relax, Jack. Try not to worry about anything. The doctors will explain when you're more recuperated, more conscious." Jack felt a hand on his arm.

"Tim Min," Jack said. "Is Tim Min here?"

"Tim Min? I don't know who that is," the voice answered.

"Who are you? Do I know you? You're voice sounds so familiar."

"You don't know who I am, Jack?"

"No," Jack replied. "I can't see you. Everything is a blur. Something's wrong with my vision."

"Well, let's just say I'm a relation of sorts."

"Relation? But you're not my brother. Wait a minute. I know now. You're Bo Mat. You're my half brother," Jack said, his voice filled with surprise.

"That's right. You must try not to excite yourself," Bo Mat said.

"How long have I been unconscious?"

"A couple of weeks. You were flown to Chungking ten days ago. I work for an American correspondent here. I write articles that sometimes appear in American newspapers. Anyway, our office gets information about American soldiers that are killed, wounded, or missing in action. I knew you were in Stilwell's Burma campaign, so when your name appeared on a list, I immediately began making inquiries. I found out you were flown to Ledo and would soon be relocated to Chungking."

"Then you've been here, by my side, all that time," Jack said gratefully.

Bo Mat smiled. "Well, you're my brother, aren't you?"

"Hey, Bo Mat, I've been meaning to tell you, all of us were so proud of you for coming over here to fight for China. When Mom read the letter you wrote her, I knew instantly that I too wanted to come to China. It seemed so much the right thing to do, since I was Chinese, and China, my homeland, was in trouble. Anyway, what I've been meaning to tell you all this time was that I'm sorry about that fight at Lowell." Jack squinted, trying to bring the face of his brother into focus.

"That's water under the bridge, Jack. It was so long ago, and so much has happened since. We've both been through so much. But thanks, Jack. I guess I owe you an apology, too. It was just as much my fault as yours."

"Hey, Bo Mat," Jack asked, "did these doctors give you any idea what kind of shape I'm in?"

"I have to be honest with you. You deserve that." Bo Mat paused and looked away.

"Sure, be honest. That's why I asked you."

"Jack, the bullet came real close to your heart. Within a fraction of an inch. There's a fragment of it still lodged in there. They're afraid there's damage to the heart itself. They don't know how it's going to heal up. There are complications. That's why they flew you to Chungking. They're going to have to operate."

Jack asked, "Do Mom and Dad know about this?"

"I'm sure they know by now. I wired them as soon as I found out. Probably the army got in contact with them too. They should be in touch very soon."

As if to boost his own morale, Jack changed the subject. "Guess what, Bo Mat, I'm married!"

"Married? That's great news!"

"Do me a favor, Bo Mat. My wife is eight months pregnant."

"Pregnant? Congratulations, Jack. You're going to be a father!"

"Thanks. You know, I'd like to see her. I don't know how long I'll be at this hospital, but by the feel of this thing, I'll probably be here awhile. Gee, this place must have a pretty good maternity ward if the best doctors in China are here. It'd be great if Tim Min could have our baby here. She'd get the best care, and besides, I'd be able to see her, and maybe, if I'm feeling up to it, I could see my own baby being born. Do you think you could find some way to bring her to Chungking?"

"Where is she now, Jack?"

"She's in Kunming. That's where we met. She's at the army base now. Tell her I'm here. Don't worry her, though. Tell her I'm going to be fine."

"Sure, Jack, I'll do everything I can to get her here. If I can rent a plane, I will fly down there myself and get her," Bo Mat said reassuringly.

"You know what? You're a good man, Bo Mat,"

Jack said. And then there was a silence. "I'm feeling kind of tired right now."

"Yeah, Jack, I shouldn't be keeping you going like this. You ought to be asleep, conserving your energy." Bo Mat patted Jack's leg.

"You'll get in touch with Tim Min?" Jack asked.

Bo Mat replied, "You can count on me."

Jack didn't hear him. He was asleep.

Bo Mat knew how good it would be for Jack's health if he could see his wife. It would give Jack such a psychological boost. It might mean the difference between life and death in a case that could go either way.

The telephone lines were jammed, and Bo Mat had to wait an hour and a half to get through. Finally he reached the army base and was connected with Mrs. Sing, Jack's wife. It was the first that Tim Min had heard of the bad news. The army really fouled up there, Bo Mat thought. Why hadn't they contacted her?

Bo Mat arranged for her trip to Chungking through the Fourteenth Air Force, whose main base was in Kunming.

That evening, Bo Mat received a phone call. It was Martin Sing.

"Bo Mat?"

"Yes."

"It's Martin Sing." There was a pause. For a moment, Bo Mat was reminded of the pain he had experienced with the Sing family, and although he had never spoken to Martin Sing, he felt that the father was responsible for much of the bad feeling that had occurred. "Bo Mat," Martin continued, the anxiety evident in his voice, "what is Jack's condition?"

"He has lost a lot of blood, and he's quite weak," Bo Mat said. "Right now, the doctors won't tell me what his condition is, but I guess he's not getting any worse. He needs to be operated on to remove a bullet fragment that's very close to his heart. The surgeons are not getting to his case. There's an unbelievable number of wounded here from just about every front in the war.''

''If he's stable, we should probably fly him to the United States immediately. U.C. Hospital, right here in San Francisco, is one of the finest in the country. They could treat him here.''

''But there's one problem. His wife. She's eight months pregnant. She—''

''Well, damn it, we could fly her to the States, too. She'd get better treatment for that pregnancy at U.C. Hospital than she would in China,'' Martin said.

''Yes, but what about the immigration authorities?'' Bo Mat asked.

''This is a wartime emergency, son. I can arrange for her to have a visa, and the problem of her getting permanent status we can solve later. I'll also make arrangements with the hospital. You take care of getting those people flown over here.''

''Yes, sir.''

''And Bo Mat . . . you come back home too, son. You belong with your family.'' Even the tinny phone connection conveyed the warmth in his voice. Bo Mat was greatly moved by the sincerity of Martin's offer.

''I will come back, sir.''

Jack awoke. He still could not focus his eyes very well. There were two visitors in his room.

''Jack,'' a woman's voice called to him.

''Tim Min!''

Tim Min carefully and gently embraced her husband.

The other visitor, Bo Mat, rose to go. "I'll leave you two alone together." He left the room.

"Tim Min," Jack said again. He couldn't believe she was here at last. He felt the roundness of her belly. "The baby feels strong." He put his ear to her stomach. "I think I can hear his heart beat."

"His? You're so sure he's a boy?"

"I'm not sure," Jack joked, "but it sounded like a boy's heartbeat." Then he grew serious. "Did Bo Mat tell you what's wrong with me?"

"A little bit, not much," she said.

"A piece of the bullet's still in there. You know, I've got to give those Japanese credit, they sure fight hard."

"Oh, Jack, I wish the doctors would hurry. You've got to get well. I don't want you to be sick. I love you, Jack, and I need you. And this baby needs you, too."

"Don't worry, Tim Min, don't worry. I'll get better."

Bo Mat returned then and said, "I don't want to interrupt anything, but I have a piece of news that might interest you. We're going to the United States."

The Sings met them at Castle Air Force Base. There was no time to talk. They had to hurry to U.C. Hospital, where Jack would immediately undergo surgery. Too much time had already been lost.

The surgeon's name was Dr. Arnold Burnstein, a renowned surgeon and heart specialist. As soon as Jack entered the hospital, he was taken to the anteroom of the operating room and prepared for surgery. The family was told to wait on the first floor. There, a lounge was available to the families of patients.

A long time had passed. Should they not have heard by now the results of Jack's operation?

Only a month ago, Martin's best friend, Peter Tsui,

had passed away. Martin had gone to the funeral for Peter held in Walnut Grove. It had been a great loss for Martin. Now his son Jack was close to death.

The family was joined by Laura Mei, Cynthia and Thomas. They were all students at Berkeley now. Laura Mei was studying biology. She wanted to become a doctor. Cynthia was a student of English literature. And Thomas was interested in economics and business. Martin had called Ronald, who was stationed in Berlin. He was arranging for a leave so he could be with his brother.

"They said the operation wouldn't take this long," Martin complained nervously.

"They were going to send somebody down to tell us," Ming Lee added.

No one said anything for a while.

Then Bo Mat broke the silence. "I'll go up there and find out what's happening."

Time passed very slowly. Martin sat where he could see the elevator, for he wanted to see Bo Mat's expression when he emerged from it. Every time the elevator door opened, Martin expected Bo Mat to come out. But it was always someone else. Why was it taking Bo Mat so long to find out what was going on?

Finally, Bo Mat appeared and started toward the lounge. Martin tried to read the state of things in Bo Mat's expression, but he couldn't.

"The operation was completed," Bo Mat said. "Jack is in a hospital room. He's asleep."

"Well? How is he?" Martin asked.

"The doctor said . . ."

"Yes?"

"Dr. Burnstein couldn't give a definite answer. He said we would just have to wait and see. He said there was more than one fragment in Jack's body. He got them all out, but the damage to the heart and the arteries around the heart was extensive. He really didn't know whether Jack would pull through or not.''

A few hours later, a nurse entered the lounge and said to the family, "Jack is awake now, but he is very weak. He calls for Tim Min. Is Tim Min here?''

"Jack is asking for you, Tim Min," Bo Mat translated. "You'd better go see him.''

Tim Min walked slowly into the sickroom. Jack was lying on the bed, his eyes closed.

Tim Min walked up to the side of the bed and looked down at him. As if he had sensed her presence, his eyes opened at that moment and focused on her.

"Tim Min,'' Jack murmured.

"Jack. Jack, darling.''

He reached for her hand. "How is everybody? I hope they're not making too much of a fuss over me.''

"No, Jack,'' she said. "They're worried, of course. But they have a lot of confidence in the doctors.''

"I have a lot of confidence in them too.'' Jack smiled weakly. "Tim Min, I think those Japanese did a pretty good job of tearing me up.''

"It takes time for wounds to heal.''

"But maybe I won't come out of this. The doctors are very good, but if I'm dying, there's not much anybody can do.''

"Don't say that. Don't even think it.''

"Honey, I've got to say it because it's on my mind. I don't want to die. I'm fighting against it with everything I've got. There's nothing in the world I want more than to be alive and to share my life with my family.'' Suddenly he began to cough. It was dry, rasping cough, and it lasted for a long time.

"Jack," she cried softly.

"My family will take good care of you and our child, Tim Min. I want you to know that you will be all right, and the child will be all right. Mom and Dad and my brother Bo Mat will see to that. This country may seem very strange to you now, but gradually you'll get used to it, and I think you'll grow to like it."

"I love you," Tim Min said.

"I love *you*," Jack said. "You're so beautiful, filled out like that. That's exactly how I want to remember you." Jack's face contorted in pain.

"Jack? Jack, what is it?" Tim Min asked anxiously.

"I don't know, but it hurts."

"I'd better call the doctor."

"Don't go away . . . just yet," Jack said, clinging to her arm.

"No, Jack. I've got to get help."

Tim Min ran out into the hall.

Bo Mat was waiting out in the corridor. "What is it, Tim Min?" he asked quickly, seeing the urgent look on her face.

"It's Jack," she cried. "Call the doctor. Quickly!"

Bo Mat ran to the head nurse on that floor. "Call Dr. Burnstein to Room 303 immediately. It's an emergency," he said.

Fortunately, Dr. Burnstein was available right away. He had been eating dinner in the hospital cafeteria, but rushed to Jack's room as fast as he could. Two other nurses were already at Jack's side.

Bo Mat and Tim Min waited anxiously in the hall while the doctor examined Jack. After a few brief, tense moments, he hurried out.

"We're taking Jack to the operating room again," he

said. "Will you folks go down and wait in the lounge? We'll let you know when we have more information."

Tim Min and Bo Mat returned to the lounge. They were greeted by Martin, Ming Lee, and the other children. Ronald had called the hospital from Berlin, saying he would try to catch the next flight to the States so he could see his brother.

After what seemed an eternity, Dr. Burnstein came off the elevator. Bo Mat went to speak with him. In a few moments, Bo Mat turned from the doctor and walked solemnly toward the rest of the family. All were anxiously waiting for the news.

Bo Mat said after a pause, "The operation has not succeeded. There was an additional complication, a hemorrhage from the pulmonary artery. The fragment must have infected the artery and caused a perforation."

"Is Jack . . . ?" Ming Lee asked.

"Yes," Bo Mat said. "Jack's dead."

Tim Min buried her face in her hands. Ming Lee, her eyes filled with tears, reached out instinctively to Tim Min and held her. "Oh, Tim Min, Tim Min, I am sorry. I am so sorry."

The caskets were lined up, twelve of them, in the army cemetery in Colma, south of San Francisco. The caskets were covered with American flags. Jack's was among them.

It was a warm day and there was a breeze. The Sings stood with other American families to listen to the sound of a bugle. A contingent of the Marine Corps Honor Guard fired a twenty-one-gun salute.

The maternity ward had its own waiting area, so the Sings did not have to sit and wait in the same lounge where they had sat and waited, hoped and prayed for Jack's life. This time, it was joy rather than sorrow that marked their hospital stay. Tim Min gave birth to a seven-and-a-half-pound baby boy.

"I want him to have two names, if I may be permitted," Tim Min told the baby's grandparents. "I want to give him an American name: Jack. And I want him to have a Chinese name, too: Leung Bing."

"Handsome soldier," Ming Lee translated.

Jack "Leung Bing" Sing slept through this decision-making. He was awake long enough to look up at his mother with wide, trusting eyes.

"Look, Jack's smiling," she said. It was the first time the Sing family saw little Jack smile. It was also the first time they had seen a smile grace the beautiful features of Jack's widow.

Chapter 33

Franklin D. Roosevelt signed the Repeal of the Chinese Exclusion Acts in 1943. By this act, Chinese could become citizens by naturalization. Birth in the United States was no longer the only way a Chinese could become a citizen. The act established a quota system based on ancestry. One hundred and five new Chinese immigrants per year were allowed in.

President Kennedy signed the Presidential Directive of May 25, 1962. This directive allowed Hong Kong refugees to immigrate to the United States. About fifteen thousand Chinese refugees were admitted under this act.

By the Act of October 3, 1965, President Lyndon B. Johnson eliminated the quota system based on national origin. Instead, each country was given a quota of twenty thousand per year.

These and other new immigration laws made it much easier for Chinese to immigrate to the United States. Men were able to bring their families. Chinatown's numbers swelled. And there were problems.

Because of the many new immigrants, competition for jobs was fierce. The language barrier made it impossible to find work outside the ghetto. When they got jobs, the immigrants found themselves working long hours and receiving scant wages. Men worked as cooks, dishwashers or bus boys. Women worked in crowded sewing factories. Their pay was less than the minimum wage. The abundance of labor made workers dispensable. The laborers would suffer without complaint or they would lose their jobs.

Crowded and substandard housing added to the difficult conditions. Large families would move into tiny rooms. The immigrants would have to rent two of these to accommodate their families. Each room was ninety to a hundred dollars a month. Both parents had to work, or the family would not survive. They would come home from work exhausted. There was little time to devote to the children.

And there was little for the children to do. There were few recreational facilities. Schools, for the most part, bred torturous experiences of failure. The language barrier made it impossible for the Chinese youngsters to keep up with the others.

Unable to make sense of their new surroundings or to communicate their frustrations to their parents, some Chinese teen-agers formed gangs. These gangs became "family" to the youth. The gangs fought each other. The provocation for a fight usually involved an insult to another gang member or an infringement of territory.

A group in Hong Kong known as the Gip Dak Tong was quick to exploit the rebellious energy of Chinatown's gangs. The Gip Dak Tong had long been involved in racketeering and extortion. They were determined to export their criminal activities to the streets of San Francisco's Chinatown. Their reasoning was that if a teen-ager was arrested, his sentence would be a lot lighter than an adult's, so why not arm the teen-agers and dispatch them to do the Tong's bidding?

In 1964, the shopkeepers and restaurant owners of Chinatown began paying protection money to teen-age agents of the Gip Daks. Now the young men no longer felt powerless. They felt that they were running Chinatown. They got free meals and movie tickets. Proprietors were frightened of them. They were paid in cash by the Tong, and with their money, the youths bought cars and cruised the streets.

The Gip Dak Tong was able to raise enough money to buy a building on Washington Street. There was a restaurant in the building, called the Silver Phoenix. This restaurant became the late-night hangout for the Lin Chings, or "The Youth" gang. The Lin Ching members were a new breed of *boo how doy* in Chinatown. It was as if the ghosts of the Tong had returned to haunt the alleyways again.

The Lin Chings had enemies. Their enemies were the American-born Chinese. The Lin Chings called them *To Jai*, little rabbits. But the foremost American-born Chinese gang called itself Pete's Boys, after "Little" Pete, a famous highbinder of the 1920s. Pete's Boys were sworn enemies of the Lin Chings. Pete's Boys and the Lin Chings fought it out in bloody cruising duels. Groups of the rival gangs would ride in separate vehicles. They'd watch out for each other on the street. They'd pull over their cars and engage in knife battles, or they'd roll down windows and take shots at each other through the windows. They used 38-caliber automatics, .22-caliber pistols, sawed-off shotguns.

The Chinese merchant companies met often to discuss Chinatown's problems. Martin Sing, now eighty years old, had long been a member respected for his accomplishments in rebuilding The Dollar Store. He had established it as a thriving discount department store. Now he was retired and his son Thomas was managing the operation. Successful branch stores were located in every major West Coast city. Martin was considered a great businessman. But some members of the merchant companies thought Martin was beginning to show signs of senility. Martin's views were too far to the left for this conservative organization. He wanted to gain its support for Chinese Third World activists. Indeed, some men feared he had become a bit of a radical, and they refused to listen to him, especially when he started advocating financial aid for new Chinese immigrants. He was convinced that by helping these people, the companies would be taking the first step toward eliminating the influence of the gangs.

He took some satisfaction from talking to his son Bo Mat. Bo Mat had always encouraged his father to use his influence in the merchant companies on behalf of the poverty-stricken newcomers.

"It's the same old story," Bo Mat said to his father on the phone. "Those men have money and power. They want things to stay as they are. Their way to deal with the gangs is just get the police to crack a few of these kids' heads."

"I cannot convince them, Bo Mat. They consider me a senile old man. Over the hill," Martin told him. "It will take pressure from the top down to get them to change, if at all. That's why your election to the board of supervisors is essential."

Bo Mat paused on the phone. Then he said in a lower tone, "You think the merchant companies might use certain information against me? I'm afraid they might try to bring up stuff about Mom and you and the past. They don't like my candidacy much. They know I belong to the Chinese for Affirmative Action, so they think I'm a radical."

"Don't worry about that, Bo Mat. They will look

pretty silly if they start using smear tactics. You helped bring Federal antipoverty programs to Chinatown. You're for improved relations with the People's Republic of China. Your record speaks for itself. I think most people agree with you. It will be a good thing for Chinatown when you're elected.''

"It would be a first for a Chinese. There has never been a Chinese on the board before," Bo Mat said.

"It's about time, don't you think so?" Martin replied loudly into the phone.

Tim Min had remarried in 1947. Low Bok Leung was now her husband of seventeen years. He was a hard worker and had built up a business as a building contractor. Bok Leung was not a family man. He didn't desire to have more children. Tim Min had only Jack Jr. to raise, but Bok Leung had never taken much interest in Jack. Time was certainly a problem. Bok Leung would work sometimes from early morning to late evening, even on weekends. He was seldom home. And when he *was* home, he was exhausted. He did little but eat and sleep. Bok Leung categorically refused any aid from the wealthier Sings. He wanted to do it on his own without family help of any kind. He succeeded, but success didn't do anything to shorten his work schedule. Long hours had become his habit, and Jack suffered emotionally as a result. When Jack was young, he turned to Martin for the companionship of a father. Grandfather was father to him. But for two years now, Jack had discontinued his visits with Martin. Martin had assumed Jack was just growing up and didn't need older guidance so much anymore.

Tim Min, however, had been very worried about Jack lately, so she paid a call at Martin Sing's home in the Richmond District on Thirty-third Avenue.

"Tim Min," Ming Lee said, "you look very distressed. Sit down and tell us what is the matter."

"I hate to bother you," Tim Min began, "but I am concerned about our son, Jack. Very concerned."

"Why, Tim Min?" Martin asked. "He's such an intelligent boy. The last time we spoke on the phone, you said that he had gotten straight A's."

"Sir, I am so worried. Yes, he does well in school, but in the evenings he goes out. I don't know where he goes. I ask him, and he doesn't tell me. Last night, he didn't come back until three a.m." Tim Min began to quiver and cry.

"Tim Min," Ming Lee said sympathetically, "tell us."

"Oh, honored parents," Tim Min sobbed, "I am so ashamed to be crying like this. Please, forgive me. I am so worried. I woke up last night when I heard the water running in the bathroom. I went in the bathroom, and there was blood in the sink. It was Jack's blood. There was so much of it. I asked him what had happened."

"What did he say?" Martin asked.

"He said he went out with some boys in a car. They were driving around, and some other boys in another car began following them. Well, he said these other boys were, for some reason or other, yelling insults. Very vicious insults."

"There was a fight?" Martin asked, trying to get the facts straight.

"Yes," Tim Min told him, nodding slowly. "The boy driving Jack's car stopped. The other car pulled over to the side of the road. Then, Jack said, the boys from the other car got out and came over. Jack's friends got out, too. They fought with fists. Somebody pulled out a knife and starting swinging it around. Jack got cut. He said one good friend of his was stabbed very badly and had to go to the hospital.''

"Who were these boys Jack was with?"

Tim Min answered, "I don't know. He wouldn't tell me. He said, 'Just friends, Mama, just friends.' He said they didn't expect that attack. They were just driving around, having a good time."

"Do you know if Jack is involved with any gangs? Like Pete's Boys?"

"I know Pete's Boys are active in the Richmond area. I asked Jack if he had anything to do with them. This was a week ago. He angrily denied it, but I don't know if he was telling me the truth or not," Tim Min said.

"And Jack's friends were attacked by these other boys without provocation?" Martin inquired.

"That's right," Tim Min replied. "I mean, that's what Jack told me. I begged him, 'Please, from now on, Jack, don't go out driving around with those boys anymore.' But Jack said it wasn't his friends' fault. It was the other boys. There was no reason not to see his friends. His friends meant no one any harm, he said. But, then . . ."

"Go on, continue," Martin prodded.

"I said, 'Jack, you don't need to see these friends. You have a beautiful girlfriend who loves you. You should spend more time with her.' Kim Li is her name. And Kim Li, I know, is worried about Jack, too."

"What happened when you tried to talk to him this way, Tim Min?" Martin asked.

"He gave me such a mean expression. I had never seen him look that way before. I immediately looked away from him. He seemed as though he wanted to kill me. Kill *me*!" Tim Min buried her face in her hands and shook with sobs.

Ming Lee put her arms around Tim Min. "It's all

right. Martin will talk to the boy. Jack trusts Martin. If Jack is in any trouble with gangs, Martin will find out and help him. Don't worry.''

"I hate to bother you, honored parents, but as you know, I just can't turn to my husband for these things. He is too busy, and he and Jack simply don't talk to each other. Right now, Bok Leung is out of town on business. It is so unfortunate.'' Tim Min looked up sadly at Ming Lee.

"And the knife wound?'' Martin asked. "Is he all right now?''

"I wanted to take him to the emergency ward at U.C. Hospital, but he wouldn't go. He said it was nothing. He just stopped it up with gauze and put some tape around it. I could tell he was hurt, but he kept saying he wasn't hurt that bad, and he wouldn't have anything to do with me when I tried to help. I think he should see the doctor. It was an awful gash. What if it gets infected?''

"I'll go to the herb store in Chinatown before I come over,'' Martin said. "We'll put some herbs on the wound and it will be okay. Don't worry.''

Early the following day, as was his custom, Martin went to Chinatown to buy meat and vegetables at the stores on Stockton Street. Then he stopped at the herb store and bought an herbal paste for Jack's cut.

That evening, Martin paid a call on his grandson. Tim Min greeted him at the door. She seemed relieved to see him. "*Fun ying, fun ying,* welcome, welcome,'' she said, bowing with respect.

The living room was immaculately clean. Tea, oranges and cookies were set out for the guest on a tea table before the sofa. Tim Min offered Martin a seat. Then she sat down herself on a chair opposite the sofa.

"Where is Jack?" Martin asked as he sipped his tea.

"I am ashamed," Tim Min said. "Jack is not here! I told him you would come tonight. He nodded as if he understood, but then he just didn't come back home after school."

"Perhaps he guesses the reason for my visit and does not want to see me," Martin frowned. "That's all right. I will just stay here until he comes back."

Martin and Tim Min waited for three hours. Jack finally walked in the door at eleven o'clock.

"Jack, at last you're here," Tim Min said. "Didn't you know that Grandfather . . ."

Martin held his hand up to stop Tim Min from criticizing her son. He wanted to put the boy at ease as much as possible. "Jack, good to see you. It's been a long time," Martin said, standing and extending his hand to his grandson.

Jack shook Martin's hand halfheartedly. Obviously, Jack's mind was on something else. "Grandfather," he said, "how are you?"

"Just fine, Jack," Martin responded. "What have you been doing with yourself? Still playing with those remote-control electric cars? Last time we saw each other, that was what you were most excited about."

"It's been a long while," Jack answered, smiling. Then he sat down. He genuinely liked his grandfather and didn't realize how much he had missed him.

Martin mussed up the boy's hair affectionately.

"Excuse me," Tim Min said, "I'm going to do some sewing. I'll leave you two to catch up on things." Tim Min left the room.

Martin's eyes fell on the bulge under the left sleeve of Jack's shirt. "You hurt yourself?" he asked.

"You know all about it, Grandpa. I know Mom went over there to talk to you. That's why you're here tonight."

"I brought something for that gash," Martin said, reaching into a paper bag and bringing out a jar with paste in it.

"I don't need that, Grandpa," Jack protested.

"Come on. Try it. It's the same stuff I put on your lip when you fell on the curb. You were eleven. You thanked me. You didn't want to have stitches. Chinese medicine was good then. It's still pretty good, you know. It's been pretty good for two thousand years. Give it a try," Martin insisted cheerfully. "It won't hurt you."

"Oh, all right, Grandpa," Jack acquiesced.

Martin took Jack into the bathroom and carefully dressed Jack's wound, using the herbal paste he'd bought in Chinatown. After he finished and they returned to the living room, Martin came right to the point.

"Tell me, Jack, who are these friends you go driving around with?"

"Friends from school," Jack answered guardedly.

"And the other night, one of these friends of yours was stabbed pretty badly, wasn't he? He had to go to the hospital, I heard."

"He died," Jack said simply, but the expression on his face was deep with disturbance and pain. "He was my best friend."

"Who killed your friend? Who were the boys in the other car. Come on, tell me. I'm not going to bite your head off."

"Lin Chings. But I'm not in Pete's Boys, like Mom thinks. Some of my friends are Pete's Boys, that's all. It's not any kind of organized gang like Lin Chings. We just don't like Lin Chings. They're outsiders. They make trouble for the American-born Chinese. They don't like us, and we don't like them."

"And the boys you drive around with? They're Pete's Boys?" Martin asked.

"Some are and some aren't," Jack replied nervously, evasively.

"You want to talk to me about this, Jack?"

"I really don't. Lin Chings killed my good friend. What can I do? I don't have too much choice. You can try to talk me out of it, Grandpa, but I have to be loyal to my brothers. If I don't have that loyalty to my brothers, I'm nothing."

"You're Chinese," Martin said emphatically.

"Ha. What's that?" Jack answered comtemptuously. "Chinaman. Buck teeth. Charlie Chan. Bent over coolies, loads on their backs, doing as they're told. Grandpa, being Chinese doesn't mean a goddamn thing in America, let's face it. You can't get anywhere saying you're Chinese."

"You've got much to be proud of in your heritage. A great tradition, richness of customs, poetry, literature. You should learn about it. Look into Chinese for Youth Alternatives. They have educational programs."

"Look, Grandpa," Jack interrupted. "Lin Chings are Chinese, too. And I don't feel anything in common with them. They're total strangers to us American-born Chinese. They are enemies."

"You have to live together."

"No. The Lin Chings must be annihilated. The Lin Chings must be blown off the face of the earth. Otherwise . . ."

"Otherwise, what, Jack?"

"Otherwise, Lin Chings will take over. Eliminate us. Crowd us out. Kill us off. It's us or them. There's no in-between. It's a fight to the death," Jack growled in low, angry tones. "I want revenge."

"Jack, you know about my past. I told you all about

the Tongs. Don't you see? A similarity between what I told you about Tongs and this gang warfare? You must learn from history that such rivalries are meaningless. The Tongs died out when Chinatown wouldn't stand for it anymore. So it will happen with these gangs,'' Martin asserted. But his words had gone unheeded. Jack said nothing. ''Okay, Jack,'' Martin went on after a silence. ''I'm going now, but I'll come back, and we'll talk some more. Okay?''

When Martin walked out, Jack didn't so much as acknowledge him.

Stubborn, Martin thought to himself. Just like his great-grandfather. Old ghost of the Tong, you've come back. But I'll beat you. I won't let you take my grandson.

Two days passed. It was a warm September evening. The Labor Day weekend was ending. It was Sunday night. Tim Min's frantic voice was at the other end of the phone.

''Honored father, come quick, it's Jack,'' the voice said. ''He's got a gun.''

Martin got in his car and sped over, running stop signs and red lights. As fast as his elderly frame would carry him, he made his way toward the house. A pretty girl about seventeen years old was coming out of the house. She was in tears.

''Are you Kim Li, Jack's girlfriend?'' Martin asked her.

''I don't know if I'm his girlfriend anymore or not. He just told me to get lost. Oh, sir, he's got a gun. I am so afraid of what will happen,'' she said, trembling.

''I'm his grandfather. I'll talk to him,'' Martin told her.

''I don't want anything to happen to Jack! I love him so much!''

"I can see that you do, Kim Li."

The front door was standing open and Martin rushed into the house. Tim Min was sitting in the living room wringing her hands.

"Where's Jack?" Martin asked.

"He's locked the door of his room. He won't come out. I went in and caught him with the gun. He pushed me out and locked the door. He was loading that gun, Father. Loading it!"

Martin went to the door of Jack's room and called, "What's going on, Jack? The leaders of Pete's Boys call out the horses?"

"That's right, Grandfather. Don't try to stop me, either. I'm going to do what I have to do. The Lin Chings owe us a debt. They're going to have to pay. That's the way it is."

"That does not have to be the way it stays, though, Jack. Where does the *Chun Hung* say you're going to meet the Lin Chings?"

"Don't push me, Grandfather. You'd better go back home. Take Mother with you. It's going to be dangerous here if you get in my way."

"Dangerous? Why? They're going to pick you up here and take you to the battlefield, grandson?"

"That's right, Grandfather. And I will go. I must be obedient to my group. If I am found to be disloyal, then my name is mud."

"When base traitor and coward turn I, slain in the road my body shall lie? That was the oath I took. Many young men lost their lives being loyal to that code of blood," Martin told Jack, his voice straining with emotion.

Outside, a car horn sounded. Martin could hear the window inside Jack's room slide open. He rushed to the front door and ran outside. Across the street was a souped up '57 Chevy. Riding inside were six young men around Jack's age. Martin could see that two of them were carrying rifles.

By this time, Jack had made it to the street and was about to get into the waiting car.

"No!" Martin cried out instinctively. Though he was old, he found a reserve of youthful strength in his desire to avert the tragedy that was unfolding. He ran toward his grandson, caught him and tackled him.

"Let go of me, Grandfather. Let go, old man."

"No. You will be loyal only to what is good and what is right! You will not kill Chinese who are your brothers! I have seen what that has done to our people, and it will not happen if I can do anything to prevent it!" Martin yelled.

But Jack's youthful strength was enough to break him out of his grandfather's hold. Jack pushed himself away. In the meantime, one of the youths in the car had rolled down the window and was aiming his rifle at Martin, trying to get a clear shot. When Jack broke loose, the youth in the car fired.

The bullet struck Martin in the chest. Then the car skidded off up Twenty-third toward Geary Boulevard.

Jack turned and saw that Martin had been hit. "Grandfather!" he cried. "Grandfather!" He hunched over his grandfather's bloodied form.

"Never mind me," Martin murmured. "Call the police. Wherever they are going. Get the police there. Stop them. Stop them."

Then Martin drifted out of consciousness. Deep in the back of his mind, he pictured a whirlpool of images: knives, shotguns, automatics and hatchets revolved in a swirling stream of blood. The faces of Lum Po, Duk Fong, Choy Wu and Larry Szeto all went around and around with the wheel of blood. A score of young men joined the wheel. They were helped onto the wheel of blood by the older Tong members. The Tong ghosts. They extended to the youths their skeletal hands. Now the blood wheel encircled Chinatown. The cooks, bus boys, seamstresses and laborers; mothers and children; merchants and politicians; all were surrounded by the wheel of blood and could not escape its confines.

At midnight, four youths from Pete's Boys entered the Silver Phoenix Restaurant on Washington Street. They were after Lin Chings. But the Lin Chings had seen them coming from down the block. One of the Lin Chings said, "*Go yan dai cheug!* Man carrying gun!" And the street-wise Lin Chings dove for cover under their table. Pete's Boys entered the restaurant and began spraying the area commonly frequented by Lin Chings with bullets. Several innocent bystanders were hit. Bob Long, a student at San Francisco State College, was killed. He had been having a snack with friends after a movie. Mary Tom was killed. She was a student at City College in psychology. She had planned to become a counselor for Chinese newcomers. Others were wounded. Altogether, eight died that night, none of them Lin Chings or individuals involved in any way with a Tong organization or a gang. The massacre was the worst recorded in San Francisco history.

Ming Lee sat by her husband's bed in the intensive care unit. Martin Sing was listed in critical condition. He was still unconscious. He had been operated on and the shell fragments had been removed. Plastic tubes were attached to his arm for intravenous nourishment and precious blood plasma. There was a device to monitor his heartbeat as well.

Ming Lee was soon joined by their son Bo Mat.

Bo Mat had spoken with the doctor.

"I'll be honest with you, Mr. Sing," the doctor had told him. "Your father's chances for coming through this alive are about one in ten. If he were younger, I would be more optimistic. But his age is working against him. He was shot badly."

"I see," Bo Mat said simply.

Bo Mat, upon returning to Martin's hospital room, related the doctor's opinions to his mother. But Ming Lee would not give up hope. "We must pray," she said to him. "We must pray together that he will recover. God will answer our prayers. Chinatown needs your father. God knows that. Martin's work is not finished."

"That is true, Mother. He has been an inspiration to those of us who are trying to make changes."

"We need him, too, son. You and I need him because we love him, and he loves us."

"I know that, Mother. But still we must prepare ourselves for bad news. We cannot expect miracles." Bo Mat placed his hand comfortingly on his mother's shoulder.

"No. Martin must not die. We must have faith. We will stay here and pray together, you and I. We will pray throughout the night and tomorrow and the next day until Martin recovers," Ming Lee argued fervently.

"But Mother, you must take care of your own health. You need to rest yourself. I have arranged for the hospital to provide a bed for you here in this room so you can be by Father."

"Thank you, my dear son, but there is no time to rest. There are prayers to be said," Ming Lee told him. There were tears in her eyes. "Will you help me?"

Bo Mat, seeing that she would not be dissuaded from

her vigil, agreed. "Yes, Mother. I will pray with you for Father."

The two of them sat in folding chairs by Martin's bed. Together, they prayed. At three a.m., Bo Mat dozed off. His head rested on his mother's shoulder and he slept. Ming Lee, however, didn't sleep at all. Her lips continued moving silently throughout the night.

They stayed the following day and night. They were joined by Martin's other children, Ronald, Cynthia, Laura Mei and Thomas. Jack and Tim Min came, too. The family stayed together in the hospital that night. They sat in the waiting lounge downstairs and prayed in accordance with Ming Lee's instructions.

It was the third day. Martin still had not emerged from unconsciousness. After the doctor checked Martin's vital signs, Bo Mat joined him in the hallway and asked earnestly, "What about it, Doctor?"

"I can't say," the doctor replied, shaking his head. But the expression on the doctor's face was grave.

Bo Mat sighed deeply and returned to his mother's side. There were deep shadows under her eyes. She seemed terribly exhausted from two nights of no sleep. Yet there was a brightness in her eyes. Hope burned there and wouldn't be put out by pessimistic news.

"Mother, you must rest. You can't keep this up. You just can't," Bo Mat insisted. "I'm taking you home this afternoon and putting you to bed. Now, no arguments! Your well-being is important. If we have to lose Father, I don't want to lose you, too!"

Ming Lee felt very tired, but she was convinced that if she could stick it out just a little longer, God would hear her prayers and Martin would get well. "Just one more hour," she pleaded with her son.

"No. Mother, that's what you said an hour ago. I

have to take you home now. I and the other children will stay. We will be sure and call you if there is any change.'' Bo Mat reached for Ming Lee's arm.

"I can't go with you, Bo Mat. I just can't, dear,'' Ming Lee said, gently withdrawing from his grasp.

Bo Mat raised his voice. "How come you're so stubborn, Mother?''

"Bo Mat! Look!'' Ming Lee exclaimed. "It's Martin!''

Bo Mat looked over at his father. Martin was moving his head from side to side, and his eyes were quivering. Bo Mat ran out into the hallway to get the doctor.

Ming Lee stood and looked down adoringly into her husband's clear, open eyes.

"Hello, darling,'' she said. Slowly, Martin reached out and took her hand, his face breaking into a smile.

The doctor came running into the room and dashed to Martin's side. He felt Martin's pulse. "Amazing,'' the doctor said, shaking his head.

Two days later, Martin was taken out of intensive care. Though still weak, his progress was steady.

His children and grandchildren visited him often. Laura Mei and her husband were both doctors. They lived in Novato, Marin County, a faraway suburb. They had a son and a daughter. Ronald was now a successful engineer living in Menlo-Atherton. He was married, and had three children. Martin's son Thomas now managed The Dollar Store. He was also married, living in the Richmond district of San Francisco with his wife, two sons and two daughters. Cynthia taught comparative literature at the University of Washington. She lived in Seattle, but took a leave of absence to be with her father during the emergency. Cynthia was married, with three children of high-school age.

But one visitor meant a great deal in particular to Martin: his grandson Jack.

Upon his first visit to Martin's hospital room, he soon started crying. "Grandfather," he said, "I disobeyed you. I didn't call the police. I was only concerned to get help for you. You saved me from being involved in that terrible massacre at the Silver Phoenix. I have quit Pete's Boys now. I will have nothing more to do with them."

"And Kim Li?" Martin asked. "I hope you reconciled with her. She is a wonderful girl."

"Yes, Grandfather. I asked her to marry me. Oh, Grandfather, you taught me so much that night. I feel so badly I have caused you to suffer, and almost die."

"I'm here. That's what's important."

"I love you, Grandfather," Jack said.

"I love you, grandson."

At the end of three weeks, Martin was allowed to go home. But he was given a strict diet and ordered to stay in bed, with an occasional brief walk for exercise.

The Sing family held a party to honor Martin and celebrate his miraculous recovery. After the party, he drew his children and grandchildren together. "I love you all," he said. "And I thank you for this celebration. Now, all of you, please stop fussing over me. You have very busy lives. Go home and continue your successful careers. And *mo daam sam ngaw*, don't worry about me."

It was an unusually warm Saturday in November. Ming Lee got up early that morning. She cooked rice and chicken and some Dim Sum delicacies. Then she prepared some of Martin's favorite tea and put it in a thermos. She transferred the meal into a basket.

When she brought the basket into her husband's room, she found him reading *The Chinese Times*.

"Isn't it wonderful?" Martin exclaimed. "Bo Mat was elected to the board of supervisors! Now the Chinese merchant companies will have to watch out!"

"Yes, that is good news!" Ming Lee agreed.

"What's all this?" he asked, looking up from his paper.

"We are going to *yeh chan*, picnic," Ming Lee said.

"Oh no we aren't!" Martin barked. "I'm not well enough for outings like that yet."

"Don't be silly. You're fine, just fine. We're going on a picnic. No more argument."

Martin succumbed. "All right," he said cheerfully. "Where are we going?"

"Angel Island," she said, keeping her eyes averted from him.

"You're crazy," Martin complained. "I vowed I would never go near that place again. I wish that whole island would just sink to the bottom of the sea."

"Oh, Martin, what are you getting all worked up about? You know Angel Island is no longer an internment center for Chinese. It's a park now. The National Park Service runs it. The old wooden building was falling apart, and now they've reconstructed some of it. They've made it into a historical monument. It's dedicated to the immigrants. That means you and me. I thought it would be interesting to go back there and take a look." Ming Lee could see Martin wasn't enthusiastic about the idea. "Please, Martin?" she asked. "Besides, the island is very beautiful. Nice views of the bay and San Francisco."

"Well, I have to admit that it sounds interesting," Martin said reluctantly. "All right, let's go."

*   *   *

As the boat left San Francisco, Martin asked Ming Lee to stand at the railing so he could take her picture with the city in the background. He took a picture of Alcatraz, too. Alcatraz Island was also a historical monument. Boats full of tourists went there on weekends, too.

As the boat cruised by the left side of Angel Island, Martin could see the old wooden building. It used to be white. Now it was yellow. The hallway and stairs leading to the dining hall were gone. The dining hall was gone, too. In its place was a large concrete area. There were also benches. And a stone pillar stood at one end of this area.

"What is that stone pillar?" Martin asked Ming Lee.

"That must be the monument to the immigrants who were interned at Angel Island," Ming Lee replied.

The boat pulled into a pier. A short walk took them to the park's picnic grounds. From there, they walked for about a half-hour until they reached the Internment Center.

There they were met by a park ranger. He was the guide. A crowd of people had gathered who were interested in taking a tour, and he escorted them—Martin and Ming Lee included—into the wooden building.

They stopped first at a lobby area. Martin remembered this as the place Murphy had counted heads before the Chinese descended the stairs leading to the dining hall. There were glass cases in the lobby that contained old immigration documents. Martin squinted and made out a set of coaching papers, now yellow with age.

The park ranger explained, "The Internment Center at Angel Island was set up to verify the immigrants' claims of legitimacy. There was a great deal of fraud in those days. Only sons and daughters of merchants were allowed to enter the United States. This ruling was set forth in the Exclusion Act of 1882. But the earthquake of 1906 destroyed all the birth records. Merchants could then claim to have many sons. These sons didn't really exist. But each name became a 'slot.' For a sum of money, the merchants would sell these 'slots' to prospective immigrants. Immigrants who entered the country illegally using this scheme were known as 'paper sons.' "

Ming Lee looked over at Martin. She could hardly stop herself from laughing. Martin was looking at the floor, afraid they were going to find him out.

"Martin," she whispered, pointing at him. "You're a 'paper son,' aren't you?" she joked.

"Hush," Martin said.

The park ranger continued, "Fortunately for these 'paper sons,' the Act of 1957 was passed. This law stated that 'paper sons' could not be deported if a spouse, parent or child was a citizen of the United States or a permanent resident alien."

The park ranger then guided the group upstairs. Martin knew these stairs well. He had been on them countless times when he was interned here. The stairs led to the men's dormitories.

The ranger took them into a large room. It was Martin's old dormitory room. The bunks were not there, only the poles to which the bunks had been attached.

"There were three tiers of bunks," the park ranger explained. "As you can see, the bunks were very close together. There was very little room to walk between them. The immigrants interned here certainly suffered greatly from these crowded conditions. And they expressed their dismay on these walls. Come this way and I'll show you."

The ranger pointed out areas on the wall that were framed by string. The areas contained faded Chinese characters. Next to the framed areas were papers on which the poems were written out both in Chinese and in English translation.

"These are poems the immigrants wrote on the walls. They were covered up by the immigration officers with paint. The authorities were afraid the immigrants would become angry and resentful reading these poems. They contain expressions of bitterness and frustration. For decades they were ignored. But when we began thinking of restoring these buildings, we became curious about the poems. We hired Chinese scholars from Berkeley to come over and decipher them. These scholars found that the poems were often very beautifully written, in the classic Chinese literary style. It is a shame, however, that some of them remain indecipherable. This one, for example."

The park ranger pointed to two characters on a part of the wall close to the floor. "All we can get from this poem is two characters, 'not' and 'is.' *Mm haih*. That means 'no' in Chinese. The poet is saying 'no' to something. But I'm afraid we shall never know what the immigrant was denying in this poem."

Martin suddenly began reciting aloud. "I have failed the interrogation. The devils now will throw me to the land of the hungry ghosts. I will be carried there like a leaf is blown, aimlessly. My lifelong ambition has been swallowed up by the monster enemy, the purple dragon, dimly visible through mists. The nightingale is quietly weeping now. The only sound is her tears. The only character left to write in this poem is the character for sorrow."

Everyone in the group had turned toward Martin and listened to him recite his poem while in his mind he was recalling that early morning in the barracks fifty-four years ago. The sky, he remembered, had signaled the morning with luminescence. Far away, he could hear the footfalls. Murphy and the other officers were coming for him. He determined that he was going to commit suicide. His life would now be over. But no! He would not let that happen.

He would not let them deport him. He would stay here, in Gold Hill. He would find Ming Lee and marry her. They would have children. And he would make this place his home.

"*Mm haih*," he concluded the poem aloud. "That means my life is not over after all. It has really just begun!" He beamed at the group. They were all regarding him with puzzled expressions.

"This is *your* poem?" the park ranger asked.

"Yes, it is," Martin said proudly. "I wrote it right there. I remember very well. I carved that poem in the wall. You see? Here is the ideogram for 'nightingale.'"

"Well, that's a beautiful poem," the ranger said. "At the end, you completely reverse the idea of sorrow. You deny sorrow and despair."

"That's right," Martin nodded.

"If you could write it out with the Chinese characters, we will put the paper next to your poem so all the visitors to the center may be inspired by your experience," the ranger suggested.

"I would be most honored and happy to do so," Martin concurred.

"Excuse me," Martin said to a young Caucasian tourist. "Can you help me?"

"Of course," she said. "What can I do for you, sir?"

"Please help me take a picture of my wife and I? We will stand in front of the monument. You know how to use this camera? It's very simple. Just press here."

"All right, sure," the young lady said.

Kwan Ming Lee and Sing Man Sum stood before the monument. Martin put his arm around his wife. Both of them smiled.

"That's right. Now, very good smiles," the stranger said. She then took the picture.

"Thank you very much," Martin said appreciatively. "Here is some Chinese homemade Dim Sum for your picnic," he offered, handing her a bag of food.

"You're both very kind," the young lady said. "I look forward to trying this. Dim Sum, did you call it?"

"That's right, Dim Sum," Martin nodded. "It literally means, 'the heart of the hour.' "

"Perhaps you could translate for me the characters on the monument," the tourist requested. "I am curious as to what they mean."

"I'll try, but it isn't easy. You see, the characters have different meanings. The inscription means several different things at once. But the meaning is something like this." Martin translated the engraved characters:

> Leaving the village well behind,
> I travel far away.
> But I find myself a stranger
> Detained in the wooden building.
> I look for the darkened sky to open,
> That I might show my face,
> Acquire new land, cultivate new fields,
> No longer as a stranger.

After finishing his recitation, he looked at the young lady and smiled.

"Very interesting. Thank you again," she said, waving good-bye.

The Chinese couple sat on one of the benches and had lunch. After they finished, Martin carefully cleaned off the area where they had been eating, throwing the refuse in the container provided for that purpose. He poured for Ming

Lee and himself paper cups of water from the fountain. Then he sat next to her.

"It feels good to be here and move around with so much freedom," he said, taking a deep breath of fresh air.

"Yes, I'm glad we came," Ming Lee smiled. "I am sentimental about this place, you know. It is because you and I met here. Here is where we started our life together."

"Remember the notes we passed each other in the dining hall line?" Martin recalled, laughing.

"I remember. I remember when I first saw your smiling face. How much seeing that face every day meant to me!" Ming Lee touched his arm affectionately.

"I kept trying to get far to the right side of the line. I wanted just to touch shoulders with you so badly," Martin remembered.

"I wanted to be close to you, too," Ming Lee said.

"Sometimes we were lucky. There were moments when we could actually hold hands."

"Yes, we were very lucky. Lucky because we had found each other." Ming Lee looked at him lovingly.

He took both her hands in his and kissed her cheek.

"Very lucky," he agreed.